Praise for Dawn Metcalf and *Indelible*, book 1 of The Twixt

"Fans of fae fantasy, YA paranormal and modern fantasy will adore this novel and find themselves willingly trapped within the Twixt. Read. This. Book!"
—Serena Chase for *USATODAY.com*'s *Happy Ever After* blog

"Regular readers will know I'm an unabashed fan of faery books, but as a fan, I've read a lot of them, and it takes a lot to impress me. *Indelible* definitely impressed me."
—Niko Silvester for *About.com*

"This exhilarating story of Ink and Joy has marked my heart forever. Dawn Metcalf, I am indelibly bound to you. More!"
—Nancy Holder, *New York Times* bestselling author of *Wicked*

"[Metcalf's] rich physical descriptions create a complex fey world that coexists uneasily with the industrialized human one. An uneven but eventually engaging story of first love, family drama and supernatural violence."
—*Kirkus Reviews*

"Dangerous, bizarre, and romantic, *Indelible* makes for a delicious paranormal read, and I for one can't wait to see more of the Twixt."
—*Bookyurt*

"I was hooked from the very first page to the very last. I couldn't stop reading. The way Metcalf's writing style flows and the way the plot is perfectly paced just left me completely obsessed."
—Gabby for *Chapter by Chapter*

Books by Dawn Metcalf
available from Harlequin TEEN

The Twixt series

(in reading order)

INDELIBLE
INVISIBLE

DAWN METCALF

INVISIBLE

•THE TWIXT•BOOK TWO•

HARLEQUIN®TEEN

Recycling programs for this product may not exist in your area.

ISBN-13: 978-0-373-21107-4

Invisible

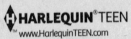

Printed in U.S.A.

This is for all the heroes around the table

(you know who you are!)

ONE

JOY STOPPED ON THE SIDEWALK AT THE SOUND OF creaking wood. It was a wintry sound, both ominous and familiar. Despite the July heat, she shivered. She was just leaving work, exhausted and perfumed in garlic, cooking oil and sweat. Joy glanced around the back lot behind Antoine's Café, adjusted her black apron over her arm and walked a little faster.

Fishing inside her purse, Joy skipped over her keys and her phone and went straight for the scalpel she kept hidden in the side pocket. She stumbled on a crack in the cement and cursed her decision to wear chunky heels to work. Clomping down the concrete, her footsteps obscured the sound of whatever followed. A prickle at her neck brought back icy memories and a half-remembered twinge in one eye. Should she shuck off her shoes or was she being totally paranoid? After all, it could just be the wind.

Right.

Contrary to the four-leaf clover in her wallet, it would be just her luck to be harassed by one of the Twixt on her way home from work.

She crossed beneath the overpass, echoes of her shoes bouncing over themselves in her haste to leave the busy downtown area. The Folk were notorious busybodies, but they could also be dangerous to humans. Curious as cats, they'd been peeking out at her from between buildings or through broken windows or from under birds' nests, wanting to catch a glimpse of either the ex-*lehman* who'd escaped her bonds to the Master Scribe or the infamous girl with the Sight who'd somehow managed to keep both her freedom and her eyes. Joy wasn't sure why she'd suddenly become more interesting over the past month, but the strange, inhuman paparazzi were getting bolder.

Those who had first appeared had been harmless, if unnerving, and Graus Claude had said the attention would pass once the novelty wore off. Then, last week, two dryads had whispered warnings to stay out of their world. Three days ago, a short, furry-haired creature had said that she should watch her back. Yesterday, a sprite wearing a floppy red cap had stood on the corner, smiling serenely while picking his fingernails with a serrated knife. The Folk were growing more menacing by the day.

Another scrape. Closer this time.

Joy's heart thudded in her ears. She'd been preparing for this.

When the shadow moved, Joy lifted the scalpel, a thin stroke of silver that identified her in the otherworld. Knees bent, she readied herself for what she might see.

An armored knight, the color of old blood, emerged from behind a large fir tree. He held a longsword at attention, sunlight streaming down its length. Joy stared at the blood-colored knight, frozen in a foggy trance of disbelief.

His foot hit the pavement, a gritty scratch of metal on stone. The sound snapped her awake.

"I'm under the Edict," she said quickly, the words tumbling out of her mouth. "The *Edict*," she said again with a bit more force. "As decreed by the Council of the Twixt."

The knight stepped forward. Joy stepped back.

"Duei nis da Counsallierai en dictie uellaris emonim oun," she tried again.

He took another step toward her.

She shook the blade in her hand. "I bear Ink's scalpel..."

The knight lifted the massive sword above his head.

Somehow she knew that wouldn't work.

The sword scythed through the air, carving a parting *whoosh* in its wake. Joy's brain stalled as the armored knight lunged. She gripped the scalpel. Her voice cracked.

"Stop!"

Ignoring her, the knight swung down at a wide angle. Joy stumbled off the sidewalk. The moment felt slow-motion surreal; she could see the sword tip passing her cheek—it was nicked and spotted with brown.

Out of the corner of her eye, Joy saw a woman push a double stroller across the street.

Screw the shoes. Joy kicked off her clogs and threw her purse. And the apron. It billowed like a cape, catching the sword and tangling it. She ran barefoot on the grass, adrenaline crackling and popping under her heels in manic bursts as she vaulted the manicured hedge into the wilder wood beyond. A steady banging followed.

Joy pounded over the uneven surface, her feet slamming into sticks and pebbles as she dived between the trees. There was a golden heat to running that soared up her limbs, shooting lightning from her soles up her spine. She had the advantage of being light and fast, but the knight charged after her, chugging like a train. She could hear his panting breath behind the metal faceplate.

Joy dodged around a tree and headed deeper into Mother Nature, avoiding broken glass bottles and bright-colored trash. She wove through the woods, putting as many trees, stumps and bracken between herself and her pursuer as possible. She cut to the north, inhaling deeply, tasting pollen and pine.

Tripping over a root, she grunted as pain exploded in her big toe and shot up her leg. Joy pushed through the injury and kept running, leaving the yellow-hot spark of agony somewhere far behind. Later, she would deal with it. Right now, she needed speed.

She broke through a small clearing, a patch of sun and weeds. She felt like leaping over the ferns and punching out a series of handsprings, but that was muscle memory talking. Her brain still equated running with gymnastics, but after her past few months as part of the Twixt, she knew that running equaled evading certain death.

The knight barreled through the woods, snapping fallen branches and lumbering up the incline. Energy frothed inside her, a flush of heat tickling over her arms and neck, filling her with a lightness, a clarity in speed. There was a heady rush to running for her life through the green grass. Joy felt like laughing. Perhaps she'd finally cracked? How else could she explain getting attacked by a medieval knight on a Thursday evening?

Whipping her tiny blade sideways, she wished that she could slice through worlds like Ink and cursed, not for the first time, that she no longer bore his *signatura* so he could not feel her panic or hear her call his name through the wind. Her skin was clean of True Names given form, so if she screamed, there'd be no one to hear.

Joy ran.

The land dipped and broke. A shelf of ragged earth loomed above a shallow crevice where the ground fell away. Joy scrabbled over the old streambed, using the smooth rocks as stepping-stones, tearing the seam of her capris as she jumped the ridge—long legs splayed out in a perfect one-eighty—stuck the landing on the other side and kept going.

The clang and sweep of metal plates crashed somewhere far below. Joy wished again for the flash of light, the spark of connection that had bound her to Ink, now severed. Gone.

She knew it wouldn't work, but she couldn't help it.

"Ink! Ink! Ink!" Joy chanted as she ran, willing him to hear her. The trees ahead began to thin, and she heard the distant roar of cars.

There was a sudden explosion accompanied by a shriek of birds. The force pushed her forward, and she shielded her eyes from several fat splinters that bit into her skin. Something slammed into her shoulder, spinning her around.

Ears ringing, Joy squinted at the dark red sword stuck halfway through a ruined tree. The trunk's shredded innards burst out in a jagged fluff of destruction. Bits and pieces of pulp peppered her entire body and most of the surrounding green. Pitter-patters of falling debris joined the snap of shattered wood. Through the ringing in her head, she could still hear the determined *clomp-clomp* of armored boots.

She blinked. The world slowly tilted. There was a deep, resonant crack as the massive tree began to list, groans and tiny clicks ricocheting off the surrounding forest as the trunk came crashing down. A gust of wind smacked Joy full in the face, blasting clouds of dirt and mulch. The knight had cut down a tree by *throwing his sword* and was now crossing the riverbed, headed toward her. Her hands tingled as terror splashed through her veins.

Joy squeezed the scalpel and spat wood chips off her lips. She tried to believe what Ink had said, what Graus Claude had said, tried to remember Inq's advice, but as the rust-crusted helmet cleared the ridge, all Joy could feel was the quiet knowledge that she was about to die in the woods in bare feet while holding a pathetic metal weapon no bigger than a pencil. She pointed the tip toward her attacker.

"Leave me alone!" she said.

The knight ignored her, reaching for the embedded sword, hand open for the hilt.

Joy shouted, *"Stop!"*

The ground spit up bits of leaf and stone as a line slithered through the earth like a whip just inches from the knight's plated boot.

Joy stared. The knight paused, and his helmet turned slowly to Joy.

The moment curled like a question mark.

Joy almost shrugged. Almost.

What was that...?

Grabbing the sword hilt, the knight swung around sharply. Joy stumbled back. The sword cleaved and clanged against something invisible, throwing off sparks that died in the dirt.

Joy blinked. *That was a ward!*

The knight tried another pass, pushing through a cloud of dust that smelled of campfire smoke. Joy could almost feel the sword's impact against the invisible shield. She smiled unsteadily, knowing that her friends must be nearby, even if she could not see them yet.

"Hey!" Joy shouted into the woods. "Over here!"

The knight drew his sword slowly in salute and charged—ten feet away, nine, eight.

Joy dived around the back of a tree and ducked. There was a punch of impact and a half-imagined grunt as the knight missed her head as she scrambled for the next bit of cover. He withdrew his sword with a snarl and pursued. Joy turned and ran faster, toes gripping the moss. She spun midstride, sweeping her tiny blade sideways—there was a grating *shing* as a piece of metal split and thunked against the ground.

The knight stumbled back. Joy sprinted up the next swell. Glancing over her shoulder, she saw that the lower faceplate had split in half, exposing a gray chin full of bristles, black gums and blue teeth.

In case she had any doubts that this was one of the Twixt.

The wash of fear came again, sparkling and brutal, pushing Joy *up up up!* through the next tangle of thorns. She bounced off a birch trunk and, misjudging the distance, tripped over a thick branch and skinned her knee. Joy wondered why she was running and not climbing. But what good would that do? The knight had made a tree *explode!*

As if the thought were a prescient tap on the shoulder, Joy turned to see the knight's elbow rise, arm cocked, shoulder back, before he hauled off and threw. The sword zinged through the air toward her. She stupidly, helplessly, raised her arms.

A ball of fire and superheated steam burst against an invisible wall. Joy's hair blew in the aftershock, and she felt moist heat coat her face. A figure dropped from a fissure in the sky, backlit by the wash of flame. He held a straight razor in one hand and her purse in the other; a silver chain swung heavily from a pocket at his hip. He glanced at her with his all-black eyes.

"Joy," he said.

She coughed and wiped a splinter off her forearm.

"Hi."

Ink tossed her purse to the forest floor. The fallen sword at his feet smoked and smoldered, dead leaves curling to ash beneath it. The knight barreled forward. The black-eyed Scribe moved, nimble and daring, drawing a complicated design in the air. Another ward gleamed into place. Ink spoke through the shimmer of gold, his voice carrying across the wood.

"I do not know you," Ink said to the wounded knight. "But you shall not harm her. She is protected under the Edict." His voice grew taut. "And she is protected by me."

The armored thing howled, charged and, with a last-moment shift, ran full force into a tree, disappearing in a shiver of pine needles.

Silence.

Joy backed away from the nearest tree, expecting a fresh attack. Ink extended his arm protectively across her body, holding his razor steady against the quiet. Joy pressed close, scanning the forest.

"Where did he go?" she asked.

Ink glanced around the glade. Branches swayed overhead. Leaves rustled. Querulous birds peeped.

"I suspect 'away,'" he said.

Joy nodded. "Away," she repeated, breathing fast. "Away is good."

Ink hadn't dropped his weapon, so neither did she. The tip of her scalpel—previously *his* scalpel—shook in her grasp. It looked a lot less confident than his straight razor. She could barely feel it in her hand, her fingers tight and numb, but she could feel him: a solid, calm presence with the gentle scent of rain. She swallowed against the sawdust in her throat.

"Can we go?" she asked. "Away?"

Ink picked up the sword and pressed her hand to his chest. "Away is good," he said as he sliced the air sideways.

They stepped through the breach with a sharp scent of limes.

Joy could feel Ink's hands on her face, the first sensation that pierced the cottony blanket of shock. They were in her room, in her house, and everything had that double-take quality of being suddenly normal, which felt strange.

"Are you all right?" Ink asked.

She coughed, tasting wood on her tongue. "Never better."

The straight razor was gone, probably back in his wallet, and Joy watched Ink pluck bits of tree out of her hair.

"I thought you said you were only receiving threats," Ink said. "This was considerably more than a threat."

"This is the first time someone's *attacked* me," Joy said,

brushing dirt from her ruined pants. "There've been snide comments, a lot of staring and some ultimatums, but Graus Claude said to ignore it. I didn't think anyone would actually *do* anything." A sigh stuttered out of her mouth. She shook her head, feeling the tension in her shoulders slip toward angry embarrassment. "I thought the Council's Edict was supposed to protect me."

"It should," Ink said and picked up the sword. The smoke curling off it was tinted with mist. He turned it over, not bothered in the least by its obvious weight. "Although this might be evidence to the contrary." Joy studied Ink's face. It was still hard to tell if he was being funny or not. He glanced over the blade at her. "Did you announce yourself?"

"Yes! I told him that I was under the Edict in English and the Old Tongue," she said. "Graus Claude made me repeat it often enough. I could say the words in my sleep!" She dropped the purse that had somehow been clutched in her hand. Her apron was stuffed inside. She still had no shoes and her feet were filthy. Joy paced her room, feeling the adrenaline ebb, leaving her weak and shaky and altogether freaked out. She didn't like it. Even with Ink's wards protecting her house, she was supposed to be able to live her life free from harm—that was what the Council had promised after she'd helped them take down Aniseed.

She stopped pacing. "Is this Edict thing for real?" she asked. "Was that what triggered the ward?"

"No," Ink said, examining the room. "That was me."

That still didn't explain what had happened before he'd arrived, when the armored knight had reached for his sword. Joy frowned. "How did you find me?"

Ink blinked his fathomless eyes and smiled.

"It is *you* who have Sir John Melton's boon," he said. Joy still had a tough time believing that her four-leaf clover actually worked.

"Good thing, too," she said, rubbing her arms as if cold. "That was... Is there a stronger word for 'terrifying'?" She shook her bangs from her eyes and paced in place. "So are we sure that the Edict's actually working?" she asked. "I mean, if it's not protecting me, then what about Dad? Or Stef? My brother's coming home soon..." The idea of putting her family in danger made Joy physically sick.

"The Edict is in place," Ink said. "I attended the Council session myself." His voice kept its steel of certainty. "Your family is safe, Joy."

Joy twisted her fingers in her shirt. "Well, if I'm so well protected, then what happened back there?"

Ink almost shrugged. Almost. The subtle cues he picked up from Joy were making him seem more and more human every day. He was learning. They both were.

"Nothing happened," he said matter-of-factly. "Which is most likely what the Council would say if we brought it to their attention." Ink held up a hand to forestall comment. "You were not actually injured," he pointed out, his black eyes sweeping over Joy. "They would agree that you look well enough. Yes, it was more than a threat, but not much more." Ink rolled a piece of wood pulp between his fingers. "Yet... this person knew about the Edict?" he asked quietly. "He knew who you were?"

Joy rubbed at the spots of mud on her ruined capris. "I said the words the Bailiwick taught me, and the guy heard me just fine," she said. "I think I can safely say that he knew *exactly* who I was." She rubbed harder as if she couldn't stop. Ink crossed the room and took her hand in his.

"You are hurt," he said simply and tapped his chest. "Here." He tried to catch her eye to confirm it, but she looked away. Her brain still twitched with firefly sparks. Her heart still pounded—she'd been so *scared!*—but it seemed as if she was only now feeling it, fierce and intense. Joy shivered. Ink squeezed her hand—it was something he'd learned how to do.

"I did not see it before," he confessed. "But I know that just because a thing cannot be seen does not mean it is not there." His voice lilted, coaxing. Joy nodded and squeezed his hand back. Her face felt hot. Her hands felt cold. She was overly conscious of Ink's worry feeding hers. He sighed. "I cannot take back what has happened, and I cannot undo it," he said. "Would that I could." He brushed the hair from her face, tucking it behind her ear, his fingers lingering there. She remembered that first touch. His voice was open, crisp and clear. "What can I do?"

She whispered, "Hold me."

Ink brought her close, and Joy wrapped her arms around him, pulling him hard against her as if she could press his solid calm into herself. Her heart thudded against his chest, an answering echo rebounding against her skin. She took several deep breaths, and it was several heartbeats later before she realized that he was copying her every move: his hand was in her hair just as hers was in his; his touch on her back was exactly where her palm rested on him. She could tell by the subtle changes of his body and skin that he was moving his senses to accommodate her—his muscles grew more pliant, his skin warmed to the touch, the strength in his arms became more like flesh than like stone. Joy smiled at herself and at him.

"Thank you," she said. "This is perfect."

He rested his chin on her shoulder. "A hug means many things," he said. "Over thirty-six, by my count."

Joy chuckled. "You're counting?"

"Yes," he said.

Joy laughed aloud, watching his smile dimple. Ink was funniest when he didn't realize it.

"You feel better," he said.

Joy nodded. "I do."

"Good," he said. "Then I will go and see what 'happened back there.'" He dropped his hands abruptly. Joy thought maybe they should work on his exits. She stepped back knowing that the wards he'd carved around her home would keep her safe, but she felt better having him there. Just in case.

Ink paused, inspecting her face. Perhaps he saw her concern? He was getting very good at reading her subtle cues.

"Do not worry," Ink said and underlined the statement with a slice of his razor, unzipping a door through time and space. He placed a slow kiss on her bottom lip, soft and tender. He felt that. She did, too. "I will return soon."

Joy nodded and was still nodding as he disappeared, realizing a second too late that he'd left the smoldering sword behind.

She yanked her bathrobe off its hook and threw it over the longsword, snatched her phone on her way to the kitchen and quickly closed the door behind her.

Just in case.

She texted Stef, asking about his ETA, then pinged Monica as she entered the kitchen and leaned her elbows on the breakfast bar.

Home at last, she typed. Shift over = FREEDOM!

It took her best friend only a second to reply, if that.

Lol! Celebrating? Happy dance?

Joy smiled. After standing on her feet all day, she hadn't gone dancing in weeks. She'd almost forgotten that places like the Carousel existed. Almost. You free?

Expensive as always, but im worth it!!!

Joy laughed as she sat down on a stool.

"Hi, honey." Her father waved from the den. "I didn't hear you come in."

"I'm a ninja," Joy said as she typed back a series of smiley faces. "It's all part of staff training. It's why we wear black."

Her father chuckled as he hauled himself off the couch with a groan. His new gym routine included heavy cardio and weighted squats. Despite the grumbling, he had lost almost thirty pounds. He looked good, if tired. "I didn't know waitresses required the art of stealth."

Joy smirked. "We're sneaky that way."

He tugged her ponytail as he passed her on the way to the counter. "Well, I'm glad you're home safe," he said. Joy felt a twinge of guilt as she hid her mud-and-wood-pulp-spattered pants beneath the counter. She concentrated on typing a reply to Monica.

Any chance u can come over? Im stuck at home.

"I wanted to talk with you about something," her father said by the sink.

"Oh?" Joy said as she read: Can Gordon come 2? Or is this estrogen-only?

Monica and Joy spent time with their respective boy-friends, but also had a regular Girls' Night since, as Monica insisted, it was always important to stand by your sisters. Monica always checked if it was a co-ed party first.

Joy typed: Gordon=good times! Will see u 2 when?

"I'm glad we've been having a great time together this summer," he said as he scraped the last of his Lean Cuisine into the disposal. "That camping trip to the lake will be one for the record books."

"Mmm-hmm." Joy nodded, still typing.

"But, you know," he said nervously, "I also want to spend

some quality time with Shelley..." As she waited for a reply, Joy imagined her father's girlfriend—Shelley wasn't a bad person, but it was still a bit weird, his having a life without Mom.

Xcellent! Will your boy be there 2?

Joy sighed. After five months, Monica was still attempting to meet Joy's mysterious boyfriend. Joy couldn't blame her, but, besides being inhuman, Ink was invisible to those without the Sight. Still, she gave her BFF points for trying. She typed back, Ummmmmmmmm, no.

"...and I made sure we'll have more family time with Stef at the end of August," her father said gently. Joy realized that he'd been talking the whole time and she'd tuned him out. She looked up and smiled to prove she'd been listening. Sort of.

"Sure, Dad," Joy said. Her phone buzzed in her hand. 1 hour? Joy hit a colon, a dash and an end parenthesis. Send. "No problem."

Her father smiled, both pleased and relieved.

"Thanks, Joy," he said, giving her shoulders a squeeze. "I appreciate it." She blew a kiss at him while scrolling through texts, her attention glued to the screen. He sighed. "And I *really* appreciate that you agreed to pay for that new data plan upgrade," he added. "Otherwise I would have to yank that thing out of your hands right now."

Joy hugged her phone against her chest and glared at him. "Hey!"

He laughed. "Well, at least I got your attention. Though why you need unlimited worldwide calling is beyond me..." Joy thought about her latest pics from Tuan and Antony's trip to Belize and said nothing. It was one of the few ways she kept in touch with the Cabana Boys. It made her feel like one of them, one of the group, included—it was something she hadn't realized she'd been missing since quitting the gymnastics team nearly two years ago, and she was more than willing to pay for it.

"Okay." Her dad kissed the top of her forehead. "I'm headed out."

"Poker night?" she asked.

"No, just a few rounds of darts with some guys from Doolin's."

Joy whistled. "Look who's Mr. Popular!"

"It starts by getting out of the house," he said. "You really ought to try it someday."

Joy mock frowned and crouched over her phone. "Outside bad! Dark. Scary. Inside good! TV. Food."

Dad rolled his eyes. "Don't wait up."

"Bye!" She waved over her shoulder. "Have fun!"

"Emergency number's on the fridge in case you decide to break another window..."

Would she *ever* live that down? Joy turned and shouted, *"Bye, Dad!"*

He grinned boyishly as he shut the door.

Joy shook her head and typed a final message to Monica.

Guys r weird.

Monica's reply came in all caps:

AMEN, SISTER!!!

With an hour to burn, Joy decided to clean her room rather than surf online. It would be tougher to tease her brother for being the family slob if her room looked messy when he got home. After filling her trash bag and emptying the hamper, Joy dusted off her dresser and wiped down the shelf that held three printed invitations to various swanky parties in

Zurich, Melbourne and Moscow (care of Nikolai, on tour); a heavy glass snow globe from Glacier Bay, Alaska (from Enrique's latest adventure); a cashmere infinity scarf (from Luiz in Paris); and an odd collection of figurines—what Ilhami called "booby dolls"—from various cultures around the world. She had eight so far, wide-hipped, big-bellied and well-endowed, lined up in a row. Ilhami thought sending them to the "Cabana Girl" was hilarious. He had even scribbled eyes on one of them in Sharpie marker, which was probably sacrilegious, but Joy got the reference: *knocked up by Indelible Ink.*

As if on cue, Ink zipped into her room through the space next to her nightstand.

"What are you doing?"

Joy shrugged and put down the booby doll. "I'm cleaning," she said into the mirror, which failed to catch Ink's reflection behind her. "I was bored."

"I see," he said with a smile. "You know, if you are ever bored, you can always call Inq."

Joy neatened her ponytail. "I'm not *that* bored."

He laughed. "Probably wise," he said. He draped her pink bathrobe across the bed and picked up the sword. He inspected the weapon closely, watching the light gleam off the nicked and pitted blade. "The Bailiwick often says to be wary of wishing for an interesting life," he said casually. "And while I have been gone, I have discovered many interesting things."

Joy twisted her fingers in her shirt. "Such as?"

Ink's eyes flicked to her. "I went back to the edge of the Glen where we fought," he said. "And you were right—I do not think this was an idle threat."

Joy crossed her arms against a sudden prickly chill. "So do you think that one of the Folk was really trying to kill me?"

"I do not know." Ink's boyish face grew serious. "To know that, we must bring this—" he hefted the sword "—to Graus Claude."

Joy scraped her bare feet against the carpet. "'We?'"

"Of course." Ink grinned and held up her discarded clogs in his left hand. "Clearly, I can't leave you alone for a minute."

"Ha ha." Joy took her lost shoes and slipped them on. "Monica and Gordon are on their way here," she said. "To keep me company." She almost added, *I wish you could meet them*. Almost. But didn't. It was impossible, dangerous and probably stupid to expose her friends to her other life in the Twixt. And Monica and Joy's motto had always been No Stupid.

"It will only be a moment," Ink reminded her.

"If that," she said, smiling. "I remember." And took his hand.

A flick and a swish of citrus-scented breeze and Joy stepped from one world into the next.

TWO

THE BAILIWICK'S GRAND BROWNSTONE WAS BOTH IMpeccable and impressive. Its stone steps were swept clean, the ironwork polished and the miniature evergreens flanking the door had been replaced with urns of hardy bamboo. The stalks rattled in the wind as Ink rapped the brass knocker twice.

Kurt answered the door in his crisp black suit with white mandarin collar. Joy was overly conscious of her dusty clothes, but she'd arrived in worse states before. The butler stepped aside, making just enough room for Ink and Joy to enter past the bulge of his gun under his jacket. Today, Joy took comfort in Kurt being cautious.

She was about to say hi but then noticed that they were not alone. A strange woman sat in one of the foyer's wingback chairs, her fist pulling a hooded cloak tightly around her face. She looked nervous, her yellow-gold eyes wide. A strange sort of squiggle ran along the edge of her jaw. She tucked her feet under her chair, politely allowing Joy to pass, but kept staring at the sword in Ink's hand. Joy quickly sat in the second wingback chair, noticing that it no longer matched its twin—it had a different, though complementary, floral pattern, and the crystal bowl of eggs was notably missing. Joy wondered if she'd been the cause of both changes to the décor.

Ink offered Kurt his calling card, but the butler held up a gloved hand and beckoned them to follow. Ink withdrew the card and nodded to Joy. She gave an apologetic smile to the shrouded woman, who'd clearly been waiting there first, and hurried down the sconce-lit hall after them.

Kurt knocked on the great double doors before throwing them wide. The windows were open, flooding the office with light, and a fresh breeze tickled the gauzy inner curtains. Twin basins of lotus flowers lent a watery scent to the air, and jewel-winged dragonflies hovered over the fat lily pads. Natural light spilled into the room, reflecting off the emerald-green lamp and the crystal bowl of roe, now resting on the Bailiwick's enormous mahogany desk. The Bailiwick himself stood up from his chair like a giant amphibious king before his court.

"Master Ink, Miss Malone, welcome." All four of the great toad's hands bade them enter. Two smoothed the edge of his tailored, pinstripe suit jacket, erasing an offending crease, while two more gestured to the chairs before him. "Please, sit."

Kurt backed out of the room, but as he closed the doors, Joy caught a quick smile and a nod, which made her feel better. His stiff, formal demeanor as butler and bodyguard felt unfamiliar to her now. She'd last seen him on a beach in Mykonos, dunking Invisible Inq in the surf.

Graus Claude settled into his high-backed chair, the great wooden throne groaning under his monstrous bulk. "I have directed Kurt to grant you two immediate audience when I am available," the Bailiwick said. "Given your recent propensity for dramatic and often untidy entrances, I thought it might be prudent."

Ink settled into a chair. "Should that be considered a 'dubious' honor?"

Graus Claude smiled, his ice-blue eyes sparkling. "Quite."

One warty olive hand plucked up a fountain pen while a second clicked the wireless mouse and the third and fourth delicately steepled their fingertips together. "Now, then, to what do I owe the pleasure of this nearly pristine visitation?" Joy wiped her hands against her pants and tried not to think about her muddy shoes. "Might I presume that it has something to do with that sword?"

"Perhaps," Ink said. "I would like to know if the Edict is still in place. The one protecting Joy?"

Whatever Graus Claude might have expected, it wasn't that. His eye ridge rose, exposing widened icy blue eyes. "Of course. Why do you ask?" he said. "Even if we had held you to your declaration that you were no longer formally involved with Miss Malone, the Council's decision was based on her service to the Twixt and not dependent on her status as your *lehman*." His eyes flicked to Joy. "Although there has been no precedent to rescind an offer due to a change in status since the role of a chosen human consort has always been a permanent one." Graus Claude's voice purred. "Yet 'permanence' does not seem to apply when it comes to you, Miss Malone."

Joy twitched, oddly chastised by his stare. Ink placed the sword on the great toad's desk with a mellow *thunk*.

"Joy was attacked this afternoon by one of the Folk bearing this," he said.

Graus Claude picked up the sword and examined it with all his hands. "It is an elemental blade," he said. "It's old. Poorly kept. Recently discharged..." The Bailiwick's nostrils flared and he glanced at Joy. "Are you certain this wasn't simply a threat, Miss Malone? I warned you that there might be those seeking to test your mettle and that you must not rise to the bait. A human provoking one of the Folk has the onus of fault." His ice-blue eyes blinked. "Do not let them taunt you into ill-advised action."

"He didn't *taunt* me," Joy said. "This armored guy showed

up after work and tried to *kill* me. When I ran into the woods, he threw that—" she pointed at the sword "—into a tree and blew it to pieces."

Graus Claude sniffed the blade. "Hmm. Definitely *not* a mere threat," he murmured and placed the sword gently back onto his desk. "This was an uncommon weapon forged once upon an age, clearly fallen into disuse, but I cannot imagine how any might attempt to use it to circumvent the Edict. The protective safeguards would be enacted almost instantly."

"That ward was you?" Joy asked. "I thought that was Ink."

"Not I, Miss Malone," the noble toad said. "But rather the Council. I am merely one of its members, the comptroller between worlds, hence my title as the Bailiwick of the Twixt."

Joy picked a flake of bark off the desk where it had fallen from the sword. "Well, I don't know why you think that some Council ruling is enough to keep me and my family safe," she said. "People break laws all the time."

"People do. *Humans* do. The Folk, however, do not," Graus Claude said. "We aren't subject to laws the way you are to yours. Human laws are collaborative suggestions that can be bent or broken, but our rules are absolute. Rules of magic dictate how our world works, irrevocably. It is part of the Twixt—we cannot change our true nature any more than our True Names." Graus Claude spread his hands across the desk. "What the Council decrees are not mere words, Miss Malone. They are laws like sunlight and gravity. They *are*."

"And yet they say that I am safe from the Folk," Joy said. "But I'm not."

"Let's not be overly dramatic." Graus Claude's voice rumbled deep in his chest. "You are safe and sound. You've simply been frightened, and for that I apologize on behalf of the Folk. As you know, subtlety is not always a valued trait amongst my people, and they delight in pushing interpretation to their advantage."

"No, you don't understand—if Ink hadn't shown up..." Joy trailed off, realizing that she still had no idea how Ink had found her in the middle of the woods. She glanced at him. It was hard to tell if he was avoiding her eyes or not.

Had she managed to call him without his *signatura* on her skin? Could that happen? Once she'd removed the mark of his True Name, Joy had severed the bond between them, much as she had cut the bonds that linked Aniseed to the millions she'd planned to kill with her magic-borne disease. Afterward, Ink had refused to redraw his mark, insisting that she was better off free, an unclaimed human, despite her asking. They'd decided to base their relationship on choice rather than magic.

But then how...?

Ink tapped the sword. "The question on the table is whether or not Joy is safe," Ink said. "Currently, the answer is 'no.' This means that either the Edict has not been implemented, has been rescinded or is fundamentally flawed." The Bailiwick's eyes narrowed, but the Scribe continued, unshaken by his employer's displeasure. "In any case, I would ask that you confirm its present state and status with the Council." Ink straightened as he added a conciliatory, "Please."

The Bailiwick sat back and reconsidered the sword on his desk. He let out a long, slow sigh. "What you ask is fair," Graus Claude grumbled. "And, in fairness to you both, I will investigate your request as well as offer you some information and advice." He shifted in his seat much like a frog settling onto its haunches. "Once you exposed Aniseed's plot to foster a Golden Age by mass human genocide, we found that, while we had apprehended many of her supporters, her guiding sentiment had gained popularity." The Bailiwick coughed politely as if it could mask his distaste. "As a martyr, Aniseed's death has given it voice." He stuffed his fountain pen into its holder in disgust. "The Council has been forced to recognize a faction calling itself the Tide, whose representatives have invoked old precepts that would grant them formal audience as well as a seat on the Council." He smoothed his four hands over the carved armrests. "If there were any who would be most interested in this sort of base revenge, it would be the Tide." Graus Claude extended one pointy claw. "And they are most interested in you, Miss Malone."

Joy gripped her chair arms. "What? Why?"

"As an extremist, separatist faction, they see you as the primary example of the danger posed by humanity," he said. "Sol Leander, the representative of the Tide, accuses the Council of negligence in allowing you to flaunt their jurisdiction by wielding power without authority."

Joy gaped. "That's not true!"

"Actually, it is," Ink said. "You ended Aniseed's reign by erasing her mark as well as Briarhook's *signatura*. As well as Inq's. And mine. Such a thing has never occurred before, and certainly never without consequence."

"But I didn't know—" she began, but Ink continued.

"In addition, you continue to wield the scalpel, an instrument exclusive to the Scribes, without anyone being able to stop you or lay claim to you, since you are already protected under the Edict. You are what all the Twixt has ever wanted to be—both powerful and free." Ink's voice remained neutral, but Joy could tell that he said this with no small amount of pride. The dimples were back.

Joy tried to put her thoughts into words. "So the Folk...are jealous of me? Or afraid of me?"

"It is enough to make anyone afraid," Graus Claude said. "Sol Leander enjoys reminding everyone that his commitment, his auspice, is to survivors of unprovoked attack, like everyone in the Twixt." He tapped his pen with one hand as another gestured to Joy. Hands three and four held the armrests. "You have abused a system that you cannot possibly understand, and without Master Ink's *signatura*, you currently exist outside our parameters, yet inside our protections, which does, indeed, flaunt the authority of the Council." He lowered his head to Joy's to impress the weight of his words. "To put it bluntly, you are considered *rogue*, Miss Malone."

He sat back with a satisfied air as Joy nervously tugged at her cuff. "And therein lies the heart of my advice," he said. "I suggest that, for the sake of peace, you consider the following options—either return the scalpel that can erase marks to Master Ink, thus negating the concern of your power going unchecked, accept his *signatura*, which would bind you to the laws of the Twixt, or quit this world, Miss Malone." Graus Claude folded his four arms together. "Walk away from this life and never return."

A heavy quiet made the room seem darker. The Bailiwick sat patiently. She blinked at him. *What?* Was she supposed to decide *now?* Joy staggered under the dual weight of Ink's gaze and Graus Claude's words. Had Ink known this was going to happen? Had she been blind not to see this coming? Or simply hopeful? How long had she thought she could go on without being forced to make a choice? The Bailiwick had warned her it was impossible to be of two worlds and, one day, she would have to choose.

She took the scalpel out of its pocket. "I'll give it back."

"You cannot," Ink said. "It was a gift and I gave it willingly." He turned to Graus Claude. "It is done and cannot be undone. Not even by the Council." Ink cast a quick warning glance at Joy. Without the scalpel, the Folk might discover that the power of erasure lay not in the scalpel, but in her.

"So you say," the Bailiwick answered. "Yet 'undoing' seems to be Miss Malone's specialty and expertise. Besides," he said, "there are other options."

Joy held the scalpel, the metal warm in her hand. It was important to keep up the ruse, protecting her magic and her life, but it was also important that she keep other things, like being human. And being free.

"Ink doesn't want me to have his *signatura*," she said.

"Because it binds you," Ink said.

"Yes," Graus Claude agreed. "Precisely its purpose, as a matter of fact." The Bailiwick tapped his manicured claws against the wood. "*Signaturae* were developed to safeguard against human entrapment, making slaves of the Folk under the yoke of their True Names. By transferring our magic to sigils, we have secured our freedom. The Scribes, Invisible Inq and Indelible Ink, were created for the sole purpose to mark humans with *signaturae*." The great toad's eye ridge twitched. "That is what they *do*."

"But it must be given willingly," she said. "A *signatura* taken by force is powerless. So if Ink doesn't agree, then that's that."

"I believe you have remarkable talents of persuasion, should you wish to employ them," Graus Claude said drily. "And it need not be Master Ink's *signatura*. It could be any-one's, but the bond does carry certain obligations and re-sponsibilities that are essential to the Twixt."

Joy hadn't realized that she and Ink had been bound to anything other than one another. When she had been marked as his *lehman*, Joy was considered to be his human lover/slave/helpmate. What other promises had Ink made by marking Joy? What did the Council know that she didn't?

"She is human," Ink said. "And, unlike us, she has her free-dom." Ink placed a hand over Joy's. She looked at their joined fingers: human and almost-human, wound together. "She should not have to give that up under pressure from the Council."

"Well, I'm not giving *you* up," Joy said, dismissing the third option. She looked defiantly at Graus Claude. "I won't."

The Bailiwick sighed around his chins. "One cannot have it all, Miss Malone," he said, giving his head a palsied shake. "Every choice has its price."

Ink regarded Graus Claude coolly. "There must be another way," Ink said. "And if anyone would discover it, I trust that it would be you."

The massive toad's great eye ridge arced in surprise. "Flattery?" the Bailiwick asked, smiling. "That is a new trick for you, Master Ink."

Ink shrugged. "I am learning." He touched the skin of Joy's wrist gently, as if remembering how her touch was his first hint at being human, the music of fingers touching, skin on skin.

Graus Claude rearranged random things on his desk before two of his hands opened a polished wood case and a third withdrew a set of gold-rimmed spectacles. "Very well. Leave me the sword—let me ruminate on the rest. See if I cannot invent some solution." He nodded to Joy. "Miss Malone, I ask that you consider the obvious alternatives within the month. By then, the Council will most likely demand a formal audience with you, and while I have labored to shield you from them, I cannot sway them from such an action as it would be well within their rights. They will customarily ask you for your voluntary acquiescence to respect their ruling and it might be in your best interest to express a preference with humility and sincerity. The Council is more impressed with a show of vulnerability than strength." He peered through his tiny lenses, his nostrils squashed flat against his face. "In the meanwhile, Master Ink has informed me that your home is still well fortified with wards of his design. You should be safest there. Wait for my summons, and we shall see what cleverness I can devise."

Ink tapped Joy's hand, but she was the first to speak.

"Thank you, Graus Claude."

"And thank you for your efforts to protect both our worlds," he replied. "For anyone on the Council to condemn you without question is poor recompense, and I assure you that I, for one, will not allow it."

Ink stood. "We are in your debt."

Graus Claude speared the Scribe with a sharp glance. "Mind your debts, Master Ink," he said. "I am certain your sister would counsel likewise."

Joy thought back to Inq's centuries-old deal with Aniseed, the one that might have first inspired the dryad alchemist to try spreading her fatal disease through *signaturae*. That one tiny trade almost destroyed all of humanity and the Twixt.

As if by magic, the doors parted and Kurt stood ready to escort them out. "Away with you, now," Graus Claude said good-naturedly. "Master Ink, always a mystery. Miss Malone, always a pleasure."

Ink bowed. "Thank you again, Bailiwick." He held Joy's hand as they left the office, exiting into the now-empty foyer with its dark wainscoting, oil paintings and ivory-colored walls. Joy wondered what had happened to the frightened robed woman. Perhaps she'd grown tired of waiting? Joy was suddenly exhausted. An eight-hour shift plus a run for your life, a hot shower and a formal audience with an eight-foot, four-armed amphibian took a lot out of a body.

"I think we're starting to annoy him," Joy said to Kurt as they approached the front door.

"Nonsense," Kurt said in his smooth tenor, which Joy still thought at odds with his heavy muscleman body. "The Bailiwick looks forward to your visits. He remarks that they are rarely dull."

"I'm so glad that my life is entertaining," Joy said.

Kurt bowed a fraction. "Most mortals' are."

Joy considered his words and his carefully neutral expression. Kurt had been a human child who'd survived the Black

Plague; his mother had called upon the Folk to save him and the Bailiwick had agreed in exchange for the boy's servitude, extending Kurt's mortal life so that he could work off his debt. Kurt had been Inq's lover, yet never one of her *lehman*, dedicating his life to killing Aniseed and recently regaining his voice by breaking her curse. He had been trained in swordsmanship, marksmanship, magic, healing and service. His eyes looked old although his face barely looked thirty, and a long scar split his throat like a gruesome smile. Kurt's life had been entertaining Folk for centuries. Joy wondered if he still considered himself mortal or not.

"You sound like my sister," Ink said.

Kurt almost snorted. "A recreational hazard."

Joy smiled. "Please tell Inq hi from me."

Kurt placed a gloved hand on the doorknob. "You know she'll take that as an invitation."

"She might, as well," Ink said. "We would welcome her thoughts on this matter."

"I'll tell her you said so," Kurt said as he nodded his good-bye and, checking the perimeter, let them through the door.

Flicking his straight razor, Ink slashed a gaping hole through the thick of the world. Black eyes hard, he shielded Joy from the open air and any who might be watching. Joy slid against his chest as he pulled her forward into nothingness.

Joy stumbled into her room, banging her shin against the side of her bed. Ink strode past her, emerging from the rent inside the closet to check his wards on the window and the door to her room before striding into the hall to examine all the exits. Joy trailed behind him, switching off the house alarm and flipping on lights. It had been barely a minute since they'd left. Time did strange things when she traveled by Scribe.

"Everything safe?" she asked.

Ink ran his fingers over the security keypad. "As safe as I left it, but not as safe as I would like." He marched a quick circuit around the condo.

"Do you think anything could happen here?"

Ink crossed the room. "No. I placed enough wards to keep the Folk at bay. Only Inq or I can enter here."

"What about Folk like Graus Claude? Or Filly?" Joy asked, thinking of the last time the young Valkyrie had appeared in her kitchen, summoned by a trill of bells. Of course, that hadn't actually *been* her kitchen, it had been an illusion, a trap, and, looking around, Joy doubted that the eight-foot-tall Bailiwick could even fit through the hall.

"Not without your invitation," Ink said from the den. "You are safe here."

"I'm not worried about me," Joy said, even if it was only half-true. "Stefan is coming home for the last half of summer break, and Dad'll be here, too." The prospect of having her family home was both exciting and terrifying. *When worlds collide...* It was almost like the idea of having Mom and Doug meet Dad and Shelley. While she didn't like the fact that her mother had left her father for a younger man and moved out to Los Angeles, Joy now accepted that her mom still loved her, but Doug was something Joy hadn't dealt with yet. When she'd gone to visit in March, he'd been conspicuously absent, which was fine by her. *Baby steps. One conniption fit at a time.* She took a deep breath. "My family can't even *see* the Folk. How are they supposed to keep safe?"

Ink unfolded his leather wallet on its silver chain. He tucked the razor back into its pocket next to the leaf-tipped wand and the empty compartment where the scalpel used to be, its shape still clearly visible, having molded into the leather over time.

"I do not believe that they are in danger," Ink said. "I have been thinking about it more. Elemental blades are most often used in ritual combat. They were once wielded against true elementals, the forerunners who ruled before there was the Twixt, back when the world was divided equally between humans and Folk. The sword we left with Graus Claude was crafted with fire and water, disparate elements—powerful, but unstable, much like its wielder," he said wryly. "I do not think he was in his right mind. The weapon was not forged for use against humans." Ink's eyes sought hers. "Nevertheless, you could have been killed."

Joy sat down. "I wasn't."

"No," Ink said. "But you could have been. Easily. Far too easily. And yet he chased you into the woods—an aged soldier in ancient armor, waving an antiquated sword. He was old, and it had been a long time since he had seen combat."

He took her hand, forcing Joy to stop twisting her fingers in her shirt. "How do you know all this?"

"I inspected that portion of the Glen, following his trail and deciphering his tactics," he said. "And I was there, with you, at the end. His endurance was waning, his reactions were slow, his aim was poor and his teeth were blue."

Joy waited, but Ink gave no further explanation. "Um, what?"

"The *Rakshasa*'s fore-teeth turn blue as they age," Ink said. "So an old soldier came out of retirement for you. Why?" Ink leaned back in his seat. "Perhaps he fought for honor or revenge, yet he fled rather than face the two of us." He tapped the wallet again. "Honor and revenge are both strong motivators, and I doubt an old soldier's pride would be weak, so the more believable incentive would be money or madness. If he were mad, he would have not retreated. Therefore, I think it most likely that he was paid to frighten you. His retreat was not out of fear, but prudence. Did you notice when he decided to flee?"

"When you showed up," Joy said, sliding her thumb against his. "When you stood by me."

"Yes—when he saw that I was there and had no intention of leaving," Ink said. "I think he was paid only to deal with you, not me, as well, and either the odds were no longer worth the asking price or he left to get further instruction, knowing that he could always try again later."

Joy withdrew her hand. "Is that supposed to make me feel better?"

"A little," he said. Joy glared. "Very little," he amended. "However, you might take comfort in the fact that if your attacker is motivated by money, then he will not be interested in harming anyone else in your family. And since his heart is not bound to it, the task may be easily abandoned."

"How?"

Ink gestured offhandedly. "He can be outbid."

Joy stared at Ink in surprise, laughter coloring her words. "You'd buy him off?"

"If necessary," Ink said. "Working for the Bailiwick has many rewards, few of which have interested me as I have found them unnecessary. But, should it become necessary, I am confident that I could offer enough wealth to sway anyone motivated merely by greed."

"Really?" Joy said, tracing the grain of the table. "So you're both handsome and rich?" She smiled. "My hero."

Ink's face melted into a true smile. With dimples. "And Graus Claude wonders where I learned flattery." He reached out a hand—one of his own Joy-like hands—and touched the edge of her eyebrow, tucking her lengthening bangs behind her ear. The touch brought back memories that made her shiver. "I cannot ask you to stay in this house," he said. "But I would prefer if you did. For tonight, at least. It is one of the few ways I know that you are truly safe."

"Okay," Joy said. "But I can't stay home forever. Aside from going stir-crazy, I can't lose my job—with cutbacks going on at Dad's office, he's working overtime and I agreed to help out."

"I could help you," Ink said.

"Thanks, but that'd be tough to explain." She tried to laugh, but it came out strained. She had been used to her father spending most of his time at work or with his girl-friend, Shelley, but he'd been making the extra effort to be around Joy and would likely notice if she was suddenly free-wheeling with lots of time and spending cash. Although the idea of quitting Antoine's was tempting, her father would ask too many questions she couldn't answer. She'd never been good at lying.

Ink brushed her skin lightly and he seemed to come to a decision.

"Then let me do this," he said, unwinding a length of string from his neck. He lifted it over his head and held it up for her to see. It was a necklace with a single metal pen-dant, a rune like a bisected Y etched into its surface. She touched the unfamiliar symbol; the metal was still warm from his skin.

"What is it?"

"It is a glyph," he said, looping it over her neck so that the symbol rested against her breastbone. "A *futhark*. It can pro-tect you against an unexpected attack. A second chance is sometimes all that you need." He pressed the tiny symbol against her skin. "I had it made after I confronted Aniseed. If I had worn this, she would not have..." His voice faltered and his expression changed as he recalled the strange sen-sation of death. "Would not have caught me unawares," he said. His eyes flicked from Joy to the wallet, and she could see the cascade of thoughts that skittered like a stone skipped across a pond: then he wouldn't have needed to give Joy his scalpel, she wouldn't have discovered that she could erase *signatura*, she would not have been captured by Aniseed and held as ransom for his mark and he wouldn't have bled to death during the battle on the warehouse floor. Of course, then Aniseed might have killed most of humanity, taking the bulk of the Twixt with it. Joy might have died. Ink might have stayed dead. Aniseed might have lived.

There was no telling what might have happened. What might have been.

That one thought scared her most of all.

"You should keep it..." Joy said, knowing how much that brush with death had shaken him, even if it had been only temporary. The memory of his eyes spilling black as his body collapsed, gushing ink onto the floor, haunted her still. But he tucked the necklace beneath her collar, his fingers lingering at the base of her throat. She felt her pulse jump as his thumb trailed over the smooth silk of her skin.

"No," he said almost hypnotically. "This can keep you safe if I am not with you." Ink drew his fingers along the chain at his hip. "I must go mark a new lama in Tibet, but I will return shortly." He tilted his face to one side. "I will always come for you, Joy."

She nodded, nearly speechless. "I know."

Ink touched his lips to hers. She felt him hover, his breath in hers, their mouths closing with delicate symmetry—withdrawing, returning, testing how they fit together—like a welcoming home, soft and warm. She felt a slow heat grow inside her, radiating out.

"I need you," he whispered, breaking their kiss. His eyes blinked open, dark wells of forever. "I need you to be safe," he said. "I need you to be free. If nothing else, and for no other reason, I need *you* to be free."

Joy paused still tasting his breath on her lips. "I don't understand."

"No, you don't. You can't. And that is good," Ink said. "There is an innocence in not knowing what you can lose."

His voice grew stern. "Do not allow anyone to place their *signatura* on you and claim you as theirs. Your body, your skin, your blood, your tears, your wishes, your dreams—they are yours and yours alone. Do not let anyone take them from you."

Joy was taken aback, wondering what he meant and wondering again what she did not know.

"I won't," she said. "I promise."

Ink looked at her strangely, almost sadly, drawing his fingers down her cheek. "You cannot promise such a thing," he said. "You are only human."

It was true, she was not bound like the Folk to never tell a lie, but his correction stung nonetheless. Before she could say more, the doorbell chimed. Joy glanced at the clock, disbelieving.

"Monica," Joy said.

Ink stood up, folding his wallet and fitting the chain.

"I will return to Graus Claude and follow the answers," he said. "In the meanwhile, please do not take undue risks. Remember, my theory is just a theory, and I would not welcome any opportunities to be proven wrong."

Joy touched the glyph under her shirt. "I'll do my best."

Ink half smiled. One dimple only. A hand on her arm. "Thank you," he said and let his hand trail, a lingering touch on her skin. He stepped back, palmed his razor and opened a neat door with a wave of his hand.

"Wait," she said. "One kiss."

"One kiss?"

"One kiss," Joy said. "Nonnegotiable."

His lips were warm and welcome and sweet, holding a promise of their own.

He rested his head against hers. His voice softened.

"I love you, Joy Malone."

She smiled. "I love you, too."

It was all she could say as he disappeared, since she realized in that moment that she no longer had his True Name.

THREE

JOY ANSWERED THE DOOR HOLDING UP TWO MAILERS.

"Dino's or Pizza Pi?"

Monica snickered as she walked in. "And hello to you, too." Gordon propped the door open with his shoulder and offered one of two lidded paper cups.

"I come bearing caffeine," he said. "One of these iced lattes is for you." He glanced down. "Nice socks."

Joy was wearing mismatched tennies, one green, one pink with daisies; it made her feel more like herself. She accepted a cup and took a sip, bowing. "You are a god."

Gordon grinned and shut the door. "It's nice to be worshipped."

"Don't let the humility fool you," Monica said, dropping her purse and giving her boyfriend a kiss. In Joy's head, she still called him "Mr. Wide" due to his quarterback shoulders and the size of his grin. Monica smoothed back her bob. "I vote Pizza Pi."

Gordon shrugged. "I'm up for anything with extra cheese."

"Don't say 'extra cheese' around me for the rest of the day," Joy said, snagging a phone and checking the number on the flyer. "If I hear one more order for anything involving extra cheese, I will seriously lose whatever is left of my mind." She flumped on the bare couch. Joy missed the old afghan, but even after several covert washings, the yarn had snarled itself around the crusted stains of Twixt and human blood. She'd had to throw it out and tell her father that she'd accidentally left it at the beach. It had been her grandmother's and she'd been grounded for two weeks. Lying sucked.

She dialed with her thumbs and kicked her feet over the back of the pillows. Monica made a face.

"Rough day?"

Joy groaned. "If this day went to the spa, it would need exfoliation treatments."

"Hey, there's an idea!" Monica said. "Spa day!"

"I wish," Joy said. "I have to earn enough to pay for my plan or Dad said he's taking my phone."

Gordon whistled. "Harsh."

Joy shrugged. "A couple of shifts a week should cover it," she said as the phone rang. "Orders, please?"

Half an hour later, there was pizza cut into long, thin strips, three empty coffee cups and a half-eaten bag of Smartfood as they chatted about the latest in Nordic bubblegum punk.

"Crushed Tomato isn't a band name," Joy said, tossing her crust in the box. "It's a pizza ingredient."

"Actually, there's a song off their new album that I think you might like," Monica said from the opposite end of the couch. Her dark legs draped over Gordon's lap and his hand rested on her knee as she stroked his blond crew cut. They looked entirely too adorable. Joy debated throwing a pillow at them.

"Oh no!" Joy said. "You've corrupted her ears! The only things she had left were her virgin ears. What will she save for marriage?"

Monica threw a pillow at her. "Well, they're a lot better than Last Dog Standing."

"Agreed," Joy said, tucking the pillow behind her head. "And twice as good as that *Der Franzen* CD."

Gordon placed a hand on his chest. "You wound me. I love that band!"

Monica patted his shoulder. "Sorry, sweetie, but I'm with Joy on this one. Your boys are into some seriously weird noise." She placed her elbow on the armrest and tugged her knees free. "Speaking of boys, when, exactly, do you expect Stef home?"

Joy shrugged. "I dunno. Sometime in the next two days."

Monica winked as the front door clicked. "How about now?"

Joy spun around to look over the back of the couch. Her brother walked in under a giant duffel bag, his face scruffy with two days of beard. He beamed at her through his rectangle lenses.

"Honey, I'm home!"

Joy squealed and flung herself at him in a full-body tackle, wrapping him in a tight squeeze. He hugged her back, smelling of open road and barbecue chips. His stubble scratched her ear, and she'd poked his glasses askew, but she didn't care. She could feel his laugh in her chest and his voice in her ear. Stefan was back! Her big brother was home! It felt like she was the one returning after being away for far too long.

"Hey, you," Joy said, letting him breathe. "Had a good trip?"

"Driving from U Penn to Columbus to Glendale? Never again. I pulled an all-nighter just to get off the road." Stef waved at their guests. "Hi, Monica." He offered a hand to Gordon. "Hi, blond stranger. I'm Stefan."

"The infamous Stef! Nice to meet you. I'm Gordon."

"Pleased to meet you," Stef said. "And you brought pizza."

"S'all yours," Monica chirped.

Stef dropped his duffel bag on the floor with a thud. "You are now officially my new favorite people." He pulled himself a double slice, and Joy beamed. Monica and Gordon held hands. Stef adjusted his glasses and took a bite. It was a perfect moment.

Stef spoke around a mouthful. "So where's Dad?"

"Out with Shelley," Joy said. "Where else? And he's going to seriously kill you for showing up before he got home. I think he was planning on there being cake."

Stef folded the second slice over the first and took another bite. "I wouldn't say no to cake."

"Yeesh. Where do you put it all?" Monica asked enviously. "Aren't you supposed to get all freshman-fifteen?"

Stef looked long and lanky, much the same as he had when he'd left with his inside-out, backward shirt, scratched-up glasses and tight-fitting jeans. "Joy and I share the Malone metabolism," he said between bites and adjusted his raggedy red friendship bracelet over his wrist. Joy was surprised he hadn't ditched the thing while at college. It was *so* summer camp. "Besides—" he swallowed "—I had to keep up. Back in middle school, Joy's appetite put me to shame." He glanced at Gordon. "There's nothing worse than being out-eaten at the school's pie-eating contest by your pipsqueak little sister."

"Ha ha," Joy said, but she couldn't help smiling. This was something that phone calls and IM chats couldn't replace— the feeling of being in the same room, riffing off one another, sharing memories, teasing, being together. She hadn't realized how much she'd missed it until just now.

Stef clapped his hands together as he swallowed the last bite. "Okay, I hate to be incredibly rude, but I need to collapse on my face," he said. "But before I go catatonic, I want to give you your present."

"You brought me something?" Joy asked.

"Yep! And it's bigger than a bread box."

Joy clapped her hands and squealed at Monica. "I'm getting a present!"

Gordon laughed. "I think you just turned six," he said. "I could see pigtails and everything."

Joy stuck out her tongue as Stef hooked her elbow, propelling her into the kitchen. "Come over to the window," he said.

"The window?" Joy asked nervously as the four of them crowded together and craned over the sink. Joy swallowed back the momentary jitters she experienced every time she came near the kitchen window. Her mind played tricks as her brain mixed a wild concoction of fear and memory, leaving Joy half expecting to find another message written in light or a monster's giant tongue about to shatter the glass.

Shaking off her first memories of the Twixt, Joy looked down into the courtyard. It looked completely ordinary with a fat couple sunning in folding lawn chairs as three kids chased each other with Super Soakers near the parking lot.

"You got me a water gun?" she guessed.

Stef pointed. "No. There. In the corner."

Joy stood on her tiptoes, spying Stef's used Kia. "Is it in the car?"

Stef dangled keys from his fingers. "It *is* the car."

Joy screamed. "I get your *car*?"

"With a quarter of a zillion miles on it. I was going to trade it in, but Mom and Dad agreed to buy it off me and give it to you." He dropped the keys into her palm. Joy bounced in her shoes. "I'll help you clean her up before I pick up my new one at the dealership, but then she's all yours," he said. "Be careful with the driver's side window—it sticks."

Joy wrapped her arms around Stef's chest.

"Thankyouthankyouthankyou!"

"You can thank me by giving me oxygen." He laughed as though pained and ruffled her bangs. "Okay! Now that I have officially won the Best Brother Ever Award, I would like to thank the Academy before I grab another couple slices of pizza and go to bed." Stef pinched his lip and nodded to everyone. "Nice to see you, Monica. Nice meeting you, Gordon. Nice surprising you, Joy. My pillow awaits."

Joy gave Stef a parting kiss on his scruffy cheek.

"Thanks, Stef! Welcome home!"

"You're welcome and good night." He waved as he dragged his duffel bag into his room, across the hall from hers. The door closed, and they all heard a thump.

"Well, he seems nice," Gordon said. "So when do I get a car?"

"Care to take us for a spin?" Monica asked.

Joy swallowed some of her excitement. She'd promised Ink she'd stay home.

"Not until after Stef helps me clean it," she said. "You know how he is."

"He's a slob," Monica translated for Gordon.

"Like you should talk," Gordon said. "My mother would kill me if my room looked like yours!" Monica poked him in the gut. He poked her back. Monica squealed. Joy tucked the keys in her pocket and sauntered back to the den. She had her own car. Stef was in his room. Her dad was due home soon, and her friends were laughing in the kitchen—it was a perfect ending to an almost-perfect night. Joy smiled as she closed the pizza box.

All it was missing was Ink.

Joy was late to work. She logged in at the exact moment she realized she'd forgotten to wash her apron. There were splashes of dried coffee and smears of dirt and what smelled like marinara on the pocket. She soaked a dish towel and hurriedly scrubbed at the stains.

"Someone's here for you," Neil said, tapping her shoulder with his cheat sheet. "Table Four. Asked for an ice water, hold the glass." His voice dipped in sympathy. He'd been her senior server when she'd started at Antoine's, and he still tried to keep an eye out for her. "What a way to start the day."

"Are you kidding me?" Joy peeked around the counter to see who was at the two-top and stared. Invisible Inq was quietly kicking her heels under her seat, chin propped on the back of her interlaced fingers, smiling.

Joy tied off the bow and grabbed her check cover, swallowing panic. No one should be able to see Inq except her. No one without the Sight...

"Don't forget your ice water," Neil said as he went to fold napkins.

Watching Neil out of the corner of her eye, Joy stopped at the fill station and scooped some ice cubes onto a saucer, placing a teaspoon on it for good measure. The freezer wasn't the reason chills swept over her body as she marched to Table Four.

The wily Scribe twinkled and waved her fingers.

"Hi, Joy!"

Joy didn't know whether to put down the saucer or not, as if leaving evidence would confirm that she was certifiably crazy to the rest of the staff. Fortunately, it was still early, and the café was all but empty.

"What are you doing here?" Joy said under her breath.

"I thought I'd come visit you at work," Inq chirped. "Make sure that you were okay. I heard pillow talk that you had a bit of excitement yesterday, and Ink asked me to check on you." She eyed the smeared black apron. "Nice digs."

Joy held her temper, knowing she had to choose her words carefully when speaking to invisible people, especially Inq.

"This is *not* a good time," Joy whispered, trying to think of some reason she could give for standing in the middle of the restaurant talking to an empty table with a saucerful of ice in her hand. Did Neil realize that Table Four looked empty? Did he have the Sight? Had Joy put him in danger by leading Inq here? Had she exposed herself by admitting that she could see Inq, too? Joy was one of the rare people born with the Sight who had managed to keep her eyes from being cut out. Joy's mind drifted to the four-leaf clover in her bag.

"Yes, well, that's the trouble with mortality, isn't it?" Inq said smoothly, opening her menu. "So much to do, so little time." She smiled again. "I hear Antoine's makes a passable frittata." Joy was about to snatch the trifold menu out of her hands when Neil walked by. Inq turned to him boldly. "Excuse me," she said. Joy froze. "Could I trouble you for a new napkin?"

Neil handed one of his freshly rolled cloth napkins to Inq and gave Joy a conciliatory "What can you do?" shrug before continuing on to Table Ten. Joy stared at Inq, who dabbed demurely at the corner of her lips.

"He *can* see you," Joy said under her breath. "How can he see you? Does he have the Sight?"

Inq blinked her innocent all-black eyes. "Do you recommend the frittata?"

"Inq!" Joy placed the saucer of melting ice in front of Inq and crossed her arms as if she could hold in her heart attack. "What, exactly, does he see?"

"He sees me, of course," Inq said with a grin. "But it's not him—it's me. I'm wearing a glamour. I look exactly like me, sans spooky eyes. It makes things easier when I want to buy something pretty or eat out on the town. Otherwise, it looks like some sort of ghost is haunting the place with stuff floating all around. So cliché." She shut her menu primly. "I'd like the frittata, a side salad and a large glass of fresh orange juice, please."

Joy flipped open her notebook and started writing to cover her racing thoughts.

"A glamour?" Joy said over her pen.

"Mmm-hmm."

A way for the Folk to be seen—in this world!—and look like normal, everyday people? The possibilities blossomed like flowers in her brain.

"You knew," Joy said.

"I suspected," Inq said. "It doesn't take a genius. Sooner or later you'd want a way to show off my brother, even if only to prove that you're not crazy." She tapped the table. "I've had more than one *lehman*, remember? I know how humans think."

Joy finished writing with a flourish. "Can you tell me where to get one?"

"I'll do better than that," Inq said. "After brunch, I'll *show* you." She handed back the menu. "Extra croutons on the salad, please."

After lunch, Joy stepped out of the ripples onto a familiar stretch of sidewalk. The reality check pushed her completely off balance. Inq caught her elbow.

"I thought we were going to see a man about a glamour," Joy said.

Inq grinned. "We are."

"Are we stopping by my house first?" Joy pointed back up the path that wound toward her condo. "We're right between my place and the mini-mart."

Inq started walking with a skip to her step. "Really? Do tell."

"Wait," Joy said while jogging to keep up. She had been nervous about being outside despite wearing the *futhark* pendant and having Inq as her guide. She was pretty sure Ink wouldn't approve of the outing, but now Joy was curious, excited and confused. "Are you trying to tell me that you can buy glamours at the C&P?"

"Don't be silly," Inq said. "You buy glamours from a wizard. And, because this is the Glen—the original one—there's all sorts of magic still around! You just have to know where to look." She spoke while almost dancing around Joy in her excitement to share a new secret of the Twixt. "You're not the only special snowflake in the neighborhood."

Joy felt a grin tug at her lips. "So we're really off to see the wizard?"

Inq nudged Joy. "You're not in Kansas anymore, Dorothy!" she said. "This is Glendale, once known as the Glen, one of the access doors to Under the Hill, and still chock-full of magic! Can't you *feel* it?" They were coming up to the mini-mart with its giant signs for the ATM, blue-raspberry slushies and state lottery tickets. They'd had a five-thousand-dollar winner. Joy blinked, trying to use her Sight to see what was hiding beneath the familiar building, but she didn't see anything unusual. In fact, everything looked deceptively normal.

Inq laughed and threw her arms out. "Here we are!"

"Wait, I thought you said that you couldn't buy them at the C&P?"

"I said you buy them from a wizard," Inq said. "But the wizard happens to work at the C&P."

Joy pushed open the door with its friendly two-tone *hello*. The smell was the same weird mix of air freshener and hot dogs. People milled about the aisles of snack bags and candy bars. Joy took a few steps inside and hugged her purse under her armpit. She was nervous about having so many humans as potential witnesses to Inq's antics, and she still had no idea what was going on. The familiar and unfamiliar started square-dancing in her head.

Inq pretended to check out the covers of magazines while Joy debated snagging a fruit-and-nut bar to eat on her lunch break. At the café she could stave off the worst of her hypo-glycemia by grabbing a roll here and there, but the carbs gave her a slow, weighty feeling that she never really enjoyed.

Her lean, mean days of gymnastics training had given her a taste for chalky protein shakes, energy bars and aspartame.

"Watch," Inq whispered to Joy as someone approached the counter. Joy's stomach clenched. Mr. Vinh, the old proprietor, picked out the numbers on his cash register as he rang up a bag of nacho chips, a half liter of Coke, a pack of peanut M&M's and a packet of gum. Mr. Vinh totaled the bill, and the customer paid cash. Before giving change, Mr. Vinh placed everything into a bag, including two small packets wrapped in leaves and tied with brown string. He hit Return on the register and counted out change, turning to address the next person in line. Joy kept her eyes on the young man who left—he looked Puerto Rican, but when he turned to shoulder the door, Joy saw that his throat was laced with pink gills and his feet in flip-flops had pale pink webs. The door closed behind him with its two-tone *goodbye*.

"You can't be serious..." Joy whispered, disbelieving.

Inq smirked. "Meet Mr. Wizard."

Joy shook her head. "It can't be," she said. "I've come here for years."

"Of course you have," Inq said, moving down the aisle. "But how often since your Sight's been active? And did you buy any gum?"

"Gum?" Joy said, wondering when was the last time she'd chewed gum.

"It's a code," Inq said and waggled a slim red-and-black packet. "Nobody buys things like clove-flavored gum anymore. And buying certain snacks in combination is really a request for...other things." Inq shrugged and pointed up. "Security cameras still work, so it's important to keep up appearances. No one wants to run our supplier out of business. And, hey—" she waved a Kit Kat "—chocolate!" She winked. "Food of the gods."

Joy stared as Inq stuffed a careful selection of things into her arms and pushed her forward. "Here," she said impishly. "Go introduce yourself!"

Joy stared at her haul in dismay. She didn't even *like* Gummi Worms...

Mr. Vinh glanced up at Joy as she spilled her armload onto the counter.

"Hello, busy girl," he said in greeting.

"Hi, Mr. Vinh," Joy whispered. He picked up the packet of spice-flavored gum.

"No sugarless mint?" he asked. It had been Joy's favorite when she'd been in training, covering the sour smell of stomach acid in her mouth—the same sort of taste that was in her mouth now, all fear and nerves and reflux. She couldn't believe that he remembered. "Maybe you want some wintergreen instead?"

Inq peeked over Joy's shoulder. "How about a dermal, fourth-circle glamour with a subvocal charm?"

Mr. Vinh's eyes lowered under his deep epicanthic folds, but he kept speaking to Joy as if he hadn't heard Inq. "You are together?" he asked.

Joy nodded as Inq squeezed her shoulders. Mr. Vinh rang up the total for the lot.

"Eight dollars and seventeen cents," he said. Joy handed over a crisp twenty. Mr. Vinh rubbed it between his fingers and held it up to the fluorescent light, all but rendered moot by the bright summer sun. Joy twisted her fingers. She felt like she was being carded. He finally nodded and made change, punching a number into the nearby phone. He spoke in rapid-fire something-ese, then hung up.

"My son will be here shortly," he said. "Please wait over there." He pointed to the lonely stack of morning papers in their thin wire display. Joy took her plastic bag, which sported a yellow smiley face and Have a Nice Day!, and stepped to the side. Inq grabbed a paper and flipped to the entertainment section.

"What are we doing?" Joy whispered as Inq turned pages.

"Waiting," she said. "It's a power thing. The Bailiwick does it all the time." Inq flipped to the back of the paper and sighed. "Men!"

A tall man in his mid-twenties wearing a blue button-up over a black tee and jeans opened a back door and loped to the counter, exchanging a few words with Mr. Vinh before taking his place at the register. He nodded to the next customer with a smile and said in English, "Next person, please."

Mr. Vinh shuffled out from behind the counter, feet scraping against the floor in black socks and worn Birkenstocks. He led the way to a sign marked Storage: Employees Only and pulled back the heavy door. Clicking on the light, he gestured for Inq and Joy to follow.

The storage closet was packed with flats of juice drinks, boxes of snacks and plastic-wrapped rolls of paper towels. A lunar calendar was tacked up on the wall above a small electric-lit altar propped with photos of dour-looking people and tiny bowls of seeds and sweets. Mr. Vinh brushed past them and ran his hand along the back of one of the shelving units, his arm disappearing up to the shoulder as the back of the closet swung open with a click.

"Less magic," he said matter-of-factly. "More secure. Come in."

He pushed the hidden door wider and beckoned them inside. Wondering what she'd gotten herself into, Joy stepped forward. Inq strolled after them, nearly skipping into the dark.

"What did the nix want?" Inq asked conversationally.

"Bah," Mr. Vinh grunted. "Modern maladies. Drink this to wake up. Drink this to go to sleep. Eat this to get fat. Eat this to get thin." He turned on a light. "It's like doing business in a Lewis Carroll novel."

Joy tiptoed into the small room lined with bamboo slats. There was an enormous armoire composed of rows of tiny drawers, each one labeled with dark red paint. Bundles of dried herbs and wrinkled things were stuffed in heavy glass jars, ceramic jugs and urns, and a large, tinted-glass mirror hung on the wall in a chunky wooden frame. A glass cabinet full of strange instruments glinted in the light of oddly twisted bulbs that hung from the ceiling. Overlapping grass mats covered the floor, shushing underfoot and swallowing sound.

Mr. Vinh shrugged on a long black robe, the edge of it catching on his C&P name tag. He tugged it loose and buttoned it closed under his left armpit. After placing a simple flat cap on his head, he drew out a long stylus, dipped it in a small bowl of water and swirled it with quick strokes into a pot of black paste. He spoke offhandedly while he worked the bristles in. "You don't really want a glamour, do you?"

"Of course not." Inq spoke first. Joy frowned at her but kept silent. "What would she do with one? She's human."

Mr. Vinh stopped swishing the brush and said nothing. He smoothed the soft bristles against the edge of the pot, creating a fine point. "Well then," he said. "How may I be of service?"

"She asked me about glamours," Inq said. "So I brought her to you."

"I don't do tutorials, demonstrations or free samples," said Mr. Vinh crisply.

"How about a sales pitch?" Inq said.

Joy stood to one side, trying to be as polite as possible. This was a different Mr. Vinh from the one she knew from the C&P. He was brisk, efficient, a little bit perturbed and a little bit scary. He was clearly in his element here in the secret wizard's back room, a place very different from the fluorescent-bulbed store.

Mr. Vinh painted himself a note in liquid script, his pen dancing in quick, soaring strokes on a roll of ecru paper. "Why are you here?" he asked.

Joy swallowed. "I'm..."

"She's *lehman* to Indelible Ink."

Joy and Mr. Vinh both glanced at Inq. She held their stares. Joy frowned. Was she? Did Mr. Vinh know what that meant? Joy felt a blush light her cheeks and twisted her fingers around her purse strap. Mr. Vinh laid his brush gently on the pot lid, balancing its length across the lip, and crossed the room to the cabinet. He withdrew a small apparatus made up of many lenses; some were tiny microscope circles and some were giant magnifiers, others were milky half domes or tinted glass or bowed optics framed in twists of wire and wood. There was even a smooth stone with a hole in its center tied to the rim with copper wire. Mr. Vinh lifted the thing like opera glasses and made some adjustments with a rotating dial.

"Remove your glamour, please."

Inq made a motion with her hand and...nothing changed. At least, not as far as Joy could see. Inq looked exactly the same.

"Thank you," Mr. Vinh said crisply. He lowered the apparatus, squinted in Inq's direction, then fitted the lenses back over his eyes. Joy got that he couldn't see Inq without them. He made a few more adjustments in silence.

"Please reinstate the glamour," he said. Inq swirled her hand again, and the wizard gave a grunt of satisfaction. He turned the multilensed thing at Joy. "Now you."

"I'm not wearing a glamour," she said.

"Of course not," he said, tweaking a lens into place. "But I cannot see their handiwork without assistance. Hold still please."

Joy tried not to squirm under the scrutiny. One of the lenses tilted. Another clicked into place.

"I am fascinated by the marriage of magic and technology," he explained as he squinted through the rock with a hole. "How it overlaps, where it repels and attracts, like two polarized magnets. It's a hobby of mine." He lowered the device and frowned. "She hasn't the Scribe's *signatura*," Mr. Vinh said. "She is no *lehman*." He shook his chin at Joy. "You have no part in this."

"But she did," Inq lilted.

"Did?" Mr. Vinh shut the thing back in its cabinet. "Nonsense. She is not what you claim. She is not a *lehman*. End of story."

"Well, I was," Joy said quietly. "But I guess now I'm just his girlfriend."

Mr. Vinh paused as he stepped behind his desk, staring at her for a long moment. Then he took up his stylus, holding his sleeve away from the wet page. "No," he said and began painting furiously. "No, no. That cannot be." He pointed his brush at Joy. "Listen to me. I do not know what this one—" he pointed to Inq "—has been telling you. But I know them. Yes, I do. I have known for many years. Them and you. And I am telling you that if you had been taken by one of the *tien*, there would be a mark on you—one that you could not see—"

"A *signatura*," Joy said. "I know."

Mr. Vinh stopped. "How do you know?"

"She has the Sight," Inq explained. Joy nodded.

Mr. Vinh's voice softened, as did his face. "You have the Sight?" he echoed and stopped to think. "Your family does not know?" Joy shook her head. Mr. Vinh drummed his fingers on the edge of the table and wiped the corners of his lips as if smoothing them closed. He spoke slowly. "You have the Sight and you are in love with a Scribe," he said. "Yes. Perhaps I have heard of you."

"You have?" Joy squeaked.

"Rumors, of course," Mr. Vinh dismissed. "Everyone comes with rumors. Rumors and requests and cash." He smiled, revealing tobacco-stained teeth. "So, yes, perhaps you exist. Strange that we have met so often and neither of us has known...but, then again, that's the way of things nowadays—rush, rush, rush. So many people so close together and yet too busy to notice one another." He shrugged and made a last careful note. "So maybe I can tell you something about glamours, after all. It is good for you to know these things. But before we get down to business, I have a question for you, busy girl, and I will tell you what I know if you would be so kind as to answer it."

Joy glanced at Inq, who nodded. "Okay."

"Good. Very good," Mr. Vinh said and came around to sit on the mats. Joy and Inq joined him on the floor. He folded to a sitting position with ease.

"So what can I tell you?" Mr. Vinh said, placing his hands on his knees. "I am a wizard, which means that I provide services for humans and *tien*. Most often spells and most often for money, although I sometimes will take trade for hard-to-find things." He opened his hands; one thumb was smudged in black paint. "My family was from a province near the Mekong River, before we came to America and brought our magic here. I make poultices and charms and small, everyday sort of spells, but glamours are my big magic—taught to me from my grandfather from his father and his father before him and so on, back centuries. It is an old craft and one that relies heavily on both art and discretion." He smiled wryly. "*My* art at *my* discretion, you understand. It is the most common way that the *tien* may pass among humans." He gestured with one hand. "You have the Sight—you understand why that is. You've seen what they look like without the veil."

Joy shifted on the mats. "What veil?"

The wizard bowed toward Inq. "The veil is the natural aura of the *tien* that lets them slip past our eyes like oiled paper—" he drew his hands quickly past his face "—without notice. It is what has kept them alive in our world for centuries. Camouflage is an effective survival strategy."

He rested his hands on his knees and continued. "The simplest glamour is not about creating something new, but dampening the individual veil, allowing humans to perceive them normally," Mr. Vinh said. "This is not an option for many, as to see *tien* in their true form, unfiltered, would likely cause alarm, breaking pacts between our worlds, so minor modifications can be made to normalize their appearance or create an entire new facade," he said. "It is a major undertaking and very expensive. Of course, in order to pass close inspection, there are additional changes necessary for masking horns, wings, tails, extra body mass." He glanced at Inq. "Or unusual eyes."

She winked.

Joy's head spun. "But...how?"

Mr. Vinh grinned. "My son is a gifted animator," he said with pride. "CAD modeling has greatly improved the quality of our glamours. We've been developing the technique since the early eighties."

"No," Joy said. "I mean, how is that possible?" She looked around the tiny room. "Spells. Glamours. Wizards. How is *any* of this possible?"

"A better question might be how are *you* possible, busy girl?" Mr. Vinh asked. "I cannot tell you how I make my magic, but perhaps you can tell me how you make yours." He leaned forward slightly at the waist in interest. "So, my question—I have heard that you managed to remove your *signatura*, freeing yourself from your Master and unraveling the *segulah*'s curse." Joy stared. Mr. Vinh was well-informed.

She didn't expect to hear these words from another human being. "Tell me," he said. "How did this happen?"

"Oh," Joy said trying to catch a cue from Inq, but she was busy inspecting the cabinet shelves. "It was an accident," she said, choosing her words carefully. "Ink threw his scalpel to me after he'd stabbed Aniseed so that it could pass through her ward. I used it to free myself." She and Ink had agreed to place the explanation for her escape and the magic of unmaking on the blade itself and not attribute it in any way to Joy, avoiding the truth that they had discovered while marking a man in a prison cell: that she could somehow erase marks that were supposed to be permanent, removing the True Names that linked the Folk to the last bits of magic in the world. "I had no idea what would happen," she said honestly. "I was just trying to get out."

"And so you did," Mr. Vinh said as he rubbed his palms against his trousers. "This is a powerful thing. A valuable thing." His eyes flicked to her. "You are full of valuable things." Inq turned her head, almost frowning. Joy wasn't sure what he meant, but she found that she'd been twisting her fingers in her lap. She flattened her palms against the mats. He pushed himself to a stand. "Like information," he clarified as he straightened. "I value information because I value *facts*. Facts are the difference between real magic and trickery. It is very important to know all of the facts," he said. "Here's a fact—you do not need a glamour, so I do not know what I can offer you, but if you have need of a wizard, now you know where to look." He fiddled with the frog buttons and placed his robe back on its hook. "I can offer you spells and remedies, and my son has a side business as a courier, should you wish to send something into the Twixt, but no discounts on store items. I still have to report to the IRS."

Joy gave a small laugh. "Understood."

He pushed open the Employees Only door back into the

pool of glaring light and garish shelves of junk food. "Thank you for an enlightening lunch break," he said. Joy's stomach grumbled. This had been *her* lunch break, too. She needed to eat. He closed the door and shuffled back up the aisle. "If you need anything, drop by. Twenty-four hours. Someone is always available." He smiled. "Busy girl is not the only one who's busy around here."

Joy rooted around her bag for something quick and edible. There wasn't much. She was considering the worms. "Thanks, Mr. Vinh."

"Anytime, busy girl," he said cheerily. To Inq, he said, "Come back later. I'll adjust the pupils. They're not tracking as well as I'd like."

"Artists!" Inq said and pushed through the door, ignoring its parting *bing-bong*. "Such perfectionists."

Joy said nothing, knowing that humans noticed the details; it was how she'd known that something was wrong with Ink and Inq when she'd first seen them with their impossibly smooth skin and penetrating all-black eyes. The Folk seemed to bother only with surface impressions, which explained how the Scribes had gone so long without bothering to add little things like belly buttons or fingernails. It made sense that they would need a human to make convincing glamours for them.

She remembered the last time she'd sat with Ink, carving the perfect muscles of his neck and chest using a human figure drawing book as a guide. They'd laughed together as they molded a little innie in his long, rippled stomach. Her fingertips tingled with the memory. Or maybe it was low blood sugar. She popped a Gummi Worm into her mouth. It squished as she bit down. *Ew.*

"So," Joy said around the orange glob. "Everyone can see you?"

"Of course. When I activate the glamour," Inq said.

"Right. So why did you tell him I didn't want one?" Joy said around another Gummi. "That is *exactly* what I want for Ink!"

Inq gave an exasperated sigh and flapped her hands. "You don't just come out and tell a wizard what you want! They'll jack up the price. Haven't you ever haggled before?"

Joy swallowed. "No." The one time she'd gone to Mexico for an international gymnastics competition, she'd been too intimidated by the constant hawking and badgering to buy anything at the market.

"Well, trust me—walking away now will make things easier for you later. Right now, it's too obvious that you want something. I figured I would help you get the ball rolling and if we started asking about glamours today, then by the third or fourth time, it will be like you were hypothetically asking."

"So—hypothetically asking—how much does a glamour cost?"

"Depends on the wizard, but he likes you. I bet we can get you a discount!" Inq winked, and Joy couldn't help but smile. What she wouldn't give to have Ink be able to meet Monica, Stef and Dad! To be visible, to be a part of her world like she was part of his. All she needed was to buy him a glamour—it would be perfect!

"I'd want to make it a surprise if I can manage it," Joy said, grabbing another worm. "Don't tell Ink."

Inq touched a finger to her lips. "It'll be our little secret." She smirked, delighted in the same way she'd been when she'd first brought Joy through time and space to her own surprise party for Lehman's Day. "Come on," she said. "Let's get you back to work. Start saving those pennies!"

She spread her hand, and the air bowed around them in concentric ripples.

"Approximately how many pennies are we talking about?" Joy asked.

Inq patted her arm good-naturedly. "Think of it this way—it's always good to have a lifelong goal."

FOUR

STEPPING OUT OF THE VOID ONTO THE ASPHALT BEHIND Antoine's back lot, Joy and Inq stopped laughing the instant Ink sprang up from the back steps and started toward them, worry and fury warring on his face.

"Where were you?" he said.

"Shopping," Inq replied before Joy could breathe. While technically true, it wasn't really the truth. Joy was amazed at how skillfully the Folk could twist words.

"Shopping?" Ink said. "You were gone and I thought..." He shook his head and turned to his sister, sounding strangely human. "It is *dangerous* for Joy to be out right now." He gestured to the heavy back door. "I cannot ward a public place like this—there are too many people! And we have not heard back from the Bailiwick yet!"

"Better, then, that she was with me and not out on her own," Inq said primly. "Isn't it sweet how he worries about you?" She winked at Joy and made a big show of adjusting her corset. "You fret too much, Ink. Everything's fine. You don't have to wait on the Bailiwick to keep living your life. It's not as if anyone's foolish enough to try anything out here in the open in the middle of the day."

Joy was about to say that this was *exactly* what had happened yesterday when she saw a rust-colored shape move from behind a parked car and the words died on her tongue.

The knight's footsteps crunched on the pavement.

Joy backed away stumbling, knees jellied and mouth gaping open, tasting air.

Ink spun around. Inq's hands blurred. The knight raised his weapon—a curved scimitar this time—and charged. Joy backpedaled against a nearby car and stumbled, the hot chrome bumper burning her leg. Ink stepped between them, straight razor raised. Inq's right hand swept down, severing the knight's blade from its hilt in a whine of sparks. The knight huffed and charged with the damaged half, a shard of razor-sharpness that caught the sun on its edge. Inq held her ground. Joy frantically fished for the scalpel, dropping the C&P bag, rooting around tubes of lip gloss and mascara. There was a dark blur of motion. Ink flashed past. The straight razor arced, but the knight swung, batting the blade from Ink's hand. It clanged off a Dumpster and slid in the dirt.

Inq dived, humming fingers stabbing straight, but the knight dodged and wove beneath her arm. Gripping the end of his sword, he tried to drive the broken bit into Inq's sternum. Joy grabbed her scalpel. Ink drew his black arrowhead. Inq's hands stilled, fingers spread wide, the same moment that Joy lifted the scalpel and Ink punched through the armor, grabbing the knight's elbow from behind. Joy stared as the metal mesh protecting the shoulder joint split, spitting broken links across the gravel in a gentle rain of rings. With a twist, Ink snapped the arm sideways, a sharp crack. The weapon dropped from the armored grip. His knees buckled. The knight heaved himself up and punched Ink in the throat. Ink's face absorbed the blow and hardened like stone. Ink frowned and slashed the arrowhead down.

There was a splash of blood and a rough scream. Ink spat a word.

"Yield."

Inq's eyes widened, a wild smile on her lips. Joy backed away from the spatter of bright blood on cement.

The knight grunted and grabbed Ink's shoulder with his good hand as if to tear it from the socket. Ink used both arms to trap the elbow and bend it back with a shriek of ruined metal. The knight's arm pulsed another great gout of blood.

"Yield!" Ink said.

"I do not yield," the knight grated from beneath his helmet. Ink's grip tightened. The armguard squealed.

"You will not touch her," Ink said. "I swear it."

"Then you, too, shall die."

Rage lit Ink's features, something pure and terrible; the hot neon light sparked like fire in his eyes. He shoved his knee forward, driving the arrowhead through the knight's back. The knight crumpled, a sagging calm of junkyard noises as he sank to his knees. Armor hit ground in tumbling percussion as the body toppled over with a crash.

The sound broke something inside Joy—it was as if the world swam into sharp focus between one breath and the next. Ink stood over the body, barehanded and calm. Inq lifted her palms warily and took a step closer. The knight was a rumpled pile of red armor, its head wrenched sickeningly back. Joy couldn't help staring where the helmet had lifted away from the neck. Pale skin peeked out from under the edge of the faceplate. No pulse beat there. It was very, very still.

Inq relaxed. "Well, that's that."

She touched her brother's wrist. Something passed between them that snapped him out of his stillness. Ink flinched away with a dismissive gesture and looked back at Joy.

"Go inside," Ink told her. "You are safe now. It is over." The words fell like stones, flat and black. He sounded lost, tired and confused—she felt the same way. She couldn't go to *work*, not now, not after this! As if he could read her thoughts, he shook his head gently. "Act normal. Otherwise, it will call attention to..." Ink stopped and sighed. "Please go. I will come back tonight and escort you home."

Joy walked around the pool of blood, speckled with gravel and tiny links of chain, and hurried up the back stairs into Antoine's low lighting and the smell of hot bread. The last thing she saw was Inq moving to touch her brother and Ink standing very, very still.

Joy waited by the restaurant's front window twisting her apron strings around her knuckles, watching the raindrops fall in a smooth sheet beyond the awning. Main Street shone like a river stippled with tiny splashes. Cars drove by, shearing sheets of spray. People walked under umbrellas. A knot of teens passed, laughing as one tipped back his face, mouth opened wide to catch the droplets. It was a fresh, clean summer storm. To Joy, it smelled like Ink.

She trusted that the rain would wash away the blood.

She'd tried not to think about the look on Ink's face in the back lot, or the armored body that had disappeared along with Ink and Inq when she'd been brave enough to check. It was as if they had never been, as if she'd imagined the whole thing, everything from the moment Inq had appeared at work to the moment when she'd walked past Neil with the scalpel still in her hand. It had been easy not to think about it while she'd rushed mindlessly between tables, but now it all came back to her in a crazy montage: ice cubes melting in a saucer, blood spouting over gravel, Mr. Vinh in a black robe behind a secret door at the C&P.

The rainy day world was as foggy as a dream.

"Need a ride?"

Neil appeared next to her, staring out at the rain.

"No," Joy said. "Thanks. I'm waiting for a friend."

Neil nodded and tapped his cheat pad. "Friend-friend or more-than-a-friend?" Joy turned and noticed him smile. "Just asking."

Ink appeared just outside the door, slipping between one flap of reality and the next. Joy watched him unzip a doorway along a parking sign and check the sidewalks and streets, heedless of the rain wetting his clothes. He raised a hand, inviting her to join him.

"I have to go," she said.

Neil frowned. "But there's no one—"

"Bye." Joy pushed out the door, hugging her purse close to her body. Ink had his straight razor in his hand and led the way past the window

"Are you all right?" she asked into her collar.

"Let's get you home," Ink said, slipping into rare contractions and walking quickly around the corner, out into the rain. Cool pinpricks tapped her arms and scalp as she walked beside him. Joy blinked through the rain on her lashes. On Ink's face, they looked like tears.

He stopped in the middle of the sidewalk and stared at her. The rain matted her hair and slid a wet finger down her back. She glanced around awkwardly and felt drops trace down her cheeks.

"What is it?" she asked.

Ink blinked in surprise.

"The water is cold," he said as a shudder passed over his body, muscles quivering under the silk shirt plastered against him. She'd forgotten how he still needed to concentrate to feel things.

"It's not really," Joy said, but Ink still looked amazed. He placed a hand against his chest. The shiver came again, shaking raindrops from the tips of his hair.

"It is cold. I can *feel* it," Ink said, pressing his palm flat. "I am alive." He said the words as if he'd never thought them before, as if their very meaning had changed. His eyes lifted and saw her with wonder. "I am alive," he said again in his crisp, slicing voice. "And you are beautiful."

Joy wiped the wet bangs from her eyes and stepped forward.

First she tasted the rain, which tasted like him—cool droplets on his mouth that melted against her tongue. The lightness bloomed into something warmer. He pulled her closer, and Joy forgot the touch of raindrops. Her arms felt heavy in her wet clothes, her fingers tangling in his hair.

He pushed her back.

"No!"

Joy stopped, confused at the sudden space between them. Her hands were empty and open, the rain running through her fingertips like a question.

Ink did not look at her as he flicked the blade with an expert motion, sliced a door and, grabbing her hand, quickly stepped through.

They spun into her bedroom with the scent of limes, the cleansing breach cocooning them between one space and the next. Her white blouse clung to her body, ripples of white cotton outlining the wet patches. She shivered. It was cold in her room. The AC was on.

Ink let go of her hand, the last bit of his warmth leaving her as he strode the perimeter, checking that his wards were still in place. His silvery shirt hung off him like a limp sail, and the spikes of his hair dripped rainwater on the carpet. He moved with a feral grace, anxious and fervent. Joy watched him circle, feeling less and less secure.

"Ink?"

"The wards," he mumbled. "The wards are whole," he said, pacing. "Your room is sealed, as is the building. I even strengthened them to repel you from danger outside your door." He was speaking quickly, almost babbling, which was unlike him. Joy had never seen him so unsettled. His nervousness crawled in her stomach, curdling her fears. "I met with Graus Claude and he said that he should have answers for us soon—"

"Ink."

"—Inq delivered the sword to Kurt—no one knows weapons better than he—though he says he cannot be certain that this is a singular act, but any formal declaration would have had to pass through the Council—"

"*Ink!*" Joy shouted, and it stopped him in his place. She dropped her purse and the scalpel on her nightstand and flipped wet bangs out of her eyes. "What's the matter?"

He looked up.

In three quick strides, he was kissing her. Their bodies pressed against the wall. He held on to her desperately, feverishly, a sudden heat washing over him that Joy could feel where they touched. She kissed him back harder, plastering her wet body against his. The fabric of their shirts slid between them, slick and wet against their skin. He held her hips, pulling her impossibly closer, matching her growing intensity with nips of teeth and tongue. She grabbed his arms to steady herself or pull him closer or hang on. He kissed the wet curls of hair at her neck.

"I cannot lose you," he said. "Not yet."

"Ink," she whispered, still uncertain of this mood, and wrapped her hands in his hair. He held her waist, and she bunched the silk of his shirt. He pulled back and lifted it like a curtain over his head, slapping it to the floor and pressing his bare chest against hers. She felt the skin of his back, imagining his *signatura* spinning there. She was spinning, too.

Clenching. Burning. Wanting. As they clung to one another, Joy felt like they were climbing the walls. Her feet kicked against the baseboard. They had nowhere else to go.

Ink slid his lips into the hollow space between her neck and shoulder. Joy leaned her head back and groaned. He lifted her easily, twisting them onto her bed. She held on to his hips with her knees, taking the weight of him as they landed. He kissed her again—her face, her eyes, her throat—pushing pillows out of the way, knocking over everything in their path as they climbed higher across the mattress, their breath filling each other's mouths. There was bumping, crashing, thumping, breaking—but none of that mattered. There was only the want. Joy could feel his kisses all over her body. Her leg snaked behind his knee, pulling him closer, tighter. He pressed against her, flattening the ripples of her shirt. She ran her hands along his ribs, sliding from his chest to his back to his shoulders. He kissed the side of her neck, her collarbone, her breastbone, her throat. He shook the dampness from his hair.

Joy squirmed. She couldn't seem to get enough air to breathe. Her clothes felt uncomfortable, stuck to her skin. She pulled at her blouse, wanting more than anything to feel his bare skin against hers, lifting the hem in bunched fists. As he kissed her cheek, she turned her head and saw the pale, glowing slash on his wrist. It hit her like ice water.

"What...?"

Ink froze. He didn't need to ask what she'd seen.

He gasped quietly into her hair, the sound of it deep in her ear, before he lifted himself up, turning his left hand over. The *signatura* looked like a jagged crescent moon.

"It's a mark," he said. Catching his breath, he swallowed. "Grimson's mark." He kissed her temple once, as if saying goodbye to the moment. "He lays claim on those who have murdered someone of the Twixt."

Joy twisted beneath him, no longer burning with need. "Did Inq put it there?"

"It is her job," Ink said. "It was my doing."

"But..." She struggled to understand. "I thought marks were meant for humans? I didn't think the Folk marked one another!"

Ink sat up, the muscles of his chest bunched and taut as if he were expecting a blow. He hung his head, ashamed. "You have seen Inq," he said. "She is *covered* in marks, proof of her experiences. I think she likes to collect them like trinkets or boys, as if they might somehow tie her tighter to the world." Ink touched the spot on his wrist as if he could feel its foreignness, someone else's *signatura* on his skin. "That is what marks are for, of course—tying our two worlds together, keeping the magic that binds us alive with so much string."

Joy traced the edge of his pinkie finger, not daring to touch the sigil. "I don't understand," she said finally. "I know you and Inq mark humans for the Folk, but not why the Folk need to mark things in the first place."

Ink turned his hand over, breaking her touch, and threaded his fingers together over his knee with a sigh.

"Imagine a dirigible," he said.

"A what?"

He paused. "A hot air balloon," he amended.

"Oh," she said, tugging her plastered shirt away from her skin and leaning back on her pillow. "Okay."

"The lines tether the balloon to the basket, or to the ship cabin. Without the ropes, the craft cannot steer or fly and the balloon will drift away, without direction. Both parts need to be bound to the other in order to sail the skies. Without strong tethers, each is lost." He leaned back, pulling his arms taut and squeezing his knee. "So, *signaturae* are what tether us, binding our worlds together and us to one another. Sever the bonds or fail to have enough of them secured, and the Council fears our worlds will fly apart. We offer our True Names as a promise to uphold our auspice and keep the world's magic alive."

Joy hesitated, uneasy and uncertain. "A promise to who?"

Ink shrugged, a play of muscles and limbs. "To those who now exist beyond our reach," he said. "And you know the Folk do not take promises lightly." He sighed, and the mattress shifted beneath him. "In the beginning, the Folk claimed the land and a few mortal bloodlines as theirs, but since much of the land has been lost or damaged, the Folk needed to mark more humans—those who possess a bit of magic or fall under someone's auspice." Ink shrugged. "If someone survives a plane crash, that person can be claimed by whoever watches over survivors of the sky. If someone is lost in the woods—" he glanced at Joy, who swallowed back the bitter memory of wet leaves and burning flesh "—then that person might be claimed by the creature that rules there. And if someone intentionally kills one of the Twixt..." Ink's voice hardened. "Then he shall bear Grimson's mark forever."

Joy stared at Ink. She barely breathed. This maudlin streak was unlike him, just as unfamiliar as his passionate crawl across her bed. It was as if his feelings had boiled to the surface, raw and unfamiliar, fresh and overwhelming, as if he'd never felt them before. And, she realized, he hadn't— he hadn't *ever*—not before he'd met Joy.

He had never taken a life or had another's sigil mar his skin. He had told her as much when he'd gone after Briarhook. Inq had told Joy that she would be his very first kiss. His first *lehman*. His first love. His first heartbreak. Everything was firsts with Ink. Life was new—wonderful, disappointing, joyous, crushing—and he was *feeling* it all because of Joy. He'd once told her that he'd been proud of his purpose to safeguard his people; it was the reason that he and Inq had been created, after all. He could be counted on to protect the lives of the Folk—that was why they'd had to pretend to be lovers, to disguise the fact that he had made a mistake in marking Joy, because the Scribes had to be infallible, reliable, always. Their world, the world of the Twixt, depended on it. That integrity was his rock, the one thing he knew about himself, and now it was gone.

He stood up and crossed the room. Joy struggled to sit up. Her skin tingled. Her legs ached. The space on the bed was fast cooling and damp.

"I have always wanted to do good work," he said, sliding the wallet chain through his fingers. "Yet I have also wanted to be *more*, and that was my failing." Ink finally lifted his fathomless eyes to Joy—the hurt and confusion there was childlike and torn. "There is no greater loss than the loss of one of our kind, if only because we are so few." His breath was coming shallow and fast. Joy felt she should do something, but didn't know what. "As a Scribe, I was created to keep the Folk from harm—from *human* harm!—and now this." His hands were open, helpless, exposing the stain on his wrist.

"Is this what it means to be more human, Joy?" His crisp, clean voice had a slicing edge. "I ended a universe of possibilities to save another universe of possibilities because I valued those more. Because that future was yours. Because *you* mean more to me than the life of someone I have never met who meant to do you harm." He struggled with it, almost pleading; his chest heaved with the need to get the words out. He touched the space over his heart with hooked fingers, indenting the skin as if he could tear the feelings from his body.

"Do you understand?" he asked desperately. "I *killed*."

The words fell like stones from the aether, heavy and burning. Even when she'd thought he'd murdered Briarhook for kidnapping her and burning his brand onto her arm, Ink had not killed him—he'd taken the giant hedgehog's heart and placed it in an iron box. She'd seen Briarhook afterward with her own eyes, fighting in the battle against Aniseed with a metal plate welded to his chest—hideous, but alive.

But the blood-colored knight was dead.

She sat, stunned silent. She didn't know what to do or say. She knew she could offer to erase Grimson's mark but that Ink would hate it if she did. There were some things that could not be undone. She watched Ink's hands cup his shoulders, his forearms crossing to hide his face; his every motion was filled with revulsion and shame. He had become something he didn't recognize, all for the love of her. Joy twisted her fingers miserably.

"I killed him," he said to the wall, to the floor. "Because he would have killed you—because I *believed* he would have killed you—because I believed he would have *harmed* you, although I had no proof."

"He was going to kill me," Joy said at last. "And he said that he'd kill you, too."

Ink bumped the back of his head against the wall and dropped his arms. "I asked him to yield," he lamented. "Why would he not yield?"

Joy shivered from more than the cold. She hugged her arms. "It was self-defense. Or in my defense," she said. "You didn't mean to kill him."

"I did," Ink said, still not looking at her. He placed his hands against the wall, studying his fingers, the lines of knuckle and cuticle and tendon they'd drawn together. The hands that he'd fashioned based on hers. The hands he'd used to take a life in her name. "I wanted to kill him and anyone who would harm you in any way." He all but growled. Joy held her breath. "And when it happened, it happened so quickly, all I could think was that it was over too fast. That I was not done with him yet," Ink said. "And then he was dead and I could not believe such a thought had ever existed inside me."

Bared to the waist, he shivered. Rain still wet his skin.

A few drops ran down the ridges of his ribs—the ones that they had sculpted together, the ones that heaved in fright. He glanced at her suddenly, pinning her fast.

"I disgust you."

Joy gasped, "No!"

"I should," he said. "I disgust me." He ran clawed fingers through his hair, throwing water to the wind. "I have never understood war or killing or death. To protect, one can wound or warn or disable. But death? Death is final." Ink rested his hands back on his hips; the chain on his left swung violently against his leg. He turned aside, rubbing his face in his hands. The sign of the ouroboros, a giant dragon swallowing its own tail, spun lazily between his shoulder blades. The scales flashed like reverse splashes of light.

"Is this what it means to love, Joy? To be loved?" he asked with bitter laughter. "To be willing to destroy anything and anyone else in your name?" He dropped his arms and looked back at her, broken, lost. It bruised something inside her. "Because, if I am honest, I would do it all again. Willingly, gladly. I would damn myself and call it love if I knew it would keep you safe."

Joy crossed the room and took his hands. "No," she said quickly. "No. It was a choice in a moment. You made a tough choice. You killed him and you saved me." She stroked the inside of his palm where they'd drawn a life line together. He placed his hands over hers, squeezing them, and closed his eyes. Joy shivered now with more than the cold. These feelings that she'd given him were crushing him. "It sounds strange to say 'I'm sorry,' because I didn't want to die and I'm glad that you stopped him, but I *am* sorry for what it's done to you. For what I've done to you," she whispered. "Even if I didn't mean to." She folded his fingers over her own. She wanted to hold him closer but felt she shouldn't dare. His pain was creating a strange wall around him as unyielding as stone. Tears threatened. Her breathing grew stuffy. How could she explain? She was responsible; she had to make him understand. She squeezed harder. "That's not love, Ink. But this is." She lifted their hands together so he could see them. *"This."*

His eyes stayed on their joined hands, fingers threaded together, like the first time.

"I love you, Ink," she said and kissed his fingers, pressing her lips gently against each knuckle. Ink swallowed, the motion flickering in his throat. His eyes slipped closed and he took a deep breath. His thick lashes parted, revealing eyes like starless night.

"I love you, Joy," he said. "No matter what, I will always love you." His fingers tightened over hers. "But it frightens me more than I thought it would."

"Me, too," she said, trying to soothe the person she'd taught to feel. They held one another in the dark. "Me, too."

FIVE

STEF'S WELCOME HOME DINNER FEATURED A VARIETY of his favorite takeout, including fried shrimp, cold sesame noodles, pulled-pork sandwiches, spicy hot wings, Greek salad, jambalaya and gooey potatoes au gratin. Stef was always hungry and Joy was hypoglycemic, but Shelley looked more than slightly alarmed at the amount of food the Malone family could put away.

"I don't understand how you can stay so thin," she said. "It's inhuman."

Joy snorted a laugh but managed to cover it with a sip of lemon seltzer.

"Dad used to say I made a pact with the devil." Stef grinned.

"No, I said you *were* a devil," Dad said. "I remember this one time Stef wanted to see if he could do stunts on his Big Wheel trike. But did he make a ramp out of a piece of wood and a brick like a normal kid? Oh no! I'm out raking the lawn and turn around to see my only son rolling down the porch banister on his Big Wheel and launch, soaring through the air with the biggest, toothiest grin on his face, and there I was—rake in hand, ten feet away, nothing I could do—and that smug little brat lands right in the middle of my pile of leaves. Stuff everywhere and not a scratch on him. I nearly had a heart attack."

Everyone at the table laughed, even though there was a tug of pain as Joy remembered the old house with its homey smells of Murphy Oil Soap, old books and slow-brewed coffee. She could imagine the back porch with its peeling white paint and the taste of real lemonade that Mom would make with slices of rind. That was before everything changed—before Doug, before Shelley, before quitting gymnastics and Dad's black depression. Before the move. Before the Carousel. Before Indelible Ink.

Stef saw the change in Joy's face and switched the subject quickly.

"So have you two decided how long you'll take off?" he asked.

Dad put his hand on Shelley's. "We're thinking two weeks."

Joy stopped chewing her spring roll. "Two weeks what?"

Dad tried avoiding her gaze, but Shelley held his hand firmly. If nothing else, Joy appreciated that his girlfriend didn't let him dodge his way out of confrontation. Another way that she wasn't like Mom.

"You didn't tell her?" Shelley asked.

"I did," her dad said. "Or at least tried to. She wouldn't stop typing on her phone."

Joy swallowed. "Tell me what?"

"Shelley and I are planning to spend some time alone this summer, and I'll be back at the end of August so we can still have some family time with Stef," he said. "Any of this sounding familiar?"

Unfortunately, it did. Joy stared back, speechless.

"I had to check the dates with work," Shelley said, taking on some of the blame. "We really didn't know anything until yesterday morning."

Joy swallowed her embarrassment along with a forkful of salad. It wasn't Shelley's fault. Joy didn't blame her for wanting some time alone with her boyfriend. And, on the bright side, maybe now she could have more time with *her* boyfriend. The knight's death and Grimson's mark had affected him a lot. She played with her fork as she collected her thoughts.

"So where are you going?" Joy asked with a conciliatory grin.

"To the shore," her dad said. "We've rented a place and a car and we'll drive around exploring. No phones, no computers, total radio silence and some lovely peace and quiet." He took Shelley's hand. "Shelley's been researching spots online and I have a tour map from triple A."

"Did you check out that *Dare to Tread* book I told you about?" Stef asked. "It's got a lot of great places that are off the beaten path."

Joy slammed down her knife and glared at her brother, falling right back into that pit of fear that always burned at the bottom of her stomach: that little-kid hurt of finding out only after the fact that she was the last to know everything.

"Wait a minute. How long has Stef known about this?" she asked.

"We had to schedule things around Stef's arrival," Dad soothed. "We wanted him to be home for you before we took off."

Joy slapped down her napkin. "What? Now I need a babysitter?" she asked. "I'm seventeen years old and have been practically on my own for years!"

"Oh, for Pete's sakes, Joy—" Dad began.

Stef reached for more potatoes. "I'm not babysitting you, so you can quit acting like a baby."

"I'm not!"

"You are."

Dad sighed at Shelley. "Did I mention peace and quiet? Less than twenty-four hours and it's like they're nine and twelve all over again." He speared a cube of feta cheese, then pointed it at each of them. "But here's the difference—I can legally leave the two of you behind as semiresponsible semiadults without the authorities breathing down my neck. So don't make me regret taking this time for myself and don't make me think twice, or so help me, I'll find a way to ground both of you for the rest of the summer. Do I make myself clear?"

Joy and Stef both chewed in their seats.

"Say, 'Yes, Dad,'" he commanded.

"Yes, Dad," they said.

"Good. And be sure to call your mother at least once a week. Now pass the chicken."

Stef lifted the plate obligingly. "You started it," he fake-coughed into his elbow.

A smirk pulled on Joy's lips. She tried fighting it and failed. She wiped her lips.

"Did not," she whispered behind her napkin.

"Did, too."

"Dork."

"Dweeb."

"Lord help me," Dad muttered, fighting his own grin as he sawed with his knife.

Shelley breathed a little easier and patted his arm. "I just love a man who takes charge."

Her dad blushed as he took a bite.

Nine o'clock. Dad and Shelley had gone to her apartment to finish packing for their trip, Stef was meeting some friends at the movies, and Joy sat alone in the condo. Surfing the web, listening to music, Joy toodled around waiting for the numbers on the clock to read one-zero-zero-zero.

The wall of her room unfurled, and Ink stepped through.

Joy's heart thumped as she removed her headphones and clicked off-line.

"Hey," she said. "I wasn't expecting you 'til ten."

Ink slipped his razor past the wallet chain at his hip.

"I couldn't wait," he said.

"You 'couldn't'?"

Ink shook his head solemnly. One dimpled smirk. "No."

Two steps and his arms came around her. She curled into his chest. He held her close and stroked her hair, breathing a sound of relief. Joy rocked in his arms, content. He was getting better at hugs. She wondered which of the thirty-six versions this one was.

"I am sorry," he said past her ear. "About before. I am still..."

"Shh," she said, squeezing him tighter. "It's okay."

"It is not," he whispered into the crook of her shoulder. She could feel his breath there, warm and gentle and sweet. "But it will be."

"Yes," Joy said, touching his face so that she could see him. "And you're here."

Ink chuckled despite himself. "Oh, I am very, very here." He lifted her hand from his cheek, cupping the back of her fingers in his. He inspected each of her fingertips: pink and perfect. A mischievous spark lit his fathomless eyes, and his eyebrows formed a question.

Joy's heart pounded. This was their game, invented at her kitchen table the first time they'd created his hands based on hers, tracing life lines and heart lines and the intricacies of each other's skin as they slowly started to become one another's—hers, his, theirs. She remembered that moment and he saw the memory spark. He smiled wider.

Joy slowly lifted his left hand in hers.

He will be learning about everything, watching you. Joy remembered Inq's words as she cradled the back of his hand, feeling his eyes on her as she brushed the side of her cheek with his knuckles, feeling the whisper of his skin on hers. He slowly did the same, sliding the back of her fingers against his cheek, smiling back at her. Joy brought his hand to her lips, opened her mouth and breathed slowly into his palm. His fingers twitched. His breath caught in surprise. She glanced up at him through his fingertips, a slow smile on her lips.

He brought her hand gently to his mouth and copied her, breath for breath, exhaling slowly into the cup of her palm. She could feel the warmth pool there and run rivers down her back.

Joy shivered. Ink smiled.

Joy brought his hand closer, tilting it back. Watching him watching her as she touched her lips to the soft inside of his wrist. His whole arm flinched. The sensation skittered over his features. Hot pink fireflies danced in his eyes.

"Can you feel this?" she asked, the words tickling his skin.

"Yes," he said. He bent his head forward and bent her wrist back. His lips touched the exact same place—the delicate, exposed skin of her wrist. Joy felt his breath hover there, warm and sweet.

"Can you?" he said. "Feel this?"

"Oh yes," she murmured and slipped her lips along the edge of his palm. She felt him do likewise. Her breath hitched in her throat. She closed her eyes even though she knew Ink still stared, watching her with impish eyes, learning, hungry, eager for more.

She kissed his skin, her tongue barely touching the barest spot on his wrist. He tasted of water. He tasted like rain.

Joy thought she might melt when she felt him do the same.

Warmth slid down her arm and her elbow twitched, a rippling she felt along the edge of her limbs. Her fingers threaded between his, tightening, drawing him closer, moving his entire arm by the wrist. Sliding her bottom lip over the slick spot of her kiss, she felt Ink's arm stretch, tighten, pull her closer, heard him shudder on the exhale. Joy scraped her bottom teeth over the dip in his palm.

He grabbed her fingers tightly, a groan slipping from his lips. She felt an answering sound somewhere deep in her throat. Joy rolled her head back as she felt his teeth graze her palm. A nip. A bite.

"Ow!"

Ink dropped her hand instantly. He looked worried, flushed.

"Are you hurt?" he asked.

Joy rubbed her wrist. "No," she said with a chuckle. "You bit me."

"And that was wrong."

Joy tried not to laugh too hard. "It was...more than I expected."

Ink cocked his head to one side. "You bit me first."

He sat on the edge of her bed, and Joy sat next to him. He took her hand back tenderly and traced his thumb over the spot, soothing it with circular strokes. Joy felt the tensions—both good and bad—pass. Glancing at each other, they both started laughing, transforming two awkward, separate people into "us, together."

"I am sorry," he said.

"Don't be," she said. "I'm not."

"I am learning."

"You are learning."

A dimple reappeared. "Some things are eagerly taught."

Joy felt the heat of the blush on her cheeks. Was she supposed to feel wrong for wanting? For showing? Asking? Knowing? Well...she didn't. So there.

Ink drew his thumb along the "7" in her palm. "I like what I have learned," he said. "I like learning with you."

Joy grinned. "I'll bet." She caught his fingers, giving his knuckles a quick kiss. His eyes crinkled in the corners. A second dimple appeared. Joy couldn't help laughing as her heart skipped a beat. His moods were so honest and wondrous and new. He didn't make her feel bad for feeling the same.

He rested their hands on his knee, a tangible tangle of Joy and Ink.

"I wanted to see you before I confront the Council," he said. "I am requesting proof of the Edict and an investigation of the elemental blade. Graus Claude has arranged an audience using his 'considerable pull,' which I can only imagine means that he will be asking me for some sort of favor later on that will undoubtedly be steeped in mystery and intrigue as the Bailiwick has a finger in every pie." Ink rubbed their joined hands against his knee, making his wallet chain jingle. He stared at their fingers. Joy squeezed. He squeezed back. "But I do not want to go. I do not want to leave you."

"I know."

"You are safe in your home. The wards..."

Joy smiled again. "I know."

His eyes lifted, his voice, sincere. "I will be back soon."

Joy nodded, unblinking. "I'm sure it will only take a moment."

Ink smiled. "If that."

He stood, the wallet chain slithering off his hip. Joy untangled her fingers and tugged the edge of his sleeve. She slid her palm over his chest and placed a kiss on his cheek that made him turn and look deeply into her eyes. He kissed her, not quite gently, not quite shyly, a moment that stretched and yielded under their lips. Their mouths lingered, his breath and hers mixed.

"Be well, Joy Malone," he whispered.

His hand slipped into his back pocket and removed the razor, drawing it swiftly sideways and down. Slicing a hole in the universe, Ink peeled away a flap of nothing at all.

He stepped back and disappeared, leaving the tingle of his words still sparking on her lips.

Antoine's. Lunch shift.

Joy sniffed her sleeve as she folded napkins around flatware, thankful that Monica had promised to help wash the car that afternoon, something to keep her mind off Ink. Stef had agreed to help, too, on the condition that Joy help him lug Dad's storage boxes out of his room and into the basement and they'd reward themselves with pizza and gelato all around. It promised to be quite the party once she could get out of here.

"Specials list will be up in five!" someone called from the back.

Joy hurried through her last five sets, knowing she needed enough time to write down the new menu items before they threw open the doors. She dropped the last napkin onto her pile and crowded next to the other servers, furiously scribbling the details of the salade Niçoise and the ingredients in the soup of the day. Food allergies were a server's worst nightmare.

"Good morning," Neil said over Joy's shoulder.

"Good afternoon," Joy said with a quick smile. "Dine here often?"

Neil laughed. "Listen, about yesterday..."

"No big." Joy shrugged. "I have a boyfriend."

"As well as a lovely Bic pen," Neil said, smoothing away the ripples of an awkward conversation before it started. "Pens are so twentieth century, don't you think? Observe." He snapped a photo of the specials board and waggled his smartphone. "Come! Join us in the modern age—half the time at twice the price."

"That's *brilliant!*" Joy said and ran to her purse. Grabbing her phone, she swiped the screen only to feel a large hairline crack under her thumb. A triangular piece of the casing was missing. She could see the silver and green of microchips. "No..." she moaned. "No no no no!" She pressed buttons, tried resetting, nothing. The face stayed blank. It must have broken when she and Ink... Joy blushed at the memory of knocking everything off her bed stand. She remembered hearing something break...

"Argh," she muttered. Dad and Shelley were leaving in a few hours! No way Dad was going to get her a new phone, and the idea of going *two weeks* without one was too horrible a fate. Dad might welcome a vacation from technology, but that would be more like a nightmare for Joy. She briefly wondered if she'd bought extra insurance. She'd have to stop by the store later and ask. Joy shuddered at the idea of having to buy a replacement—one more thing she'd have to save up for, not including a glamour for Ink.

Tossing the useless hunk of plastic back into her purse, Joy hurried back to the specials board, whipping out her pen.

"Forgot your phone?" Neil asked.

"I wish," Joy said, scribbling words like *ahi tuna* and *anchovies* and smearing the blue ink. "It's broken."

Neil whistled through his teeth. "Sorry. That sucks."

Joy grumbled and scribbled down the last details as Neil tucked away his cell. He lingered by the board.

"Can I ask you something?" he said.

Joy double-checked the prices. It was a mistake she'd like to make only once this summer. "Yeah, sure."

"That friend of yours, the one who stopped by the other day? Miss Ice-water-hold-the-glass?"

Suspicion prickled up Joy's arms. "Yeah?"

"Is she seeing someone?"

Joy laughed. "Um...no. I mean, yes. She's seeing someone..." Joy thought about the Cabana Boys—Luiz, Tuan, Antony, Enrique, Ilhami and Nikolai, as well as the indomitable Kurt—all hard bodies and exotic faces. Joy was afraid Neil didn't quite fit the bill. "Um...*several* someones, in fact."

Neil raised his eyebrows. "Really?" he said, patting his stiff spikes of hair. He went back to texting and shook his head. "Man," he whispered under his breath. "That is *so* hot."

Goodbye, Shelley! Goodbye, Dad! Hello title transfer! And now for a hot date with a sponge...

Joy scrubbed the last crusty bits from the windshield. She wasn't sure if it had been bird poop or squashed bugs from the road, but she planned on throwing the rag in the garbage and soaking her hands in bleach.

"I'm washing it right now," Joy said into the house phone tucked by her ear. "There are Cheeto stains on the ceiling, Mom. The *ceiling!*" She sighed in disgust. "Your son is the messiest driver who ever lived."

"Is he there?" her mom said. "I told him to call as soon as he got there."

"He went out to get Turtle Wax," Joy said and wiped her bangs out of her eyes. "Why does anyone need to wax turtles? Their shells are already so shiny."

"I'm sure I don't know," her mom said. "You never had any interest in pets."

"Does an iPad count as a pet?"

"Har-har. Just tell him to call me later, okay?" she said. "I have to go meet Doug at the gallery. I love you, I'm glad you have a car, I'm proud of you, please remember to eat something that does not have a foil wrapper and—oh, by the way—I love you. Did I mention that already?"

Joy squeezed the rag in her hand. "I love you, too, Mom."

"Bye, Joy. Hugs to Stef."

Joy hung up and slipped the phone into the glove compartment to keep it dry. Soapy water ran by her feet and into the gutters, trickling over her toes. She still felt damp after using the hose—Monica and Gordon's offer to help was much appreciated but also far soggier than she'd anticipated—but they'd agreed that the outside of the car had been a lot easier to clean than the inside. Stef's car was a free gift in a very smelly wrapper.

They'd attacked the Kia with sharp-smelling fluids and thick, bubbly suds, using rags and old toothbrushes and toothpicks along the seams. They'd played "spray tag" across the backyard, yelling and ducking, before Stef bequeathed the hose to Gordon and ran to the C&P to get more wax. Monica was scrubbing the rear bumper, soaped to the elbows. Gordon aimed a tight spray near the back wheels.

"Hey!" Monica's voice spiked from behind the trunk. "If you spray my feet one more time, I swear I'm going to come over there and force-feed you this sponge!"

Gordon fixed Joy with comically wide eyes, then sprayed again. Monica shrieked.

Gordon winked as Joy laughed. "Oops."

Monica less-than-gracefully stumbled to her feet, her orange tank top soaked over a flower-patterned bra. She threw the sudsy sponge at her boyfriend, which Gordon dodged easily. He sprayed her again in self-defense, laughing and backing up, but not fast enough to avoid getting tackled into the yard. Bits of freshly mowed grass clung to their bodies as they rolled over the hose, fighting for the nozzle and getting drenched. They yelled and squealed as Joy wiped down the side mirrors. She ignored them until she got a cold splash across her back.

"Hey!" she shouted and whipped around. Monica waved a *sorry* and went back to wrestling her beau.

"Ah, young love," Stef said, approaching with fresh rags and a plastic bag. "Or, in this case, a mating ritual courting massive allergies."

Joy picked at her pruney fingers. "Mom called while

you were gone. Call her back. There! My deed is done." She pointed at the bag. "Found the car wax?"

"Yep. Stored cleverly between the rat poison and boxes of cornflakes. Don't confuse the two." Stef held up the small red tin. "Okay, so—first we have to rinse all this off, towel it dry and do an even coat of this stuff. Wait an hour—then wipe it off. Not too hard."

"Says you," Joy quipped. "My arms are killing me."

"Oh, please. I've seen you flip twenty times in succession to the operetta from *The Fifth Element*," Stef said. "Your wimpy arms can take it."

"Yeah, well, it's been a while." She sniffed. "I'm out of practice."

Stef crossed his arms in his I'm-coaching-you way. It was so familiar, it made Joy's stomach lurch with performance butterflies; her body psyched up for a Level Nine routine. For a split second, she was back on the mats with a panel of judges, a crowd in the backdrop and her family near the bench. She could feel the air-conditioning, smell the chalk dust and sweat. It was as if she'd been plunged back years at a glance: her brother's coaching from the sideline.

"Is that an excuse?" he barked.

"No," she said. It was her line. "No excuses!"

"That's right," Stef said, wagging a finger at her. "You can do this."

Joy dropped her dirty rag and toed off her flip-flops. Tossing her ponytail, she rolled her shoulders and bounced on her toes. The backyard was open and empty and as green as Abbott's Field. She whispered words to no one.

"I know I can."

Dipping her chin, Joy ran for the yard, bare feet clearing the parking barrier and touching wet grass. She felt it tingle up her spine, sending electric pops through her toes. Joy sprang in the dirt into a quick roundoff and slammed a series of back handsprings, fast and tight, in a snapping cycle that felt like flying. She landed in a corner. Everyone had stopped, stunned.

Joy was still moving. She pivoted left, right, and took off again, her mind's eye imagining the triple twist, double back before it could happen, both knowing that the ground wasn't a spring floor and that she could do it, anyway. She could *feel* it. Warmth pulsed up her legs like golden wine, warming her hip joints and filling her lungs, pouring liquid light out her palms.

She ran forward and dived, her fingers squelching in mud and wet grass, slippery and dangerous, but the rush was upon her—she wouldn't stop, *couldn't* stop!—and tucked herself through the spin, landing with an impossible stick. Present left, present right, a split leap and a long, stretched pose, reaching for the sky and straightening her knees, rolling the energy from her heels to her toes, pointing in crisp formation.

Final measure. She lifted her chin: *finis!*

There was a scatter of applause from other windows in the complex. A couple of whistles and a hooting shout. Joy blinked. She'd collected quite an audience. She stood up shyly as she lifted out of her performance trance, doing a little bow and a wave for the kids in the corner condo.

Monica and Gordon clapped wildly from their spot in the grass.

"*WOO!*" Monica hollered, spinning fists over her head.

"Wow!" said Gordon. "That was incredible."

Stef ran over, eyes wide, mouth open, caught somewhere between awe and concern.

"What was *that?*" he said and patted her arms as if checking to be sure she was all still there. She breathed deeply, bright and beaming, and wiped at the grass sticking on her palms.

"That was awesome!" she said.

"That was *insane*," Stef snapped. "Are you kidding me? You could have broken your neck! This is soft ground with loose grass and way too small..." He shook his head and helped wipe off green bits with a rag. "Seriously, Joy, what were you thinking?"

She picked bits of weeds off her tank top. "I wasn't thinking," she admitted.

"Yeah, got that." Now that the shock was over, her brother sounded angry. "I thought you said you haven't hit the mats in over a year," he said, turning her around to wipe her back. "I've never seen you that crisp. Not in ten years—maybe ever. You looked Elite. I have *no* idea how you got that air..." He stopped as she shook out the end of her ponytail. She turned around curiously. His eyes had gone flat, his mouth a tight, thin line. She hadn't realized she'd made him so upset.

"Sorry," she said.

His eyes flicked up to her eyes. He held her shoulder hard, either steadying her or ready to shake some sense into her. "Are you okay, Joy?" he asked suddenly. "Do you feel okay?"

"Yeah," Joy said, confused and suddenly every inch his little sister. "Just winded. Adrenaline crash imminent, but otherwise, I'm fine."

Stef's face was pale. The rag fell from his hand. He bent to pick it up and his voice was strained and strangely subdued. "You should go inside and eat something."

At the mention of food, her whole body tingled. "Good idea," she said and examined his face. "Are *you* okay?"

Stef looked alarmed by the question.

Monica slammed into her back, throwing her dark arms around Joy's neck.

"You were *amazing!*" she gushed. "A one-woman show!"

"That was seriously awesome," Gordon said. "I never knew you could trick."

"Eleven years of gymnastics," Joy murmured, still looking at Stef, who was busying himself with the wax. She felt like she was seven years old, the day after the talent show, ashamed and self-conscious for showing off at school. "I'm going inside to grab an apple," she said. "Anyone want anything?"

"How about another towel?" Gordon suggested as he sprayed Monica's toes. With a squeal and a shout, they were at it again. Stef shook his head.

Feeling oddly chastened, Joy nodded and left.

She rubbed her hands together as she took the stairs, the tight tingling in her fingers and a slight woozy sensation telling her she'd burned too much too fast and needed to refuel. Of course, she should have expected the glucose drop after her wild little stunt in the yard—no warm-up, no practice and on inadequate turf—Stef was right, she'd been stupid. And her and Monica's motto was No Stupid. She could have easily slid into the pavement or hit the fence or landed on her head. She still nursed the injury of two broken toes from that time she'd blown an aerial, and that was back when she was in top form, with her coach in the gym and all the safeties in place. Today, she had just been...reckless. Maybe she could blame it on summer? Ever since she'd been barefoot outside, she'd been itching to really *move*. She'd barely enjoyed any sun since she'd started working at Antoine's. The long days had become all about earning money, which sucked, but now there was a promise of obtaining a glamour: the carrot at the end of a very long stick.

She hopped onto the landing and let herself into the condo, entering the security code and thinking maybe she'd invite Monica and Gordon to go out dancing and blow off some steam. Neil had said that there was some party going on at the beach. She hadn't considered going because she didn't want him to think that he was asking her out.

That was the trouble with having an invisible boyfriend; it was hard to appear to be a couple when the guy in question never appeared.

Joy grabbed one of the oranges out of the bowl on the counter, but it was gushy to the touch. She put it back, opting for a couple of bananas and a stack of whole wheat crackers. She checked the fridge for some cheese, making a mental note to add sharp cheddar to Stef's growing grocery list. As she shut the fridge, Joy caught a glimmer on the very edge of her Sight.

It wasn't the flash of splintered light that she'd experienced when Ink first cut her eye, but it brought the same chilly wariness that she could feel in her lungs, edgy and tight.

She kept her hand on the fridge, replaying her footsteps in her head: Had she accidentally stepped over a ward? Dialed a combination? Triggered a key? She swore at herself for being lazy; she couldn't forget how easy it was to become someone else's plaything, someone else's prey. In the Twixt, Folk were cats and humans were mice.

But she was no mouse.

Joy cautiously let go of the handle and tried to locate the source of the spark. It had the same sort of shimmer that she associated with the Twixt. If she could catch sight of it again, she'd probably know for certain—she, like Ink and Inq, could see *signaturae*, unlike the rest of humans and Folk—but there shouldn't be anything here inside Ink's wards. He'd checked them so carefully. No one could be inside the house!

She retraced her steps, drifting past the counter, opening the fridge, carefully peeking around the corner while keeping her eye on the kitchen window to catch any reflections. Joy wondered how she'd ever felt safe with her head stuck in the fridge. She closed the door and saw it again.

It was reflected in the stainless steel, milky and indistinct.

Joy looked behind her—nothing. Even with the Sight, there

was only her ordinary kitchen with her ordinary snacks on the ordinary countertop. She edged closer to the refrigerator; the sunlight from the kitchen window was bright on her shoulder, warming her skin through the air and glass. Maybe that was it? A flash of sunlight on skin?

Not likely.

As she turned, she saw it again: a flash reflection. Her whole body tingled. It was something *on* her.

Joy remembered when she'd been first marked by Ink, when he'd attempted to obey the law of the Twixt and blind a human with the Sight, but he had missed, accidentally scratching her cornea instead. The wink of light that had speared her eye hadn't been the wound; it had been his *signatura* drawn directly on her eye. She remembered the sort of *Flash! Flash!* she'd had when seeing things in the Twixt for the first time: horrible monsters and fabulous creatures and the glowing shapes of *signaturae* on skin. This was the same sort of flickery brightness, the same sort of echo of light.

Her stomach dropped with an odd twist of shame and nervous dread. She ran to the bathroom and switched on the light. Removing her shirt, she sat on the sink with her back to the mirror and, twisting awkwardly, tried to see what it was.

There was a ghostly smear stuck to her skin.

Joy reached her hand over her shoulder and tried to touch it, but it was too far down her spine. She tried reaching behind her back, but it was too high, out of reach, like an impossible itch. She pulled the skin at her shoulder and saw it move. There was definitely something there. Joy squinted, but it was cloudy and vague, unlike the clear designs of True Names. It wasn't the black of Ink's marks or the pale watermarks of Inq's reverse-henna tattoos, but Joy recognized what it was just the same.

A chilly sort of horror crept up her arms. She knew.

She'd been marked with someone's *signatura.*

*   *   *

Joy sank to the floor, her legs weak with fear. She'd been marked—not by Ink or Inq or anyone that she knew. The knowledge squirmed inside her, setting off sparks in her brain. How was that possible? She hadn't seen anyone! She hadn't seen it happen, and for some crazy reason Joy thought, after everything she'd been through, she ought to have *felt* something happen, at least.

She crumpled against the wall. After all Ink's efforts to keep her safe, to keep her unclaimed and free, she'd been marked, tied to some stranger in the Twixt. Her mind spun with the implications: Who? How? When? Why? With someone already out to kill her, the mark on her flesh felt like a beacon. Joy felt inexplicably violated, exposed. *I can't believe this! What happened?* What could she do? What would she tell Ink?

Oh my God. Ink!

Joy remembered his rage when Briarhook had branded her. He'd been livid, a sharp, deadly quiet, and when he'd returned to Graus Claude's, his arms had been soaked to the elbows in blood. She'd thought for certain he'd killed the gruesome hedgehog and his sneering accomplice, Hasp. She'd been horrified at his violence and herself for feeling avenged, but she had felt it all through a woozy thickness that had been her healing trance that night. Whatever Kurt had given her had left her memories both foggy and bright, but she could still see the vivid streaks of blood against the sink's porcelain knobs and what it was like to see Ink's *signatura* for the first time: an ouroboros, a living tattoo winding over his back.

Yet Briarhook lived because Ink valued life, instead cursing him to earn back his heart, now kept in an iron box. Ink said that he had never killed another living being...until now. What would he do if he found out that she'd been claimed by

some stranger? Would he hunt down whoever was responsi-
ble, only to later be crushed with self-loathing and remorse?
She pictured him hugging his arms over his head in misery.
Joy never wanted to see him like that again.

Grabbing her purse from the hallway, she took out the
scalpel. She returned to the bathroom, turned her back toward the mirror and tried catching the edge of the blade
under the newfound mark. The blade head slipped, snagging
nothing. She tried again. Either she couldn't get the right
angle or she was doing something wrong. Maybe it wasn't a
real *signatura?* Maybe it was too fresh? Maybe it was something else? Joy wasn't completely clear how *signatura* worked,
and since she didn't know whose it was or where it had come
from, perhaps that made it impossible for her to erase? She'd
only ever removed four *signaturae* from her skin: Ink's, Inq's,
Briarhook's and Aniseed's. Of course, that was four more
than anyone else had ever managed, and the reason that the
Council was interested in her still. She felt stupid for having
assumed that removing anyone's *signatura* would be just as
easy and then furious to be proven wrong now.

Why NOW?

She kicked the linen door in frustration and stretched her
arm farther, straining her shoulder and wrist. She felt the
blade skip against her skin and realized that she'd probably
cut herself before she'd do any good. She tried to remember
what it felt like to slice Briarhook's brand off her arm, erase
Aniseed's mark in the air or slowly fuse Inq's belly closed—
that oily, slick, reverse-spark of undoing.

Whatever it had been like, this wasn't it.

She dropped her arms and examined the shape: it was a
roughly circular blob, runny and blurred. She blinked and
tried another angle. Squinted. No use. She couldn't make
it out and she couldn't risk asking Ink. Joy knew she had to

get rid of it before he found out and did something...horrible. She didn't want to be responsible for hurting him again.

Dropping the scalpel back into its pocket, Joy picked up her brand new phone—replaced thankfully under warranty—and prayed that all her data was retrievable from the cloud once her transfer was confirmed, but she couldn't access her contacts list until then. She ran to her room and opened her desk drawer, rifling through old papers, library cards, business cards, magnets and Post-it notes, excavating the one she'd hoped to find: a crisp piece of card stock with exquisite penmanship. Graus Claude's voice mailbox was a convenient 800 number.

She dialed quickly, waiting for the automatic voice stating its standard instruction that she could please record her message after the beep.

"Hi, this is Joy," she said, feeling foolish. "I have something I have to show you." She added, "Alone. My cell phone's reestablishing voice mail, so please call or email. I'll check for messages until I hear from you. It's kind of urgent. Thanks." She recited her phone number and spelled out her email address and hung up, wondering if she was making things worse.

Ink trusted the noble toad absolutely, but Inq was suspicious. *The Bailiwick already suspects something,* Inq had said when they'd been passing off Joy as Ink's chosen, his *lehman.* But that was before Joy had proven herself, undoing Aniseed's pandemic curse, potentially saving both worlds, and falling in love with Ink. Graus Claude knew that she was on their side, didn't he? He counted her as a friend. A niggling voice chased that thought through her mind. *Well, he didn't actually SAY that he considered her a loyal friend—he'd implied it—but the Folk twist the meanings to suit their own ends. The Bailiwick is no different.*

Joy trembled with more than apprehension; she still hadn't eaten.

Hurrying back to the kitchen, she peeled a banana, took a huge bite, pulled on her shirt and scooped the random assortment of crinkling snack bags into her arms. She took the stairs in twos, finishing the banana before she hit the courtyard, and managing to open a lemon water as she rounded the corner into the back lot.

Her car's windshield gleamed in the sun. Matte-white smears of wax had dried in semicircular patterns. Stef was gone, Gordon was gone and Monica sat on the parking stop, picking at the sponge in her hand.

"Hey," Joy said, looking around. "Where did everybody go?"

Monica looked up as if she hadn't realized she was alone. The wet splashes across her shirt and shorts spoke of an earlier giddiness that was now notably absent. Monica's voice was low and subdued. "I didn't see where Stef went, but Gordon went home."

"Figures that the guys leave us to do the last bit of dirty work," Joy said and handed a bottle to Monica. Her friend didn't touch it, didn't even lift her hand to take it. Joy frowned. "Are you okay?"

"No," Monica said to the asphalt. "Definitely not okay."

"Okay. Not okay," Joy repeated as she sat down on the concrete riser, plucking at her friend's wet clothes. "Did Gordon push things one step too far?"

"You could say that," Monica said and stretched out her legs. Soapy water sludged past, the bubbles only the tiniest froth, the edge of the puddle evaporating in a long, gray smear. "Gordon asked if he could meet my folks, get our families together for a picnic." She threaded her fingers and stretched her arms in front of her, turning her palms inside-over, light versus dark. "I said I didn't think it was a good idea," she said and cracked her neck to one side, then the other. "Then he asked if I had a good reason why not."

Joy took a swig of her lemon water. "Is there a good reason why not?"

"Yes and no," Monica said. "Mostly no." She leaned back on her palms, keeping her eyes on the water. "First of all, I figured that would officially make him my boyfriend and I wasn't really looking for a boyfriend right now, you know? We hooked up. We had fun. I never expected to fall for him." She shrugged without conviction. "He's the first guy who's stuck around long enough for me to wonder 'what if?' And, okay, yeah, I shouldn't be surprised that he wants to meet my parents—I should be flattered, right?—but honestly, it freaks me out." She tapped her flip-flops in the puddle, sending tiny splashes across the asphalt. "I've never brought a boy home before, and that sounds pretty serious," she huffed. "It *feels* pretty serious, so I guess I just freaked." She glanced over her shoulder at Joy. "I'm happier having things stay the same."

"Trust me—I'm an expert here," Joy said. "Things *never* stay the same."

Monica slipped off her shoes and dipped her toes in the water. "I know."

"So what's the other reason?" Joy prompted. Monica tried to look like "what?" but they both knew there was a "what" so why bother saying "what?" They knew each other well enough to not go down the path of play-pretend-friend.

"The *other* reason," Monica said, "is stupid."

Joy sipped her water. "And our motto is?"

"No Stupid."

"Right," Joy said. "So spill." Monica evaded her eyes. There was another long, sunlit pause. Monica stomped on a soap bubble, killing it. Joy leaned closer and nudged her friend's shoulder. "You know you can tell me."

"Anything?"

"Anything," Joy said, feeling the first flutter of serious worry in her stomach. Monica's face was pinched and drawn. Something was really, really wrong. Joy nudged her again. "Really. Honest."

Monica grimaced and leaned back on her fists. "Okay. If I bring Gordon home, then the first guy I'll be introducing to my mom and dad will be white."

Joy waited for the punch line. It didn't come.

"So?"

"*So?*" Monica said. "I thought we just said, No Stupid."

"I'm not being stupid," Joy said. "I just don't get what's the big deal." She gestured with the bottle. "Your folks are cool. They don't care about that stuff. I mean, they like me, and I'm white." But as soon as she said it, Joy suddenly wondered. Was that true? Did the Reids not like her? Did they not like her because she was white? Had she somehow never noticed during almost ten years of friendship? A catalog of imagined faults and worries flipped through Joy's mind. She suddenly felt small and slightly ill. "We're okay, right?"

"Yes, of course," Monica said peevishly. "But I'm not *dating* you. And it's not a question about whether my parents are cool with white folks or not—they aren't racists or anything. It's just...They've never actually said, 'Don't date a white guy,' but after what my dad went through growing up in Arkansas, it was kind of implied." She rubbed her arms as if she was cold.

"Really?" Joy said doubtfully, scraping her shoes through the puddle.

"Yes, really," Monica said, sounding annoyed. "Ask Stef how many times people asked him whether he had a girlfriend or if he thought some girl was hot or if he planned on having a wife and kids someday?" Monica flicked her fingertips like she was banishing the world. "Not many people will come out and say, 'Don't be gay,' but the way they talk means that everyone expects boys to bring home girls—or blacks to bring home blacks or Jews to bring home Jews—parents expect their kids to be basically like themselves. That's not racist or sexist *on purpose*, but it's still there all the same."

Joy sat quietly, knowing that she'd made a lot of those same mistakes with Stef. It was uncomfortable realizing that she'd fallen into the same trap as "everybody else." How had her brother felt every time she'd asked him about having a girlfriend? Or teased him about some girl on TV? She'd never meant to be mean. She'd never meant to be insensitive or uncaring, either; she'd just been...stupid.

"My dad grew up with people spitting on him while he stood in line at the grocery store and while he waited for the bus," Monica said. "He and Mom didn't want me to ever feel different that way—that's why we moved to Glendale." She carefully stared at the sun glinting off her toe ring. "And it worked. I was never told that I couldn't do something or that I wasn't good enough being a person of color. I got good grades, got early admission into a good college, I have my own car and I know I'm pretty privileged. I get that. But I'm not so privileged as to be blind to the world or think it's not out there waiting to judge me." She spread her arms as if to encompass everything out there. "So when you say 'So?' like it's no big deal, it pisses me off because, let me tell you, it is most certainly a *very* big deal!"

Joy felt a push button of panic. "Why are you getting mad at me?"

"I'm not *mad*," Monica snapped, her eyes flashing at Joy. "Okay, I *am* mad, but I'm not mad at you—no, wait. I'm mad at you, but not *at* you, personally, just what you are doing, being you." She shook her head angrily. "That's not coming out right." She took a deep breath and set her hands on her thighs. "You're my friend, and I know that. That's what makes this hard, okay? But I trust you to hear me out and think about what I'm saying before you write me off as a hor-rible person." She took another deep breath, eyes fluttering. "Right. Here's the deal—I'm angry that you are in the position to think that this is a big deal or not because to you, it may not *be* a big deal. But given how you got all wound up about your brother coming out and you still haven't introduced your own boy to me, let alone to your parents, I think maybe these kinds of things are a bigger deal than you let on, even to yourself. But see, *you* get to call it." Her words came out in a rush. "You're the majority, the default, the Pretty Young White Thing. Maybe it *wouldn't* be a big deal if you brought home a brother or a Muslim or a Jewish Puerto Rican butch chick with piercings and introduced her to your family at dinner. It's not like they could throw stones. But this stuff is all—" she grasped for the right words, shaking her hands in the air "—*messy* and *rude* and *ugly* and *stupid,* and I don't like it, but that's the truth. I don't know how my folks would feel about it." Monica sighed and picked up her lemon water; beads of condensation dripped down the sides. "I know they want the best for me and if the best is Gordon, then every-body wins, but if it's not..." Monica unscrewed the top off her bottle. "I just don't want anybody getting hurt."

Joy watched a thin trail of suds slip down the storm drain. "I think it's too late for that," she said. Monica shrugged and wiped her nose.

"But are you getting what I'm saying?" Monica asked.

"A little, maybe," Joy said. "I guess I don't know." Joy leaned sideways, touching elbows with her best friend. The honesty didn't hurt as much as she thought it would. It felt better to be trusted to share an ugly, rude truth. And Monica was right—Joy ought to understand, and, truthfully, in some ways, she did...and, more truthfully, in many ways, she couldn't. She felt guilty about it and, also, not.

She and Monica were many things, but they were also best friends.

Joy picked at her nails. "So how long do you think he'll wait around?"

Monica stared at her toes. "Oh, I'll call him eventually," she said. "I'm just waiting for the perfect moment."

Joy shook her head and drank some more water. "There are no 'perfect moments,'" she said. "There are only 'moments.' And then they're gone." She poked her friend with her elbow. "What about you? What do you want?"

Monica stepped half-heartedly on the sponge. It squished. "I don't want to have to choose."

Monica dropped her head against Joy's shoulder. Joy rested her ear on Monica's hair. Their knees touched: dark brown and pink-peach, both scuffed and speckled with soap and grass. They splashed their toes in the water. Joy let out a sigh.

"Amen, sister."

SIX

I am intrigued. Will send the car for you at 5pm EST at the corner of Wilkes and North Main. Please be prompt. -GC

JOY LOGGED OFF HER ACCOUNT AND CHECKED THE time. She really wanted to stay and coax Monica out of her funk, but this was important.

Stef had gone grocery shopping, leaving Joy to wash the dishes. Pizza and gelato had been shelved in the wake of the Monica–Gordon drama. Joy left a note—"Out. Be back soon!"— and gave herself five minutes' lead time before she locked up the house, jogged down the stairs, crossed the courtyard and shut the gate behind her, fully aware that she was going beyond the protection of Ink's wards. She ran her thumb over the *futhark* pendant at her neck as she crossed Wilkes Road.

She stood on the corner and checked her phone again. If Graus Claude said he wanted her on the corner at five, she wasn't going to risk being late. She glanced around, gripping her purse strap, wondering just how long three minutes could possibly take. She kept glancing at the screen out of habit, twisting it awkwardly in her hand. This was probably the reason that old people wore watches.

A classic Bentley whirred up to the corner. Joy recognized its long, clean lines of chocolate-brown and caramel-gold with white-rimmed tires that looked like they'd never known dirt. Joy opened the back door and eased into the buttery seats, her feet sinking into thick carpet. The air smelled faintly of mint.

"Miss Malone?" the driver spoke over his shoulder without turning around. "Please make yourself comfortable."

"Thank you," Joy said as she placed her purse beside her on the seat. She missed having Ink next to her, but she had to do this alone. She squirmed nervously against the leather, trying to get comfortable. She'd only formally met with the Bailiwick once or twice before, and he intimidated the heck out of her. Still, it was better this way. She had to protect herself...and Ink.

The car slid from the curb as her eyes slid slowly closed.

Joy woke to the car drawing level with the brownstone's front steps, surprised in that half instant to be somewhere outside Boston. It took her mind a moment to catch up to the present: ghost image on her shoulder. Graus Claude. Bentley. Driving. Brownstone. Kurt. Ink. She shook her head to clear it. She must have been more tired than she'd thought, but Joy didn't remember feeling tired in the first place. It was disconcerting and surreal.

The driver held her door open as she awkwardly stepped out onto the sidewalk; a brisk wind made the world feel more real by the moment. She took a few cautious steps, and, satisfied, the driver returned to his post. He tipped the brim of his cap as he got into the luxury vehicle, which slowly rolled away in a hush of ghostly wheels.

Joy touched the handrail, the cool grit under her fingers convincing her that she really was awake and in front of the Bailiwick's house and was climbing the steps at this very moment of her own free will. It was strange to be there without Ink or Inq; she'd never come there alone before and the steps were unreasonably wide for one person. Remembering how Ink had hurried her through the breach, Joy ran quickly up the steps, knocked the knocker and hopped inside as Kurt opened the door.

The emptiness of the foyer was welcoming, and Joy was grateful for the silence as Kurt led her down the hall and knocked a quick double rap upon Graus Claude's office doors. Joy blinked the sleep from her eyes and wiped her palms on her pants.

"Come in, Miss Malone," the Bailiwick's voice thrummed, in no way muffled by the heavy ironwood. Kurt opened the doors, and Joy stepped through. The room was once again nestled in comfortable shadow, its heavy curtains drawn and the emerald lampshade aglow. The great toad looked up from his paperwork and sat back in his throne-like chair. "I hope your journey here was pleasant?"

"Very," Joy said, slipping into a chair. "I slept all the way here."

"Of course," Graus Claude said almost glibly as he motioned Kurt to pour some water with two of his hands while the other two shuffled a stack of papers into a neat pile. "The Bentley has a soporific effect when transporting passengers across large distances. Cuts down on the unnecessary strains upon the mental facilities when dealing with transdimensional shifts. I would think you might have noticed given how often you've been driven to and from my address during our brief association."

Joy sat down slowly, uncomfortable with the knowledge that she'd been put to sleep on more than one occasion without her prior knowledge or consent. She listened to the gurgle as Kurt poured water from a crystal carafe. Maybe she shouldn't drink the water? Maybe Inq was right to be wary?

Kurt set a silver tray with small china plates on the desk. Each had slivered vegetables and two tiny bowls of green-

and-white sauce swirled in delicate yin-yang designs. Joy accepted a plate and glass of water, but she waited for the Bailiwick to take the first sip.

Graus Claude motioned for Kurt to be dismissed. Joy didn't look at him as he left, professionally slipping the doors closed in his wake. The Bailiwick settled back in his chair, one of his hands dipping a slice of jicama in sauce. "I discovered that the elemental blade belonged to Jaiveer Sungte, a mercenary from the Old Wars. He had long been retired from active service and was known to occupy the cliffs of Varkala," he said. "No reason at all could be found for his desire to attack your person. If I had to guess, I would surmise monies or a long-overdue favor was involved."

"Ink thought the same thing," Joy said.

"Then let us consider the case closed and say no more about it. As I understand it, Master Ink would prefer it that way." Joy squirmed and tried not to think about the look on Ink's face if he knew why she was here. "In any event, you came to address a different concern." Joy nodded and the Bailiwick leaned over the desk, his eyes like sparkling sapphires. "Show me."

Joy removed her jacket, exposing the back of her spaghetti-strap tank, turning around in her chair to show the gleaming smear between her shoulders. The air was cold and stippled her spine.

"Can you see it?" she asked.

"A moment." She heard him move, a scraping of nails and the groaning of wood followed by a delicate sound of thin metal clinks. "Yes," he said. "I can see it."

Joy swallowed. "Do you recognize it? Do you know whose it is?"

Another aching creak of wood and she could feel the damp heat of his breath on her back as he leaned closer to take a better look. Joy shuddered at the great beast literally breathing down her neck. He might look like a respectable four-armed amphibian in an immaculately tailored suit, but she'd seen him eat an attacking soldier whole.

"I do not know," he said. She could feel his words on her skin. "I can barely make out any discernible detail." Joy turned back around to face the giant comptroller. He wore his tiny pair of gold-rimmed spectacles perched above the nostrils of his nonexistent nose. They flashed in the light of his desk lamp and reminded her, oddly, of Mr. Vinh's multi-lensed contraption. Now she understood how Graus Claude could see marks without the gift of Sight.

"Normally, I would expect those of the Twixt to know the identity of those who marked them, and a mere human to be ignorant of the entire affair." The Bailiwick drank his water and picked up two ice cubes with his tongue, crunching them in his massive jaws. "As a human with the Sight, I expect that you see what I see, which, I am guessing, is a half-formed *signatura*."

"Is that normal?" Joy asked.

"It happens," he said. "The form of a True Name can be different for everyone, a fact of which you should be well aware. Your acquisition of Master Ink's mark was significantly different than Briarhook's—the one, nicked with a knife, the other, burned into your flesh." Joy winced at the memory and touched her upper arm. "However, I imagine there must be a few that develop over time. When did it appear?"

"After I did gymnastics in the grass."

Graus Claude rumbled. "Somehow I doubt that falls under anyone's formal purview," he said drily. "The Folk are more interested in babies born with eleven fingers or those who can spin straw into gold."

Joy peeked back over her shoulder. "Can people do that?"

"Hardly at all anymore," he said sadly, then shrugged both sets of shoulders. "Should you wish to disassociate from it, you are in the unique position to do so. Why not simply remove it and be done?"

"I tried," Joy said. "It didn't work."

Now Graus Claude looked surprised. Or possibly intrigued. "Really, now?" he said. "It was my understanding that you could remove *signatura* from the flesh with the scalpel of Master Ink."

"Yes, well, I thought so, too," she said. "I don't know who did this or where I got it, but I don't think Ink would be too happy if he found out." Some of the worry seeped into her voice. She pulled her arms through the jacket sleeves. "I thought you might at least be able to tell me whose it is."

"I'm sorry, Miss Malone, that I cannot be of more service," he said. "I do have extensive records from the Scribes' client list, but I'm afraid, given what I see here, there isn't much to go on."

Joy shrugged her jacket back over her shoulders, hyperconscious of the feel of the fabric against her spine. "It's okay. I'm just...I'm worried that I can't seem to remove it. This hasn't happened before, and now I'm wondering if I've somehow..." She didn't know how to end the sentence without giving too much away. Graus Claude didn't know that she had the power to remove *signaturae* and that it wasn't a magical property of the scalpel itself.

"Broken it?" the Bailiwick suggested.

She swallowed back the unspoken lie. "Or something."

"And you don't want Ink to find out," Graus Claude said. "How very adolescent. I'd forgotten how trivial relationship dramas can be. It's refreshingly mundane." He lumbered to his feet with a great shifting of things. "However, I believe that I have the good fortune to offer you an opportunity to test your theory before there are any undue histrionics. If you would be so good as to follow me?"

Joy finished a wasabi-cream carrot stick in two bites and

followed the Bailiwick as he made his way down the hall, the stinging heat of the spicy mustard zinging inside her nose. Graus Claude's great head swung methodically from his hunched spine as his wide, flat feet shuffled forward in shiny leather shoes. They made their way down the hall, passing gilt-framed portraits and highly polished mirrors, until he came to a wide, decorative archway faced in scalloped wood, layered like dragon scales from frame to floor.

"Step lively, Miss Malone," Graus Claude advised as the scale under his hand popped inward with a push and the entirety of the wall slid sideways, revealing a luxurious elevator with velvet benches and brass fixings. The walls were sheets of smoked glass and a small, crystal chandelier hung from the ceiling. Joy stepped inside, and the door slid closed behind her.

"Are we going upstairs?" she asked.

"To my private apartments?" he said, quirking his browridge. "I think not." He grasped the brass lever in the corner and wrenched it four notches to the left. The opposite wall slid away. "But I do trust that you can appreciate the significance of these rooms. There are few I would trust access, beyond the mere knowledge that they existed at all." He handed her a Japanese-style robe of pale pink silk with embroidered cherry blossoms. "Here. Wear this." He slipped on a smoking jacket of red silk with black lapels while two hands tied his belt. He opened a side door in the antechamber. "This way."

Joy hung her jacket on a hook and slipped the cool silk over her goose-pimpled skin. The hidden room was colder and draftier than the foyer with high, vaulted ceilings and white-on-white walls. The clean lines were accented here and there with glass bowls of river stones or small bonsai trees. An upright slab of slate propped with green copper wires trickled water over its surface. The tables were glass and the couches were white and a woman sat with a book of

Ansel Adams photography open on her lap. There was a familiar squiggle along her jawline and a score of angry welts at her throat. Joy could see a *signatura* glowing through the bumpy scar tissue.

"I believe I foretold a short respite before a solution presented itself," Graus Claude said as the woman closed her book. "I trust you have been comfortable during the interim?"

"Yes," the woman said, glancing furtively to Joy. "Thank you."

The Bailiwick nodded and threaded his four arms behind him. "Excellent. May I present my associate, Miss Malone? Miss Malone, this is Mademoiselle Ysabel Lacombe." Graus Claude turned to Joy. "Mademoiselle Lacombe came to me with a conundrum that, I confess, exceeded my abilities to address, but one which may be well suited to your unique talents." Both women exchanged glances. The injured woman spoke first.

"You can free me of Henri?"

Joy glanced at Graus Claude, who said simply, "Perhaps." He settled himself onto the white chaise, which barely gave under his weight as he poured green tea into three delicate handleless cups. "Why don't you enlighten Miss Malone as to your predicament?"

Joy was about to ask Graus Claude how any of this was supposed to help her, but the dark-haired Ysabel was quick to comply, her amber-golden eyes hungry and wide.

"I was chosen by Henri Dubois, alpha of the Ridge Pack, and marked as his own when I was fourteen." Her voice had a strange, nasal accent, almost French but not quite. "I don't remember much before then, honestly. It's mostly a blur of tiny bubbles and noise." She glanced sideways at Joy. "My people are from the Saint Lawrence River," she explained. "We are defenseless River Folk, and human encroachment has meant that we must barter for protections." She calmly placed the coffee table book beside her on the couch, one hand lingering upon it. "I was offered as tithe to the Northern Ridge Pack in exchange for my peoples' continued safety. I obeyed without a thought." She placed thin fingers against her scar-riddled throat. "I knew nothing but obedience and cruelty under Henri, but I considered it my duty to be loyal to *ma famille*." Her eyes burned along the edges, turning the irises a shocking coppery red. Joy felt an unsettling squeeze of sympathy and fear. "But then I met Lucius. He was a packless loner from All-Snow and..." Ysabel did not finish, but she didn't have to. Her story was written all over her face: she fell in love with her savior and wished to leave with him. Ysabel raised her chin and dropped her hand. "I came to appeal to the Bailiwick to help me escape, but with Henri's mark upon me, he said I had a very short lead, one which could be reclaimed at any time, should Henri choose to drag me back. I have made it this far but do not know how much longer my freedom will last."

Graus Claude glanced meaningfully at Joy, who shifted her purse, almost hearing the scalpel rattling in its side pocket. She remembered how the Bailiwick had once told her that while *signaturae* must be given voluntarily, they were not always received that way. Part of her understood Ysabel all too well—Joy had been branded with Briarhook's mark, burned into the flesh of her arm, and it had carried the illicit addition of Aniseed's *signatura* secreted beneath her skin. Both had been forced upon her, neither one wanted. That feeling of helpless horror still haunted her dreams.

"*Signaturae* are sacrosanct," Graus Claude said gravely, his words reverberating like a gong in the room. "Designed as a matter of safety and precaution for all the Folk. The removal of a mark could breach our world order as well as the Council's decree and, as such, should be considered a nigh impos-

sible feat and, perhaps, an act of treason within the Twixt."
Joy watched the cords in Ysabel's neck flicker, her face tight.
Her hand trembled against the book cover, a sort of miserable bravery. "And yet," he said magnanimously, "here is
Miss Malone." Ysabel shifted to look at Joy, who wasn't sure
whether to smile or bow. Graus Claude's eyes fixed hers with
enviable confidence. "She might be willing to make the attempt on your behalf."

Joy froze. *What?* She had no idea if she could do such a
thing! The only marks she'd removed from other people had
been Ink's—*signaturae* hidden in the scars or birthmarks that
some of the Folk required for earning their favor; wounds
and experiences that were etched permanently on their skin.
Okay, she'd erased Aniseed's *signatura* (in the air) and Inq's
(by accident) and Briarhook's (on purpose), but she had only
removed that which had been drawn by the Twixt onto *humans.* She had never tried it on Folk who marked one another!
She hadn't even realized that could happen until recently.
The glimpse of a serrated crescent moon sliced through her
memory. She hadn't offered to remove Grimson's mark, because she'd known Ink would refuse...but what about this
river woman who had never asked to be sold into slavery as
a girl? She wouldn't ask—and wouldn't refuse—because she
didn't know that it was possible. Ysabel looked at her with
hope-filled eyes.

"What do you say, Miss Malone?" Graus Claude purred.
"Are you willing to try?"

Joy called the Bailiwick several bad names in her head as
she opened her purse and set it on the table. She took up the
scalpel in her hand.

"Show me," Joy said.

Ysabel loosened the neck of her robe, baring her long
scarred throat. She shed her thin covering, exposing her
chest as a patchwork of claw marks, rents and gouges over

uneven skin; layers of red and purple shone darkly against scores gone white with age. She'd been torn repeatedly, her breasts and belly systematically mutilated over the years, and yet there was a strength in her spine that shone on her face. Ysabel lifted her chin in a submissive gesture, one Joy could only imagine she'd grown accustomed to since she was fourteen.

Beneath it all, the *signatura* burned.

Joy tried to ignore the sickening landscape of scars, trying to see the beginning of the mark buried there. Beneath the bulb of Ysabel's chin, a long, thin shape like a zipper of teeth etched down the length of her throat and ended in a teardrop between her breasts. This was the dreaded Henri's *signatura,* shining like quicksilver drawn with a serrated knife. Just looking at it gave Joy a glimpse of his true self: severe, brutal, vicious, absolute. If she'd had any reservations about removing it before, she had none now.

"I see it," Joy said and lifted the scalpel. "Can you lie still?"

Ysabel nodded and willingly offered her neck to Joy and the blade.

Joy glanced back at Graus Claude, who observed without comment, his four arms tucked behind his massive back in polite interest. Joy wasn't certain if she was really about to commit treason or if it was merely another one of Graus Claude's grandiose statements, but in any case, he was making her nervous. A tremor shuddered along her limbs. Joy was about to attempt something she would have never dared—and in front of the Bailiwick!—in order to free a stranger.

Smug toad, she thought and touched the scalpel to Ysabel's skin.

She felt it working, the familiar sluice as the tip of the instrument nudged itself under the mark. She worked at the tiny space between the *signatura*'s teeth, tracing the phantom image, following the elegant sweep of Ysabel's throat.

Joy moved the scalpel slowly over the ridges of breastbone and sinew, slipping past scar tissue and bloodless wounds to curl into the final droplet shape in the center of her...

Graus Claude said, "Wait."

Lumbering forward, he opened one of his clawed hands. Joy hesitated, her pulse jumping thick in her throat.

"I believe you may have missed something," he said, blue eyes flashing. "May I, Joy Malone?"

Ysabel, eyes closed, did not move a muscle. Her face had turned toward the paper screen, her bared torso stretched across the couch. Joy knew she should not give the Bailiwick the scalpel but couldn't think of a way to refuse. He waited patiently, like a parent for the stolen cookie or the keys, and Joy felt her hand move out of some instinct or obligation. Graus Claude did not touch the scalpel until she'd set it in his palm.

He withdrew his set of gold-rimmed spectacles from an inside pocket and set the blade against Ysabel's white throat. Joy twisted her fingers, feeling her hands go numb, wondering what would happen next.

The Bailiwick pressed the tip of the scalpel into the exposed breastbone. A sharp inhale from Ysabel did not sound like pain, but mild surprise. Below the *signatura,* a bead of blood welled to the surface. Graus Claude lifted the tainted blade and withdrew.

"My apologies," Graus Claude said, handing it back. "Please continue."

Shaking, Joy accepted the scalpel under the great toad's icy glare. She tried to ignore his searing gaze as she continued where she'd left off, sweeping to close the last curve of the droplet, completing its design.

The line of teeth and tears flared once and disappeared.

"Splendid," the Bailiwick said, making Joy jump. "Miss Ysabel?" He offered her a thin tissue and a circular magnifying mirror for her inspection. The woman wiped away the spot of blood and ran disbelieving fingers over her throat and down her chest.

"It's gone?" she said in a disbelieving whisper. "It's really gone?"

"It is," Graus Claude said gently, pocketing his glasses. "As is your confinement." He ambled forward, the palsied shake of his head returning as he bent nearer. "You are free to leave the premises and are encouraged to do so, although you understand I must advocate that you not return to Île d'Orléans. I trust you can find residence elsewhere." Another hand produced a sealed envelope. "In this, I have listed a number of locales, including contacts, should you find yourself at a loss. Each comes highly recommended. Once you have found yourself situated, I expect that you will inform me of your relocation and we can settle accounts."

"Yes. Yes, of course," Ysabel said, taking the envelope. The smile on her face wobbled between disbelief and radiance. Her shining eyes sought Joy's. "Thank you! Words cannot express..." Her fingers clutched the robe's hem closed. *Merci. A ma coeur.* Thank you!" She touched Joy's hands, the scalpel all but forgotten, and pressed a kiss to each of her cheeks, first one then the other. Tears of happiness ran shining trails down the river sprite's face, wetting her skin, almost—thought Joy—like the missing mark of quicksilver that was no longer at her throat.

Ysabel traded two kisses with Graus Claude and collected her things out of the white-and-glass cabinet. After pulling on a sundress, she pressed the envelope to her chest and threw her cloak around her shoulders as she gave a last, burbling whisper in her liquid language. *Thank you!* Hugging the envelope again, she quickly withdrew.

Joy sat on the couch, thoughts whirling.

"I would say that was an unparalleled success," Graus

Claude said. "I had previously mourned my lost opportunity to observe your work with Master Ink's trademark instruments during our last adventure, being somewhat preoccupied with battle at the time, but I am pleased to have the lapse rectified at last." He finished his tea and set the cup on the table with a delicate *ting*. Joy felt the note shiver down her spine with dread. "I must say I am duly impressed, Miss Malone." He paced the room, tucking two of his four hands into their pockets. "What you have just now demonstrated is both the ability to undermine our world's most sacred precepts while simultaneously proving that you have been cloaking your actions in such a manner that has kept you anonymous and alive." He nodded. "Very impressive, although it is now evident to me that the power to erase *signaturae* resides within you and not in the scalpel, as the Council and I had previously been led to believe." He smacked his lips. "Brava."

There was no use trying to deny it. Joy blew the blade clean, just like Ink, watching the tiny droplets of red lift and disappear under her breath. She placed the scalpel on the glass table. It settled with a click.

"Ink thought it best," she said.

"He was quite right."

"So," she said. "What happens now?"

The Bailiwick puffed up his chest as if about to croak. "I have already given my counsel on what I believe you should do, Miss Malone. I do not appreciate repeating myself as it implies that the recipient of my sage advice is not doing their part by heeding it and therefore not worth the bother of repetition," he admonished. "My answer has not wavered in the slightest—give back the scalpel, accept a *signatura* or remove yourself completely from the Twixt." Graus Claude loomed over her, his head dipping down, somehow stilled of its palsied quiver with the severity of his words. "Now more so than ever I would urge you to make a decision and take action quickly…before someone gets hurt."

"I have a *signatura*," she grumbled.

"You have *something*. That is certain," he said. "But you would be hard-pressed to convince the Council of its authenticity without one of the Folk willing to come forward to claim you." Graus Claude rumbled deep in his chest. "Without a claimant, I doubt that you would have sufficient proof that you have fulfilled that requirement. And after seeing your display with Mademoiselle Lacombe, I would have to consider the possibility that you somehow created a clever forgery."

Joy glared. "That's ridiculous! Even if I knew how to do that, you said yourself that *signaturae* couldn't be forged or counterfeited."

"I also said that *signaturae* were permanent and could not be removed," Graus Claude said. "There are many once-sacred facts that are currently suffering revision under your hand, and if I could surmise the possibility of forgery, certainly anyone on the Council could do so, as well. Especially Sol Leander. He would be eager for the chance to prove that humans remain a significant threat, especially those with the Sight or power, considering his auspice." He placed the mirror upon a shelf and adjusted its glass to a more pleasing angle. "I am finding myself in the distasteful position of beginning to see the wisdom in some of the Old Ways."

Joy cringed. She didn't like the sound of that. She knew that once the Folk and humans had shared their world with one another, but something had happened that had forced the nonhumans into hiding, preserving the last bits of magic in places and people—the secret remnants now known as the Twixt. They also advocated plucking out the eyes of any human with the Sight. Joy was not a fan of the Old Ways.

"I can't give back the scalpel—you know that," Joy said, rubbing her eyes. "Ink gave it to me and now it's mine, like it or not."

"You could refuse to use it," he suggested.

Joy ground her teeth, feeling heat flush her face. "Yes, well, that seems a little hypocritical since you basically ordered me to use it just now."

"I did no such thing, and I resent the implication," the Bailiwick said mildly. "As a human, you purport to value free will. If I put you in a strategically uncomfortable position, then that is the nature of war, Miss Malone, a state that currently exists disguised in these modern times in civilized pursuits such as etiquette, polite society and chess. You simply allowed yourself to be put into check." He gestured with his lower two hands. "You wanted to test your abilities, and I gave you the opportunity to do so, or not, as you desired. It was your hand, not mine, that did the deed." Graus Claude shifted his ice-blue eyes to the door through which Ysabel had gone. "If it gives you comfort, I think you did a kind service to a lady who has endured much unkindness, which is no small thing to weigh against my discovery of your hidden talent."

Joy nodded and felt a bit better. "Are you going to tell the Council?"

"Certainly not," he said, affronted. "Why implicate both of us as well as poor Mademoiselle Lacombe?"

Joy flumped back on the couch. It was stiff, cold and unyielding. "So I can't prove this thing is a *signatura,* I can't give back the scalpel or promise not to use it and I'm not giving up Ink." She reached behind her shoulder as if she could touch the spot where the ghostly symbol stained her own skin. "I even *asked* Ink to mark me and he said it was more important for me to stay free, but it feels more like I'm trapped, like I'm running out of options." She checked for the Bailiwick's reaction, but she was no good at reading the face of a toad. She sighed. "I don't feel very free."

"We rarely value freedom until it's lost," said Graus Claude.

She picked up the scalpel and tucked it back into her purse, maneuvering around the uncomfortable silence. "Were you telling the truth that removing marks was a treasonous offense?"

"I might have exaggerated slightly for the benefit of our audience," the Bailiwick said. "Although it has never come up before the Council as a point of address since, as I've stated previously, no one has ever demonstrated the ability to negate what was designed to be permanent." He smoothed his collar with a single hand. "*Signaturae* are our True Names given form, an elegant solution to the danger of humans shackling Folk to their will by speaking their Names."

"But isn't that exactly what Henri did to Ysabel?" Joy said. "Bound her by a True Name? There doesn't seem to be much of a difference, and you asked me to undo that."

Graus Claude said nothing for a long moment, rotating the white teapot on its trivet with a tiny scraping sound.

"An astute observation, Miss Malone," the Bailiwick said as he made minute adjustments to a small arrangement of cacti in a glazed bowl. "As the intercessor between worlds, I value maintaining the balance above all things—keeping the Twixt and its inhabitants alive, safely ensconced amidst the greater human world, is paramount—and, given that priority, it requires that I allow a certain...*leniency* for absolutes, which requires a delicate hand as well as an iron fist, when necessary." His icy eyes sought hers. "I cannot, myself, bend or break the rules that govern my world, as I am a part of it—more so than most—but there are those who can smooth over the gaps and the cracks that occur under the normal stressors of time and politics. It is a treacherous dance, I'll admit, but by no means one born of treachery or treason—merely a necessity when keeping an eye on the greater picture." He cleared his cavernous throat with a polite cough. "I understand you have met with the Wizard Vinh."

Joy swallowed. "Did Inq tell you?"

"No. Your purse reeks of his malodorous incense."

Joy flipped the shoulder strap. "I did meet him—well, I knew him already, but this was the first time I met him knowing that he was a wizard."

Graus Claude nodded. "Mr. Vinh is a person such as I, serving both worlds with magery and craft and exchange," he said. "Again, I might have exaggerated that no one can successfully split their existence between worlds. I would amend that statement to specifically discourage *lehman* from the attempt. Love with a foot in two bedrooms has very few happy endings."

"But I could find work—is that it?" Joy said. "If I could do something that served both my world and the Twixt, then the Council would get off my back?"

"Such a life has its own hazards, but, essentially, yes."

"So...there's another option." Joy leaned back on the white couch, the leather popping and groaning as she moved. "Maybe I could remove marks for a fee?"

"Certainly not!" Graus Claude snapped and ran a warty olive hand over his face. "Goodness blessed, what a ghastly mess *that* would be! You still fail to understand the purpose of *signaturae*. This is exactly the sort of talk that whips the Tide into a froth!" He shook his head and lifted his many chins. "What I meant to suggest was that perhaps you might offer yourself as a courier for Mr. Vinh, disguised as a cashier or stock girl or the like, *not* to become..." His voice rumbled like distant thunder. "The mere suggestion of such an enterprise..." The Bailiwick trailed off again, clenching his hands slowly; then he shook his great head as if coming to his senses. "No. Absolutely not. If the Council learned of such a thing, your life wouldn't be worth a holly leaf!"

"But then why let me try it now?" Joy said.

Graus Claude sighed again, heavy and reluctant. "You presume that this was my will, Miss Malone, but I assure you that the entire situation was outside my control." Joy found it hard to imagine anything the high-ranked amphibian *didn't* control. He seemed to sense her thoughts and gave a rueful grin full of shark's teeth. "Though I am the Bailiwick—a role I accepted both willingly and with favor—I am also one of the Twixt, bound to my Name and to my auspice as much as any other." His smile was almost wistful. "When fortune smiles or frowns or looks askance, I must be there with open arms to answer it." He pointed one manicured claw at Joy. "You came to me twice asking for counsel on this matter, both times on the heels of Mademoiselle Lacombe. It is a pattern that I recognized at once for what it was—you would both continue to circle one another, spiraling tighter and with greater consequence, until I permitted your paths to cross and forge their own conclusion. Once addressed, the tensions dissipate, conflicts resolve, the coincidences cease and you each may continue on your separate journeys. Thereby balance is restored."

"Wait, what?" Joy's mind spun. "You're saying that I had to be given a chance to remove her mark? That it was fate?"

Graus Claude chewed a celery stalk thoughtfully. "An oversimplification, I assure you, but for our intents and purposes, that is correct. And I always reap the rewards following good fortune." He shifted his feet and added reluctantly, "I will, of course, forward you a percentage of Mademoiselle Lacombe's fee, once the particulars have been settled, and we will speak no more of it."

Joy let the implications sink in. "So...that was a job?" Joy said.

"No," Graus Claude said. "It was merely fortuitous chance."

Joy waved a hand between them. "No, no, no. If I've learned anything about the Folk and the Twixt, it's that there are no mistakes," she said. "By your own logic, my coming up with this idea had to be something I would think of *after* I first tried it on Ysabel. I'd successfully remove her mark and then come up with the idea of doing so for a fee, a job, as a solution to my problem with the Council—something I have now come to you twice about—and it sounds like I will keep coming back to it over and over again until it's resolved, right?"

"That is *not*," Graus Claude said darkly, "at all the case." He picked up the photo book, snapped it shut and slid it into its place on the shelf. "Do not look for fate as an excuse for folly, young lady, for you will then soon find it, whether it is there or no." He sounded disgusted. "Free will always trumps fate if one demonstrates sufficient will, which, I admit, is not often the case with humans." He gazed at her sternly, but to Joy it sounded as if he was trying to convince himself more than her.

She sensed weakness despite his words as the mighty politician flailed his four arms with uncharacteristic dismay. "Given your ability to fabricate, justify or otherwise convince yourself that your own desires are, in fact, destined outcomes by a power greater than yourself and that you are entirely powerless is not only foolish, but dangerous," he said. "This is why Master Ink wished you to remain unmarked, to exercise your free will. Like a muscle, it needs to develop reliably with practice. Humans take their freedoms for granted." He sighed. "Alas, all for naught, but still..." he added somewhat more gently. "You should leave such matters to the experts."

Joy sat on the pristine couch in the secret chamber of the giant toad's residence and considered what the Bailiwick had said and not said. After years with her mom and dad quietly not saying the most important things in her life, she'd learned to listen to the weight in between words. She remembered the eagerness in Mr. Vinh's eyes as he'd studied the scalpel and the look on Graus Claude's face as he'd studiously ignored it.

"Well," she said. "Since I am currently speaking with the resident expert, I wonder what he might say if I offered to work for him, removing unwanted *signaturae* from a select number of clients, prescreened at his discretion, for a percentage of the fee?" Joy looked up at him with careful neutrality. "Theoretically speaking, of course."

The Bailiwick crossed his many arms. The air became still. There was the soft chuckle of water off slate.

"You must know that such a proposition isn't strictly legal."

Joy smiled her Olympic-class smile. "What I notice is that you didn't say no."

Graus Claude's browridge quirked. He took four strides across the room. "It would be a delicate business," he said, adjusting a bowl of cacti. "One that could be neither discussed nor discovered, done strictly off the record, disavowed and unknowable. It treads dangerously close to crossing the Council's decree."

Joy brushed her ponytail over the back of the couch. "I notice you're still not saying no."

The Bailiwick stopped spraying the succulents and turned fully to Joy.

"Indeed," he said. "I accept."

Joy exited the Bentley and walked into Antoine's in a daze. She'd been fully awake for the last few steps, her mind whirling with all that Graus Claude had said. She'd stared at his widescreen computer at the amount of her first deposit check made to an offshore account. The number still bobbed behind her eyes as she opened the door and was enveloped in the smell of hot garlic oil.

She'd have her own workspace, set her hours—Monday

through Friday, noon to four—and had the right to refuse any client, for any reason. It was the freedom she'd always craved at a price she could hardly believe. Graus Claude had explained his system for exchange rates, automatic deposits and the necessary tax exemptions, adding that, in the Twixt, it was customary to expect tips, which she could keep. Kurt would contact her when the arrangements were complete.

The line of zeroes still danced in her head.

She hung up her jacket and picked up her pen. She had to play it cool—not do anything rash. Joy was still employed at the café until she could find a reasonable excuse to leave. This was still something on her résumé and it wouldn't be good to burn bridges. Her parents' career advice had been a one-liner that still rang in her head—"If you can't be a yes-man, be indispensable"—meaning that she should be good, be loyal, don't make waves, be agreeable, be quiet and work extra hard.

But look how well that worked out for them.

Meandering up the aisle, Joy took her place among the clustered waitstaff jockeying for position as the manager finished writing the evening's specials on the board.

"Joy, nice of you to join us," the floor manager said, not looking up. "Don't ask me about nights again for at least two weeks."

Nearby, Neil's face pinked in sympathy. Joy turned her head with infinite slowness. Neil kept his eyes down as he typed with his thumbs. Everyone else seemed to avoid her gaze, too, as if her bad luck was contagious.

Little did they know she had a John Melton's boon.

"Actually," Joy said loud and clear, "I quit."

The look on all their faces was worth every lost tip.

SEVEN

JOY THREW HER KEYS IN THE DISH AND DROPPED HER purse on the kitchen table, then celebrated her last day at Antoine's with a Lindt chocolate truffle. She popped it in her mouth and savored the mouth melt of buttery milk chocolate. So much for two weeks' notice!

Neil had given her his number and told her to keep in touch, which was nice but unlikely. Her world was so much bigger now! Joy plugged her new phone into its charger and checked the mail for anything Cabana Boy related. Now maybe she could make that party in Moscow. Or meet Tuan in Acapulco? The possibilities were endless.

She smeared the smooth, greasy buttercream around her mouth as she dialed the house phone, tucking it into her shoulder as she walked around the kitchen. Like Inq, Joy appreciated the difference between chalk dust and chocolate. And as soon as she earned enough to buy one of Mr. Vinh's glamours, she and Ink could enjoy Lindt chocolate truffles together along with all her family and friends. The idea was as dizzying as the sugar rush and made her smile.

Monica finally picked up on the third ring. "Hello."

"How are you?"

Monica sighed. "I had a fight with my boyfriend."

Joy swallowed the last of the chocolate. "I just quit my job."

Monica groaned. "Jeez, Joy! So much for No Stupid," she said. "Does your father know?"

"He and Shelley called from the road earlier," Joy said, flopping onto the sofa. "But I might have forgotten to mention it."

"So, what? You have three weeks to find a new job?"

"I've got it covered," she said, hoping that she'd come up with some sort of excuse before her father came home. Again, it amazed her how her mother had managed to keep her affair with Doug a secret for so long. Joy had a hard time telling lies. "How about you?" she said, kicking off her shoes. "You talk to your folks about Gordon yet?"

"No," Monica said. Joy could hear the sound of flipping channels. "They figured out that I'm upset over someone. They know the signs—I get a sudden craving for Twizzlers and Emily Dickinson."

Stef entered the kitchen in torn jeans and an inside-out shirt and mimed a phone by his ear, mouthing the word, *Dinner?*

"Emily Dickinson?" she said to Monica while nodding to Stef. "Really?"

"Hey, the woman knows pain," Monica said as Stef flipped through the file folder of delivery menus. He held up a Sushi Ocean and a Curry Hut. Joy pointed to the second.

"You're scaring me, Mon," she said.

"I'm scaring myself," she confessed, and there was the whooshing sound of the phone switching ears. "This is my breakup routine. I know this dance—I can feel it. But, the truth is, I don't want to break up with him. I like Gordon."

Stef waved the menus to get Joy's attention. Joy turned her back on him, concentrating on Monica. "You *like* Gordon?" she said sarcastically.

"Okay! I *love* him. I love Gordon," Monica said, her voice sounding stuffy. It hurt Joy to hear Monica hurting. Her best friend's voice cracked as she started crying. "I love him a lot."

"Then you know what you have to do, don't you?" Joy said, batting away the papers thwacking against her head. Stef loomed over the back of the couch, wielding rolled-up menus with dire intent.

"I'm *hungry*," he whine-whispered.

"Shhh!" Joy hissed.

"What?" Monica snuffled.

"*Don't* break up with him," Joy said, glaring a warning at Stef. "You love him, you don't want to break up, so don't. It's that simple."

Monica sighed. "It isn't that simple."

"Yes, it is," Joy said, remembering how easy it was to discount Graus Claude's suggestion that she could simply abandon Ink. That was never going to happen. She loved him, he loved her, end of story. "It really, really is." She tried to grab the menus, but Stef waggled them out of reach. She strained to snatch one. He bapped her on the nose. Joy snarled into the phone, "Can I call you right back?"

"Okay," Monica said. "I'll be here reading Miss E.D.'s *Collected Works*."

"Sorry, Monica!" Stef called as he ducked Joy's wild swing with a couch pillow. "Guys suck!"

Joy spat a quick, "Later," and hung up, launching off the couch and chasing Stef around the kitchen counter. He dived around corners and sidestepped with small feints and bursts. Joy swung the pillow wildly as he swerved out of the way, laughing. She threw the pillow, which soared overhead, knocking into the lamp above the sink.

Joy froze.

The kitchen light swung erratically, tossing broken, dancing shadows, reminding her of icy nightmares, shattered glass and a monstrous tongue. Stef rose from his crouch and glanced behind him.

"Whoa," he said. "Nice shot, William Tell. Good thing you

didn't break anything or Dad would've..." He turned around and stopped talking. "Hey. You okay?"

"I'm fine," Joy said, smoothing down the hairs on her arms. She felt a cold, dizzy déjà vu. She blinked her eyes expecting a *Flash! Flash!* but there was nothing. No one was at the window. Nothing strange was there. She pulled off her hair band and rewound her ponytail, wishing Ink was with her now. He'd described some secret society initiation in Belgrade that "might take some time." Considering his work took a moment, if that, this was not an encouraging sign.

Stef reached up and stilled the light. The frayed red bracelet on his wrist looked like it was on its last threads, sawing against the edge of his archaic wristwatch that Dad had gotten him for graduation. She'd teased him about it mercilessly. He'd laughed and said that's why it was called a Fossil. She wished her brother would laugh like that now, but he looked too serious, his eyes half shades of worry.

She wanted to ask him about it, but he just as pointedly looked like he *really* didn't want her to ask him, so she didn't. The Malones were the champions of things unsaid. Still, it prickled like static between them.

"You want Curry Hut?" he asked, smoothing the menus flat with his hands.

"Sure," she said. "Chicken curry sounds fine."

He nodded as he dialed. "So? Still trouble in paradise?" he asked as he waited for someone to pick up. "Monica and Gordon didn't look too good when I left."

Joy wanted to ask him what he'd seen or heard, but he started ordering green and red chicken curries, medium-hot, a Buddhist Delight, two orders of roti, two mango lassis and an extra side of sticky rice. It was only while stewing in her forced silence that she remembered where he'd been.

"You went to the C&P," she said as he hung up. "To get the car wax?"

"Yeah," he said. "So?"

"Do you know the owner? Mr. Vinh?"

Stef took out some plates and snagged a few napkins, folding them into proper triangles.

"Hard not to," he said with a shrug. "Seems like the guy knows everybody in the neighborhood." He gave her a look. "Why?"

"I don't know," she hedged. "He's kind of weird."

Her cell phone buzzed in its charger. Joy hurried to pick it up, feeling guilty that she hadn't called Monica right back and expecting to see some angry emoticons, but it wasn't a text from Monica. It was from Kurt.

Expect you at this address tomorrow at eight a.m.

Stef stepped around the counter. Joy killed the screen.

"Love note from the boyfriend?"

Joy thought of Kurt. "God, no!" she said too quickly. "I mean, it's from work."

Not technically a lie.

"They text you from work?" Stef said as he grabbed a Mountain Dew from the fridge. "That's harsh." He popped the top and gestured at the door. "Delivery'll be here in twenty minutes. Money's in the drawer. I'm going to online chat until then, so try not to set anything on fire, okay?"

Joy twisted her finger in her shirt hem. "Yeah, okay."

Stef disappeared into his room as Joy reached into the drawer and started counting out tens before realizing that while she'd successfully evaded any sticky-subject conversations, maybe Stef had, too.

Joy was only mildly surprised the next morning when she pulled up to Dover Mill. The address in Kurt's text matched her phone's GPS. The sight of the worn building curdled her stomach. It was as if the past few days had been filled with old ghosts. She shut off the engine and listened to the wind rattle the shutters. The sound off the river was a faceless moan. It was part of the reason that kids whispered that this place was haunted. Joy knew that the truth was much stranger than that.

She got out of her car, shouldered her purse and slammed the door; the sound was all but swallowed by the wailing, hollow breeze. Stray seeds rushed past, buoyed like skipping stones off the river, dipping over and down the man-made falls. The peeling green paint and weather-beaten stone were somehow even less welcoming than the riverbank's red warning signs about mercury levels and hazardous waste. There was no fishing in this river and the mill's wheel never turned, but that wasn't the reason for Joy's sense of dread.

Whatever wards had been in place when she'd first been to Aniseed's secret cache were gone; Joy could see the overhang clearly—wide, jutting beams full of sharp, thorny brambles curtained railway steps that led down into darkness.

She stepped one foot over the dangling chain marking the edge of the property, shoes crunching through the layers of dead and stubborn crabgrass. Kurt emerged from the sublevel wearing a faded work shirt and pants and wiping his hands on a rag. He looked entirely too large for ordinary clothes.

"I've just finished cleaning up," he said, his mild tenor carrying over the wind. "I think you will be pleased."

Joy kept her hands deep in her pockets to hide her growing panic. Even the smell of the place set her teeth on "grind."

"Great," she said, glancing above her head at the thicket, unseen and unknown by most human and Folk. Thorns as long as her pinky curled from the black branches like ominous fangs. "Couldn't Graus Claude have found somewhere less...horrific?"

Kurt flipped the rag onto his shoulder and crossed his massive arms. "Personal history aside, this happened to be a vacant, cloaked location within a reasonable distance of your warded household and was already familiar to you. Once the Council confiscated Aniseed's belongings, what remained was a perfectly usable space."

Joy pushed back her curtain of windblown hair. "All right," she said, swallowing some of her jitters. "Let's see what you've done with the place."

There was already a huge difference, Joy noted as she and Kurt descended the stairs; the steps had been scrubbed clean and plucked of errant shoots growing through the grain. The walls were plastered smooth and painted a cheery yellow-gold. The makeshift table that had dominated the center room—a sagging wooden door propped on dingy cinder-blocks—was gone and had been replaced with a sleek leather massage table and a matching padded stool. A mounted dental tray set on a swivel arm stood next to an adjustable shaving mirror and a sharpening block. Tiny LED track lights ran across the ceiling, and the rickety shelves once full of rune-labeled, wax-stoppered bottles had been replaced with slick suspension units sporting a small collection of nature photographs, a digital clock and miniature speakers. The only thing that remained in the cache was the giant slate wall, wiped clean. Joy ran her fingers over the slightly uneven surface, remembering how it had once been riddled with the True Names of those who had traded their *signaturae* for whatever potions or promises Aniseed had offered. Inq's had been one of them; the Scribe's *signatura* had paved the way for the Grand Plan: to unleash a magic-borne pandemic and cull humanity from the earth. The massive map of death had been sketched here, the evidence that the aether sprites—who had led them on a merry chase, smashing windows and windshields—had wanted Ink and Joy to see. Touching the bare slate, Joy thought about how much had changed between that day and this.

But beneath the paint and plaster, she could still smell a whiff of licorice.

"The Bailiwick said that you would work weekdays, noon to four, with a suggested minimum of four clients per week. A client list will be available here." Kurt tapped a mounted filing pocket on the wall. It held several colorful file folders. "You may reject any client at any time, at your discretion. Drop-ins are discouraged for security reasons and can be directed back to the Bailiwick." He touched the three hanging file cubbies. "Completed transactions go in the second file, rejections in the third. Collections will take place every Friday, and payment will accrue biweekly. Do you have any questions?"

Joy shook her head while running a finger along the shelves. The edges were sharp and left an indent on her skin.

"The Bailiwick also advises against withdrawing large amounts of cash at any one time to avoid raising red flags and making your family suspicious. You are, of course, welcome to keep any tips as is customary amongst the Twixt, but try to exercise caution. The Bailiwick expects that the Folk will pay handsomely for your skill as well as your silence, so be circumspect," Kurt said with a gentlemanly bow. "I believe his exact words were, 'Don't let it go to your head.'"

Joy sat on the stool and adjusted its height to the table. It didn't make so much as a squeak. She rested her elbows comfortably on the cushion. "No swimming in cash, no raising suspicions, no going to head," she said. "Check."

"There is both electronic and transcribed security at the mouth of the entrance and the steps themselves. A polite 'etiquette cloak' is in place for when there are already two people inside the room, and it can be lifted by your hand, although I'm certain that Ink will want to add his own protections."

A slippery chill settled in Joy's stomach. She didn't know how she was going to explain this new arrangement to Ink. How long would he be tied up in Belgrade? "That won't be necessary," she said and glanced at Kurt. "I mean, I trust the Bailiwick."

Kurt simply folded his hands behind him. "Very good, then," he said. "I trust you have your scalpel with you?"

She took the blade from its pocket and hung her purse on a convenient hook. The light sliced off the scalpel as sharp as the blade itself. Joy was suddenly very nervous. This wasn't just some crazy idea she'd cooked up with the Bailiwick, some theoretical loophole; this was *real*—she was about to begin an underground side business removing *signaturae* in order to keep her toehold in the Twixt as well as remain a free human being in order to keep Ink. This was all to keep Ink. He'd have to understand, know that this was the best option, but Joy had the sinking feeling that she'd have to be pretty convincing. If she could pull this off, the Council would leave them alone. She could have a place, a job, in this world and the Twixt—it could let her have the life she wanted. She could have it all.

But all of a sudden, it didn't seem like a very good idea.

Kurt wiped an imagined smudge off the wall with his rag. "Well, then, if everything is satisfactory, I'll leave you to your work."

Joy blinked. "That's it?"

"The Bailiwick has agreed to your terms—you will not have to remove any *signaturae* performed either by Ink or Inq, solely the Folk's marks upon one another," he said. "That was your one stipulation, correct?"

Joy nodded. "Yeah."

"Then that's it." Kurt placed a foot on the lowest step.

"Aren't you going to stay with me?" Fear pricked her voice

higher. She wasn't thrilled about being out there alone. This place still gave her nightmares.

Kurt flashed a disapproving glare. "No." He sounded annoyed, so she didn't push it, but her fingers twisted into the edge of her shirt. He pointed to the wall. "If you have any concerns, press the glyph here—" he indicated a carved sigil, nearly camouflaged, beneath the corner of the second shelf "—and the Bailiwick will be alerted immediately. Tap it twice to disengage. The glyph on the opposite corner will trip a basic warding across the entryway. That ought to keep anything disgruntled at bay." Kurt circled the familiar-looking squiggle. "Tap it once to activate, twice to disengage. Simple enough?"

Joy stared at him helplessly as she cut off the circulation at her knuckles. *Disgruntled?* She didn't like the sound of that. "Um…"

Kurt shook his head and sighed.

"Give me your phone," he said. She took it out and handed it over. He opened her contacts file. "Here is my number, my *personal* number," he emphasized while typing it in. "Don't abuse it."

"I won't," Joy said. "Thank you." She listed him as Cabana6. She hit Done and flashed him a grin, but the butler-bodyguard wasn't smiling. He turned scathing eyes on Joy.

"Remember, Joy, I am *not* somebody's *lehman*. And neither are you." His voice simmered with scorn. "Don't forget that."

Taken aback, Joy pressed her phone against her leg.

"I won't," she said. "Sorry."

He snapped the rag between his hands and mounted the stairs, but stopped—his body poised halfway up the steps as if he debated whether to say something else. Joy waited, wishing he wouldn't go, wondering how she could do this alone, if she was really making things right or worse. Kurt lowered his voice and the edge of his chin.

"Good luck, Joy Malone."

She remembered the four-leaf clover still in her wallet with a little flutter of confidence. "Thanks," she said. It was the wrong thing to say. The almost-question snapped shut like shutters behind his eyes and he left without speaking. She wondered if she should have asked him what he thought about this and whether Inq knew about it or if she would tell Ink. Joy had the unsettling feeling that there was something more to this arrangement that she should know, but now it was too late to ask. She was alone in the strange office room with whispers of Aniseed sunk deep in the walls.

She slid her hands over the leather table cushion, feeling the flawless surface whisper under her fingers. It reminded her of Ink—the touch of his skin, unmarked, slick and without blemish until they carved the details together, a swirl of an earlobe, the whorl of a fingerprint. She missed him. Even in the quiet moments, especially in the frightening ones, she missed him. She looked at her own hands—his hands—moving as she daydreamed. *This is worth it, isn't it? To keep us together? It's a way that we can have everything: love, freedom, each other.* Joy's hands stopped, resting on the table's edge. *What if it isn't? What if what I think will keep us together only breaks us apart?* Fear grabbed her heart and squeezed. She stood up, knocking the chair back, uncertain whether she was about to bolt out the door or slap her hand on the glyph, tell the Bailiwick that she'd changed her mind...

The *shush* of feet made Joy turn, hoping that Kurt had come back, but the feet that gripped the steps had talons for toes. The legs bent backward at sharp angles like a bird's. A woman's torso balanced with eagle's wings, her hair a mess of speckled feathers framing a quizzical face. The harpy looked impossibly young with a thin smear of oil on her cheek. A livid *signatura* blazed like a lash across her back.

"Is this the place?" she asked, descending the stairs awkwardly. "Graus Claude sent me here."

Joy took one look at her, smiled and patted the table cushion.

"Yes," she said. "Please come in."

The edge of the blade completed its circle and the sigil dissolved into nothing. Joy blew on the tip of the scalpel out of habit.

"That's it," she said, patting the bumpy shell. "You're done."

The old woman slid slowly off the table; her enormous ridged shell lumbered lower as she drooped to touch the floor. The elderly creature moved like the snail she resembled. Both her face and the nacre of her shell were yellowed with age. Baubles and trinkets hung in ropes around her neck and long, wispy braids decorated either side of her head. The two bulbous antennae stretched as she worked out a kink in her neck. She looked up at Joy with watery eyes.

"Thank...you..." Her smile spread over her soft wrinkles like honey, slow and gold and sweet. "It's...been...*such*...a burden."

"It's over now," Joy said kindly. She'd read the client file and knew the mollusk woman's story; claimed as property of a taskmaster who was now years dead, his *signatura* still bound her to return to the cells beneath his storeroom each night, condemning her to a dank place where she'd been lost and forgotten, an elderly servant tethered to a long-dead master's whim.

"Wasn't...a...bad...sort," the shelled woman muttered as she made her way toward the stairs. "Just...*lonely*," she said, smiling again as she passed, her shellacked back throwing off a fresh, pearly light. Fumbling behind her neck, her thick fingers counted the knots of her various charms. She removed one beaded strand riddled with tiny stone birds.

"For...you..." she said. "For...youth."

The woman placed it in Joy's hand, her skin preternaturally soft and boneless. A bulbed feeler brushed Joy's cheek. She tried not to flinch.

"Thank you," Joy said, ignoring the cool kiss of slime. "I hope you like your new home."

The woman began crawling up the stairs, a smooth, escalator climb, but turned her head enough to give a toothless laugh.

"I'm...*always*...home," she said. "Now...I'm...*free*."

Joy smiled self-consciously and scribbled a note in the file to hide her flush of pride. Sliding it into the outbox, she considered the time. It had been a good day, but it was getting pretty late.

She dropped the necklace onto the small pile at her left. She'd converted the dental tray into a tip jar, spreading out a cloth napkin onto which she'd placed her haul. There was some crumpled paper money, a handful of raw amethyst chunks, a polished gold coin that looked like it was pirate's treasure, a beaded bag of shiny pinfeathers, a long droplet of milky glass and several gift cards good at local stores and for online shopping. Joy wondered if they'd been activated. It had been a good week, overall. She picked up a set of earrings that may or may not have been real pearls and admired them against her ears in the mirror. Maybe she'd wear them when she saw Ink tonight?

"You," a voice croaked. "*Lehman* to Ink!"

Her heart stopped. She whirled around.

No! Graus Claude would have known better, but the smell of rotting leaves left no doubt; the stench burned her throat and stung her eyes.

A giant hedgehog squatted at the base of the stairs, fleshy cheeks sagging and piggy eyes beetle-bright. Its quills stood out at all angles, speared with last season's leaves, the tips blackened, sharp and caked in mud. Its clawed fingers picked absently at the thick metal plate set into the center of its chest; the skin around it was puckered with scars and scratched-open sores.

Briarhook dipped his head in a subservient gesture. His obscene earthworm tail waggled, smearing pollen on the stairs.

"Get out," Joy said, barely above a whisper. She squeezed the scalpel in her hand. "Get out now."

He was already in the cache room. The ward trigger was useless. How had he gotten in here? How had he known?

"You. My heart," he said, shuffling forward. His fetid stink filled the air. "Have it, you?"

She raised the scalpel, and Briarhook stopped. She had to swallow three times before she trusted her voice to work.

"No," Joy said, which was not altogether true. It wasn't here, in this room, yet Ink had bequeathed it to her—how did Briarhook know that? She backed against the table, nearly tipping it over in her haste to get away from the thing that had tortured her on the ravine floor. She was shaking so badly, the scalpel vibrated. "Get out. Get out or I'll burn it to ashes, I swear it!"

"No, no." Briarhook halted and raised his claws. He pointed to the dental tray. "Client, I."

Joy squeezed the handle of the scalpel. "No," she said. "Never."

He plucked at his mealy shirt. "Freedom want," he said. "Free as you. No?" His piggy eyes squinted into menacing slits. "You know, you, freedom. Ex-*lehman* to Ink." He pounded a fist on the plate in his chest. "Want my heart! Want it, you!"

She experienced a full-body shudder, from the hairs on her arms to the marrow of her bones, with all the soft things trembling in between. She couldn't forget what he'd done to her. How Hasp had kidnapped her and held her down in the freezing slush, how Briarhook had threatened her and tortured her, taking his revenge on Ink by burning his mark into her arm. She couldn't forget how the smell of her own skin mixed with her pajamas melting as they burned. She felt that helpless, sick, red rage all over again.

"GET OUT!" she screamed.

In the silence, they stared at one another. Briarhook sneezed in annoyance, a fine mist of pollen scattering from his quills. He plucked a tiny cloth satchel from between his toes and tossed it on the tray. It was tied with a clean pink ribbon that curled.

"Briar seeds," he said with a growl. "Grow quick." He clicked his claws in a scissorlike snap. "Thick. Sharp. Touch soil, then—" another snap "—grown!" His voice was low, grudging. "A gift, you." He held up a single claw as he turned away. "You think, freedom this? Know this, you—" He tapped the metal pointedly. "Want my heart, girl. Message mine, you—want my heart. Will earn it, you."

Joy gulped for breath, but her stance didn't change. The trembling had become something hot-cold-numb. After another long moment, Briarhook mounted the stairs, his flabby bulk swaying, bristles clicking and clacking as he went. She had the crazy notion to stab him in his fat tail, but she couldn't seem to move. She was frozen in the grip of horror and flashback and questions.

Briarhook shook himself in the doorway, backlit by a blue sky. He traced a claw tip against the wall, then pointed it at her.

"I, client, I, 'til my heart mine," he said and shuffled out of the mill.

Joy pulled into her parking spot and shut off her music. She squeezed the steering wheel in both hands and took a deep breath. She'd driven fast and furious. Now she was home. Safe. It was over. It was all behind her. Her purse was heavy and rattled with strange things, the seeds from Briarhook pushed into her pocket. She didn't trust them but hadn't known what to do with them. She couldn't leave them in the cache office in case they wrecked the place, sprouting from the floor. She didn't want to bring them home, but where could she leave them? She debated hiding them behind the plant urn by the stairs. Her phone buzzed. Text message.

Things r NOT going well!

    Joy frowned in sympathy, momentarily distracted from her own worries, and typed back to Monica: *hugs*
    The next words were long in coming: This is the 1st first fight that I DON'T want to be the last. How do I do this???
    Joy sighed. Keep talking, she typed. Should I call?

Not now. Later. When less sobby.

    The idea of Monica sobbing was disturbing. Joy had trouble imagining it.
    Joy quick-typed another *hugshugshugs* and tossed her phone into her purse. She rolled up the windows and flipped her keys over in a fistful of metal and plastic grocery tags. She got out and shut the door with her hip, her sneakers sucking the hot asphalt, the sticky-squelching sounds mocking her steps as her mind wandered to Monica, Gordon, Briarhook, Ink and air-conditioning, not necessarily in that order.
    A clang of sound and light slammed her forward. She flew into the hedge and felt something break under her shirt. Dazed, she spun around to see a pointed, red helmet cocked to one side—the knight's weapons had been thrown clear, a pair of narrow swords stuck winking in the grass. Empty

hands fisted with the heavy scrape of armor. The disarmed knight faltered in that moment of surprise.

Joy ran.

She burst into the courtyard. Bolting for the steps, hooking her fingers against the handrail and propelling herself upward. The clanking behind her forced her feet to move faster. She pounded up the steps knowing she had to get through her front door, had to get there first and quickly—Ink's wards were the only protection she had against the red-colored knight. There wasn't time to grab the scalpel. There wasn't time to think. There was barely time to breathe. Air dried her teeth as she gasped, climbing higher, faster, eyes locked on her goal.

She hit the second-floor landing and kicked a floor plant down the stairs. It bumped and bounced, coughing up dirt and broken pottery. She kept running. The knight was close, faster than she remembered; she could hear the long pulls of breath echoing in his helmet.

Joy vaulted the next steps by twos. She heard the crashing on the stairs behind her, heard the *thump-thump-thump* as armored footsteps hit the carpeted hall. She grabbed the next landing's floor plant with both hands and threw, showering herself in dirt and smacking the knight square in the chest. She needed distance. She needed room. She grabbed the satchel in her pocket, and the cloth burst in her hand. She flung it at the knight.

Seeds hit dirt. Brambles exploded, instantly clogging the stairwell in thick knots of branches with wicked black thorns. The knight slammed to a halt, trapped at the edge of the thicket. He began hacking with both swords, bits of briar flying. With a fresh wave of panic, Joy ran down the hall.

Fumbling with her keys, she struggled to fit one in the lock. It wouldn't go! She couldn't get the door open! Her hands wouldn't work! A high, thin whimper clawed in the back of her throat. She had to get inside! *Get inside! NOW!* Keys jostled in her fingers; metal scraped the keyhole, the door-knob, her skin. A flash of red burst around the corner. She dropped the keys, stumbling in the bits of dirt. A searing jolt shot through her limbs like pain or fear.

The knight appeared, holding twin swords, and charged.

Joy kicked the door. Hard. It snapped at the jamb. Throw-ing herself at it, she dropped inside, falling face-first into the foyer as the security alarm screamed. A gold ward shim-mered to life behind her, washing the doorway in fairy light.

Sprawled on the floor, Joy gaped up at the knight. He stood in the hall, shoulders heaving, a sword in each hand, the thin eye slit fixated on her. Joy scrambled backward, the tile slippery under her palms. The knight glared through the sheen of Ink's ward as the security alarm wailed. The phone rang. Joy lay on the floor. Everything was shrill and bright and numb.

"He killed you," she heard herself say. "He killed you."

The knight raised its swords, the voice beneath the face-plate booming under the din.

"It cannot be done," he said.

A splice in the overhead lights, and Ink landed, crouched over Joy with an outstretched arm. He held the obsidian ar-rowhead in his fist and growled like a wolf. She felt every-thing from fear to relief to delight through a haze of tingling shock.

The knight crossed his swords and retreated slowly, three steps, out of sight. They heard his footsteps echo in the hall and on the stairs.

Uncurling, Joy stared at the broken door. It took a sec-ond for the pins and needles to fade from her fingertips and legs. Ink stood in the doorway, checking the wards, swing-ing the black blade back and forth in mute frustration, trail-ing a deep gray smudge of power behind him like charcoal smoke. He smacked the arrowhead against the keypad. The alarm stopped.

Joy ran for her room, pressing a hand to her stomach. She felt ill—not queasy, but something deeper. She was too aware of her insides still being on the inside and her mouth somehow tasted how very close she'd come to death. Two swords loomed in the back of her mind while she knew that the knight was probably lurking somewhere just outside. Waiting.

"Joy," said Ink, appearing in her doorway.

"You felt the wards?"

"I felt the wards," he confirmed.

"Is he still there?"

"Perhaps. But he cannot come in."

"I don't think..." Joy swooned, and she caught herself on the back of her desk chair. She wobbled on her feet as the room darkened at its edges.

Ink crossed the room swiftly. "Are you hurt?"

She blinked. "Yes," she said. Then, "No." Her eyes focused on his. "Ink?"

"Yes?"

"You didn't kill him"

"Yes, I did," he said and held up his wrist. "Inq marked me, and there was no mistake. I murdered a member of the Twixt, as per Grimson's auspice." He shook his head. "This knight bears the same mark, the same *signatura* as the one I killed, but everything else—his height and bearing, his skill, his weapons—have changed. I cannot explain it. To have the same True Name..." Concern laced his voice. "It makes no sense. But you are safe." He brushed her hair from the side of her neck. She glanced up at his touch as his fingers slid along the chain at her neck and withdrew the tiny pendant from beneath her collar. Only half the rune was there—broken, snapped in half, a ragged edge bisected the glyph. The rest of the shattered pendant was grit against her skin.

"I am glad you had this," he said.

The first blow had not killed her. The *futhark* had served its purpose. It had saved her life.

"I...I didn't see anything," she said. "I never saw it coming. He was... He must have..." She shut her eyes, a quick erasure of what might have been. Her body heaved with a sudden, sickly jolt, but she held herself still. "He attacked me from behind," she said, swallowing bile. "I would've... He could've..."

And Ink did something that surprised her: he gathered her into his arms, held her tightly to his chest and stroked her hair. She closed her arms around him and tucked her head into his shoulder, two puzzle pieces sliding together until they fit. He was warm and strong and smelled like summer rain. She wondered who had told him that this was the precise right thing to do, and then realized that he had probably learned it from her, watching her. Her heart swelled, then contracted to the size of a pin.

Cupping her hair, he lifted her face and kissed her mouth with reverent sweetness as if she were something precious, as if she could break. He stroked her lips with his mouth, barely touching her. His eyes squeezed shut. His fingers stilled against the side of her throat, and when he breathed, it was a slow, shuddering breath.

She kissed him back, winding her fists in his shirt and pulling him closer. He leaned her against the wall and held her face by the tips of his fingers, cradling the sides of her jaw. Joy's mouth opened. The next kiss drew him deeper. Her hands kneaded his shoulders through the silk of his shirt.

Ink's hand traced her arm, her ribs, her hip. Joy squirmed. His fingers tentatively followed the thin line of bare skin between her shirt and her jeans. Joy arched her back. She was drinking breaths in the gaps between kisses, eyes closed, head full of sparks. She tugged at his shirt, aching to touch his skin. He paused, stilling her scrabbling, hungry fingers. Joy moved to pull away—ashamed, afraid—but his hands held hers, his eyes searching her face, swollen-lipped and gasping.

Ducking his chin, Ink peeled his shirt over his head. The muscles moved catlike over his body, hints of ribs and chest and sculpted abs. He'd matched his body to his face, lean and strong and boyish. Dimples appeared along his smile as he tossed his shirt aside. Joy caught a hint of the dark scales of his *signatura* that wound a dragon-circle tattoo across his back.

He returned to kissing her. The scent of summer rain filled the room like a squall; she could feel the crackles like lightning raising the tiny hairs on her face and skin. She touched his chest, fingers slipping into the furrow they'd created, her thumbs sliding between the unnaturally smooth muscles of his pecs before they were off exploring on their own. He *felt* like silk, like polished stone, strong and ageless. She moaned into his mouth and slid a little as her legs loosened, drawing them down onto the floor, onto her purse. She made a small sound of protest. Ink stilled.

"Wait," he said, voice slicing and urgent, eyes wide. His body stiffened against hers, arms locked at rigid angles. "I am..." Ink blinked with effort. "I have not yet..." The look on his face was almost comical, but it was a painful confession. Joy understood. How far had he gone to make himself look human?

Joy licked her lips, sweaty and embarrassed; her want was far too big for her too-tight skin. His eyes were so wide that she could see stars. Joy inched aside slowly, pulling her purse out from under the small of her back, feeling the seams of her jeans stretch and pull as she moved. Ink sat up, the play of muscles over his chest and shoulders a languid shudder. His whole body shifted as he sat on his haunches, lithe and long-ing. He tore his hungry gaze away from her with an effort.

"I should go," Ink said.

"No," Joy said. "Stay with me." More than wanting him, she knew that if he hadn't killed the knight, keeping him close would help keep it that way. She did not want him to kill. *Again?* "We're safe here, right? He can't come in?"

He shook his head, struggling to compose his breathing. "No."

"Then stay with me," she said. "Please."

Ink dropped his arms and heaved a sigh. "All right," he said. "I will stay here, with you, until I must go." He pushed a hand through his hair, running lines through the black thatch.

She crossed her legs and squeezed them together, still try-ing to fend off the hot, pulsing energy that strained against her clothes. It didn't help that he sat shirtless on her floor, his arms sculpted with long, lean muscle, his chest chis-eled and slender and narrowed into hard abs. He'd added a belly button and deep creases at the pelvic bone that disap-peared beneath the waistband of his jeans. His long black bangs shielded his eyes, and his boyish face was tense. He was so beautiful it was easy to believe he wasn't human. But all the subtle changes he'd been adding were making him more and more familiar, more humanlike, enough that she sometimes forgot.

Propping herself against the wall and trying to distract him from murderous thoughts, she said, "Exactly how far have you gotten?"

Ink hesitated as if debating how to answer.

"Feet," he said finally, his voice soft and low. "They are proving difficult."

Joy scooted back, creating distance and cooler air between

them. She flipped her ponytail from the back of her neck, sticky with sweat, and smiled.

"Show me."

Glancing at Joy through lowered lashes, Ink tugged off one black boot and then the other, dropping them to the floor. His silver wallet chain snaked into a puddle on the carpet. His eyes watched her watching him.

His feet were new, masculine and perfect; clearly the most complex thing he'd done yet. Joy crossed her legs and placed both his feet in her lap, examining his toes, from biggest to smallest, secretly liking that he'd chosen to make a full-scale version of his littlest toe instead of a tiny apostrophe like hers. It was almost as if her tiniest toe was an added after-thought. He had used another model, and she was secretly glad; she'd never liked her feet, damaged after years of gym-nastics abuse. With two bent and broken toes, chapped heels and split nails, they were her least favorite part of her body. Hence why she wore crazy socks—it deflected attention from what lay underneath.

Joy looked at the pair of feet in her lap, trying to recognize them but couldn't. *So whose feet are they?*

Ink leaned on one arm, angling his right foot, then his left, watching the bones slide around the axis of his ankles and flexing his arches back. "Not half as useful as hands, less flexible, less precise, but require exacting balance and ki-netic harmony for a bipedal gait in order to work properly," he said, turning his knee to one side. "I used a number of models. What do you think?"

"They're perfect," Joy said, which was true: his feet were smooth, uncalloused, impossible—a podiatrist's dream feet. "Except the nails," she was forced to add. He hadn't finished making the toenails yet, just outlines drawn on the nubs themselves. For a long time, neither Ink nor Inq had had fingernails; it was the first detail she'd noticed that made them truly inhuman. That and their fathomless, all-black eyes.

"Well..." Ink shifted his chain to the side and drew out the leaf-tipped wand. "We should work on that, then."

Joy took the scalpel from its inside pocket, ready to erase anything that Ink didn't like. It reminded her of the first time she'd held the naked blade and they'd discovered, quite by accident, that she could remove whatever he'd drawn. In the case of *signatura*, it was an awesome power—one forbidden and feared—but with Ink, she had removed scars, closed wounds and even straightened crooked nail beds for her boyfriend, the perfectionist.

She smiled to herself, hearing Inq's voice, *Artists!*

Maybe Ink would understand her new role in the Twixt? But while she had the urge to tell him everything, she didn't want to break this moment. Not yet.

He bent over his knees, and she crouched by his head, getting lost in the details as he drew his feet into living human shapes. They sat molding and erasing and rebuilding them like children making sand castles at the beach. Ink convinced Joy to remove her shoes, and they compared the shapes of their toes and bent knuckles, widening the small hollows of skin between digits, debating whether the second toe should be longer or shorter than the first and how much nail the baby toe should have. Ink discovered Joy was ticklish when he traced the inner swell of her arch. She kicked and squealed and grabbed his ankle, but he was unsurprisingly immune.

"No fair!" Joy said. "You aren't ticklish!"

"No," he said, smiling. "I do not know what that feels like."

"It's..." Joy stumbled, trying to think how to describe it. "It's sort of an uncomfortable squiggling that makes you laugh. Like a silly little itch that prickles."

Ink's lip quirked. "Sounds delightful."

"Try it," Joy said. She put a finger on the arch of his

foot. "You can feel that, can't you?" She drew a line from toe to heel.

"Yes," he said, concentrating where her finger started and stopped. Joy knew he was rearranging his senses, something that Inq had once told her allowed them to feel hot and cold, become hard or soft and taste the difference between chalk dust and chocolate. He flexed his foot and moved it closer in her lap.

"Okay." She made her touch featherlight. "Can you still feel that?"

"Yes."

"And this?" Lighter still.

"Yes."

His voice blurred, soft as down. Ink was staring at her without blinking. She'd only just noticed. And now that she'd noticed, she couldn't look away. He didn't say anything. It was as if his eyes had grown deeper, darker, cavernous. She remembered first falling into those eyes, reflecting bits of glow sticks and carnival lights.

"Does it tickle?" she whispered.

He shook his head very slightly. Only the very tips of his hair moved.

"No."

Her fingers played over his skin and found the rough edge of his jeans. It was as if she couldn't stop touching him. As if she couldn't help herself for what happened next.

Joy ran her fingers along his ankle, over the swell of carved bones and muscle, running her nails along the cuff of his jeans, pinching the denim where the seams met. She lifted the scalpel and held it up between them, eyebrows raised. Ink raised his eyebrows right back, curious. Joy tugged his jeans and touched the scalpel there. A single yellow stitch popped undone. They kept their eyes locked on one another, an unspoken question, a silent dare. Joy did it again: *pop*.

Then another. *Pop.* And another. And a third. *Pop. Pop. Pop.* Joy unzipped the seam of his jeans in a slow, upward stroke, eyes on his, slicing the thick fabric neatly in half. Her hand slid up his leg, gaining access, feeling his calf and the slope of his shin. He didn't move. She spread her hand over the crest of his knee. His bare skin under the denim felt hot to the touch.

Ink stared at her with something like hunger or thirst—his eyes, deep and dark, swallowed her whole. She leaned forward, touching the side of his thigh, and kissed him, but not just a kiss.

Their lips met, tongues touching. He groaned a soft sound in her mouth, and Joy felt it hum deep inside herself. He could *feel* her. She could feel him. Her hand tightened on his thigh. He leaned closer, grabbing her shoulder, squeezing encouragement, pulling her nearer.

"Joy? You in here?"

Joy froze. *Stef!* Ink closed his eyes and turned his face toward the wall, breathing ragged. Joy's hand stuck between tight denim and skin. Her brother was in the hallway, and Joy's door was ajar. She couldn't quite think, her body tingling and feverish, a part of her brain wondering whether she should quickly get up and sprint for the door or stay still and pretend her hand wasn't pressed inside Ink's invisible thigh.

"Joy?" Stef said as he pushed her door open wide. Joy tried to look innocent as if she had been painting her nails or had some other reason for sitting shoeless on the floor.

She tried to smile and breathe normally. "Hey, Stef..."

Her brother's face darkened, and his arm blocked the door.

"What's this guy doing in your room?"

EIGHT

JOY GAPED AT STEF. INK GLANCED UP, SURPRISED. THE color drained from her brother's face.

"*Joy!*" Stef screamed, and Joy turned, half expecting something like Hasp to be crawling through her window. She felt Stef grab her wrist and yank her to her feet, pulling her down the hall and into the kitchen before she knew it.

"Stef?" Joy gasped. "What...?"

"Trust me!" He grabbed the carton of Morton Salt and, popping the spout, poured it over the floor, turning in place while holding Joy's hand in his fist.

She struggled, confused. "What are you doing?"

"Sit down," Stef said, pushing her shoulder. Grabbing a steak knife from the butcher block, he sliced the tip of his finger as Ink rounded the corner.

Joy screamed, "*Stef!*"

A thick drop of his blood sank into the salt. He whispered something and the ring around them lit with crystalline flame. Ink slammed against it, knocking himself back into the fridge.

"Ink!" Joy cried and tried to get up, but Stef clamped his hand over her arm, smearing her wrist with blood. Ink stood up warily, hands raised, one pant leg hanging as loose as a skirt.

"You stay back!" Stef warned Ink, his words cracking like a whip. "Get out of here! Leave her alone!"

"Stef, you don't understand..." Joy tugged at his arm. "He's—"

"He's not real," Stef said bitterly. "Stay in the circle."

"You can... You can see him?" Joy stopped yanking. She felt cold. Icy prickles bubbled over her body as she stared at her brother. "You have the Sight?"

"Stay in the circle!" Stef shouted and licked his bloody fingertip, angry and confused. "Wait. You know what he is?" he asked warily, his eyes on Ink. "He's not wearing a glamour?"

Ink spoke up. "No," he said. "She has the Sight." Ink added, "Just like you."

Stef blanched and shook his head. "No. That's not possible," he said, pointing the knife at Ink. "I don't know what you've done to her, but it stops *now!* This is *my* home and *my* kin and under the Accords, I have discovered you trespassing and you will dismiss yourself immediately!"

Joy sputtered. What was Stef talking about? Ink glanced between them.

"My wards are all that protect her here," Ink said.

"Really? Is that what you've been telling her? That you could 'save' her from whatever's out there?" Stef said, waving the knife at his homemade ward, a circle of salt and blood. "And I thought that your kind could not tell lies."

Ink weighed Stef's words carefully and took three steps back.

"I cannot tell lies," he said. "And I have no wish to harm her." Ink turned to Joy and tucked his hands behind his back; Joy knew it was to remove one of the blades from his wallet, but he did not want to seem a threat.

"Talk to him," Ink said to Joy. "I will return. Later. After I speak with Graus Claude."

He bowed to Stefan, swept his arm in a half arc and, with a flash off the straight razor, disappeared.

Joy sagged against her brother. Her arm hurt where he held it.

"You know about the Bailiwick?" Stef said.

"Dammit, Stef!" Joy stood up, eyes stinging. "You've had the Sight all this time and *you didn't tell me?*" she screamed at him. *"AGAIN?"*

"Hey," he shot back. "I'm not the only one! You have the Sight?"

Joy yanked her arm out of his grip. "Yes!"

"Since when?"

Joy had to think about it. "Since February. About five months ago."

Stef wiped the back of his hand across his mouth. He looked damaged, lost. His hair was a mess, his face blotchy with emotion; a smear of red stood out on one cheek.

"I don't understand," he said. "You can't... Did something happen? Did someone...? Oh." Stef sank to his knees inside his salt circle and pinched the bridge of his nose. "The E.R. visit. You told me—a scratched cornea, right? I never put it together..." He sighed and gestured with a bleeding hand. "The boyfriend."

"You *lied* to me, Stef!" Joy shouted past the fear in her voice. "You knew about *this* and you knew about *Mom* and you knew you were *gay* and *what else don't I know?*"

"Whoa, whoa. One conniption fit at a time," he said, placing the knife on the floor and sucking his cut. "Damn, that stings."

"How long, Stef?" Joy asked.

"How long have I been seeing them?" he said around his finger. "Since I was five."

Joy stared at him. *"Five?"*

"Yeah. That's how I know you couldn't have had the Sight long. You would have seen things way before now, and you can't really hide that sort of thing when you're a kid," he said. "Besides, I think if you'd seen Mr. Buggles for real, you would've said something."

"Mr. Buggles?" Joy said, barely remembering the name. "That was...?"

"My rabbit. My imaginary friend," Stef said. "Except he was real. Mr. Buggles is a phooka, but they were all real. Lime Slime, the Toothless Fairy, Dmitri, all of them. Especially Dmitri." His face flickered through many emotions, none of them easy. "They were *all* real." He glanced back toward the fridge. "Or at least as real as that guy. What did you call him?"

"Ink," she said. "His name's Indelible Ink."

Stef's lips were a tight, pale line. "And that's why you couldn't tell Dad? Because he's an Other Than?"

"A what?"

"A nonhuman," Stef said. "One of them."

"Yeah," Joy said. "That and the fact that he's invisible."

Stef grimaced at the cut that still leaked blood. "Few of them are actually invisible—they just don't like to be noticed. Especially by humans—humans like us." He rubbed his palm against his knee. "Other Thans don't take kindly to being seen without permission."

"Yeah, I got that." Joy shifted her shoulders, trying to keep from the crackling line of energy. She'd had bad experiences with wards. "So...are you a wizard?"

"What? No!" Stef said and adjusted his glasses. "Who told you about wizards?"

"Inq," she said.

"Indelible Ink?" he asked.

"No. His sister, Invisible Inq," she said, making a breath of the *q*.

Stef shrugged. "Hard to hear the difference."

"Trust me—they're not at all alike," Joy said, lowering her head as if they'd be caught whispering. "Does Dad have the Sight?"

"No."

A pause. "Mom?"

Stef sighed. "No. But her mother's mother did."

"Great-Grandma Caroline," Joy said. "That's why they locked her up?" She'd known her great-grandmother had been put into an asylum by her family shortly after arriving in America. Joy had had a childhood fear that she could have inherited some mental disorder and be locked away like her great-grandmother, and that was *before* she'd started seeing strange stuff on her own. She tucked her hands against her gut. "But she wasn't crazy! She had the Sight!"

"Well, she wasn't exactly sane," Stef said. "I used to visit her with Grandma. But as soon as she spoke to me, she knew that I could see them, too." He shook his head and wiped his finger on his jeans. "She'd been in the institution for a long time—almost forty years. They'd given her drugs, shock treatments. I think her formal diagnosis was paranoid schizophrenic. By the time we talked, she wasn't making a whole lot of sense, but she insisted I not tell anyone about the Other Thans. I think she wanted to protect me from...ending up like her." Stef's voice trailed off as he saw the look on Joy's face. He played with the threads of his frayed friendship bracelet. "She told me what she knew about the Accords and the Council and how to protect myself from getting my eyes gouged out." Stef looked at Joy through his rectangular lenses. "I guess you weren't so lucky."

Joy picked at her thumbnail. "I've kept both my eyes," she said. "But how did you do it?"

"I shielded them," Stef said and removed his glasses, pointing at the joint. There was a tiny row of glyphs scratched into the finish. What she'd taken for damage she now recognized as runes. Stef sighed. "Dmitri said when he met me, he thought my glasses were wards and that he couldn't pierce them. He was too young to know, but it gave me the idea, and I managed to trade for some protective glyphs until I could handle things on my own." He rubbed his clotting finger and thumb together, making small rolls of sticky blood. "Other Thans are sticklers for rules, and messing with order tends to drive them nuts." He tugged at his shirt. "Wearing clothes backward or inside out is physically repulsive to them," he said. "So is the color red. Sometimes green. And things that defy the natural order of things, like a solid rock with a hole in it or trick candles that won't blow out." He held up his wrist. The ratty red bracelet was held together with a dark metal bead. "And cold iron can burn them." He dropped his hand. "I started trading for knowledge in fourth grade. I wanted to protect myself, and I did." Stef touched the knife with a finger. "Now they leave me alone."

Joy felt a cold rush like a cupful of water poured down her back. She knew something about trades in the Twixt. "What did you trade, Stef?"

He smiled the way he did when she'd nailed a routine on the mats. "You're smart," he said. "Luckily, so am I. We are something valuable, Joy. Rare. We have the Sight. We're born with a little extra, like the sort of magic that still lives in the Twixt. It's in our blood," he said, gesturing to the crystalline ward. "Not everything Great-Grandma Caroline said made sense, but she knew what worked." Stef adjusted his seat on the tile floor. "When I met her, she'd been blind for over sixty years. They'd come for her right after she was married—she must have been close to your age." Stef rapped his knuckles on the floor tile. "Maybe that's when she started seeing things, too. Maybe it happens later for girls."

Joy shrugged. "Maybe." The idea of getting married at sixteen was almost as frightening as being able to see monsters. Or losing both eyes. She watched the ward shimmer, remembering Aniseed's trigger-traps. "Maybe they just like to be cruel."

"Yes, they do," Stef said, pinching his lip. "So you have the Sight?"

"Yes."

"And your boyfriend's one of them?"

Annoyance colored her voice. "Yes."

Stef sighed and hung his head for a moment before he straightened, the ward flickering behind him, reflecting off his glasses. "Listen, I know what it's like. What you think you're feeling. They're...unreal. Powerful. Beautiful, even. And I know how it feels to have all of that attention focused on you, fascinated by you."

Joy snapped, "You don't—"

"It feels like drowning."

Joy swallowed her next words. That was *exactly* what it felt like when she looked into Ink's eyes.

"I know," he said. "It happened to me, too."

It was one of those fragile soap-bubble moments that Joy so rarely had with her family, a moment that pressed against her chest and made it hard to breathe. Her mother and Stef were the ones that talked about *feelings*—they were the ones who made her laugh the hardest, scream the loudest or cry the longest because they knew where she hung her heart away from prying eyes—but they also made Joy uncomfortable. She was more used to things going unsaid. Still, she had to ask.

"What happened, Stef?"

He pinched his lip again and then crossed his arms protectively. "What happened is that I forgot that they aren't human," Stef said. "None of them are. And that no matter what they look like or how hard they try, they aren't anything like us." His voice hardened. Veins stood out on his wrists.

"Is that bad?" Joy asked.

"They're not good or bad, Joy," he said. "They are so *different* that it's impossible to explain what 'good' and 'bad' means to them. We want to match feelings to what they look like they're feeling, or guess their motivations and reasons to what is really more like a whim. We'd like to have them make sense—but it's an illusion, Joy, like camouflage. They only *look* like people, but they're not," Stef emphasized. "It isn't real. It took a long time before I understood what they are capable and not capable of."

Having stood on Aniseed's burning floor, Joy was under no illusions. "But it's not like that," she said. "Ink's not like that."

Stef wore a strange expression. "They never are, until they are."

Joy frowned. "Hence, the ward?"

"Hence the ward," he said, glancing at his fingertips. "It was a fair trade."

Joy made a face as understanding dawned. "You traded your *blood?*"

"No," Stef said. "Well, once. But that was an extreme circumstance." He clearly didn't want to say more and licked his cut again. "Mostly, I traded tears."

"Tears?"

"They're valuable," he said. "Blood is nastier, more basic. It's how I can make a ward so quickly without glyphs."

Joy watched the salt sparkle, throwing fissures of light. "How?"

Stef shrugged. "You saw the quick and dirty version—a salt circle, a drop of blood, a word to seal the deal. That's it." He scraped a line through the salt with the steak knife. The scintillating fire collapsed and disappeared. "It's not much, but it's enough to keep your boyfriend out."

"You didn't have to do that," she said as he went to the kitchen sink to wash up. "You don't even know him."

Stef took his time cleaning the knife. "You think you know what you're doing," he said, shutting off the water. "You think you know him, but you don't. You can't. And while I don't expect you to drop him on my say-so, I want you to at least think about the fact that I know something about this, about them, and that I'm your brother." He slid the knife back in the butcher block. "You *know* that I care about you."

Joy felt grit grind across the tile as she stepped through the salt.

"Ink loves me."

Stef took out the broom. "Of course he does," he said in the way only big brothers could.

He tossed her the dustpan. Joy held it against the floor as the stiff bristles scraped salt onto the plastic scoop. She dumped it into the trash, letting the salt slide in. A single red-brown bead stippled in crystals rolled out last.

"They're dangerous, Joy," Stef said. "To everything and everyone they touch."

Joy stared at her brother, wanting him to say more, wanting him to tell her why, but her phone rang. It was the fifth call in a row from a number she didn't recognize. She moved her thumb to answer it. Stef put his hand over the phone.

"I want you to be safe," he said. "And if this guy really loved you, he'd want you to be safe, too."

Joy pulled free and answered the phone.

"Hello?"

"Joy?" A resonant voice said her name. "This is Enrique. We need your help, honey. Ilhami's in trouble. Can you meet us outside?"

This was clearly the opposite of safe.

Joy felt danger hum in her arms as she sat in the sports car with a black backpack tucked between her knees, twisting the straps around her fingers as Enrique explained again what she needed to do to get Ilhami out of New York.

"His name is Ladybird," Enrique said from the driver's seat. "He and Ilhami go way back, but Ilhami got careless and bound himself to the locale. He's been stuck at Lady-bird's for over a month."

"Which is a problem," she guessed.

Enrique sighed. "Which is a problem."

Inq's oldest *lehman* was in his seasoned fifties, silver-haired and dashing like a James Bond from south of the equator. Even though he wore an Oxford shirt and gray slacks, Joy always pictured him in a suit. He had that kind of air about him: confident, high-stakes, first-class. He'd picked her up in a white Ferrari 458 and explained the situation, but Joy still couldn't wrap her head around what was happening. Even flicking some gizmo that made the Blue Ridge Parkway tunnel empty out on Flatlands Avenue made more sense than what he'd been saying during the drive. Her stomach fluttered, either from the jump, her growing fear or the steamy cup of hot caffeine in her hand.

"Tell me again why I'm here?"

Enrique checked his mirrors. "We wouldn't have called you if we hadn't run out of options."

"So what happened?"

She felt the powerful engine growl as Enrique took a corner. "We ran out of options."

Joy frowned. "I mean what happened to Ilhami?"

"Call it an unfortunate by-product of being a tortured genius," Enrique said, taking a sip of his coffee and placing it back in its holder. "Ilhami is a gifted artist, you know, but I think if Inq hadn't found him, he would have been lost in the *gecekondu* ages ago. He had no family, no money, only his art. The way he describes it, his talent 'burns.' He has few who understand him this way and Ladybird is, unfortunately, one of them. He knows it is very hard for Ilhami to endure ordinary life."

Joy sipped her latte thick with cream. "*This* is an ordinary life?"

Enrique smiled as he switched gears. "Well, maybe not," he said, his voice jovial, light. "Still, we can't *leave* him stuck in Brooklyn. Besides halting your fascinating collection of Venus figurines, Inq wouldn't like it."

Joy didn't like it, either. She needed to get back to Ink and explain what had happened with Stef and why. "I don't see why she can't get him out," she said.

"I'm not certain, but she made it clear that she will not be going," he said as he slid up the road. "Confidentially, I think she can't. Maybe the place is warded against her. Maybe it's some old agreement between her and Ladybird, who knows? What I do know is that Ilhami told him his sister would come and bring his backpack and, since his host is a member of the Twixt, those words are binding."

"Why would Ilhami say that?"

"He meant Inq," Enrique explained. "We never call them by their names so we use replacement words like *sister* or *cousin* or *good neighbor* for the Folk." He checked his mirrors before changing lanes. "It's considered polite."

"So he calls Inq his *sister*?" Joy said. *Ew!*

"Yes, well," Enrique said. "I'm sure he didn't know that she wouldn't come. I tried to reach Raina, but no luck. That leaves you." He turned onto a side street. Joy didn't ask who Raina was—it wasn't important if she couldn't help. Enrique sighed. "One of the problems with the Twixt is that the Folk take things very literally. Ilhami's words are binding—he cannot leave Ladybird's until the conditions are met—his sister must come get him, bringing his backpack. Fortunately, there can be more than one interpretation of the word *sister*. That's why I grabbed his backpack and called you, Cabana Girl. You're the little sister in our brotherhood, so it should work."

It wasn't a question of whether she'd do it or not; the question was...why was she so afraid? When she'd been in trouble, the Cabana Boys had been there for her—Nikolai had left an exotic shoot somewhere in Russia to come steal a car in Glendale, North Carolina, in order to drive her home before she and Monica had to deal with the police or, worse, a mob of angry aether sprites. She knew that if any of Inq's *lehman* needed her, they could call and ask for help and she would try her best because she was once one of them—an exclusive club of mortals chosen by one of the Folk, in this case, a harem of drop-dead gorgeous men from all around the world and her. The fact that she had removed Ink's mark, freeing her from *lehman*-ship, didn't mean she forgot her friends.

And if they needed her to bust one of them out of New York, she would.

Joy bounced her head against the headrest. "All I have to do is walk in with this backpack and bring Ilhami out? That's it?"

"That's it," he said. "That should satisfy the conditions of his release, and I'll be waiting outside to take you both home." He had the grace to look embarrassed. "I wouldn't have asked you to do this if we weren't desperate. It's been many weeks."

Joy's hands wrapped around the cup as Enrique completed another turn. She was feeling pretty desperate, too. She was glad she'd told Stef that she was going with Enrique to get another protective pendant—not a total lie as she planned to ask him to drop her off at the C&P afterward. Her brother had let her go with reservations and a promise to come home soon.

"And we have to do this now?" she asked, still thinking about Ink.

"Best as soon as possible," Enrique said, checking his mirrors. "The longer he's in there, the worse it can get. Who knows what he'll say next? No, better to get him out now." The older man thumbed the side mirror up with the touch of a button. "You still willing to do this?"

"Yep," Joy said without feeling.

"All right." Enrique turned away from traffic and drove deeper into darker, less populated roads, whose buildings cowered away from the glass-and-steel downtown. It was shadier here, subdued and cool. The borough felt sinister. Trash speckled the gutters, windswept and crushed. Joy tensed in the passenger's seat out of some urban instinct and checked that the doors were locked.

"Over there," he said, nodding toward a gray building. It looked ignored compared with its neighbors, devoid of greenery or decoration, aloof and alone. "Go down to the basement floor. Let them check you in. They should bring you to Ilhami when you get there," he said as he slowed the car at a red light. "Try to avoid talking—that's how we got into this mess in the first place. Take Ilhami, come out the front door and I'll be waiting to pick you up. In and out. Simple as that."

"You're trying to make it sound easy," she said.

"I'm used to corporate takeovers," he said. "This should be easy."

Joy put the coffee in the cup holder. Her hands were shaking. "Then you should be doing this."

"I know. I would if I could. I'd do just about anything for one of my brothers, but a hasty sex change isn't one of them." The traffic light ahead changed, and the cars began moving. "I'm sorry I can't go in with you, Joy."

"It's okay," Joy said, which it wasn't. She took giant sunglasses and a pink lipstick from the bag on the floor. It had been in the passenger's seat when she got in, in case she didn't want to look like herself given cameras could record her time-stamped image being both there in New York and at her condo moments before. Joy bypassed the wig and the high-heeled shoes. She wanted to run unencumbered if she had to. She folded down the sun visor and used the mirror on the back. Her trembling fingers smeared the lipstick and she had to start again.

Enrique pulled over, and Joy slid on the sunglasses, keeping an eye on traffic as she opened the door. She almost stumbled into the street and watched more than felt Enrique hand the heavy backpack to her.

"In and out," he said. "I'll be right outside. If there's a problem, come back here and we'll figure it out."

"Okay." The shoulder strap felt slippery in her hand. She squeezed the fabric and walked away from the car with a backpack, a pair of CK sunglasses and a tight tingling in her stomach.

East New York smelled hot and chemical, the buildings crowded together and looking grumpy about it. Joy felt surrounded by the dark facades and cheap smells, smears of old chewing gum and splashes of waste spackled the sidewalk. Pale, weak grass pushed out of the cracks in the pavement, and there were far more cracks than pavement. Joy walked quickly to the gray building and, holding the backpack over one shoulder, pushed the call button by the door.

"Name?" said a loud voice from the speaker. For a million and one reasons, she didn't want to say her name.

"I'm here for Ilhami." She raised her face to the camera. The door buzzed. She pulled it open and ducked inside.

The lobby was dark, cold and quiet, a concentrated bubble of the outside. The door closed behind her like an air lock, sucking her in. A large balding man sat behind a security desk, pale and flabby and bored.

"Name?" he asked again.

Joy hesitated, squeezing her fingers. "Ladybird?"

The man pointed with a ballpoint pen. "Downstairs."

She walked to an open stairwell of chipped blue paint and thin, weak light. Her footsteps echoed softly as she made her way down.

The smells changed subtly from canned air freshener to something smoky and spicy, slightly sweet and acrid like burned orange peels. Another whiff of something petrochemical felt oily in her mouth. She blinked through a foggy haze before she found the bottom floor.

The door to the basement was missing. A beaded curtain hung from the frame that filtered the scene beyond the stairs. Noises shivered through the beads, low voices and a plinking, plucking sound that might have been Middle Eastern music or leaky water pipes. Joy's heart hammered in her ears as she thought of Ilhami somewhere in there and wondered if Nikolai had felt like this as he'd stepped into Inq's stolen car to save her. *What we* lehman *won't do for one another...*

Joy pushed her hand through the curtain, feeling something other than the beaded strands part. It sparked along the tips of her fingers and sizzled. *A ward.* As she passed into the large room, the soft babble became louder and the smells overwhelming. She hesitated on the edge of an elaborate carpet dyed in vivid yellows, blues and crimsons, breathing in through her mouth, trying to adjust.

The basement was one large studio filled with white columns and hazy kaleidoscope lamps. Dismantled cubicle partitions lined the opposite wall, built into a sort of haphazard maze with LED constellations projected on the ceiling. There were seats everywhere, from hard wooden church pews to pale fainting couches that looked like they'd been salvaged from some wealthy estate. More beaded curtains hung from the ceiling, creating small booths around a row of papasan chairs lining the back. Long bolts of sheer fabric hung from exposed pipes, slowly wafting in thick eddies of smoke. The whole place looked like a cross between a backstage bohemian theater and a salvage furniture warehouse, and there were people strewn absolutely everywhere.

A fat black man with a homemade cigar blew an enormous cloud of ill-flavored smoke at her feet, his lips puckered wetly around the tip of his tongue. Two shaved-head teenagers sat in a tangle of limbs on the floor, passing a rolled joint back and forth and giggling, while a white-haired woman lounged over the length of a stippled silver chaise, sucking delicately on a bone pipe that exuded bluish smoke. There were two men in embroidered caps and billowing sleeves gesticulating madly, their language both scratchy and strange. Someone cackled from somewhere off in the maze. Five twentysomethings sat in a circle, staring blankly at each other, the ambient light of a crystal lamp lending color to their faces. There was a snort. Something olive-green rustled under a pew, snoring loudly, and Joy guessed that whatever it was was sleeping it off.

That's when it hit her: she was in a drug den of the Twixt. As soon as Joy noticed the green creature's tail, she became aware of all the other Folk in the room. There was a feathered figure nesting in one of the papasan chairs with colorful wings as bright as macaws. A reedy person with multiple spindly arms played a stringed instrument next to a brazier of coals riddled with hissing leaves. What looked like an elf from *Lord of the Rings* sipped purple wine from a crystal chalice while a furry sort of creature snuffled around a dish of steaming broth. A chubby girl hung from a chrysalis glued to the ceiling, her wings shining wetly, dripping thin rivulets of mucousy drool. A bubbling fish tank connected to a number of thick pipes and wires sat in a corner, and a small generator chugged next to it on the floor.

Joy stepped forward, if only to get beyond the cloud of noxious smoke. A thick slab of a man guarded a door on her left, his square face impassive. Behind tiny yellow John Lennon glasses, his eyes were stone. Joy didn't immediately see Ilhami, so unless he was in the office-partition maze, she guessed he was behind the door.

She stepped to the side, bumping into someone; she turned to apologize but instead stared at the horned man whose head hung back over the edge of the couch. A thin orange mist hovered over his face, turning with galactic, sparkling slowness.

"Don't touch him, Nightingale," a smooth voice warned. "Sunset Dust plunges one into dizzying dreams." The voice grew closer, forcing her to turn around. "One touch is all it takes, and it doesn't come cheap."

Joy clenched both fists as a tall man in a crimson greatcoat stepped into the room, stabbing out a cigarette into a hand sparkling with rings. His dark hair hung about his head in thick waves, eyes sparkling in either delight or madness. There were small black spots dotting the edge of his hairline as well as his jaw and the sides of his throat. His smile was golden and sharp. His skin had a glossy, chitinous sheen.

Ladybird.

"You're here for Ilhami." He said it less like a question and more like he liked the feel of the words in his mouth. His eyes brightened as he neared. "My, my, you are a pretty bird. But there's hardly any family resemblance." Joy said nothing as he came closer. His skin rippled. The greatcoat flared. He waited politely for her to answer, and eventually inclined his head and directed a ringed finger at the backpack. "Is this my payment?" he asked. "Ilhami said that you would bring it."

The penny dropped. Joy had never checked the contents, but she guessed the amount must be quite a lot given the weight on her back. This was Ilhami's *dealer* and she was the drop. She wanted to thrust the backpack into his arms, away from her, and run—but she needed something first. It took her a second to remember why she was in this grubby, bohemian basement on the wrong side of East New York.

"Where is he?" she said, finding her voice.

"He's here," Ladybird said, full of authority. He didn't even turn his head to address the beefy hulk by the door. "Bring him."

The guard disappeared into the office. Giddy laughter trilled from somewhere in the divider maze. The cigar smoker hawked and spat into a copper spittoon by his feet. Joy tucked her hands behind her to keep from crossing her arms. *Get Ilhami. Get out. Get in the car. Go!*

"Will you sing for me, Nightingale?" the dealer purred. "I bet you have a pretty voice."

Joy bit the insides of her lips. Pink lipstick felt like margarine on her teeth.

There was a collective sigh and the circle of humans collapsed like dominoes, the crystal lamp in the center sputtering out. The guard's glasses winked in the dying light as he came back into the main room holding Ilhami by the arm as if to keep him from running away or, perhaps, to help him walk. Ilhami swayed, his street tattoos blue-black over his tan arms and neck, his jeans hanging loose and his T-shirt sweat stained and tight. He pulled himself upright, sniffed and ran a finger over his teeth. He smiled until he saw her standing there—he blinked owlishly, dark lashes fluttering.

"Joy?"

"Joy," the drug dealer said, clapping his fingers together, rings chiming. "What a delightful name! I daresay it suits you."

She didn't trust herself to speak—she could feel a quivering tic next to her mouth and a telltale flush of heat on her face. She couldn't risk Ilhami saying more of her name. She knew without anyone needing to tell her that it would be more than dangerous to say it here.

She put down the backpack and gestured for Ilhami with an outstretched hand. He looked bewildered. Ladybird smiled.

"Come, come, dear boy. Give your sister a kiss."

Ilhami slowly eased past the two men, his pupils wide with drugs and dismay. He took Joy into his arms for a brief hug, placing a chaste kiss near her ear. He smelled oddly of roasted chestnuts and candle wax.

"You shouldn't be here," he whispered.

Joy nodded, jaw tight. She couldn't trust herself to say anything; she was furious, terrified. She could barely imagine the words she would use—but not here, not now. She let go of the shoulder straps, and the pack sank to the floor. Her fingers were cramped and damp as she took one of Ilhami's hands in hers.

"The conditions have been met," she said, voice tight. She

backed toward the exit. The guard didn't move. Ladybird watched, touching the tips of his fingers to his smile, the black spots pulsing up the tips of his ears. She and Ilhami were almost to the doorway. Five more steps. Four. Three. Two.

"One moment," Ladybird said. Both Joy and Ilhami stopped dead. Dread lodged in her throat as Ilhami's hand tightened on hers. The greatcoat brushed past the eclectic collection of seats as Ladybird drew closer, completely ignoring the backpack as he studied her with interest. "Joy is hardly a Turkish name. Did you change it when you came to America?"

Joy didn't speak.

The man tipped his head to the side and sang a string of syllables that bounced off his tongue. Joy tensed, expecting a spell of some kind. The men in the back stopped arguing and the thin, pale woman slipped the bone pipe from her mouth.

Joy glanced at Ilhami. His hand tightened on hers.

"She does not know your native tongue," Ladybird said in English. "She is no more your sister than I am." The dealer turned thoughtfully, his greatcoat swirling. "Yet the name rings in my head like the toll of a bell." He tick-tocked his forefinger. "Ding. Dong. Ding. Dong. Now where have I heard the name Joy before?" His face leered closer. She could smell tar on his tongue. "You can see me," he said and puffed a breath in her face. She flinched and blinked. "And there is no sheen of elixir in your eyes." He grinned and hissed, a low giggle. "Ohhh, yes, I *know* you!"

Ilhami placed a hand over her shoulder. Joy could barely feel it there.

"She brought the money, Ladybird," Ilhami said. "That's all. We're done."

"Oh, no," the tall man said and waved his ringed finger.

"Oh, no no no no. She has brought me something more precious than gold. More precious than diamonds." He wrinkled his nose in delight. "She has brought me *blood*."

Joy stumbled back from Ladybird's face; Ilhami's hand tightened on her arm. Her hand itched for the scalpel that wasn't there. Her purse was in the car! *I'm so stupid!* The dealer tipped his head back and crowed with mirth, his Adam's apple jumping in his speckled throat.

"Dear me, what a catch! Two birds with one stone," he said, eyeing Ilhami as the young man darkened with rage. "Tell me, precious, are you the one the Scribe calls 'love' and the Council curses behind velvet walls?"

All eyes turned to Joy, human and not. She staggered under the unwanted attention. The fringe of carpet felt precarious, like the edge of a cliff. She tugged on Ilhami to keep steady, to keep moving. He inched toward the beaded door, his hand hot and clammy in hers.

"I think you are! I think you are!" Ladybird flung himself into an ergonomic office chair and let his heels drag on the floor. "A human with the Sight," he said, delighted. "In all my days..."

Joy and Ilhami reached the door. The bead curtain rattled behind her back, the ward skittering sparklers against her palms. The guard had moved a fraction of an inch, right shoulder turned slightly, rock eyes gleaming. The dealer's voice dropped an octave, suddenly serious.

"I will pay you handsomely for three drops of blood, willingly given."

Joy was surprised that he expected some response.

"Um." She licked her lips to wet them. "No."

"I'll forget the debt." He gestured to the backpack.

Ilhami paused, his face hungry with want. Joy's voice was surer now. "No."

Ladybird stilled as if frozen by the audacity. His guard waited, eyes clicking behind yellow lenses like a mechanism engaged. The dealer's wide smile shattered his face like glass.

"Very well then," he said and sprang to his feet, crossing the room in two great strides and pinning Joy with a sudden swipe of his multiringed hand. "My card—" he said with a flourish "—should you ever change your mind."

Joy didn't move to take the card, black and gold in the light. Ilhami nudged her shoulder. She took it. The card was glossy and smooth.

"Oh, very good," he said, retreating to the camelback couch. "Very, *very* good!" Ladybird stuck his face in the pale orange cloud above the horned man's head, inhaling deeply. His eyes closed in ecstasy and his fingernails bent the upholstery. His eyes snapped open and he tilted his head. "Off you go, then."

Joy tucked the card into her pocket and tugged Ilhami to go. The other occupants of the room had gone back to their distractions, puffing or plinking or dozing on the floor. Joy's hand touched the beaded curtain. She felt the ward part.

"Ah, one more thing," Ladybird said with a twirl of his coat. The dealer smiled and stage-whispered, "You are all under arrest."

NINE

RED-AND-BLUE FLASHES PIERCED THE SMOKE THROUGH the high basement windows. An electronic siren outside wailed. A whining bullhorn coughed and shouted.

"This is the police! You are under arrest! Stay where you are and put your hands in the air!"

The domino circle on the floor scrambled to their feet, scattering like roaches in different directions. The black man pushed past Joy and Ilhami as the two robed men dived behind a set of lounge chairs. There was a stampede for the exit, a shivering of sparks and bodies and beads. A surge of sound, and a girl with purple tattoos bounced off the beaded curtain as if it were brick. The crystal lamp shattered. Someone threw a punch. The brazier toppled over, spreading hot coals onto the carpet. A twentysomething guy got kicked in the ribs to get him clear of the door. There were terrified screams as Joy slammed against the wall. Ilhami threw himself around her and pushed her down.

In contrast, the Folk glanced around lazily, bored and amused. The pale woman blew a thin trail of smoke from her bone pipe and smiled. The feathered person in the papasan chair cackled, an alien sound, and the chubby girl on the ceiling started cawing, wild and obscene. Ladybird rocked gently in his office chair with a self-satisfied grin.

"It's a raid! It's a raid!" he mocked in a high, squeaky voice and laughed. "I find it's good to clean house once in a while," he said, staring straight at Ilhami as the humans fled past. Ladybird grinned as he rocked in his seat. "Keeps things interesting."

"You called the police," Ilhami said.

"What if I did?" Ladybird asked. "Cops are human. They can't see me and mine." He leaned a little forward and winked. "But they'll most certainly see you."

The embroidered caps resurfaced, bearing machine guns aimed at the windows. Joy inhaled to scream but lost her breath as Ilhami yanked her behind a column as they opened fire. Glass shattered under a hailstorm of bullets, chunks of drywall and concrete block. Rebel yells warbled. Answering fire rained down. Nearby couch cushions exploded in spurts of stuffing and wood.

Ladybird twitched his fingers as if conducting an orchestra.

"You're insane!" Ilhami shouted over the automatic gunfire. "Bullets can kill you as well as anyone!"

"I very much doubt it," the dealer said. "Besides, my boy, people come here to feel *something,* and while it might hurt, pain is undeniably something."

Joy shuddered as several shots punched through the back of a pew. The olive-green creature on the floor snorted awake and yawned. It had far too many teeth.

Another chattering blast shot out some of the overhead lights. Joy cowered between Ilhami and the floor, wishing that Ink would appear and take her away. But she was far from him and his wards. It was up to her to get them out. She clung to Ilhami and tried to think.

One of the armed men flew backward with an "oof" of arterial spray. His companion kept shooting until he'd exhausted the clip. In the breath of silence, there were curses.

Breaking glass. Thumping. Shouts. Something sailed through the window, trailing a stream of yellow smoke. The guard in the sunny-tinted glasses placed himself next to Ladybird and calmly handed him a black remote. Ladybird smiled and licked his finger, making a big show of choosing a button.

Ilhami didn't wait. "In here," he said and pulled Joy by the shoulders, pushing her toward the office door. "There's a back exit."

Joy grabbed the doorknob, coughing. Her eyes stung. She pushed into a dark room painted black with phosphorescent plants under blue lights. She couldn't see a back door. Ilhami wasn't behind her, and she turned to see him running into the main room. There was a low *boom* and screams of surprise and pain. Before she could react, Ilhami scurried back, pulling his backpack behind him. The firefight renewed with a series of pops and *brat-a-tat-tats*. There was a shrill cry followed by the sound of something crashing. He closed the door with his foot.

"What are you doing?" Joy snapped.

Ilhami lifted the backpack with a goofy grin. "Who says you can't have it all?" he said. "Let's go!"

Ducking behind the desk, Ilhami slid his fingers against the underside, searching for a button or a switch. Joy couldn't think through the anger and fear. Noises filled the hallway; she could hear them coming closer.

"Ilhami," she whispered.

He grunted. "I can't reach it."

"Move over!" she ordered and flipped onto her back, slipping her arm under the desk and running her hands over every surface. Finding a button, she pushed it hard.

"What are you worried about?" Ilhami said. "Ladybird's right. They're just bullets."

"Just *bullets*?" Joy said.

Ilhami helped her up. "You're protected, aren't you? Ink drew a Tyche glyph on you, right?"

Joy yanked back her hand and shook with rage. "No!"

Ilhami's eyes went white around the edges. *"What?"*

A shelving unit sprung open. There were stairs leading up into light. Ilhami pulled them against the wall. There were shouts in the main room, another exchange of fire. They both flinched as the office window sprouted a hole. Joy could see dark shapes through the tinted glass. They were almost there.

"Go!" Ilhami pushed her toward the stairs. "I'll cover you." Joy hesitated. He shoved her again. *"Go! Go! GO!"*

Joy launched up the stairs, a set of concrete back steps climbing to a side door. She looked back through the one-way glass behind the shelves and watched Ilhami raise his arms and shout something, his tattoos flashing, his stern face in profile.

And Joy saw him snap backward as someone shot him in the chest.

Joy muffled her scream against her palm, biting the skin between her thumb and finger. The back of her legs scraped the edge of the secret exit steps as she collapsed, her knees giving out. She squeezed her eyes against sudden tears. She saw him hit. She saw him fall. It was like the warehouse battle all over again, Kurt crushed under Aniseed, the torn puddle of Ink...

They shot Ilhami!

Whether it had been the police or the armed robed men or Ladybird's pebble-eyed guard, it didn't matter: Ilhami was dead and she'd be found soon. She'd be next. Joy pushed herself away from the hidden door, cowering on the stairs. Her ears roared. Her legs wouldn't move. She had to get out! *Get out! GET OUT!*

"Ink," she whispered as though he could hear her. "Ink! Ink! Ink!"

Joy squirmed on the concrete stair. She couldn't feel her feet.

The door swung open. Joy gasped. Adrenaline splash. She felt a stinging slap against her head.

"Joy! Let's go!" Ilhami hauled her up by the elbow and started climbing the stairs. He held the backpack in his left hand. His shirt was a mess. A vivid bow-shaped glyph glowed low on his ribs. Joy's brain stalled.

"But...?"

"Wait." Ilhami shoved the backpack into her arms and peeked out the window. He tapped his side hard three times. The glyph flared. "The car'll be here any second."

Joy squeezed the backpack to her chest. "You were shot."

"Hmm?" Ilhami kept scanning the alley.

"You were shot. In the chest."

"Yes. It's unpleasant," Ilhami said and shouldered the backpack. "Move!"

He pushed open the door and held Joy around her shoulders, ushering her before him, using his body as a shield. Joy didn't see whether there were cops or Folk or gawking bystanders as she was shoved into the passenger's seat of the Ferrari and immediately fell backward as Ilhami pulled the seat lever and threw himself across her lap, spilling cold coffee, slamming the door and tucking his body clear of the stick shift.

Enrique peeled out onto the street.

Joy coughed out a sound. Ilhami's weight rocked against her. She felt sick and dizzy and desperately confused. Enrique gunned the engine. Police sirens sounded somewhere not far behind.

Joy strained under Ilhami's not inconsiderable weight, her limbs rigid, feeling cold latte trickle down her shin. She

nto the g-force pull, sinuses straining under pres-
ey were obviously going very fast. She could hear the
hifting gears, Enrique switching lanes and squeal-
ugh stops, slamming them sideways and around
e floor of the car and the seat leaped uncomfort-
r her legs. She couldn't see past Ilhami's muscular
d the smell of roasted chestnuts pressed into her
ns blared. Sirens wailed. Traffic signs sped by in a
shoulder smashed against the door as they made
uick turn. Ilhami braced himself against the arm
senger's seat so he didn't crush her with every jolt.
happened?" Enrique shouted.
rd called the cops," Ilhami said before barking a lot
ounding garble. Joy thought that Turkish sounded
on Ladybird's lips, lots of lilting liquid noise. She
ery time Ilhami's weight bounced against her gut.
Enrique spat.
u were the one who sent her in without a glyph!"
," Enrique said, turning a hard left. "Honey, you
h, don't you? Inq said Ink gave you one."
pendant," Joy said through clenched teeth. "A
t broke."
hifted gears. "What about his *signatura*?"
t."
e," Enrique muttered and downshifted, gun-
he car roared.
lice cruiser flanked them on the parallel street;
the lights between buildings, hear the sirens
doors. The sound buzzed against the windows.
d off the locks. She anchored her shoulders
at and Ilhami tucked himself tighter, bracing
nst the passenger door. It probably looked like
ng the cops. *Great.*
heavy whooshing sound that she could feel

through the metal. There were a
over!" in English and in Spanish. S
the door handle. Her head rattle
rumble strips.

"We're going to die," she said
"Don't be ridiculous," he said
"Hold on!" Enrique shouted a
shifting gears, spinning hard a
direction. Joy's neck strained a
head slammed hard against t
and kept going. The side of her
smacked against her leg. Ilhan
chin scraping her arm. The si
and Enrique gunned the car

"I need a little distance," he

Joy's stomach burned w
doing?"

Ilhami laughed in her la
His eyes were all pupil. Jo
smacked his forehead. Har

Enrique hit the turn, sv
sheering of metal and tire
past the windshield. He
into an underpass and fli
in the dash. It blinked tw
windows went dark. Joy'
rique hit the brakes. Th

They appeared under
space, smooth as warm

Enrique jumped out
and yanking Ilhami of
the car with steady, st

"Get the plates," he
off his shirt, popped t

leaned i
sure—th
snarl of s
ing thro
turns; th
ably und
arms, an
face. Hor
blur. Her
another q
of the pass

"What I
"Ladybi
of angry-s
a lot nicer
coughed ev

"Idiot," E
"Hey, you
"I did no
have a glyph

"I had a
futhark. But

Enrique s
"I erased i
"Que madr
ning right. T

Another po
she could see
through both
Lights flashe
against the se
his knees agai
he was mooni
There was a

case. He began unscrewing the license plates with practiced ease and replacing them with new ones. Enrique steadied Joy on her feet and frowned into the car.

"You're paying to get it detailed," he told Ilhami. "And why'd you take the backpack?"

Ilhami finished replacing the back plate. "Spending cash," he said, smiling, and winked at Enrique's scowl. "Relax. It had her fingerprints all over it. With the cops there, I thought I should grab it for safekeeping."

Enrique grunted and patted Joy's shoulders. "You okay, honey?" She stared at him, hearing his words from a long way away. She blinked. "Everything's all right now," he said. "Let's get you inside." He folded her against him with a fatherly arm, took out his keycard, then slipped it through the slot. The door buzzed open and Ilhami jogged in after them, tucking his ruined shirt under one arm. Enrique waved to the doorman in the glass-and-fern lobby and pressed the button for the elevator. Joy could see her reflection in the steel. She looked scared.

Funny, she didn't feel scared. Oddly enough, she didn't feel anything at all.

Her phone buzzed. Text from Mom.

Hi, honey! Writing from work. How was your day today?

Joy stared at the words and let out a horrified giggle. Hearing herself, she stopped.

Joy put her phone away, unanswered, and moved when Enrique moved, stepping into the shiny elevator and watching the doors close, curiously detached. Ilhami, bare-chested, stood on her left, holding the backpack over one meaty shoulder and scratching the glowing glyph on his ribs. It was hard to believe that no one else could see it—the glyph looked as if it were drawn on his skin in molten light.

Enrique pressed a button and the elevator slipped upward. Joy felt the little drop in her stomach as they rose.

"She's not going to be happy," Enrique said over Joy's head.

Ilhami glanced at Joy's slack face. "No."

The doors opened and they walked quickly down the hall. Enrique slid the keycard through the lock as Ilhami walked cautiously backward, watching the elevator close and descend behind them.

"Clear," he said. Ilhami's fingers twitched and he had a bounce to his step.

Enrique opened the door and escorted Joy into a spacious apartment featuring a sprawling view of the city below. A curving kitchen bar and semicircular sofa split the great room into two sloping halves of masculine elegance. A wall-sized flat screen dominated the living room, and there was an outdoor stone fireplace flanked by hanging plants on the deck. Everything was done in shades of mocha, polished granite and tinted glass. The room slid off her eyes like rain.

"Sit down," Enrique said softly. "I'll get you some tea."

Joy thought she should probably say something but couldn't think what. She sat mutely on the leather couch. It barely creaked. Her phone buzzed. She took it out and stared at the text: Need to talk!

Monica? Joy didn't answer. Couldn't answer. She tucked the phone back into her pocket. Monica was as far from her as Mars.

Ilhami pulled the zippers of the backpack and gave a low whistle.

"Would you look at that?"

"Yes," Enrique muttered as he poured a cup. "All up your nose."

The air wobbled and warped as someone entered the room wearing a long black evening dress slit up the leg. Inq grabbed Ilhami's shoulders and turned him around, smoothing a hand over his bare chest and holding his chin, inspecting his eyes one at a time.

"Are you all right?" she asked.

He answered, contrite and childlike. *"Evet."*

Inq kissed him once, like a tender threat, and released him.

"Go sleep it off."

Without a word, Ilhami walked into the back of the apartment. Joy heard a door click closed.

Inq nodded to Enrique. "Thank you, Enrique." He gave a noncommittal sound. She smiled with pride as she crossed the room, arms outstretched. "Joy," Inq said and lifted her to her feet. Joy didn't protest and simply stared as she slowly recognized the familiar black-eyed, heart-shaped face. Inq touched the side of Joy's cheek. Joy barely felt it. She felt strangely outside her body, watching things happen to it from somewhere far away.

Inq sighed and called over her shoulder. "How is she?"

"Most likely in shock," Enrique said as he returned with a smooth ceramic mug. "It'll wear off soon enough and then there's bound to be weeping and screaming and the like. I'll get a towel." He gestured with the steaming cup. "She was brave enough, but completely unprotected. We should never have sent her in there." He pressed the drink into Joy's hands and curled his fingers around hers. She saw all the lines in his knuckles bend smooth as pearls. That's what she'd been attempting to show Ink: knuckles needed ridges that could smooth out and reform. She stared up at Enrique, wondering how she could explain why this was important and how to thank him for showing her precisely what she meant, but his eyes looked worried and guilty and old so she stayed silent.

"I'm so sorry, Joy," he said. "I would never have asked you if I'd known."

"Don't be silly," Inq said. "Of course she has a glyph. Ink

protects her like a lion." She held her hand before her eyes and inspected Joy through the space between her fingers. Inq frowned delicately and dropped her hand. "My brother is an idiot."

She circled Joy with measured steps, her high heels tapping on the hardwood, and pulled back her hand as if singed. "What...?" She touched Joy's shoulder, tracing her finger along the bulge of Joy's spine, stopping at her bra strap. Joy remembered that was where the ghostly mark burned. She suddenly felt a cold fire. Joy turned around. Inq's eyebrows asked a question. Joy said nothing.

"Can we borrow your guest room for a bit?" Inq asked politely.

"Of course," Enrique said and shared a slow kiss with Inq, hand resting gently on her hip where the slit in her skirt began. She ended it with two pecks, one on his bottom lip and one on the top.

"Thank you, baby," she said as she took Joy's hand and led her down the hall. Halfway there, the heat from the mug registered. Joy quickly switched hands.

"They shot Ilhami," she said. The cup in her hand shook.

"I know," Inq said. "Serves him right." She pushed open the door to a neat little room with a wide bed tucked with sharp military corners and stylish silver-gray pillows spread along the headboard. The fixtures were sleek and silver, the vertical blinds alternately black and pale gray. Even the lamp looked built for speed.

"Sit down," she said. Joy sat. Inq brushed back her hair. "Do you want your tea?"

Joy looked at the mug in her hand. "No."

Inq took the steaming cup and put it on the nightstand, then sat gently next to Joy. She spoke as if Joy were frightened, but she wasn't frightened—she was numb.

"I thought that I had found a neat solution to our little

problem with Ilhami, but I had never considered the possibility that Ink hadn't given you protections. I knew he didn't want you to wear his *signatura*, but I thought he'd at least give you a shielding glyph." She gave a sigh that strained her dress top. "I admit, I didn't think to ask, but then again, I never thought he'd be so careless."

"He did give me something," Joy said, moved to defend him even though she felt like screaming. "A pendant. It broke when I was attacked last time."

Inq cocked her head. "Who attacked you?"

"That guy in the suit of armor," Joy said.

"Him again?" Inq said, sounding surprised. "I thought Ink killed him once already."

"He did." Joy didn't want to think about that. She could hear the clanking footsteps, the sound of swords hacking through briars, the rush of blood in her ears. "Ink went to ask Graus Claude about it. He thinks the knight was hired by the Tide." *The Tide.* Even the word sent a quivery chill through her limbs. To know there was a group of people out there that hated her enough to try and kill her...

"The Tide?" Inq waved her hand dismissively. "Pshht. They know the Edict better than most and follow it to the letter, if only to prove to the rest of us that they can. Higher and mightier are the zealots! However, Ink knows that any charm can be broken," she said. "I meant that he should have drawn one *on* you. That's what we do, after all, but instead of using *signatura*, we can use protective glyphs, like wearing a ward on your skin. A personal shield."

Joy blinked. "That...sounds like a good idea."

"I'd like to think so," Inq said, smirking. "It was my idea. But let's ask Ink before we do anything, shall we? Asking permission first would be polite." She winked one all-black eye lined in thick lashes. "You're not even a little bit mine, anymore." Inq placed a hand low on her belly and Joy knew the three concentric circles of Inq's *signatura* would be there. That mark had once flared on Joy's bottom lip.

A rent flashed in the air and Ink stepped out of nothing, taking in Inq and Joy and the contents of the room.

"This is New York," he said.

Inq nodded. "Enrique's apartment in Battery Park."

"What is Joy doing in Enrique's apartment in Battery Park?"

"The boys needed a little help with an errand," Inq said. "The better question is why isn't Joy protected with a Tyche glyph?"

Ink's voice darkened. "And why would Joy need a Tyche glyph?"

"Because there's an armored knight trying to kill me!"

Joy's words exploded out of her mouth and with them came feelings. It was as if a heavy blanket had been thrown off her shoulders, leaving her shaky and hot and cold and bright. She felt suddenly naked, exposed to the world. The reality of the past hour burst through her skin. Her teeth chattered. Her eyes stung. Ink knelt next to her, concerned.

"Did he come again? He didn't hurt you, did he?"

Tears flung from her eyes. "No."

Inq placed a gentle hand on Joy's shoulder. "Honestly, Ink, have I taught you nothing about keeping your *lehmans* alive?"

Ink growled, "She is not my—"

"You know what I mean," Inq said. "Joy is your love, not your harem girl. I know the difference," she said smoothly. "It is the difference between Kurt and the boys."

"I thought the pendant would be enough," he said earnestly, smoothing a hand over Joy's trembling arm. "I'd purchased another. And...I did not want to mar your skin." He ran his thumb over the back of her hand, eyes on her veins. "Remember, my marks are meant to be seen—I would have had to draw something like a birthmark or a scar, something every human might notice. And I am no expert—I know how to ward a place but not a person. A glyph might have been hard to explain."

"Oh, really, now," Inq said, exasperated. "I'm all for aesthetics, but you put Joy at considerable risk out of vanity?" She threw up her hands, sparkling with black polish and diamonds. "You could have simply asked me."

Ink glanced at his sister. "Asked you what?"

"To draw on her for you, of course," Inq said. "Unlike you, I *am* an expert—I know a thing or two about personal wards. And my marks are *invisible*, so no one will see them, and since they are protections, she will be left unclaimed. Unmarred." She smiled at Joy. "Still pretty as a primrose."

"A wildflower," Joy mumbled. "With bite."

Ink's hand tightened on Joy's knee. "You would do this for me?"

"Anything for you," Inq said and glanced to Joy. "And certainly this for her. What kind of sister do you take me for?" She swatted her brother lightly. "Joy is one of us, after all. She's family."

Ink leaned closer to Joy. She could smell his clean scent of rain.

"Do you want this, Joy?" he asked. "Inq can protect you in ways I cannot."

Joy nodded as if the nodding would never stop. "Yes," she said. "Yes, please!" Knowing in the back of her mind that anything Inq did to her could be undone made her feel less vulnerable, more in control. While Invisible Inq had shown her every kindness since taking down Aniseed, Joy had never felt on settled ground with the wry and reckless Scribe. Inq wasn't above getting Joy into trouble; in fact, she seemed to enjoy it a little too much.

"Very well," Ink said. "Thank you."

Inq clapped her hands and bounced on the bed, making her breasts jiggle. "Excellent!" she said and pulled Joy's sleeve. "Now strip!"

Joy snapped out of her fog. "What?"

"Fine, spoilsport, you can just take off your shirt and lie down on the bed," Inq said as she kicked off her high heels and hiked up her dress then crawled over the mattress toward Joy. "I'm going to draw it on your back since it's been such a tempting target."

Glancing at Ink, Joy hesitated, twisting her fingers in the edge of her shirt. Inq looked back and forth between them and smirked.

"Oooh! Do I get first peek?" Inq laughed and bounced on her knees. Ink opened his mouth, but his sister pushed him toward the door. "Go on, shoo!" She hugged Joy around her shoulders and rested her chin near Joy's ear. "This is between us girls."

Ink ducked his head and smiled. Dimples appeared.

"Do not let her get too carried away," he said to Joy. "Only for protection, you hear?" he warned his sister and slipped into the hall, closing the door behind him.

Inq waited for the click. "He doesn't know."

"Know what?" For a split second, Joy was completely serious.

Inq made a face and tugged impatiently at Joy's shirt. "Take this off and show me what that is on your back." Joy hesitated only a moment, then pulled her shirt over her head and turned her back to Inq. The Scribe considered the blurred mark in silence.

"Whose is it?" she said.

"I have no idea," Joy said. "All I know is I can't remove it."

"Really?" Inq said, leaning out of the light. "Hmm. Lie down."

Joy stretched out on her stomach and grabbed a pillow to prop under her armpits, her breasts smushed against the decorative buttons. She felt Inq's all-black eyes searching her bare skin. It was too quiet for too long.

"Is it a *signatura*?" Joy asked.

Inq considered it. "If it is, it's like none I've seen before. And that's saying something."

Joy sighed. Her belly sank into the mattress. "Graus Claude said the same thing."

"You've shown him?"

"I thought maybe he'd recognize it," Joy said. "He says he has records of all the Folk who have ordered your marks."

"Does he now?" Inq said slowly. "And Ink hasn't seen it yet?" Joy shook her head. Inq chuckled. "Well, obviously not. He hasn't seen much of anything under that shirt, has he?" Joy felt Inq's finger trace her spine, the tickle of her breath as she leaned closer. The sheets whispered under the shifting weight. "Mmm. Shame. You have very soft skin."

Joy swallowed a squeamish flutter. "Do you mind?"

"Not at all," Inq said. "Don't worry, Joy. You're not my type." Joy could picture Inq's face as she smiled and withdrew.

"So what do you think it is?" Joy said to cover her awkward embarrassment.

"Well, I don't think it's a *signatura*. And I should know," Inq said, rubbing her palms to make them warm. "It's my job, after all."

"Well, what is it then?"

"I'm not sure," she said. "Maybe a marker? Like tagging a bear for later study. Or, in your case, a mouse." Joy frowned and Inq raised her palms in mock innocence. "It's just a splash. *Signaturae* were developed to replace True Names, and that takes a complicated ritual involving lancing Folk with alchemical fire and asking them to offer up a token of themselves to seal the magics—it's a requirement, and not something taken or given lightly."

"A requirement?" Joy said into the pillow. "You mean it's forced?"

"Everyone had to do it. Everyone in the Twixt," Inq said. "Everyone but Ink and I."

Joy twisted around to look at Inq. "Why not you?"

Inq smoothed her hands over Joy's back. Her fingers, devoid of ripples or fingerprints, slid frictionless as feathers. "Like Ink told you, we were made, not born," she said. "Our *signaturae* were designed along with our bodies. We didn't have to give up anything because we aren't Folk. We are their instruments, created with one purpose in mind—to draw *signaturae* on humans in their stead." She stroked her palms over the mark on Joy's back. There was a cool tingle like snowflakes. "You don't ask a paintbrush to give up its bristles."

Joy tried not to think about the slippery satin feel of Inq's inquisitive hands. "So what kinds of things do the Folk give up?" Joy asked. "You and Ink didn't have to give up anything—what about Kurt?"

Inq pressed her fingers against Joy's spine. "Kurt's human."

"Sort of."

"Sort of," Inq admitted.

"Well, what about Graus Claude?" Joy said. "What did he have to give up?"

Joy felt Inq trace the blurry glow with her fingertips, exploring its edges. "I don't know. It's an interesting question, but it's considered impolite to ask," she said. "Sort of like 'what color is your pubic hair?'" Inq grinned. "So what color *is* your pubic hair?"

Joy tried to act unruffled, half-naked on a stranger's bed. "None of your business."

"See what I mean?" Inq said. "Well, whatever this thing is, it looks...sloppy, unfinished. Perhaps it has to set first before you can erase it?" She slid her hands over Joy's back like smoothing a canvas flat. It was a rich, liquid feeling like swallowing warm custard. "What were you doing when you noticed it?"

"I noticed it after I did some flips in the grass," Joy said quickly, feeling more exposed by the minute as Inq's fingers roamed lower. "After we washed my car. After I talked to my mom."

"Those hardly seem the sort of things that qualify under an auspice," Inq said. "It somehow lacks the drama of being claimed by one of the Twixt." She shifted on the mattress. "Then again, what do I know? Perhaps someone claims to be the guardian spirit of used vehicle maintenance? Or the solemn sisterhood of grass acrobatics?" Her voice held a tickle of laughter. "Or perhaps they realized who you were a tad too late and wisely withdrew before finishing up. In any event, I wouldn't worry about it—no one but Ink and myself and those with the Sight can even see it. An unfinished claim will simply fade over time. Now let's see," she said as she straddled Joy's waist. The bed sank deeper, pushing Inq's knees against Joy's ribs. Joy hugged the pillow tighter and tried not to freak out. "Don't worry—you won't feel a thing. But lie still. Even if others can't see it, I take pride in my work."

Joy gasped as a warm heat touched her back, radiating out from where Inq's palms rested against her skin. The sensation sank deeper into her body, a low buzz of warmth spreading under her shoulder blades, dripping down her ribs and pooling in a bead behind her navel. Inq moved her fingers. Joy felt her insides squirm. The almost-heat traced inquisitive tendrils through her muscles, pouring liquid light slowly through her torso and limbs. Inq gently nudged Joy's organs, weaving around her kidneys and stomach, her heart and lungs, her intestines and groin and tracing the insides of her thighs down to her toes. It became difficult to breathe—the air suddenly heavy and thick—before the tension snapped; the smothering weight lifted like champagne bubbles frothing out the top of her head. Joy half imagined a hissing whisper off her scalp and lips and ears. Her eyes fluttered as she took a deep breath.

Inq lifted her fingers from beneath Joy's skin.

"There now," Inq said. "That wasn't so bad."

Joy's lungs pressed against her rib cage as she took a deep breath, pushing Inq's knees wider. Inq sat on the small of her back.

Joy blinked back winks of firefly light and wet her lips.

"How...how does it look?" Joy asked for something to say.

Inq leaned forward, taking her weight off Joy's hips, and lightly touched the length of her spine. The Scribe whispered against Joy's ear.

"Beautiful," she said. Joy tried to look at Inq, but she was pinned. Inq giggled and climbed slowly off Joy. The sudden lack of weight and heat left its mark, cool against the open air. Joy's body was slow to move, woozy and warm.

"That should be enough to counteract your basic gunfire and blast damage, but blunt impacts can still hurt. I can't do much about mortal physics." Inq tugged her dress back into place and regarded Joy clinically. "It's too bad we don't have more glyphs," Inq said. "I bet I could protect you from whatever the Tide could throw at you."

Joy twisted on the rumpled sheets, still holding the pillow to her chest. "What do you mean?"

Inq leaned back on her hands. "The Tyche is a general protection glyph. It should keep you from most worldly harm— weapons, collateral damage, that sort of thing—but it can't keep you safe from those in the Twixt who are intentionally seeking you out. Folk are too specific. Bound to narrow rules, they have specialized—hence their auspices—and so they have become *very* good at their jobs." She scootched over to sit on the edge of the bed, her dress opening along the length of her thigh. She wore an old-fashioned garter

with a black lace rosette. It made her seem older. "If someone intends to harm you, then we could build a ward against
them. Using specific sigils, I could block all those Folk from
harming you."

Joy frowned. "Don't I need their permission for those to
work?"

Inq shook her head with a feline grin. "Protections aren't
the same as invoking someone's True Name—for that, you'd
need them to give their *signaturae* willingly, to be part of their
pact, to share some of their power, give up some of their
control. A ward is like a fence or a shield. To ward off a specific attack, I would just need to link their *signaturae* to the
Tyche glyph. It would repel a specific person's attack. And,
technically, everyone grants me permission to draw their
signaturae as their proxy because I'm one of the Scribes." She
drew a finger in the furrows of the mussed top sheet. "Of
course, I shouldn't do any such thing. You're just a human
girl, after all, and rumored to be a dangerous one at that."
Inq winked. "But I think us 'dangerous girls' should stick together, don't you?"

"You know everyone's *signaturae*?"

"Not off the top of my head," Inq admitted. "It's been eons,
and I've drawn a lot of True Names, many of which are similar but not exactly the same. Every one has to be perfect, so
it would help to have a visual."

Joy scooted up on her left elbow and fished her phone out
of her back pocket. She scrolled through the memory download. Clicking through her photo file, she searched the dates
and tapped an image, then turned the result to Inq.

"Like this?" Joy said.

Inq picked up the phone as Joy enlarged the photo with a
sweep of her finger and thumb. Aniseed's chalk wall zoomed
to fill the screen. Hundreds of *signaturae* shone against the

dark slate, scribbled in white chalk. Inq smiled slowly, the tip of her tongue between her teeth.

"Yes," she said, eyes sparkling. "Exactly like that."

Joy walked out of the bedroom feeling larger than life. Her footsteps hovered on the carpet and her swaying arms left shimmery echoes in their wake. Her center of gravity felt lower, her senses sharper, her shoulders squared under an invisible suit. Turning her head caused sparkles to wink on the edges of her vision, reminding her vaguely of the splice of light that had first introduced her to the Twixt. Magic beat in her heart and sang on her skin. She could taste its burnt-sparkler-candy tang on her tongue.

"Joy?" Ink rose from the couch where he'd been sitting with Enrique. Both men looked at her as if she were back-lit onstage. Ink drew his fingers along the silver chain at his hip, his eyes wide and uncertain.

Inq appeared from behind her and smirked. "How are you feeling?"

For a long moment Joy forgot to answer, her eyes full of stars and wonder.

"Amazing," she said. The word bounced along the backs of her teeth. She lifted her hand and saw the pale sigils swimming on gold-colored currents. If she concentrated, she could almost feel them humming over her skin.

"What took you so long?" Enrique asked. "It's nearly dark."

"It's complicated," Inq said, wiping a hand over her forehead. "It took some time, but I wanted to do it right. I want to keep Joy safe." She smiled at her brother, exhausted and proud. "Isn't she gorgeous? And I'm not finished yet. It'll take one more session to complete the design." She poked Joy in the shoulder. Joy was rooted to the spot, as if her feet were magnetized to the floor, the steel girders of the building and the foundation deep underground. "Now don't you go undoing all my hard work this time. With these in place, it'll be hard for Folk to sense you, sort of like a dampener field or a masking scent. But if you suddenly remove one, you'll light up on their radar like Boxing Day no matter where you are." Inq squeezed Joy's shoulder and winked. "Next time, I take your pants."

Inq had covered Joy's back, chest and arms with sigils; her knees to the soles of her feet had undergone similar treatment. Inq had drawn on her palms and her lips and in between her toes. It had felt like floating in a bath of effervescent bubbles, ripples lapping and popping all over her skin. Inq's fingers had looped scripts of sparkling wine over her bare body for hours. Joy lay back on the pillows, drunk on it. Inq had talked in low lullabies about the Cabana Boys, the Dark Ages and her earliest memories of transmuting herself from a hollow Scribe into the person who called herself Inq. She'd last been speaking about someone named Maimonides from Cordova as she'd drawn liquid squiggles between Joy's breasts.

Now, even fully clothed, Joy felt naked in a way she hadn't felt since she was small: unashamed and glorified, hyperaware of her body as a miracle, too vast and unique to ever wither or die. She felt connected to a stream of living music that ran through everything in the universe. She felt like she could walk through walls, like she could call down rain, like she could fly.

"Joy?"

Ink's voice reached her across the chasm of awe and she glanced up. She'd somehow missed him, musing at the light flickering along the back of her mind. She looked into his fathomless eyes and felt a fire ignite inside her. She smiled from the heart. It struck him—the shock was plain on his face.

"Are...are you ready to go home?" he stammered. Joy had never once heard him stammer. It made her smile.

"Yes," she said, her voice thick with heat and magic.

"Wait a moment," Inq said, tapping Ink's shoulder. "I'd like to discuss what else I'll need to complete her armor. But first, I need some ice." She simpered at Joy. "You're quite a workout." The Scribes strolled into the kitchen together, a matching set of black-and-silver instruments like his and hers knives.

Joy stood in the main room, drinking in the New York skyline with hazy eyes. She felt the immensity of it—the surreal beauty of the city as the sky turned indigo-black-orange with a million square fireflies of light.

Enrique handed Joy a glass of water. She drank it as if she'd never tasted liquid before. She felt the cold sliding down her throat, spreading from her stomach out to her limbs, keenly aware of everything the water touched and the gentle transformation happening inside her as water became blood and energy and Joy.

"I'm sorry for bringing you into this," Enrique said softly. "I should have known better."

"No, it's all right," Joy said. It was better than all right. She felt *incredible*. Ink kept stealing glances at her as if he couldn't look away. "Where's Ilhami?"

"Still sleeping it off," Enrique said, sipping a beer. "I'll kick him out once he can get back to the studio on his own two feet. I'm certain there's some masterpiece brewing in that brain of his, whatever's left of it." He sipped again and turned his shoulders away from the Scribes. "But that wasn't what I was talking about. I hadn't realized that you'd been kept clean of the Twixt. Now you're covered in it."

Joy had forgotten that Enrique had the Sight. All the Cabana Boys did. And although it was a rare elixir that had given it to him and not a genetic inheritance like hers, it still meant that he could see all the changes Inq had wrought with her fingers and their diamond-studded tips.

"It's to keep me safe," Joy said.

"There is no 'safe,'" he said back. "You're part of the Twixt and it is a part of you. And while I'd be the first to admit that I've been incredibly fortunate, as well as exceedingly spoiled, being a *lehman* is not without its price." He took another sip. "It means that you are far from safe." Enrique downed the rest of his glass and set it gently on a marble coaster. "You are young, but look at Ilhami. Look at Raina. Look at me. A life that burns twice as hot burns half as long."

Joy frowned, his words poking cracks in her new glorious armor.

"I don't understand."

"You will," he said. "And that is why I am sorry." Enrique opened the hall closet and shook out a coat. He slipped it over her arms, buttoned the front and smoothed the collar. It smelled expensive, of cashmere and cologne. "We may live charmed lives full of sights and sensations few will ever experience and none would ever believe, but that is only for as long as they choose to bestow it and only for as long as we escape the notice of our enemies." Enrique picked at a bit of errant fuzz as he whispered in her ear. "The Folk are passionate and also jealous. Whatever they feel, they feel it sharply, and are as quick to adore and anger as well as strike back." He smiled his handsome, 007 smile. "I am fortunate to have been her favorite for so long."

He tugged the edges of her collar so that Joy looked up into his eyes. She'd never noticed that one of his eyes was slightly larger than the other. It made him look oddly lopsided, owlish and wise. "You do not have the advantage of being old and unimportant," he said softly. "And I have forgotten what it feels like to be young and invulnerable, but I'm old enough to know the difference between what is real and what is not." He settled a hand onto her shoulder. "This is not real, Joy. Not really. But time *is* real. What seems like a moment in our world is still time passing in theirs, and your mortal clock knows it." His voice was insistent. "You will *age*, Joy, and quickly—it is a price they cannot fathom because it is one they cannot pay." He patted her shoulder thoughtfully. "Do you have any family?"

"Yes," she said, dimly thinking of her brother and mother and Monica and Dad, all of them older and therefore more mortal than her.

"Good. I have no family and so never had cause to want one, to miss it, to wonder 'what if?'" Enrique turned her with his fatherly arm. "Keep them in your thoughts. Let them anchor you in this world—the real world. Do not forget what is important to you as an ordinary girl even though you've been given an extraordinary life. It is *your* life, after all, to live as you like. Remember that." He kissed her on the forehead as if she were his daughter. "Good night, Joy. And thank you from Ilhami in absentia."

The Scribes were watching them from the leather-topped stools at the end of the bar. Inq popped the remnants of her ice cube into her lowball glass. Enrique placed Joy's hand in Ink's and touched the back of Inq's neck, massaging the spot with strong, rolling strokes. Inq smiled luxuriously.

"Thank you, again," Ink said to his sister.

"My pleasure," she said and blew a kiss to Joy. "See you soon!" Joy saw the glint of mischief in Inq's eyes before Ink tugged Joy sideways into a tear between worlds scented with cologne and rain and citrus spice.

TEN

JOY'S ROOM LOOKED SOMEHOW SMALLER THAN WHEN she'd left it. It was as if she'd grown a few inches taller or her eyes had developed telescopic vision; the bed looked lower, the ceiling higher and the floor seemed very far away. She gazed at her computer, thinking that her fingers might now be too big for the keys.

When she moved, she thought the sound of her footsteps might knock things off the shelves.

"Do you want to sit down?" Ink asked quietly.

Joy shook her head. This feeling was too big for her body. Another part of her mind, the reasonable part, knew that nothing inside her had changed, but she *felt* different, a buzzing aftereffect of Inq's glyphs on her skin. It was almost as if she could feel the protective armor as she moved, scales of power overlapping, chains of symbols linked together and moving as her body moved, hot and liquid-smooth. She stood in the middle of her room, staring around with curious eyes.

"Does everything look different to you?" she asked.

Ink placed a hand over the back of his neck, smoothing the hairs there. It was a human gesture, both foreign and familiar.

"Everything looks the same," he said. "It is you who look different."

"I do?" Joy had barely had time to look at herself since getting off Enrique's guest bed. The echo of the rumpled sheets mixed with the smell of her own skin and Inq's strange, dry rose perfume. "What do I look like?"

Ink swallowed. "A goddess."

Joy smiled. "Have you met many goddesses?"

Ink grinned shyly as if he wasn't certain he should. Only one dimple teased his cheek. "Given that your people have often worshipped the Folk as gods, I should think that I know quite a few." He leaned against her closet door, his hands tangling in the wallet chain. "You glow like light on the water, taking shape in the waves."

Joy looked at her hands and feet. She saw the symbols as he described, a golden glimmer moved as she watched the calligraphy shifting. She'd seen a similar effect on the ouroboros on Ink's back. She remembered his *signatura* had been Inq's handiwork, too.

"This is not usually what happens, is it?" Joy asked, exploring the play of light on the backs of her knuckles. She remembered watching Inq mark a girl in a blue bikini, a cut-paper-snowflake pattern unfolding under the girl's skin. "Is this normal for Inq?"

"Maybe it is not Inq," he said. "Maybe it is you."

Ink reached out and brushed the hair from Joy's neck.

"It starts here," he said, his touch featherlight. She leaned her head to the side. He traced lines slowly, weaving his fingers along the filigree that connected the glyphs. His hand faltered at the collar of her coat; the sloping lines disappeared beneath the neckline. Joy stared into his eyes and undid the buttons, one by one, peeling layers away, exposing more of her flesh to his touch.

Ink opened his mouth to say something but instead slid his hand against her skin, as if unable to help himself. The warmth sent her mind swirling. Liquid sunshine dazzled along the ceiling and the floor. Mesmerized, Ink watched the light play through his fingers, dancing to her quickening pulse. She felt it thrum and pound in her veins.

Dipping his head, he touched his lips to the cleft of her throat as if to taste the honey-colored light. Joy gasped at the softness, the surprising stillness; anticipation heightened the almost unbearable moment—sensations lit crystal sparks behind her eyes. The kiss hovered, incomplete; she felt his parted lips barely brush her skin before the warm tip of his tongue traced one of the glyphs.

Joy's hand fastened to the back of his neck, grabbing his hair. She felt the soft moan in his throat, the edge of his teeth and his body pressed against her hard enough that she thought they might fall.

There were three pointed knocks on her door.

Joy wet her lips, dry from gasping. Ink dragged his chin upward and rested his forehead against her jaw.

"Joy?" Stef called through the door. "Tell him to go."

"You've *got* to be kidding," Joy muttered. She could barely keep her balance, crushed against him. Ink's hands tightened on her waist, his breath barely a moan.

"Joy," Stef warned.

Joy's hands opened and closed in impotent fists. "Go. Away. Stef!"

"It's late. And I have to talk to you," Stef said calmly. "About the front door." Joy's head spun, trying to remember the door and the knight and the kick and Ink on the floor. But Ink was in her arms, willing, needing. Her body felt swollen and burning with *more*. "I expect it might take a while," Stef added drily.

"I'll go," Ink said, a husky hush in his voice. His hands were hot and tight against her skin. She'd never heard him sound so human. She had never wanted him more.

Joy kissed the side of his cheek, his jaw, his ear. "I'm sorry," she said. "My brother..."

"Is right," Ink said, his fingers releasing their hold all at once, an act of will and deference. "He is right. It is late. And I am still..." Ink stopped, facing her, a golden stardust in his eyes reflecting her strange light. He smiled at her ruefully. "New...at this."

It was a gentle withdrawal, a subtlety she hadn't thought him capable of. She suspected that Inq had helped. Was there anything in her life that Inq hadn't touched first?

"Okay," Joy said softly and took a deep breath. She added a louder, "Okay!" aimed at the door. Joy adjusted her coat and her shirt and shook out her hair, damp and sweaty at her neckline. "I'll be out in a minute."

"I'll be waiting right here," Stef said from the hall.

"*Stef,*" she warned.

"*Joy,*" he mocked back.

Ink slid his fingers along the silver chain with a caress that she envied. She twisted her hands behind her back, her body aching for another touch.

"It seems our siblings have much in common," Ink said. "However, if it were Inq, she would be far less polite." His breathing steadied; his hands stopped shaking. "So I will go now and see if I can procure what she needs to complete your wards." He stared at her. "To keep you safe, I will do anything. Even leave you like this. You must know that."

He unfolded the straight razor. Joy crossed her arms.

"What more does she need?"

Ink paused. "Your attacker's *signatura*." He'd stepped through the breach to another place entirely, a line in space invisibly cutting him off at the knee. "Do not worry. I will find it, Joy. I will not fail you." He straightened. "I love you."

She touched his face, wanting to kiss him again. He

kissed her palm on her heart line and stepped into nothingness. Gone.

Joy's breath fluttered in her chest for a long, lingering moment before she stomped over to the door, twisted the knob
and flung it open.

"Do you *mind?*" She sneered into Stef's face. He stared at
her, openmouthed.

"Holy..." He reeled back and bumped into the opposite
wall, surprise derailing his tirade. *"Joy?"* His voice sounded
scared, broken. "What have they done to you?"

Joy's anger one-eightied into chagrin. "It's nothing."

"Nothing?" Stef gestured to her in the hall. "You look like a
walking Christmas tree!" He snatched her wrist and pushed
up her sleeve. "It's all over you, isn't it? What did you do? Roll
naked down the Hill through everyone's domain?"

She yanked her arm back. "I *asked* them to."

"*Asked* them? Are you *insane?*" Stef said. "I thought we
talked about keeping a low profile, not making ourselves
out to be any more of a target than we already are."

"I am taking precautions," Joy said. "That's what this is."

"By being a banner ad in Times Square?"

"I know what I'm doing!"

Stef fumed. "You haven't a *clue* what you're doing!" He
paced the tight width of the hall. "Let me ask you something—
did you come up with this clever plan all by yourself or did
one of *them* bring it up?" Stef's sarcasm was a living thing
scuttling over her spine. "A simple suggestion? A tiny precaution? Maybe wondering how things could be better if
only they had this one thing that only you could provide?"

Joy's attitude flipped instantly—suspicion curling into
embarrassment thinking about Inq's uncharacteristically
generous offering and the pic of Aniseed's wall. *Did I just do
something incredibly stupid?* She wanted to rail at Inq, but her
brother was closer.

"You don't know what you're talking about! You don't know them! You don't know him!" Joy shot back, although it sounded like he did. In fact, it sounded too close for comfort. "Ink and Inq are helping protect me against whatever it is that's out there..." Joy winced as she felt a hot twinge on her back, like a burning mosquito bite where the splotch of light burned. The non-*signatura*, or whatever it was—something was happening. She tried to feel over her shoulder, but it was just out of reach.

"I wouldn't be surprised if your 'attacker' was one of those two in disguise to pressure you into doing this," Stef said. "Using a mask or a glamour to throw you off."

"Don't be stupid," Joy said as she pushed past him in the hall.

"I'm not being—*Joy!*" Stef shouted her name as she grabbed her keys, her glyphs flaring, throwing sparkles across the ruined door. Her brother looked desperate, as if he were trying to talk her down off a ledge. The golden shimmer bounced off his glasses, outlining the tiny sigils scratched there. "Have you ever seen the guy's face, the one who attacked you?" he asked quietly. "Do you know for sure that it wasn't one of them?" Joy bit her inner cheek and said nothing. She remembered seeing the knight's exposed throat after Ink struck him down, knowing that he was no longer breathing, seeing no pulse beating there. She remembered a flash of blue teeth and gray stubble and how the knight later struggled past Briarhook's briars on the stairs. She'd thought that he was dead, but she wasn't sure of anything anymore.

Stef pressed her arm, bringing her back to the present. "Take a minute," he said. "Think about it. You know I'm right."

Joy grabbed her purse and the doorknob, blinking back tears.

"You're *wrong*," she said. "And I'll prove it."

She slammed the door, which wobbled on the ruined jamb. Anger felt a lot better than doubt.

Joy stormed into the C&P, whipping open the door, which utterly failed to give a satisfying slam as it eased gently closed, greeting her with its two-tone *hello*.

She grabbed a diet bar and a chocolate bar, figuring they'd cancel each other out, and snatched a sports drink, craving its chemical salty-sweetness. Joy deliberately waited for the last customer to leave before adding the pack of clove gum.

Vinh's son, Hai, glanced up when he saw the gum. "You're the one from before? Back room?"

She nodded. "Yes."

"One moment," he said as he dialed the phone. He hit the keys on the register. "Total comes to six thirty-two."

Joy dug out a twenty from her last stint at the café. This was petty cash now. She wondered if she might go straight to Dover Mill and get some work done. *What day is it?* Enrique was right: time worked differently. While she might be hours in the Twixt, she was only gone moments here, and it threw her off her schedule. She needed to get out, go out, go *do* something—get away from the house. And Stef. And everyone. She'd have to get someone to fix the broken door before Dad came home.

Mr. Vinh emerged wearing his usual blue shirt and loose black pants, but he was holding the multiple-lensed contraption in his hand. He adjusted it as he walked, glancing through a ring of three lenses as she accepted change from Hai. The wizard frowned.

"You look different, busy girl," he said. "You look like one of them."

Joy took that as a compliment. Hai squeezed by them and opened the freezer, facing the ice-cream labels forward. She tapped the counter with her pack of gum.

"Remember the thing I asked about last time?" She saw him remember. Saw him frown. "I'm curious—how much?"

Mr. Vinh slid behind the counter and removed a notepad. He scribbled a number on the page, tore it off and handed it to her. She read it. It was clearly not a discount.

"Done," she said, folding it up again. "I should have it in a week."

The wizard's expression didn't change. "Will that be cash or trade?" His tone wasn't judgmental, merely curious. He had no doubt that she could pay, which was a compliment of sorts. Her new glyphs flared and spun.

"Cash," she said, tucking the slip of paper in the pocket behind the scalpel.

"Very well," he said. "I will see you in one week." He handed her the plastic bag of snacks. "Have a nice day."

She worked for hours at Dover Mill, but she didn't feel caring and generous; she felt ruthlessly efficient, angry and defiant. Joy nearly crackled with energy as she poured her frustration onto her table and into Folks' skin. As if sensing her mood, her clients were quiet and polite, no excess words, no life stories or elaborate thanks; strangers simply came in, sat down, had their glyphs removed and left. Some placed a tip on her tray, but most bowed out wordlessly and climbed the stairs with haste.

Joy was *not* in a good mood.

She methodically ran through her list of files. She texted her status to Graus Claude and punched her earnings into her phone calculator. Three more days like this and Ink's glamour was in the bag. Add another day for the door and she could have everything in place by the time Dad and Shelley got back. Then, maybe, she could think about detailing her car.

Or buying a vacation. Or paying for college.

There was a rumble of thundering boots down the stairs. Joy turned just in time to see blue tattooed eyelids and a wide grin up close. Joy backed into the table.

"Filly!"

The woman whooped, "Joy Malone!" She set her hands on her hips and threw back her chin. "I heard that I might find you here."

Joy nodded, thoughts spinning. Filly was good friends with Ink. It was hard to imagine two people less alike, but she was sure that they spoke often. Filly was nosy and brash and brassy and altogether too proud to be the first to know gossip.

"I'm..." Joy struggled to think up an excuse for what she could possibly be doing there that wasn't precisely what she was doing there.

"You are removing marks," Filly said. "For payment."

Joy's heart stopped. *Too late.*

Filly shrugged back her rattling half cape, the finger bones clacking like bamboo chimes. She twisted her horsehead pendant to hang behind her neck and pointed to a sigil high on her shoulder. "This one," she said and promptly hopped up on the table. "Remove it."

"Um. It's by appointment..." Joy said weakly.

Filly glanced around the empty room. "I am here now," she said. "Remove it."

Joy took out her scalpel and blew on the blade, buying seconds even as her scalpel drew nearer, almost against her will. *I really shouldn't be doing this...*

"You should really go through Graus Claude," Joy said. She'd begun to sweat, her palms hot and moist.

"The vainglorious frog?" Filly barked a laugh. "He's had enough of my coin. He can fill his belly elsewhere. Remove it," she said again. "Please."

Joy wiped a smudge of mud off the woman's shoulder. Her

fingers were shaking, nervous and stiff. She was going to get in *serious* trouble for this.

Filly kicked her heels impatiently. "Well?"

Joy still hesitated, resisting the urge to do as she asked. Why was saying no so hard? Why not kick her out? Why not just give in? "Aren't you going to tell me how it happened?" she asked in a last-ditch attempt to stall for time. "Explain how it was a mistake? Why you shouldn't have it? Why you need it removed?"

Filly thought about it for a moment, licking the tattooed spot under her lip. "No."

Joy gave up. "Okay, then. Hold still."

She traced the fractal five-pointed star, carefully unwinding it one triangle at a time, almost relieved to be doing it now that she'd begun. When she finished, the sigil collapsed into what looked like crumpled glass before disappearing completely. Filly rotated her shoulder and smiled.

"Excellent!" she crowed. "Many thanks, Joy Malone!"

Joy didn't bother to point out the tip tray or mention payment due. Somehow she was certain it wouldn't matter in the least. Mentally, she chalked it up to owing Filly big-time. Filly had fought off a dozen of Aniseed's monsters after having been summoned by Joy autodialing her phone. The young horsewoman had been most upset that the battle was hardly worth the call, but it had undoubtedly saved Joy's life.

"Don't mention it," Joy said wryly. "I mean that. If Graus Claude found out I was giving away freebies, he'd...well, I have no idea what he'd do, but I'm betting it wouldn't be pleasant."

"Undoubtedly correct," Filly agreed. "However, you have nothing to fear." She hopped down off the table and adjusted the ram's horn at her belt. "Besides, whoever said I would not be paying you? I thought to save you and I a bit of headache and give it back in trade. Take this."

She thrust a drawstring bag into Joy's hand. It had a spiral pictogram stitched on its front and it was filled with tiny rolls of paper, brown and thin and scaly.

"That's vellum," Filly said helpfully. "Draw that there—" she swirled her finger around the tiny bag's decoration "—on the back. Write a message on the other side and burn it in a fire and it will appear here." She showed a similar pouch attached to her own belt. "You can send messages to me without risking my wrath by ringing a bell. And I can write you without raising your ire." She smiled. "I've seen your ire. It is most impressive!"

"Thanks," Joy said, wondering why the young Nordic warrior was offering to be pen pals. "But why do you want to hear from me?"

Filly tapped the side of her head with her knuckle. "I *hear* things, lots of things," she said. "Lately, lots of things about *you*. And I like to be the one to hear things first. Especially straight from the horse's mouth."

A creepy chill writhed in Joy's stomach. "What sort of things?"

"Nothing you can't handle," Filly said and laughed at Joy's expression. "Relax. You've got heart, Joy Malone, as well as Ink's plums in your pocket. What do you have to fear?"

Joy hid her blush by wiping the scalpel against her jeans. She didn't want to think about what she feared. "What sort of things would you expect me to write?"

Filly leaped onto the stairs like a joyful colt. "Well now, I imagine most often you will write things like 'Help! Help!' but if you care to share anything else, I'm always interested in knowing what Folks're going on about."

"You want me to spy for you?"

Filly whickered a sly raspberry and crossed her arms, vambraces shining under the track lights. "Don't be daft," she said. "You're about as subtle as a stampede. Spying's sly work and neither of us are good at it. But things *happen* around you—things are *drawn* to you, yah?" She winked. "Well consider me to be one of those things, and I like to know the company I keep. You're a friend of Ink's and a friend of Inq's and now ensconced with the likes of the Bailiwick." She leaned over and took a deep sniff. "And you reek of wizards. That's quite a package, hmm? So keep me in the loop and I'll watch your back. Fair enough?"

"More than fair," Joy said, relieved and pocketing the pouch. "Thanks."

"I'll be looking forward to your messages," Filly said and waved. "Good night and good morrow, Joy Malone!" she sang as she vaulted the stairs and jumped out into a characteristic clap of light and thunder, which set off Joy's phone. Joy switched it off, debating whether or not she should introduce the blonde warrior woman to the wonders of AT&T.

Her phone buzzed. Glancing down, she read, Sorry, Cabana Girl. Thanks for saving my skin.

Joy smiled. Ilhami.

Sokay, Joy typed back. Just don't do it again.

No promises, he texted back. But I'll be more careful next time. Joy snorted. "Next time," already? I owe you.

Joy shook her head and typed back, Put it on my tab.

She hit Send, feeling that she was getting more tangled in entanglements. In a world of checks and balances, she was digging herself in deeper by the minute. She glanced at her other text message, swore and hit Call Back.

"I'm sorry!" Joy said as Monica picked up. "I'm sorry, I'm sorry, I'm sorry!"

"That and a packet of peanuts won't even get me into the circus," Monica said drily. "Where the heck have you been?"

"Out. Busy. Dead. Skydiving." Joy struggled to think of something plausible. Anything but the truth. She felt a stabbing pain that had nothing to do with guilt. "Mostly fighting with Stef."

"About?" Monica prompted.

"I broke the door."

"You broke the door? What door?"

"Our front door," Joy said around the sudden twinge in her side. "I sort of broke it and Stef wants me to pay to get it fixed before Dad comes home." She traced her finger against the clean slate wall. It was cold.

"That sucks," Monica said. "Waitressing lunches doesn't even pull minimum wage."

"Oh," Joy said. "Didn't I tell you? I have a new job. I didn't even have to wait the two weeks." Her words were tripping over themselves as if running downhill. Lying made her heart race. "The pay's great, but it's still going to take some time to save up."

"A new job?" Monica asked. "Doing what?"

Joy winced. Monica had helped her with her résumé when she'd applied to Antoine's for the summer. Her best friend knew *exactly* how unqualified Joy was for any sort of work, let alone anything that could pay well. Joy scoured her mind for something suitably outlandish.

"Um, remember that guy that picked us up at Evergreen Walk?"

"The hottie with the accent and the GPS? The one who's dating the sister of your mysterious tattoo artist boyfriend whom I have still never met? Your 'significant-other-in-law'?" Monica said. "No, I can't say that I recall."

"Ha ha," Joy said, feeling her gut twist. "Well, he got me a job...as a personal shopper." Joy wanted to throw up. The lie tasted like spoiled sour cream on her tongue.

"A personal shopper?" Monica said. "For who?"

"His sister," Joy said. "Back in Russia." She grabbed her water bottle to swallow something clean. "She's got money to burn and likes American things." The words kept coming as her brain screamed *Lies! Lies! Lies!* How was she supposed to keep track of them all? She sat on her hand to still its trembling, scrunching her eyes against a sudden panic-attack headache. How many times had her mother lied like this? How did she do it? Was it worth it? Why? Joy rubbed her scalp. "She tells me what she likes and her sizes and I send her links." It felt like she was about to get a nosebleed—the pressure was like a bubble of phlegm. Joy squeezed the bridge of her nose. "If she likes stuff and buys it...I get a percentage." The feeling passed. Joy breathed through the tightness easing behind her eyes. She blinked a few times. *Ow.* At least now she could think clearly.

"Sweet setup," Monica said. "Go you."

Joy rested her face in her hands, her legs feeling weak. "Yeah," she said, wiping away her sweaty bangs. "But we're not supposed to be talking about me, here. We're supposed to be talking about *you.*" She took another deep drink to clear her mouth and her head. This was important. This was Monica. "This, here, talking? You wanted to talk, and I know it's late, but if you still need to talk, I'm here. Or I can just listen. Anything you need." She paused self-consciously. "I'll stop talking now."

There was a pause, then a stuttering sound like static on the phone. It took a moment for Joy to realize it was Monica breathing through a sob.

"I think I just broke up with Gordon," she said.

Joy rubbed her forehead. "You think you did? Or you did?"

"I'm not sure," Monica said. "We went for a drive and said a lot of things and I ended up yelling something awful, but I can't remember what most of it was. I just remember the look on his face and I said I couldn't take it, so I left." Joy was having trouble understanding most of what Monica was saying. The words were coming very fast and squeezed through the phone, choked up and thin. "We'd taken my car." Monica sniffed. "And I didn't go back to get him. I left him stranded at the park!"

Joy twisted her fingers in her lap. That sounded bad.

"Did you *want* to break up with him?"

"No," Monica said slowly. "It was just...easier. To be mad." She inhaled a great gulping sob. "But it's *awful!* He won't answer his phone, and I've sent a hundred texts and emails to apologize and so far, nothing." Joy heard her friend's voice muffled by tissues. "I *deserve* the silent treatment, okay? I get that. I was a brat. I own it. But I can't say I'm sorry if he won't pick up the phone!"

"Have you gone over to his house?" Joy asked.

"No. That seems a little too sparkly-vampire-stalker for me," Monica said. "I'm desperate, yes, but not so desperate as to have the door literally slammed in my face. I have some pride." She sniffed again. "Okay, not much, but some."

Joy kicked her heels and sighed. Sometimes having an invisible boyfriend was easier than having a flesh-and-blood one. "I wish I could tell you what to do."

"Yes," Monica said. "Please! *Please* tell me what to do! You are my best friend and Gordon's a great guy and I screwed up and I really need someone to tell me what to do because I'm out of ideas and I feel miserable knowing that he's miserable and mad at me, too, and this whole time everything was perfect until I opened my big mouth and started being scared." She took a deep breath. "How do I fix it, Joy? How do I take it back?"

Joy rubbed a hand over her eyes, feeling her sugar levels dive. Stress did that to her, and things had been more stressful in the past forty-eight hours than they'd been in the past four months. She took a deep breath. What would Monica say to her?

"Say you're sorry," she said, wiping the drying sweat off

her forearms. "Keep saying you're sorry over and over until he hears you. Until he gets it." Joy tucked a hair behind her ear. "If he loves you, he'll forgive you. That's what good boy-friends do."

Monica sighed and sniffled. "I'm a lousy girlfriend."

"Everybody makes mistakes," Joy said. "Try harder next time."

She could hear the tears start again. Monica's voice was damp.

"I really want there to be a next time."

"So tell him that," Joy said. "You are beautiful and funny and smart and an awesome dancer and a very best friend. What's not to love?"

"You should tell him that." Monica laughed.

"I will the next time we all get together," Joy promised. "Meanwhile, I think we both need a breather. Take a break from groveling and I'll meet you downtown for coffee and shoes. I think we need some girl time, just the two of us."

Monica hesitated. "That almost makes up for blowing off my phone calls."

"I'm sorry..." Joy said.

"I know. I get it. Apology accepted," Monica said, taking a cleansing breath. "Okay. How about tomorrow?"

"Tomorrow. You got it," Joy said. "Ten a.m. First purchase, my treat."

Monica chuckled weakly. "My, my, Miss Moneybags. Do I hear some new shoes calling my name?"

"I was thinking more like caramel lattes."

"I think you need your ears adjusted," Monica said through a last stuffy sniffle. "Thanks, Joy. You're BFF gold."

Joy looked at her arm, humming with honeyed glyphs. "Anytime," she said, and she was surprised to find that she was smiling. "Love you, lady."

"Love you, too."

"And remember," Joy said. "No Stupid."

"Pshht." Monica sighed. "Too late."

Joy thumbed off her phone, feeling better. Exhausted but better. Enrique was right: real life was really all about this.

There was a polite tap at the top of the stairs. A uniformed driver held an armful of file folders and tipped the brim of his hat.

"Here for the files," he said. "And for you, Miss Malone." He straightened at the waist as impeccably as his employer. "The Bailiwick sent the car for you, miss. You should come at once. Master Ink is waiting."

She'd heard all she needed to hear. Joy grabbed her purse and vaulted the steps, pausing only to say two words: "Let's go."

She woke when the car rolled up to the brownstone steps. Kurt was waiting by the curb, a hand in his jacket, looking stern. Joy let herself be pulled from the car and whisked through the front door and into the lobby. She hadn't even registered her feet touching the stairs.

There were no courtesies, no greetings, no rebuke—Kurt escorted her swiftly into the Bailiwick's office, sat her down and shut the doors.

It was dark. The shades had been drawn, the cheery sunlight shunned. Water still burbled from the flanking fountains, but it took a moment for Joy to register any other sound. Graus Claude was not at his desk but in the corner of his bookshelves, consulting a large tome on a pedestal. Ink stood next to him, holding the sword. They both looked up as Kurt departed.

Joy dropped her purse on the floor and crossed her ankles. She always felt like she ought to be wearing a skirt here. With hose.

"Miss Malone," Graus Claude rumbled. One of his hands

flipped the page. Two others crossed their arms. The fourth scratched the side of his cheek with one claw. "I trust your journey was uneventful. I apologize for the necessary inconvenience, but it was urgent that we speak." He glanced once at Ink and made his way across the room, his giant feet shuffling over the hardwood as his massive head swayed back and forth. He eased himself down behind his desk and smoothed his calloused hands over the carved armrests. "Ink and I have been discussing the matter, and I need you to describe this obstinate attacker in your own words." Four sets of fingers threaded together as his pointy teeth flashed. "Please."

Joy glanced at Ink, but his face was blank and his eyes of bottomless night told her nothing. Graus Claude similarly gave no indication of what he expected other than what he'd requested. She wondered who was suspicious of what and who was proving what to whom. She felt a knot of guilt in her stomach as she imagined Ink's opinion of her secret joint venture with the Bailiwick at Dover Mill. She knew she could never lie to Ink if he asked.

"It...he looks like a knight in a red suit of armor. He usually has a sword, although this last time he had two. When Ink..." She trailed off. Ink didn't move, but his body language screamed guilt and warning. Joy switched pronouns quickly. "When we thought it was over, I remember looking at the guy's throat—for a pulse—there was no movement."

Graus Claude watched her with those icy-blue eyes like shards under his protruding browridge. "Are you sure it was a 'he'?" he asked.

"I think so," Joy said, recalling details. "The way his voice sounded, how he moved, other things." She was familiar enough with kinetics to recognize gymnasts from their routines on the floor. She knew there was something different about the last knight from the way he moved: his gait had been different, his fighting style changed.

The great toad was inhumanly large, especially up close. "Did you ever see its face?"

"No." There was a twinge in her shoulder as she sat up in her chair, and something shifted in her body and her memory. "Wait. The first time I saw it, his lower faceplate came off. It..." Images clashed. Something wasn't right. "He had a gray, bristly jaw." She looked at Ink, whose eyes were flat as plastic. "And blue teeth."

The Bailiwick sighed. "And did you check the dead man for blue teeth?"

She didn't know. Ink shook his head. They hadn't.

"No," Ink said.

"But the second time, he was clean-shaven and pale," Joy said. "When I looked at his throat...for a pulse..."

The Bailiwick's attention shifted to Ink. "And what did you do with the body?"

"Inq offered to take care of it," he said quietly. "I was not familiar with what to do in the circumstances." Joy winced.

"Indeed," his employer replied. "In any case, I surmise that his teeth—should you have taken the time to check—would not have been blue." Graus Claude picked up the old sword as he addressed Joy. "A blood-colored knight, always bearing a weapon, whose clear intent was on nothing else, no one else, but you. Is that correct?" Joy nodded. The Bailiwick's hands fanned in a hopeless gesture. "It's the Red Knight."

No one said anything, so Joy spoke up. "Who?"

Graus Claude ignored her, shaking his head in dismay. "I apologize for my gross oversight," he said. "It seems I underestimated the severity of the sentiment against you and the lengths to which it had been pursued. It does, however, explain the elusive quality of our quarry having been able to supersede the Edict and evade Ink's swift justice, but—as Sir Doyle so aptly observed—'once you eliminate the impossible, whatever remains, however improbable, must be the truth.'"

"That's Sherlock Holmes," Joy said.

"A character *written by* Sir Arthur Conan Doyle," Graus Claude said evenly. "In any case, it explains everything except your inestimable ability to remain alive, Miss Malone. It quite defies probability." The toad's eyes turned to slits. "You still have that boon, don't you?"

"The four-leaf clover?" Joy said. "I keep it in my wallet."

His great arms spread as if to say, *Well, there we are, then*, and rested all four on the desk. "Unbelievable," he said. "I am forced to admit that I am completely astonished by either your auspicious luck or the whim of blind providence."

"But who is the Red Knight?" she asked.

"An assassin," the Bailiwick said. "The ultimate assassin. The Red Knight possesses a flawless record, a daunting reputation, and exists for a single purpose, which, in this case, is to kill you." Graus Claude grumbled as if it were a personal insult and not a chilling death sentence. Joy squeezed her elbows to keep still. "Unfortunately, the Red Knight is not so much a 'who' as a 'what'—since the Red Knight is a title, an auspice that is taken on willingly within mercenary leagues. Anyone can assume the auspice and become the Red Knight. If a Red Knight dies, another manifests its *signatura* with slight alteration and takes its place, resuming the task that the previous knight left unfulfilled." The great toad shook his head. "There is no stopping the Red Knight once it has been assigned—it will keep coming, returning again and again as different mercenaries, until the terms of the contract have been fulfilled." He groaned with exasperation or effort to move himself in his chair. "You see, now, why the knights you saw did not act similarly nor carry the same weapons nor use the same tactics? They were *different* Red Knights. It explains Jaiveer Sungte and his elemental blade— he must have been the last Red Knight since the Old Wars, enjoying his golden years, which is the last recorded sight-ing of one hunting in the Twixt." He cocked his browridge in Ink's direction. "Once he saw you, Master Ink, he must have realized what protected Miss Malone—not only a Scribe, but the Edict, as well. He could not have hoped to succeed, so he fled to incarnate the next Red Knight." He tossed the sword aside. "So much for retirement."

Joy tightened her hold on herself. "I don't understand. How would that change anything?"

The Bailiwick stroked the edge of the desk, an almost self-conscious gesture. "The Edict binds all within the Twixt to the Council's decree by their *signaturae,* the leash of our True Names. For Jaiveer Sungte, this prevented him from doing you harm because he, as the Red Knight, was bound to obey the Edict because he was the one bearing the *signatura* at that time. Yet the Red Knight's contract is binding, as well, and he could not fulfill it. In order for the Red Knight to succeed, a new Red Knight would have to take his place, one who would 'refresh' the *signatura,* conveniently outside the original parameters of the Edict." Graus Claude stretched for an analogy. "Are you familiar with *seppuku?* An honorable death to avoid disgrace?" Joy shook her head mutely. "It is the closest equivalent, but imminently more practical since with the death of Sungte, the next Red Knight could take his place. Because the Red Knight's *signatura* is transferable, it changes slightly, binding itself to the next individual's own *signatura.* While Sungte as the Red Knight was bound by the Edict, the newest Red Knight was not. Nor would be the one after that. Nor the one after that." The Bailiwick sniffed. "A neat loophole the Council has not considered before this." He cast a baleful eye at the blade on the floor. "You can keep killing them, Master Ink, but the Red Knight is innumerable, unstoppable. He is a death sentence."

"He is an assassin," Ink said. "They are each—whomever they are—hired killers." He looked like he wanted to reach out to Joy. "Anyone solely motivated by greed can be dissuaded by wealth."

"Master Ink, you cannot simply 'buy off' the Red Knight," the Bailiwick said. "The knight is not motivated merely by riches. He is bound by contract, inviolate until either the contract is fulfilled or the order is rescinded, forfeiting the not-inconsiderable fee." A single claw tapped the desk. "Should you offer to bribe the Red Knight, he would most likely use that moment of parlay to kill Miss Malone or, should he take the money, be obligated to kill her at another time, fulfilling the terms of his contract and then killing himself shortly thereafter for breaking an agreement with you. He is bound until death." He glanced between Joy and Ink meaningfully. "I assure you that none who bear the Red Knight's mark would consider such an offer for even a moment."

Joy sat against the back of the chair, her body exhausted from its near-constant exposure to fear the past few days. She felt a helpless cry bubbling in the back of her throat. She swallowed hard and rubbed her eyes.

"Our one advantage thus far is that it has had difficulty finding you," Graus Claude said. "Usually it tracks an individual by its *signatura*, like a bloodhound, but you are human so it must be stalking you, learning your patterns of movement, lying in wait for you to appear or to mark you in some manner in order to track you." Ink missed the subtle insinuation, but Joy understood, thinking of the ghostly mark still ablaze on her back. Could that be it? Not a *signatura*, but a tag? A tracer? A target drawn directly on her skin? "But as that is not the case," he added smoothly, "there is an opportunity to keep you safe by removing your set patterns and order of operations—unless you plan to remain in your home until this matter can be resolved?"

"I thought no one could stop the Red Knight from fulfilling its contract," Ink said.

The Bailiwick clicked his wireless mouse and the computer monitor sprang to life. "I said it must either fulfill its contract or have its orders rescinded," Graus Claude said while opening various applications. "I intend to alert the Council about this gross infraction and the loophole and force a retraction. We won't even have to identify the culprit, although I would dearly like to pursue that vein, but time is of the essence and an Amendment can produce the necessary results that a lengthy investigation cannot. We will have to sacrifice identity for immediacy."

"How long will that take?" Joy asked.

"To pass an Amendment?" Graus Claude said. "I'd rather not presume."

"It cannot wait," Ink said.

"Indeed not," the Bailiwick agreed, typing with two hands as the third kept hold of the mouse. "Miss Malone will be brought before the Council as soon as the charges levied against her are next in queue. She must present herself and her preference of choice regarding judgment, and we must assure that she lives long enough to make her appearance. The Council does not abide delays." His fourth hand scratched the top of his head. "I will use that argument to boost its rank on the agenda."

"I have another idea," Joy said.

Both Ink and Graus Claude looked at her. Ink's face did say something this time: *speak carefully*. Joy took a sip of water to buy a second to think.

"Ink gave me a protective pendant, but it broke," she said. "That one thing saved my life."

"You wish to have another such protection?" Graus Claude asked.

"No. A better one," Joy said. "I'd like to use the Red Knight's *signatura* in a ward." Joy carefully avoided saying too much. She didn't want to get Inq into trouble in case Graus Claude disapproved. Without his pair of gold-rimmed glasses, he couldn't see the invisible golden armor already drawn on her skin. "If I could use it in a protection, then I don't need permission, right? I could safeguard myself against the Red Knight until the Amendment passes."

"Whoever ordered the Red Knight broke the law defying the Edict," Ink added. "This could be reparation until the matter is formally addressed by the Council."

The Bailiwick stopped as if caught with a flashlight under glass. He glanced suspiciously from Joy to Ink and back again, his four arms rigid in their positions of efficient task management. He seemed utterly perplexed.

"That would be...an elegant solution," he said. "One that I imagine the Council would support in the interim to avoid any further abuse of their decree." He paused another fraction of a second. "Yes, I believe that could be managed if the proper details were in alignment." One hand gestured to Joy. "To obtain the current Red Knight's *signatura* will be difficult but not impossible," he said. "Although it might prove to be an...expensive...venture and one which, once it was discovered, will only buy you time until the next Red Knight emerges."

"I will pay for it," Ink said.

Graus Claude's eyes never wavered from Joy. "Although I have no doubt that your earnings could adequately cover whatever costs were involved, Master Ink, the truth of the matter is that this transaction now resides well outside your purview, and is firmly within mine. And while the young lady continues to be your mortal paramour, Miss Malone is regrettably no longer your *lehman* and, as you both have quit the pretense of her ever accepting your *signatura* and thus your formal claim, she is—in a manner of speaking— no longer your affair. While she may accept your offer, this conversation and contract is between Miss Malone and me."

Joy felt as if her seat had tilted out from under her, but she thought she understood. Graus Claude was giving her a convenient cover story, if she was willing to take it.

"I'll pay for it," she said. "I can do some work for you." She suggested it casually, as if it were merely a passing thought, but many unsaid things passed between them just then. And all witnessed by Ink. Joy felt her insides harden. So much for the glamour. Or the door repairs. Or her cut of the fees. The Bailiwick had trapped her neatly. She was too angry to be impressed...or too impressed to be angry, and all too aware of Ink standing there listening to every word.

"Very good," Graus Claude said with an ill-disguised grin. "Then I shall discover the Red Knight's sigil for you and give it—"

"To Inq," Ink said. "It would be safest."

Graus Claude paused the merest instant. "Do you agree, Miss Malone?" Joy was ashamed and embarrassed that he was ignoring Ink while asking her permission and that Ink felt he must interject himself on her behalf. In a world of favors and influence, she appreciated that Graus Claude acknowledged her as her own person and not an extension or property of Ink, but she *really* wished he'd simply let her boyfriend throw money at the problem. She understood that this way she could explain her working for the Bailiwick in terms Ink could understand when she got around to telling him. It was all growing so complicated! Ink looked both surprised and confused, but she felt too awkward juggling so many unsaid things to be suitably reassuring. She simply nodded.

"Very well, then," the Bailiwick said. "I shall bend every resource toward these efforts and offer my personal assurance that they shall be completed to your satisfaction." He smiled again, looking quite satisfied already. Joy groaned internally. *Arrogant frog.*

Ink bowed at the waist, both stiff and formal. "Thank you again, Bailiwick."

"Yes," Joy said flatly. "Thank you."

"It is my duty, my honor and a pleasure, as always, to help those in need," he said without even a hint of irony. "But do take care to keep yourself intact so that we might all enjoy the fruits of my labor as I toil to correct the mistakes wrought against you." His ice-blue eyes glittered. "Pray do nothing too foolish in the meanwhile."

Joy pressed her purse to her stomach. "Oh, don't worry," she said. "My best friend and I have a saying, No Stupid."

"A wise friend," he said. "Now off with you—back behind your wards. I'd not appreciate the Red Knight blustering in here. It would be a terror on the woodwork and most likely soil the carpets."

Ink strode to the door, but Joy lingered to shoot a hot whisper across the desk.

"I take it I should log in some extra hours?"

Graus Claude was busy typing on his computer and clicked the mouse with a third hand. "Why wait?" he purred with a smile and clicked a button. "As a human, you should appreciate that there's no time like the present."

ELEVEN

JOY WAS OPEN FOR BUSINESS WITH EXTENDED HOURS, and, according to the files delivered by courier within moments of her arrival, she'd have plenty of clients lining up at the door any minute. Joy's mind boggled at how Graus Claude could possibly keep this well-known secret a secret for long. She readied herself for a long shift reminiscent of late-night cram sessions for school. She could hardly believe that summer was almost over and senior year was almost here. Of course, before then she would have to answer to the Council, make a decision to keep her freedom or Ink and somehow manage to pay for—at last count—a *signatura,* her cell phone bill, another tank of gas, a glamour and a front door. She sighed and took out her scalpel, already regretting calling off her date with Ink.

He'd been hurt. She'd never broken a date before—they'd been too precious, too rare, too brief—and couldn't come up with any good excuse so gave a lame, "Something came up," which was true, but didn't make it any easier. It was as if Ink could feel her withdrawal, catch the scent of withholding, the slightest pulling away, watching a strange distance yawn between them that he was uncertain how to avoid.

He had hesitated, watching, looking for clues, but she'd

given him none. He'd left her at her door without another word, safe behind wards.

And she had left that safety as soon as he'd gone, taken the Kia and the scalpel and driven out to Dover Mill.

So much for No Stupid.

Joy shuffled her files and scanned the first entry just as her phone buzzed. She looked at the screen.

Where are you?!?!?

It was Stef, and Stef sounded pissed. Joy thumbed off the screen and plunked it into her purse. Let him find her, if he could. He could download an app. Or hire Kestrel to track her. She was staying here until she'd chipped away at some of her debt.

There was a sound on the stairs.

"Come in," she called up and waited for the footfalls to draw closer.

And when they did, there was Ink.

Joy froze, her body tingling in all-over shock—scalpel in hand and hand on table—caught. Ink's eyes were flat, reflecting none of the light, and his expression, which had always been hard to read before, was as blank as the slate wall.

"Ink—"

"No," he said flatly. "No more lies."

She swallowed. "I didn't lie." It was a stupid thing to say.

His chin tipped infinitesimally to the left. "What interesting things you say," he said. "It is almost as if I am talking to the Bailiwick himself."

She left the scalpel on the table and twisted her hands in her sleeves. "I wanted to tell you, but I didn't…" She shook her head, rattled and rambling. "I just didn't."

"You 'didn't'?"

"Not that I couldn't," she said with honesty. "I could. And

I didn't. And I'm sorry I didn't tell you—I didn't know how or when or what to say..." She groped for the right thing to say. "I'm sorry!"

"You are sorry," Ink said, more a statement than a question as he stepped around the table and examined each of the shelves with mild interest. "For what, exactly?" His fingers traced over the dental tray, the mirror, the minispeakers, the slate wall. Joy's heart pounded hard and heavy with guilt. "For not telling me about this? For keeping it secret? For getting caught?" His face turned to her again, deadly calm. "Or for doing any of this in the first place?"

Joy trembled at his anger, but she deserved it. She deserved every bit. She knew this feeling—the feeling of betrayal, of being the last to know, having been kept in the dark, to have been lied to, even if only by the evasion of the whole truth. It suddenly dawned on her what she had really done. She had a sudden split perspective of being her mother or her father or her brother and herself all at the same time: angry and guilty and ashamed and at a loss. To have caused *that look* on someone's face—someone that she loved—was awful.

She understood more in that moment than she'd ever wanted to know.

"All of it," she said truthfully. "Everything."

Ink strode past her, not touching her, his absence made more poignant by him being so clearly out of reach. Joy cringed. He went to the file boxes but didn't touch them. He merely stared at them.

"This is the Bailiwick's," he said. "Color-coded, alphabetized, fresh labels in bold type."

"Yes."

Ink looked at her like she was an open file, spread bare under the overhead lights. "You are working for him."

She closed her eyes a moment. "Yes."

"Erasing." He said the word as if it were squeezed out of his body. "Removing marks."

"Not yours," she said hastily. "Or Inq's. They're marks of the Twixt on one another—ones that should never have been made or are old or forgotten or cruel. Graus Claude checked. *I* checked. And I never had to do any that I didn't..." But even as she said it, she heard her own arrogance, her own excuses, and it sounded just like her mother on the day she'd left, trying to explain that she had "needs." No matter what she called it, she had still abandoned her family for her young lover across the country. Nothing could undo that. Nothing could change the facts.

"It doesn't matter," Joy said, swallowing pride and blame. "None of it matters because I should have told you. I should have asked you what you thought about it first."

"Yes," Ink said evenly. "Why didn't you?"

Joy let out a long, tight breath. "I was stupid."

"Obviously," Ink said. "You are not heeding your friend Monica." He placed both hands on the table, across from Joy, the scalpel winking in the light between them. "But what I meant to ask was, why do this?" And Joy knew that he was asking many things: *Why do something so dangerous? Why do something so foolish? Why not tell me about this? Why risk getting caught? Why indebt yourself to the Bailiwick and become ensnared in his web? Why agree to willingly endanger yourself and others? Why mess with things beyond your understanding? Why try to lie about it? Why not trust me?*

"I thought..." she started and was frightened to find her feelings had lodged in her throat, making her voice tight and thready. "I thought that I could earn my way in the Twixt, that I could do something valuable that let me into your world—something only *I* could do—that would keep the Council from forcing me to choose your life or mine." She spread her hands, tears threatening to betray her idiocy. "I

thought I could figure it out by myself and solve all our problems and then everything would be perfect."

"Not like this," Ink said, something other than hardness
tingeing his words. "No, Joy. Not like this."

"I *know!*" Joy said, defeated. "But I thought I was doing
something *good*. But then the Bailiwick—"

"The Bailiwick is many things," Ink interrupted smoothly.
"But above all, he is self-serving. One of his most admirable
qualities is his loyalty, but one of his greatest failings is his
capacity for greed." He gestured offhandedly to the cache
office. "It is part of his auspice, part of his nature."

"That is...pretty harsh," Joy said. In fact, it didn't sound
like Ink at all. "Did Inq tell you that?"

Ink gave a half shrug. "More or less."

"I knew that Inq didn't trust the Bailiwick, but you always
did," Joy said. "I thought I could work him."

Ink frowned. "Work him?"

Joy sighed. "Maneuver him to my advantage."

Ink laughed, which was surprising, and shook his head.
"No one can 'work' the Bailiwick and come to a good end. It
is his auspice—his very essence—to be fortune's beneficiary.
He is a Luck Child of the water, that element which stretches,
touching all corners of the world. There is no point pitting
yourself against him, which is why he is so powerful and
commands such respect in the Twixt. He has chosen a role
that serves both our worlds as well as himself, but he would
be the first to admit it is the money and the status that most
appeals to him." Ink looked at her, and she was relieved to
see that some of the warmth was back in his voice. "I imagine that you were surprised to find that he had orchestrated
all of this to his own benefit?"

Joy sank into her seat. "You could say that."

"And I have," he said, leaning against the table. "The
Bailiwick knows many things—the shadows of politics are

foremost among them." He shook his head, and a gentle sympathy slipped back into his voice. "I know that it is his hand that drew you here and it is his debt that holds you to it, but I also know enough to realize that he has his eyes trained on greater things. If he wishes you to be here performing this—" he tasted the word like vinegar "—*service,* then I can only trust that his doing so is part of a larger plan that I cannot fathom in which you are equally blameless. Your being here is no accident." He trailed his fingers over the silver wallet chain, his boyish face thoughtful in profile. "But I do not like it."

Joy leaned her elbows on the table, denting the plush. "So do you think I should stay?"

He glanced at her out of the corner of his eye. "I think you cannot leave."

"Oh," she said into the tense quiet. "Well, if it helps, I was also trying to earn enough to buy you a present."

Ink cocked his head. "A present?" he said. "Your freedom should not be considered a gift for me, but for you."

"I don't mean the Red Knight's *signatura,*" Joy said. "I meant something for you."

"For me?"

"And me," Joy admitted.

"What...?" he began and dropped his head, looking oddly embarrassed. His fingers twitched on his lap. Her hands, her fingers, now his. "What did you have in mind?"

"A glamour," Joy said. "Inq showed me hers and I thought... well, obviously I thought a lot of things and most of them were wrong." She placed her left hand near him on the table. "But I wanted to introduce you to my family and friends. To let them finally meet you, to show you off to them." It sounded stupider than she'd thought it would, having now said it out loud. *I'm* such *an idiot.* "So it wasn't just the Bailiwick that was being self-serving. I wanted to do something for you."

"And for you."

"For us," she said, and when she said that word, she felt the tension melt between them. *There is still an "us,"* she thought. *And that's what Monica's missing right now, what Dad missed after the divorce: suddenly, no "us."* Joy came around the table and stood as close to Ink as she dared without invading his space. The light caught the chain at his hip and the tips of his hair. "Can you do something for us?"

He looked up, his eyes curious and a little afraid.

"What can I do?" he said. "For us?"

"Forgive me?" she said, her heart beating quickly. "Please, *please* forgive me."

It was the longest pause she'd ever known without breath.

"You hurt me," he said gently and pressed two fingers to his chest. "Here."

"I'm sorry," Joy said again, and this time, tears fell. "I am so, so sorry. I never meant to hurt you." She wiped her hands over her cheeks. "It hurts me that I hurt you." She held both hands out, palms up, helpless. "Ink, I am sorry. I am sorry, Ink!"

He stood up and took her hands, placing them around him, folding her against him and completing the circle with his arms. He rocked her, breathing slow, deep breaths, and whispered into her ear. "I forgive you, Joy," he said. "I love you and I forgive you." Joy closed her eyes and tried to press him closer, so she could not be certain if he said the last words or if she'd invented them in her heart:

"I forgive you, Joy, but I do not forget."

Where are you?!?!?!

Joy scrolled past Stef's text as she sat on the guest bed in Enrique's apartment, stifling a yawn. It was his sixth text, copied and pasted and resent. She couldn't even try to explain, so why bother? Her brother clearly didn't approve of her involving herself in the Twixt or being with Ink or getting protective armor, but it wasn't like he was going to run and tell Dad. She mentally chuckled at the thought of being grounded for getting magical, invisible tattoos without parental permission.

"Thanks again for coming to get me," Joy called over the splash of water. Inq had hopped into the shower as soon as they'd arrived. "Ink had to go to some farm town in Poland and I hadn't realized that I'd run out of gas. I didn't know who else to call." While not strictly true, she had decided to leave Stef out of this and keep Filly and her magic message pouch out of the picture for now, too. She was beginning to think the less Folk like Filly and the Bailiwick knew about what she was up to, the better.

"I still can't believe he just stormed in," Inq said in her voice that sliced through white noise. It didn't even sound as if she'd raised her voice—it slipped through the air like a knife.

"I think he was mad," Joy said. "Not mad, exactly, but disappointed."

"I think he's being an idiot." The water shut off, quick and final, without any faulty last drips. "He still thinks of you as perfect and this has thrown him off, but hey—no excuse. He knows you're being hunted by this Red Knight and he knows you agreed to work for the Bailiwick. I bet he's just sore your life's not all about him. Men are such babies." Inq huffed as she walked into the room, wrapped in a thick, fluffy bath sheet, her *signaturae* flying over her water-warmed skin. Joy remembered that her marks were temperature sensitive. Inq grinned at Joy staring at her.

"You ready?" she asked impishly and then opened her bath sheet, flashing Joy.

"Hey!" Joy shouted, averting her eyes.

"I thought it only fair," Inq said, tucking her towel back into place. "I show you mine before you show me yours? I thought it would make you feel more comfortable."

"Yeah, well, it doesn't," Joy said, trying to scrub the mental image of a perfectly formed alabaster statue out of her head. "Get dressed and *then* you can complete the armor, okay?"

"Of course," Inq said, opening a drawer. Joy shouldn't have been surprised that Inq kept some clothes in Enrique's apartment. "That's why I brought you here. I thought if I couldn't get past the wards in your room, at least this would feel more familiar." She zipped on a sleeveless silver leather corset and picked up a thong. "Besides, I warded this place seven ways from Sunday." She glanced at Joy as she tugged on skintight black jeans. "Why are you still dressed?"

"Is this a trick question?"

"Well, I thought it was pretty obvious from the last time," Inq said. "Anything we didn't get to before we're doing now." Joy crossed her legs and hunched forward. Inq frowned. "What?"

"Is that strictly necessary?" Joy asked.

Inq laughed. "You're wise to ask, and while I admit to getting a teeny tiny thrill out of making you squirm, the truth is that, yes, we want to shield you from head to foot and everything in between. Ever heard of Achilles? We don't want you dying of a crotch-shot. So," she said turning magnanimously around. "You get undressed while my back is turned, slide under the sheet and we'll take it from there." Joy could hear the grin in her voice. "I promise to be gentle."

"Ha ha," Joy said, but she didn't feel like laughing.

Being on a team full of girls had nullified Joy's body shyness years ago, but even having one of her teammates ask her out on a date hadn't weirded her out nearly as much as the thought of having Inq draw on her skin a second time. As much as Joy understood the logic and that Inq was doing her an illicit sort of favor, she *really* wished there could have been another way. Even the memory of floating on waves of warm light didn't comfort as much as terrify her now. Her stomach dropped out, releasing butterflies of panic. She tried to swallow her nervousness along with a mouthful of spit.

Joy removed her clothes with her back to Inq, folded them neatly into a pile on the floor, adjusted the sheet to be certain it covered everything and tried to imagine this as getting a massage to save her life.

"Ready?" Inq chirped.

"Sort of."

"Don't be nervous," the Scribe chided and bounced over to the bed. "We'll start with something simple. Strictly first base."

Joy laughed and that helped with some of the jitters. Turning up Enrique's surround sound helped more. He had sophisticated tastes in music that were distracting as well as soothing. Inq, as promised, was professionally distant and Joy finally relaxed under the feather touches of languid, liquid heat. She lost herself to the thrum of the music as Inq traced something on her hip.

"You seem to be doing better," Inq said.

"Amazing considering someone's trying to kill me," Joy said, checking to see if Monica had called to keep her mind off what Inq's hands were doing. No new calls or texts. Joy debated whether that was a good sign or not. "Actually, I'm currently feeling pretty good about my chances at beating this thing."

"Especially now that I've got this." Inq waved a little paper in front of Joy's face; it had an elaborate scribble with three arrows jutting out of its base. Graus Claude had produced it within hours—"impossible" clearly being a matter of mood. She wondered how much the sigil was going to cost her in American dollars. "With the Red Knight's *signatura*, there's no way he can touch you." The Scribe was almost giddy, as if she were a kid sneaking cookies instead of thumbing her nose at the Council's failure. Joy didn't know what Inq had against authority, but she wasn't complaining.

"I'm hoping that Graus Claude can call him off first," Joy said. "Not that I doubt your work, but I'd rather not have it put to the test."

"No offense taken," Inq said. "I'm impressed that you've gotten so much out of the Bailiwick. He must like you." She drew a sloping line down Joy's thigh. Joy squeezed her knees against the awkward tickle. "I've barely gotten more than a civil smile out of him in years. I don't know how you do it."

"Must be my feminine wiles."

Inq squinted down at Joy. "Obviously," she said. "Now roll over. I want to put the keystone at your throat."

Joy obediently turned over, holding the sheet to her chest, adjusting the pillow under her head and keeping her eyes on the ceiling so she wouldn't stare up Inq's nose. It was sort of like being at the dentist or the gynecologist, although the way Inq smirked at her would be considered totally unprofessional in the medical community.

The Scribe placed her thumbs along Joy's collarbones, pressing firmly down. The almost-heat spread between them like a circuit humming under her skin, a strange electricity pooling and trickling down her chest. Inq consulted the slip of paper, tracing the shape of the glyph with her forefinger, holding Joy in place with a touch of her left hand. Joy felt the *signatura* growing, heard it crackle, sizzling softly and sinking into her body as the power took shape. She swallowed it back, thick as honey. Closing her eyes, she concentrated on the feeling, like a handprint over her heart. She tried not to panic. There was a deep tugging, like magnets being kept purposely apart but inexorably drawing together.

"Almost done," Inq whispered, more to herself than Joy.

Inq moved her thumbs, and Joy could picture the three arrows as they were drawn with aching slowness. The edge of Inq's fingernail scraped the final stroke. Joy felt it drag along the backs of her knees, a single hairline of pain cutting through a haze of the strange compulsion gripping her limbs, torquing her bones. Her whole body shuddered as the armor coalesced, links clicking together, sparks snapping into place. A wave of scorching heat brought a thin sheen of sweat to the surface. Joy gasped, eyes wide, and half sat up.

Inq winked. "Was it good for you, too?"

Joy bunched the sheet under her chin and blushed uncomfortably. "Ha ha."

"Seriously," Inq said. "How do you feel?"

Joy flexed her arm, watching the filigree threads of power slide with clockwork grace. Glyphs shone at her major joints, strung along her limbs and bones like beads. They tangled together in clusters of cursive hieroglyphs, thin tendrils burning delicately over her fingers, eyelids and mouth. She touched the Red Knight's *signatura* at her throat as if she could feel it there.

Indelible. Indomitable. Invisible Inq's.

"Amazing," Joy said. The heady rush that she'd experienced before, warm and wonderful, had intensified, focused down to minute detail. Her eyes swam with colors absent in the silver-black room. It was as if the lights had fragmented, throwing off bits of rainbows that shimmered behind her eyes. The walls had ripples. The music shone.

Inq smiled, pleased. "And here is my gift to you," she said and opened her hand. Joy offered up her own and Inq turned it over, drawing two circles in the center of Joy's palm. It tickled as it cooled. "It's not part of the armor. It's a ripple," Inq said. "A push. Just a little one, but enough to give you some space if you need it." She folded Joy's fingers over it. "A little something from me to you. A girl can't be too careful."

Joy curled her fingers as if holding a secret. "Thanks."

"I couldn't do anything with that ugly splotch on your back," Inq said. "I had to draw over it."

Joy sighed. "Yeah, well, I can't seem to remove it, either," she confessed. "I've tried over and over and still nothing."

"Maybe it'll stay until the contract is up or the Red Knights are all dead."

Joy pulled the pillows closer. "Great."

"Oh, and one more thing." Inq tried to sound casual. "Do you want Ink's?"

Joy frowned slightly. "Ink's what?"

"Ink's *signatura*."

"What?" Joy balked. "Ink would never hurt me."

"True," Inq said. "Although 'never' is a long time and you hurt him today." Joy shifted under the covers and wondered how much Inq knew. Bargaining with Graus Claude for the Red Knight's *signatura* was equal parts protection and cover story, but Inq didn't know that; she probably thought Joy was still saving up for the glamour. "But that's not the sort of hurt I can shield you from, anyway. That's Ladybird's domain," she said with a sneer. "I was thinking more along the lines of tacit permission—a lock instead of a ward, separate from the armor. Not to be indelicate, Joy, but my brother's taking this whole trying-to-be-more-human thing very seriously now that you're in the picture, and he might not realize what he's getting into *if* you know what I mean." Joy didn't like to think that she knew *exactly* what Inq meant. She blushed. The Scribe shrugged. "Think of it as magical birth control. I won't lie to you—halflings happen." Inq leaned close to Joy's face, black eyes glinting. "And, like I said, a girl can't be too careful."

Joy imagined Ilhami's enormously pregnant booby doll with the scribbled-on eyes. "But what if..." Joy stopped. She didn't want to sound naive or slutty.

"Relax. You of all people could erase any one of these glyphs or the whole thing, if you chose. I wouldn't link it to the others. You could unlock it anytime," Inq said. "That's the point—it would be *your* choice. No one else could take that from you, even by accident," she said as she propped herself up on one elbow. "Guys get a little 'overwhelmed' their first time doing just about anything. Normally, I'd use your *signatura*, but since you don't have one, I could use his to the same effect. Warding him off instead of locking you to yours—make sense?" Her face went a little funny. "Ink is the only one right now, right?"

The heat on Joy's face had nothing to do with the glyphs. "Yes," she said. "I mean, he hasn't...we haven't..." Joy glared at Inq's snorting fit of giggles. "There's no one else, no." Joy tucked the sheet under her armpits. "But I trust him. I don't think we would do anything 'together' unless we decided it together."

"Ugh, monogamy." Inq might have rolled her eyes, but the effect was lost with all-black orbs. "I'll never understand it. Thankfully, immortality releases you from all those pesky human definitions." She rolled onto her belly, staring over her bare shoulder at Joy. "After eons, trust me, *nothing* is off-limits."

Joy tried to sound neutral. "I am."

Inq blinked. "Of course you are, silly," she said, spanking Joy's arm. "You're Ink's and he's yours. I'm the one who put you two together, remember?" She clapped her hands in rapid glee. "This is just a little insurance. Personally, I can't *wait* to see how things turn out!"

"Yeah, well, we're not picking out baby names yet," Joy said, regaining her composure. "I think I really shook him this afternoon."

"I know," Inq said. "But you can make it up to him in a minute. He's waiting for you outside in the hall."

"*What?*" Joy whispered and grabbed the sheet, yanking it over her glowing body pulsing with light. "He's here? Now?" Joy grabbed for her stack of clothes.

"Well, I wasn't about to do something like this without him here," Inq said reasonably. Joy once again marveled at the wide range of meanings of *something like this.* Inq shrugged. "He's my brother, after all." The timbre of her voice dipped lower. "But, just between us girls...do you want me to draw his sigil on you or not?"

Inching back, Joy pulled on her shirt and let go of the sheet.

"Okay," she said. "Do it."

Inq grinned, waggling her fingers. "Don't worry. It'll be our little secret."

Joy emerged from the bedroom to find Ink pacing the kitchen. Enrique watched him from the bar with casual interest. Both men turned as she and Inq entered the room, their expressions revealing everything Joy suspected.

Ink's face went slack, alien with awe. He stared at the light shining off her in undulating waves. It surrounded her in gossamer threads, suffusing the walls and filling his eyes— she could see herself in them and the thoughts that swam there: she was glorious. A goddess. Her skin warmed like sunlight, outlining his body. She smiled as she shone, a golden angel on unsteady footsteps.

"It will fade in due time," Inq said from behind Joy's shoulder. "It is freshly made and should settle in soon. Enjoy it while it lasts." She glanced at her brother's face with a sympathetic moue. "Don't they act adorable when you're so pretty?"

"Ink," Joy said from miles away. She saw his eyes follow the shape of his name on her lips. "Are you okay?"

The word came from him, unbidden. "Yes."

She did not feel reassured. He was worshipping her every

word—it was a little unnerving. "I wanted to tell you...I wanted to say again that I was sorry," she said. "About this afternoon."

"This afternoon?" he said, as if unfamiliar with the words.

"Yes," she said. "At the cache."

Ink nodded very slightly, a dip of his chin. "He said it was to keep you safe," Ink said, reaching out as if afraid to touch her, as if to verify that she was real and worried that she wasn't. "When I asked him. The Bailiwick." He looked dazed, possibly dazzled. Joy was unsure what to feel. Fumbling to find where she was in the world—she still felt like she was floating, tethered with ribbons of light. It was as if she were looking down on herself from above, spliced tunnel vision hidden in the crown molding. Ink was acting strange. His eyes were intense, their warmth palpable. Or maybe it was the glyphs? Or, like he'd said, maybe it was her? Her armor sang a chorus of goose bumps on her skin.

"I promised that I would keep you safe from the Red Knight," he told her. "I am bound by it, Joy." His fingers caught a curl of hair by her ear and he fanned his fingertips on the very edge of her cheek. She watched him watching her, transfixed, mystified; his words were both frightening and eerie with desire. Joy couldn't help but feel undeserving and oddly wished he'd kept his simmering anger rather than this sudden, smitten awe. But the way he looked at her was all truth and adoration. Love was written in his every movement as plain as the *signaturae* on her skin. She was shy without words to keep him at bay.

He stepped forward, hand still hovering, still not quite touching—what space left between them growing more heightened, charged.

"Please. Not in the hallway," Inq said, squeezing past with an indulgent smile. "Go home, Joy. Go home, Ink. P.S. Enrique says, 'Hi.'" Joy spied the silver-haired gentleman by the bar giving a sly salute. Inq tapped her brother's shoulder. "She's running very hot right now," Inq whispered by his ear. "Do be careful not to burn up all at once."

He gave no answer but reached behind his back and opened his straight razor, his eyes and fingertips never leaving Joy. He tore a long incision in the universe and guided her toward him by the intensity of his stare, stepping back and through and out and away. Joy followed willingly, gratefully, playfully, eagerly.

She walked into her room and into his arms.

His hands folded around her, curling into her hair, holding the back of her neck and cradling her jaw as their lips met, brimming and full, murmuring sounds of relief. Joy melted. Forgiven. Forgotten. Permission granted. Her arms closed about his waist, the wallet chain delicately sliding against the side of her wrist.

"I love you," Ink said between kisses. "I missed you. I was worried. I thought..." He couldn't stop kissing her, and Joy chuckled against his lips. He smiled self-consciously while stealing another kiss. "I thought, perhaps, now that you have your own protections, your own powers, your own place in the world, that you no longer needed me." He paused in his confession. "That you would no longer want me the way I want you."

"What?" Joy pulled back an inch or two and stared into his eyes framed in thick lashes. "Ink, *this* is wanting. *This* is needing." She squeezed him closer, as close as she could, suffusing herself in strong limbs and the scent of rain. "I love you, Ink, and I want you—*only* you. Being strong doesn't mean I don't want you, too. You are the only person who knows every part of my life, every part of me in it, the good and the bad and the horrible, and you *still* love me." She rested her forehead against his, the tips of their noses almost touching. "You are always with me, even when you're not there.

And when you're not there, I can feel it, like an empty space where you ought to be, and I can hardly wait until you're back to fill it again. Neither world feels like it fits, but *we* belong. Here. Like this." Joy kissed him long and slow and sweet, breaking apart only to catch a breath. "You have never let me down. You are always there for me. You are the best part of me, who I want to be, and every time I look at you I can hardly believe how lucky I am to be with you and I hope you know that." She squeezed her eyes shut and swallowed hard. "Never let me lose you, Ink. Never let me screw this up. And never think for one moment that I don't love you, need you or want you with me."

He stared at her, open and pure.

"Joy," he said. And then ran out of words.

He slid his lips over hers, kissing the end of each filigreed glyph and teasing a gasp from somewhere in her chest.

His hands loosened and slid down her arms, soothing as raindrops, trickles of touch. She tightened her hands on his back, needing something to hold on to, her senses on overload, head swimming, eyes closed. Having been naked for the past hour or more, her clothing seemed unnaturally restrictive now. Her body strained against the seams, hems catching at the buttons; breathing deeply, she felt the fabric pull. He held her so softly, almost reverently; it was *maddening*. Too much was in the way, too many layers between them—sweat wet her bangs as her body burned.

He turned his head to the side, kissing the sigil at her throat, following its curve down the length of her neck as if he could catch droplets of water from the tips of the glyph. His hands held her steady as she bent back and back and back. She unfolded like a dancer, gymnastics had given her a dexterous curve; his forehead rested on her chest as her legs twined in his, her knee clamped over the swell of his hip.

"Joy," he murmured and lifted her, holding her hips and

sliding his hand up her spine to help her look into his eyes. She was dizzy, head ringing, eyes wondrous and wide. "You are my everything," he said to her solemnly, his crisp voice breathy and hoarse. "You are everything that matters to me." His hand gathered her hair at the base of her skull. She was pillowed in his arms. "Tell me you understand," Ink whispered. "Tell me that you feel this, too."

"I do," she said. The room was still whirling. Her lips were kiss-swollen. Her hands held him tight.

"I am *feeling* more," he said as a shudder passed through him, a trickle from the tips of his hair down the slide of his spine. "I feel *everything* more." It was a confession teetering over an exciting precipice. "I cannot express it. I can hardly keep track of it all." He swung her around, dimples framing his wide smile. Sparkles swam in his fathomless eyes. "It is you! All you! Everything!" He leaned his head back and laughed. She hugged him, laughing, too, unsure why, but happy all the same. Ink was happy! He was *happy!* Because they were together. Because of *her.*

"I love you," she said with a smile.

"Yes! I feel it—" he tapped his chest hard with two fingers "—here."

She rubbed the spot tenderly as their circling slowed. They watched her hand rest against him. Here it was: a perfect moment.

"Can you feel this? All of this?"

He inhaled sharply. "Yes."

"What do you feel?" she asked.

He smiled at her and squeezed.

"Joy," he said, laughing. "I feel Joy!"

TWELVE

SHE WAS SKIPPING. JOY COULDN'T BELIEVE THAT SHE was actually *skipping* down the plaza with an armful of designer plastic and stiff paper bags. They rustled and banged as she walked with a bounce in her step. She tipped back her head and twirled around, prompting Monica to laugh.

"Come on, Twinkletoes, let's go!" Joy said. "You said 'shoes' and somewhere I hear platform straps calling our names!"

"I can't believe you bought me these." Monica held up her Nordstrom Rack bag. "Seriously, are you high?"

Joy laughed. Stef had asked her the same thing, even though he knew better. "I said the first purchase was on me," she said. "And so it was. Besides, consider it an investment in us having fun." Joy glanced back at her friend, who looked unsure and tight-lipped. Joy tsked. "I know things have been not-so-fun lately and we haven't had a lot of time to hang out. I'm worried about you."

"You keep spending money like this and I'll be more worried about you," Monica said. "This isn't more guilt checks from your mom, is it?"

"No," Joy said. "Ever since my birthday visit, she seems to think all is forgiven." Oddly enough, Joy thought she might even be right. Since coming home in May, Joy hadn't brooded as much about Mom ditching the family and running off to California with Doug. Joy didn't even think twice about calling to check in. They were growing beyond civil, sounding more and more normal and less and less afraid. Stef and Joy took turns answering the phone—Stef enjoyed making up outrageous lies about trashing the house, but Joy didn't like telling even silly little lies anymore. It wasn't worth it.

"I told you, it's my new job," Joy said, swinging her purchases. "This is a long-overdue celebration blitz."

"Personal shopping," Monica said. "Seems we are making our new job into a new hobby?"

Joy chose her next words carefully. "I am happy and deserve something pretty. And so do you."

"No, I don't." Monica sounded uncharacteristically bitter. Joy always thought of Monica as Miss A-#1 Fun. But there was an unmistakable Gordon-sized hole in the air, and it was all the more present as they shopped around the mall. He was usually the one toting the bags.

"You sound unhappy," Joy said.

"I *am* unhappy," Monica said. "I have a *right* to sound unhappy! I'm breaking up with my boyfriend because he's too nice and understanding and I have only just realized that I'm a politically incorrect hypocrite." She swung her bag for extra emphasis, nearly knocking over a display. "You've been hogging the Unhappy-Pants for the past year, so now I'm pulling a Sisterhood and it's my turn to wear the pants!"

Joy whistled. "Whoa. Did the apology not go well?"

"We're talking. On the phone, anyway," Monica said. "That's better than not talking, right?"

Joy nodded. "Yes, definitely. Don't worry. You'll work things out," she said, spinning in place. "You're both still crazy about each other—the rest is just head games." She shook her head sympathetically. "They're not real."

"Coming from the expert on head games," Monica said, doing a quick double take in front of some lime-green pumps.

"Speaking of, have I recently needled you about my continuing quest to meet your Someone-A-Guy, Ink?"

"You have not been neglecting your duty," Joy said, circling to look at a window display full of long summer dresses and tiny mirror balls. She'd told Monica his nickname as a sort of condolence prize. It was kind of nice hearing her best friend say it out loud. "He's been out of town a lot lately—" *true* "—and I thought we could do a big get-together this summer, but something came up." Joy adjusted the bags in her hand. "He might not be available."...*as opposed to visible,* she mentally added. Joy still didn't like thinking about having to cancel her order with Mr. Vinh so hadn't gotten around to it yet. She worried that there might be consequences, like cancellation fees. She tried not to think about it. "It all depends."

"Depends on what?" Monica said. "Does it have to be a blue moon or solar eclipse or something?"

Joy was about to return serve when something caught the edge of her Sight: the multimirror reflections turned shiny rust-red. Joy dropped her purchases and turned, hand raised.

"Move!" Joy shouted and mentally *pushed!* Her palm bowed inward around Inq's glyph as a pulse of air knocked Monica sideways, out of the path of the Red Knight. There was a moment of blind fear as the twin blades came down. Her golden halo flared. A blinding clap of lightning shattered all the surrounding glass and mirrors into a fireworks display. Joy cringed, shielding her eyes, blinking back colors, but remained standing amid the wreckage, unharmed. The Red Knight had been thrown back against the anachronistic backdrop of Forever 21, regaining its balance on pointy, plated feet.

Joy hadn't time to be shocked that no one else could see what was really happening. She fought for her scalpel, her wrist tangled in plastic handles. There was a blur of movement. The knight swung again. Joy flinched, too late...but there was no pain—nothing but gold sparks and the scraping squeal of metal on stone. Again and again the blades rained down, a hailstorm of slicing silver death that never came close. Joy's armor sparked on impact, defiantly gold. Joy uncurled slowly, standing straight, watching the dual swords arcing toward her face, her chest, her neck, her sides, coming at her like 3-D special effects, a blur on fast-forward, and...nothing. Nothing at all. She squared her shoulders, the glyphs singing against her skin. Her fingers curled into fists, one tightened over the scalpel in her hand. She was a fiery angel in a nimbus of unseen golden light.

She was unstoppable. Unbreakable.

There was a pause as the knight withdrew a wary step, swords held parallel to his shoulders, his body loosened to spring. The helmeted face was inscrutable. Joy flashed her Olympic-class smile.

"You've been hired to kill me," she said quietly. "It cannot be done."

Joy took one step forward.

The Red Knight eased one step back.

"Go," she said, holding the scalpel close in her right palm. A small voice in her head reminded her that security cameras, videophones and humans could still see her, but she had to make her stand. "Go." She raised her left palm and *pushed!* The Red Knight staggered against the gale. One of the swords blew from his grasp.

The knight crouched with surprising agility, snatched up its weapon and ran for the thin spiral evergreens flanking the plaza. Diving forward, he was swallowed up instantly in a shudder of manicured branches. Joy watched him go, gleaming invisibly, and held her scalpel against her thigh. She scanned the area haughtily: nothing. Not a hint of him. Nothing dared approach. The only red visible was the shopping logos of major department stores.

Joy grinned. It was over.

It worked! Her heart leaped inside her, buoyant and proud. She was alive! She was safe! Better than safe: she was *invincible!* Inq was right. The Red Knight couldn't touch her. *Nothing* could touch her! No one would ever hurt her again!

Relief spread through her like cold soda, bubbly and effervescent and chilly to the bone. She hadn't realized how scared she'd been, how stressed she'd been, how much worry she'd been carrying around with her all this time until it was magically gone. When the Red Knight hacked at her uselessly, when she stood uninjured and untouched, Joy felt taller and stronger and more confident than she ever had in her life. She felt as if her legs had been part of the floor, part of the framework, part of the building sunk deep into the earth—strong and immovable as a mountain, huge and impenetrable and defiant. She'd stood her ground and the Red Knight was powerless.

Joy lifted her arms and pumped them once, the same feeling of winning the gold hot through her veins, blooming bigger than life, larger than what her body could hold. She bounced on her feet as the glyphs darkened, quieting to normal. Only then was Joy aware that nearby shoppers were staring at her and starting to close in.

Joy's smile faded with her unearthly light and she fumbled for her bags.

"Time to go," she muttered and waved her friend over. "Monica?"

Talk bubbled in at the edges of the crowd. Some male voices called to one another. An old lady cried out. The sound zinged up Joy's spine, alarming her. She slipped.

Joy looked down. Red smeared her shoe.

"Monica?"

That's when she saw her best friend. And that's when she screamed.

* * *

It was the smell that made Joy want to get up and leave. She didn't, of course, because you can't leave when you're in the waiting room of a hospital expecting news. You have an obligation. You have responsibilities. You have to stay in the stink of chemical cleansers and body odor and powdery latex and that curious, sterile smell of something that can't exist outside in nature because it's about as natural as toxic waste. Joy crossed her feet beneath the hard plastic seat, wondering who'd design a place to be the least comfortable environment possible for the people who needed to be comforted most. Why were funeral parlors so much cozier, when the person everyone had come to see was already dead, and yet when the same person could still be alive, they stick you in a cold, unwelcoming, vomit-colored room filled with clear plastic tubing and bad filtered light?

She hated hospitals.

Even though she sat with Gordon on the orange-colored bench, she felt alone, numb behind a thick layer of glass. Maybe that was the armor? Maybe it protected her from feeling anything that could harm her? Somehow she doubted it. She remembered Ilhami's recklessness in New York, his daring escape, the drug money and the raining bullets, running safe and secure behind a single glyph. Joy wore a couple hundred of them now. Monica hadn't had even one.

Joy was so stupid.

There was a hollow echo replaying in her head, the words she'd kept repeating to the paramedics and the police and then to the Reids and the doctors and Gordon and the receptionist behind the counter when she'd first gotten to the hospital and they'd said she couldn't go in because she wasn't family and she would have to wait. Joy kept talking as if the words were a passport, a tithe, a secret code that would allow her to explain what had happened without saying in any way what had really happened because, of course, she couldn't say that. It even tickled on her tongue when she sat in the pool of blood, carefully not moving Monica's head because the long gash across her forehead had cut through her nose and Joy wasn't sure if she would drown in her own blood and stop breathing. She'd watched air bubble through the fissure of blood and bone thinking if she kept her eyes on it, she was certain Monica would keep breathing. She couldn't die from that, could she? A severed nose? A long gash? It didn't seem possible. But none of this was possible, which was why Joy had invented the story of some psycho with a knife that rushed past them, slashing as he ran.

After she told that story, she'd thrown up in the toilet.

Joy squeezed the warm gel pack nervously in her hands. Lies were stupid. No camera would show any attacker in the mall. Joy knew that she had a scalpel in her purse. She didn't know what might happen, but the childhood fear of being locked away in a psychiatric ward loomed somewhere, screaming in the back of her mind behind a black curtain of guilt. If she listened, she could imagine the faint sounds of Great-Grandmother Caroline beating blindly at the bars on her door.

"Joy?"

Joy glanced up and stood, feeling Gordon do the same. Mrs. and Mr. Reid were standing in the double doorway, faces the color of deadwood, bleached with fear and hospital lights. Their eyes were twin cameras set on "record" as if they were filming the moment from a long way away, storing it for later viewing because this couldn't possibly be happening now. Joy knew she should say something, but their faces stole her voice.

Gordon stepped up to Mrs. Reid, and Joy watched her puffy eyes spill over. Gordon's wide rugby arms came around her, hugging her shoulders, and Mrs. Reid hugged him back, sobbing unreservedly into his shirt. Gordon's face was hard and soft at the same time, jaw clenched but eyes peacefully closed as if in prayer. Joy watched the two of them like a nature show. Mr. Reid rubbed his wife's back. Joy's stomach tightened. Mr. Reid noticed her through his rimless glasses.

"She's all right," he said. Joy wanted to be sure which "she" he meant. Joy wanted to hear him say her name. She needed to hear it said. She needed it to be real in the way only a dad could speak things into being. Mr. Reid nodded as if he understood. "Monica will be fine."

Joy's breath came out in a cough with a sob hooked at the end like a worm. Her inhale was too loud and her exhale brought tears. She ran to Mr. Reid and hugged him hard, wiping her face across his power tie. He patted her back and kissed the top of her head.

"It's a miracle," he said. "They said it was a glancing blow. It missed the eye and only scratched the bone of the orbital ridge. Whatever it was..." He squeezed Joy as if to smother the thought. "Well, it could have been a lot worse. A lot worse. But it wasn't." He patted Joy's shoulders and she let go, rubbing her face with her hands and reaching for one of the ever-present boxes of flimsy tissues. "We have a lot to be thankful for."

"There was so much blood," Joy said, as if that meant anything.

"Head wounds bleed a lot," he said calmly and tapped a spot on the side of his head, permanently dented from some brick Monica had told her had been thrown from a truck while he'd been walking home from church. No matter how many times she'd heard the story, Joy had never once thought about the blood. "Ask the vascular surgeon. Trust me—these things usually look worse than they are."

"Can we see her?" Gordon asked, still holding Mrs. Reid.

She must have cried herself out and was now transferring self-consciously to her husband's arms.

Mr. Reid hesitated for the barest instant. He exchanged a glance with the police officer who stood waiting against the wall.

"Soon," he said. "She's sleeping right now. And I don't want you—" he looked at Joy and Gordon "—*either* of you, to see her like that. I won't want to lie to you—seeing Monica will be a shock." Mrs. Reid started crying again, quieter than before. Mr. Reid hugged his wife, his own eyes growing shiny. "Most of the damage was a single laceration, a clean cut, but she'll need corrective surgery. They've already called in a neuro-surgeon, a plastics physician and a facial specialist who's re-paired her septum, the bridge of her nose that was severed, and we've approved the use of a new laser technique that should minimize her scarring and the hospital stay, but..." His voice faltered. He rubbed his cheek against his wife's hair. "She won't look the same. They wanted to prepare us. She'll be scarred for life."

"I don't care," Gordon said. "I don't care what she looks like. I..." He raked his wide hands through his stubbly blond hair, calming himself with effort. It was as if his wide arms didn't know quite what to do. "Mr. Reid, sir, please, can I see her?"

Mrs. Reid placed one of her delicate hands on his shoul-der. She was a piano teacher and her every move was musi-cal. "We know that she's special to you," she said. "And that you're very special to her, too. But let's try to think about Monica right now. She hasn't had a chance to see *herself* yet. She doesn't know what's happened. I don't want her think-ing we let you in to see her when she didn't feel ready to be seen." She patted her husband's chest. "Some ladies don't like their men to see them at less than their best, even after twenty-two years." She unwound herself from Mr. Reid and rubbed her hands together. She smiled at Gordon. "Would you be so kind as to escort me to the cafeteria? I think I'd like a cup of coffee. Would you like one?"

"Of course," Gordon said automatically. His manners were impeccable, boarding school bred. "Right this way, Mrs. Reid."

Joy watched them head for the elevators while she stood alone with Mr. Reid, the policeman's eyes boring an itch into her back.

"She's still got it," Mr. Reid said, looking after his wife. "Miss Southern Belle. Only girl to win two years running and Homecoming Queen, besides. Always a lady, even in the most difficult times." He shook his head and didn't bother to wipe his eyes. Joy wondered how men kept all the tears in. He sighed. "You know what I'm going to ask you, don't you, Joy?"

"I wish I had seen him," Joy said, totally unsuccessful at keeping any of it in. The tears bubbled over; the lies stung worse. If she thought about wanting to know the identity of the Red Knight, it hurt less. "I really wish I did, but it happened so *fast*." She wiped her face with the thin-as-lint tissue and grabbed another, balling the first in her fist. "We were shopping and we stopped to look at the window display and I saw something in the mirror balls and he was there and gone." All true, but too much else ran through her mind—all of what happened after. Joy was aware the silence had gone on too long. Mr. Reid stared at her. Confession wet her lips.

"I shouldn't have pushed her," she said.

Mr. Reid stayed calm, but she could tell he was listening intently. The officer had moved away from the wall, crossing the hall toward them.

"You pushed her?" Mr. Reid said.

"I pushed her," Joy admitted. "I said, 'Move!' and I pushed her. I thought I was pushing her out of the way." She wasn't lying: she had and she did and the security cameras would probably show that much, but nothing else would make any sense. There would be no attacker. There would be no Red Knight. And if anyone saw that she'd held a scalpel in her hand, she'd logically be suspect. She hadn't cut Monica— would never—but on tape, no one had. Joy imagined being recorded talking to herself and waving a scalpel in the air while her friend lay bleeding on the floor. It wouldn't take a genius. She knew the policeman was right behind her. She could feel the closeness of his uniform like static on her skin.

"I thought I saw something coming and I pushed her out of the way," Joy said, her voice thick and tough to swallow. "I pushed her. I shouldn't've pushed her. I didn't mean to... I thought..." She started sobbing, wishing she could tell the whole truth, wanting the Reids to believe her, to understand that what she *meant* was true. "I'm so sorry! I'm so so sorry!" And she said something she hadn't meant to, but it was the truest thing she'd said all day. *"It should have been me!"*

Mr. Reid grabbed her hard by the shoulders. "Stop that, Joy!" he said, snapping her silent. "Don't say that. Don't talk like that. Don't let me *ever* hear you talk like that!" He leaned forward so that Joy couldn't help but meet his eyes, teddy bear brown and growling-proud. He spoke to her fiercely and kindly at once. "You might have saved her life, pushing her like that. You might have just *saved her life* and you're lucky you didn't get hurt, and my little girl in there? She would tell you the same thing." Joy shook her head. He was so wrong. This was so wrong. She wanted to tell him, and she didn't. She daren't and she couldn't.

"Mr. Reid?" One of the doctors appeared with a clipboard, a white coat and a mask of professionalism. "I'd like to speak with you and your wife about the next forty-eight hours, if that's all right with you."

"Of course," he said, rubbing Joy's arm and letting go. "My wife's in the cafeteria. I'll go get her."

"Can I see Monica? Just for a minute?" Joy said.

"She's sedated," the doctor said kindly. "She can't hear you right now."

"Please," Joy said, first to the doctor, then to Mr. Reid. "Please, I want to see her. She knows me. I want to tell her..." The words were plain on her face: *I'm sorry.*

The doctor, sensing the father's hesitation, added, "Family members only."

Mr. Reid held her gaze and gave a small nod. "It's okay," he said and glanced at the doctor, then the policeman. "She's family." He gave extra weight to the words that made Joy feel more honored, and more guilty, than ever. "Excuse me. I'll go get my wife."

The doctor hugged her clipboard and turned to Joy. "Room two-eighteen. Bed nearest the window. Three minutes, okay?"

"Two-eighteen," Joy said, grabbing her purse and wiping her eyes. "Thank you."

Joy walked down the hall, feeling the policeman's eyes on her all the way. She ran up the flight of stairs instead of waiting for the elevator, a habit born of exercise, her shoes thudding on the poured stone. The concrete steps felt nothing like the bleachers at school or the ones at home, which, in her mind were littered in potted topsoil and chipped paint on the second-floor landing. Joy pushed into the two hundred hall with a bang of the door.

It was quiet in the hospital wing, amplifying the beep and whirr of machinery and the efficient bustle of the nurses' station. Everyone spoke in hushed voices—forced, soothing monotone drones, their footsteps too loud despite paper booties clomp-clomp-clomping in the hall. Everything smelled sterile and was colored eggshell-whispery white. Lights glared off the Formica and the curved mirrors mounted in ceiling corners. Joy passed many doors, regular as clockwork, as she made her way under the exit sign to room 218.

The beds were separated by a sunny yellow curtain and sunlight streamed in through the open blinds, but all the other colors were otherwise bleached thin; pale peach walls and powder-white sheets, metal poles and clear plastic things and boxy gray monitors with shiny red buttons kept vigil by the head of the beds. Everything hung limp. Everything had wheels. Joy bumped against a cart as she eased her way past the molded plastic footboard with handles. A lanky girl lay in the first bed, bandaged from the neck down, wheezing quietly. A drip disappeared beneath the blanket. Joy quickly looked away and ducked behind the curtain.

It was Monica. Or what looked like Monica. The top of her face was under bandages, crossing the bridge of her nose and circling behind her head. Her carefully straightened hair was bunched and bristling in patches, her eyes were sunken into dark circles and her generous lips were slack and chapped. She looked fragile and frail and altogether a stranger, drained to a color that wasn't quite sepia, like a very old movie or a tea-stained cup.

Joy picked up the chair in the corner and placed it gently on the floor. She sat and stared at her best friend's hand, which lay half-open, the coral paint on her fingernails chipped in places. Joy held her breath to keep from making noise. She pushed a hand against her mouth to keep her cries inside. As she leaned back against the chair, everything started spinning. The seat tilted. Her ears rang. Sweat prickled her skin. She forced herself to look at Monica's eyes, half-moons framed in thick lashes that curled up like a doll's. They didn't flutter. They didn't wink. They were as closed as hospital doors.

Joy squeezed her fingers and crossed her knees. She wanted to twist herself up like a wet towel and wring out the pain—looking at Monica ripped something inside her. She felt ashamed for having even once thought of herself as invulnerable. She was incredibly vulnerable and this was proof. She was frail, she was mortal, but she *knew*—Joy *knew* what had been lurking out there, what was coming for her, and Monica hadn't. She'd led Monica into danger while she was shielded, safe. Joy had been courting it, daring it, secretly hoping that the Red Knight would show itself and be thwarted. If she was being honest, she'd been half expecting it. And when it had come, she'd laughed. But Monica had been busy thinking about Gordon; she'd been worried, distracted. She had come along at Joy's prodding, out buying shoes. She'd had no idea. She'd been totally unprepared. Joy had invited her along to cheer her up, even knowing she was a target. Joy had known about the danger. And, now, which of them was bandaged and broken in a hospital bed?

Joy curled her fingers into fists that shook and clenched her jaw to keep from sobbing, feeling the hot rush of blood across her face and neck, burning with shame. Guilt throbbed behind her eyes. She wanted to apologize, she wanted to take it back, but she also wanted to hit something very, very hard. *Revenge!* She wanted to tear the Red Knight apart, piece by piece, rip apart the metal armor and stab whatever breathed beneath it into the heart of its True Name. She wanted him to hurt more than Monica, more than her, more than this. She wanted so very, very much to make it all untrue.

Opening her eyes, Joy saw the tiniest speck of black beneath the cotton gauze. A little puckered tug stretched along Monica's cheek and disappeared into the fluffy bandages. Joy leaned forward. It was a stitch. A single tiny thread. The first of what must be a zipper line of stitches running from the middle of her right cheek, across her nose, through her left eyebrow and into her hair. The edge of the wound. The beginnings of a scar. It reminded her of Ysabel and Henri and what she'd done in the white room at Graus Claude's.

A tingle of realization cascaded over her scalp and spine. She could remove scars.

"I can fix it."

She bit her cheek after she'd spoken aloud. Long moments passed under a soft, steady beep behind the curtain. Joy counted five before she stood up and slowly drew the curtain around Monica's bed, hiding them from the doorway and any curious cameras. She opened her purse and took out the scalpel, squeezing it in her fingers, and leaned closer to her friend's face.

She lifted the edge of the gauze, smelling the chemicals and sticky ointments and the sticky red blood. The stitches stood out like railway tracks, and extra cotton batting covered the bridge of Monica's nose. She could see a glow peeking there—what must be the Red Knight's *signatura*. She'd deal with that later. Joy sat carefully on the edge of the hospital mattress and steadied her arm.

Touching the scalpel to skin, Joy had the momentary flash of worry that maybe it would be like the ghostly mark still on her back, all but lost under the filigreed network of her armor, unable to be removed—but she had to try. This was *Monica*. This was her best friend. And she'd never be in here if it weren't for Joy.

The very tip of the blade touched the puckered skin to the right of her lips. There was a familiar feeling, a cool, shearing grace. The scalpel slid upward. The stitch popped. The skin beneath it shone clean.

Smiling, Joy followed the line of the Red Knight's sword, tracing where it had sliced through skin and bone. Shallow at first, the wound deepened, requiring Joy to bend over the bed, nearly in half, concentrating on slowing down to erase every last trace of the gruesome wound and the glowing True Name that burned beneath it. She smoothed her thumb over her friend's cheek, smooth and perfect. Monica lay in drugged sleep, unaware. If Joy could do this quickly, it could be over before she woke.

I can do this. I can make it untrue.

Joy peeled back the extra padding supporting the reset cartilage. Monica's nose was purple-black and stitched up and swollen. Joy lifted the bandages with her fingertips, wondering if she should just cut it off with the blade. She had only minutes. Probably two. Maybe one.

The curtain flew back on its rings.

"Joy!"

Panic slapped her. Then she realized who it was.

"Ink," she said gratefully, heart slamming. "You scared me."

He stared at Joy and Monica with horror.

"What are you doing?" he said.

"The Red Knight attacked me in the mall," Joy said. "I'm fine. The armor worked—he couldn't touch me, but Monica—"

"I know," Ink said quickly. "I know what happened." He sounded shocked and angry. Upset. Joy was touched that he felt so much for her friend, even though they'd never met, like Gordon and Mrs. Reid. He understood how much Monica meant to her. But as she watched, his shoulders bunched tighter like a hissing cat's, ready to spring. He squeezed the back of the abandoned chair. "I did not ask what had happened—I asked what were you doing?"

"I'm..." Joy raised the scalpel—it seemed obvious. "I'm erasing it."

"No!" He sounded furious. Joy frowned.

"But...it was an accident," she said. "It was meant for me."

"Joy!" Ink said, clearly furious. "You cannot do this."

"No, Ink, I *can*," Joy said happily. "I mean, it's *working*. I can fix it!"

"No!"

Joy jerked back, alarmed, forgetting for an instant that no one else could hear him. Ink was livid, the deep lines around his mouth and eyes sharp as knives, his dimples chiseled into stark crevices—he looked stricken, pained beyond anger. The chair back creaked under his tightening fingers.

"You *cannot* do this," he said flatly. "You will undo everything."

Joy stammered, "It's a scar—"

"It's a *mark*," Ink said, eyes flashing. "I put it there."

Baffled, Joy shook her head. "No," she said. That made no sense. Her skin prickled with sick nerves and fear. "It was the Red Knight," she said. "I saw it. I would have..." She swallowed the doubt that whispered with Stef's voice. "I would have seen you..." But she stared at the naked flesh under the bandages and could see what Ink meant: a spear-shaped *signatura* pointed like a compass through Monica's dark skin, striking down her face like a slash. It wasn't the Red Knight's. Joy didn't recognize it.

"It was on the way to the hospital," he said, "once the drugs had entered her system, guaranteeing that she would not wake." Ink ran his fingers along the length of silver wallet chain, back and forth like stroking a cat. "Yes, the Red Knight had struck her, scored her flesh, and she was not his target, but it left a mark—a mark that everyone would see—a mark in the scar that would be left behind." He placed his other hand on the bed to steady himself. "Think, Joy. Your friend is a mortal who has been wounded by one of the Twixt and survived, which puts her in a very small category of humans living in this world. It places her under an auspice. It is a mark that she has earned and which she will bear for the rest of her life." He slapped a hand on the cushion. "Who do you think put it there?" He stabbed two fingers angrily into his chest. "Permanent. Indelible. Indelible Ink." He pointed at her. "You *know* that, Joy. *I* am the one who places the marks that can be seen. You *knew* that this was one of mine."

"It was a mistake," Joy said.

"It is an experience—*her* experience—that cannot be undone." He glanced at the scalpel in her hand, once his own. "It should not be undone."

"But in the cache, those were strangers, and you understood..." Joy groped for some strand of logic, some sense in all of this. "This is *Monica*."

Ink shook his head, fairly quivering in frustration. "Those were the Folk marking one another—auspices claimed within the realm of the Twixt—*not* my work, *not* on humans and no longer legitimate claims, correct?" He shook the chair back in emphasis. "These circumstances are nothing alike."

Joy felt a strange flush of frustration, although she kept her voice calm. Ink *had* to understand. She wasn't explaining it well.

"It was meant for me," she said.

"Perhaps by intent, but not by design," he said. "My orders were clear—both the who and the when."

Joy was horrified. "You *knew?*" she said, furious, betrayed. "You *knew* this would happen?"

Ink sighed. "Scribes cannot know everything about the auspice or the claimant, but I know this," Ink said over Monica's body on the bed. "That is my work you are erasing."

Joy stared from the scalpel in her hand to her friend's half-bandaged face and Ink's tempered fury. "I didn't know..." She shook her head. "I didn't realize..."

"I understand," Ink said tightly. "But now you do. And now you realize why you must stop."

The scalpel quivered in Joy's hand. Monica's face was slack and purple, the gauze still slick with antiseptic and oxidized blood.

"No," she said. "No, I don't."

Ink's eyes flattened to matte; he sounded annoyed. "She is meant to be marked and I delivered it—a mark and a scar that was meant to be seen. That is my work that you are undoing—precisely the sort of thing that we wished to avoid when first we met. My mistake—any mistake or failure to deliver—throws my work into question and places Inq, myself and you at risk." He slammed a hand against the chair, startling her. "You *know* this, Joy! This is why we created our first deception, not to mention all the ones that we, together, crafted thereafter!"

Ink came around the chair and stood near her, close enough that she could smell his crackling rainwater scent. "You know that I live to protect myself and Inq and you. Yet this sort of irresponsible selfishness can undo us all!" He waved his arm, setting the curtain rings rattling against the rod. "Inq and I must remain dependable, reliable and loyal, marking humans with *signaturae* in the stead of our people so that the Folk do not try to do so themselves, risking discovery or capture and sowing chaos between our worlds. *That* is what you were undoing in Dover Mill—the Folk's misuse of power. But this? You know that the Council must believe that the power to erase marks exists within the blade and not within you in order to keep you from deeper inquiry and harm. The Council will soon address the Tide's claims that you pose a danger to the Twixt—that you are potentially the most dangerous human alive—a human with the Sight who has not been blinded or killed, who is not only aware of our existence, but wields a terrible power over us without restriction." He spread his hands, echoes of her hands, in appeal. "By removing legitimate human marks, you undermine the system of *signaturae*—you cut free the balloon, you ground the ship, you sever our worlds. And you not only discredit the work of the Scribes, you prove Sol Leander right that you are not simply ignorant, but unwilling to abide by our rules, which places us all at cross-purposes and puts everyone at risk!"

Joy's face grew darker. "Did you just call me 'ignorant'?"

He snarled and made mad slashes with his bare hands as if unable to contain his frustration. He spun around, pressing his fingers to his lips.

"Unbelievable human arrogance..." he muttered and dropped his arms. "Listen carefully," Ink said, clearly struggling to impress upon her the severity of the moment. "By erasing my work, you are threatening me—and my sister—as well as my ability to protect you...or defend your actions to others who might take offense."

Joy stared at him. He straightened and calmly offered a hand to help her stand.

"Come away, Joy. Now," Ink said. "Please."

Joy gazed down at her friend, half-bandaged, half-healed.

"But it was an accident," Joy insisted.

"There are no accidents," Ink said. "You once told me that."

Joy was fixed to her seat. It was unfair to ask her to do this—to ask her to *not* do this—to condemn Monica to disfigurement and to wear Joy's mistake on her face for life. Her best friend knew nothing of the Twixt or the Red Knight or the Tide! She had only wanted Gordon and her parents to love her and get along despite their differences—and everything *was* fine with them—but Monica didn't know that because she was lying in a hospital bed, unconscious, and it was all Joy's fault!

Monica lay still as an accusation between them, half of her bloody slate wiped clean.

"No," Joy said, gripping the scalpel hard. "I was wrong. This is *wrong!*" Hot tears filled her eyes. "Monica has nothing to do with any of this! She was never meant to be there. She was never meant to get hurt—she was just in the wrong place at the wrong time and it was *my* fault that it happened and

I *won't* let her pay for my mistake!" She shook the scalpel for emphasis. "Please, Ink, I *can't* let that happen. I can't let her be scarred for life—not when I can do something about it."

Ink both grew and shrank, his face looming closer, his eyes growing wider.

"Joy." Her name strangled from his throat. "Do *not* do this."

Then something strange happened: he cried.

The hot pink light that danced in his eyes wobbled and ran, not in black rivulets, but with real tears. Clear drops of water spilled off his lashes, running down his face and hugging his jaw. Joy stared, disbelieving. She'd never seen him cry. It felt like a kick in the stomach. As she watched, she somehow recognized the tiny scintillating flashes in the droplets that caught the light.

The Sight.

They were *hers*—her tears—once cried into his eyes.

Joy remembered after the battle with Aniseed, sealing his severed throat closed and praying that he'd open his eyes and *look* at her, she'd cried—her tears splashing onto his face, over his eyes, into his eyes and he'd held on to them all this time and he was giving them back to her now. It was the same aching, heart-wrenching sadness that brought its salt to the surface, and she relived that stabbing loss all over again.

She was losing him. He was losing her.

Ink.

He was crying her tears back at her, but she couldn't give in.

"You said you didn't want me bound by the Twixt and its rules," she said. "You said you wanted me to have my freedom." She sobbed for breath to say the right things, the ones that would make him understand, make them an "us" again, whole. "I want that for Monica. She deserves anything she wants. She deserves to be beautiful and safe and loved and free." Joy placed a soft hand on the patch of Monica's hair sticking through the web of gauze. "She deserves better than this."

"You do not know what she deserves," Ink said. "You only know that you love her."

"That's right," Joy said.

"Despite what is right?" Ink said. "Despite who else it may harm?"

"This won't hurt you, or Inq, or anybody," Joy said with conviction. "I wouldn't do that. I love you, Ink. You *know* that." She turned the scalpel in her hand "No one will find out. No one will know."

His voice hardened. "*I* will know."

Joy stopped, fingers trembling. Her tears changed from anger to heartbreak—she felt the difference even though they tasted the same on her lips. Her hands shook as well as her words. "Don't ask me to choose," she begged him. "You can't ask me to choose between my best friend and you."

He stepped back. "I have never asked," Ink said quietly. "And you always had to choose. Now you have made your choice clear." He gestured toward the hospital bed. "Love has made you blind and foolish," he said as his straight razor snapped open and swept a line of nothingness clean in half. Ink turned away and snarled over his shoulder. "You and I, both."

He marched through the breach and disappeared, the yellow curtain zipping closed behind him.

The rattling settled. Machinery beeped. Joy stared at the curtain.

Ink was gone.

THIRTEEN

HER BODY JOSTLED AND BOUNCED IN THE PASSENGER
seat of Stef's new Nissan. She'd left Monica's bedside and wan-
dered into the hall, into the lobby and into the parking lot,
following the walking path along the river until her brother
pulled up a timeless time later. Even sitting in a moving car,
she felt like she was wandering. Her feet knew they should
be doing something even when her mind didn't.

Gordon had stuffed Joy's purchases into the backseat. One
of the white paper bags had a tiny spray of brown blood.
Stef and Gordon had exchanged words in low voices; Gordon had said something to Joy and she'd smiled. He looked
at her uneasily. That was okay. None of this was real. She
couldn't have left Monica's face half-finished, the *signatura*
half erased after Ink had left her sitting there, battling guilt
and anger on her own.

Ink had left her.

"It's for the best," Stef said.

Joy could vaguely remember saying something that
prompted this sentence, but she couldn't quite remember
what it was. They'd been in the car for some time, so she
couldn't be faulted for forgetting. Everything was hazy. What
was it? Joy sifted through the foggy memory of getting into
the car. She'd seen Stef drive up, waited for the shiny silver

Nissan to stop, opened the door, put her purse by her shoes, fastened her seat belt and said something. She remembered the dull shape of the words in her mouth.

She'd said, "He left me."

That couldn't be right. Stef was mistaken. That couldn't be for the best.

Joy struggled to remember what else she might have said when her phone went off. She watched her fingers automatically answer the text.

Miss Malone,
I have been notified of your recent indiscretion and regret to inform you that such an action constitutes a breach of magnitude that I cannot abide. As you have elected to perform services on clients proscribed by our mandates, I must consider your decision an end to our association. Therefore, this notice serves to terminate our agreement as well as your employment, effective immediately. Your prior earnings have been allocated to alleviate any outstanding debt and all other accounts are closed as of this date. I need not remind you that further contact is prohibited in accordance to our laws. Do not attempt to reply to this message.

May you succeed in other future endeavors.
Sincerely,
GC

Joy smoothed back her hair from her face. She was surprised that her fingers came away wet. She laughed or sobbed or made some noise that sounded like both.

"What is it?" Stef said.

"I just got fired," Joy said, knowing Stef would think she meant the café, but it didn't matter. She let her hand fall. None of it mattered anymore. "I've lost my job, my best friend's in the hospital and my boyfriend left me all in one day." She streaked her tears against the windowpane. "That's everything. I've lost everything."

Stef squeezed the wheel, looking absurdly like her father, minus thirty years and sixty pounds. "I know it feels that way, but it's not true," he said. "You have your family and your friends—real ones—the ones that matter." Stef stopped at a yellow light, something he rarely did. He was being extra careful with her. Joy didn't know how to feel about that. "Monica's going to be okay, Dad will be home soon and you can always get a new job." He signaled and turned. "I know things feel officially out of control, but it's over now. This is life going back to normal."

This is normal? Joy kept her fingers on the glass, imagining she could feel the whip of leaves and twigs, of shrubs and grass speeding past. What if she just opened the door? What if she tumbled out into the blurry landscape? She'd want it to sting. To hurt. To break things. To wake her up. Words slipped from her lips.

"Did life go back to normal after Dmitri left?"

Stef's knuckles whitened. He drove the last two turns sharply, pulled into their lot and parked the car with a jerk, cutting the engine off with a twist of the key. His voice was quiet and flat.

"No."

He got out and grabbed her bags from the backseat. She followed, vaguely wondering if the Red Knight would appear.

There was no one waiting for her as she made her way across the lot. There was no one in the courtyard or standing on the stairs. There was no one by the door, which had recently been repaired, or lurking in the hallway or slicing through space. There was no one in her kitchen or in the hallway or in her room.

There was no one there.

No one at all.

* * *

Joy couldn't sleep.

The feelings raged—bigger than her body, bigger than her room—too big and terrible to contain inside the four walls of her house, and so she kicked off the covers, slipped on her shoes, grabbed her zip-up and keys, unlocked the alarm and went outside. She fumbled down the stairs into the courtyard. Slammed the gate. Started to walk. Started to run.

She didn't know where she was running—running to or running from—but she tried to outpace the tiny voices in her head whispering doubts and recriminations, running a little bit faster when they turned to shame or blame, pushing until the only sound in her head was the gasping of her breath and the pounding of her blood in her ears. Her feet slammed into the pavement, her pores open and weeping sweat, her face hot and cold and dripping, her bangs sticking to her face. She swatted them away like summer flies.

Joy ran knowing that something would pursue her. She ran like prey. She ran like bait.

If it was the Red Knight, good. He couldn't touch her and she wanted to break him! If it was Indelible Ink, good. She wanted to scream at him and cry. If it was Invisible Inq... Joy slowed down a notch. She had no idea what the female Scribe would do, but she was sure it wouldn't be pleasant. Perhaps Graus Claude would take care of it on behalf of the Council. Perhaps Kurt would shoot her.

You are considered rogue, *Miss Malone.*

Joy kept running, feeling the beat of her body match the cadence of her playlist; from classic soundtracks to Lady Gaga, she filled her head with music to drown out the noise. She revisited years of routine tunes that went on and on and on, half remembered twitches in her body as her limbs relived impacts and jumps, springs and twists, and her stomach switched places with her head in the trance of no-mind as she flew. The white noise of adrenaline. The pull of gravity. The smack of landing again and again. Joy gratefully lost herself in herself for a while.

She should have known the thump of music would bring her here.

It was night and the moon was fierce. The Carousel sat on the hill, built of long shadows and solid shapes, a quiet theater for the night, a modern Pantheon for gods. There was something huge and awesome about the massive six-row carousel even though it had been gutted, converted into so many other things over the years that never stayed, although the Carousel itself did.

She circled it, wondering how old it was.

Joy leaned against the temporary fence that surrounded the Carousel on the Green, threading her fingers though the links and hanging her head to catch her breath. The metal shivered, rattling cold and hard against her skin. She wiped her forehead against the back of her arm and stared into the darkness of the central pillar. She couldn't remember what music had been playing when she'd first seen Ink, but she felt it all the same.

She closed her eyes, afraid to say his name, afraid he wouldn't care, afraid he wouldn't come.

An ache squirmed in her belly like cold snakes and *twisted*.

Ink.

She walked slowly along the chain-link fence, staring into its depths. Mottled shapes played tricks with the moonlight, sliding along the floorboards, peeking in and out of the mirrored beams. Things *moved*, but not as she moved, which was strange. It was as if the carousel horses were lingering ghosts. Joy remembered riding a painted mare with wooden flowers and inset glass jewels. As a little girl, she'd thought that they were magic. And, perhaps, she'd been right. Hollowed out, the old Carousel still hummed with an echo of merry-scary music.

Something on two legs moved.

Joy stopped.

"Hello?" she whispered, trying to see who it was. Was it Folk or human? Enemy or friend? Stranger or lover? "Hello?" she said again.

"You shouldn't be here," said a voice that she didn't recognize. Joy was worried that perhaps it was some beat cop or a skater kid from the streets, which frightened her more. She was protected against magical assault, but still wasn't too sure about bullets or a hit to the head, no matter what Inq said. She remembered Ilhami in a blaze of semiautomatic fire and light. She stepped back. A face came closer to the fence, crisscrossed with shadows.

"You're Ink's girl, right?" the guy said. "You can't come in."

Joy swiped her hair out of her eyes and took a quick breath. It was the DJ from Carousel's Under 18 Nights, but there was something wrong with his face. With the way he said words—the shape of his lips as he said them. Or maybe it was the weird curly half-beard poking off his chin. *Ink's girl.* Joy stared. He knew about the Twixt—maybe was one of the Twixt, or a human handler, like Mr. Vinh.

"I'm not here for the club," she said. "I'm..." What was she doing? What did her feet know that she didn't? She ran here. She'd been running. She'd been running to him. "I'm looking for Ink."

"Yeah. I got that," he said, leaning one elbow against the fence. They made a strange parody of a mirror with no glass. "What I'm saying is that you can't come Under the Hill, *persona non grata,* so you might as well go home."

"The hill?" Joy said, glancing down at the well-trampled grass. "The hill is hollow?"

The guy laughed and shook his head full of curls. The

chuckle sounded patient, if exasperated, but okay with it, like he was used to having to explain. "Boy, I hope you're smarter than you are pretty or the Council's gonna eat you for breakfast," he said, tucking a curly lock behind his pointed ear. His elfin ears had tufts of fur at the tips that could be neatly hidden beneath his giant headphones, which he now wore around his neck. She recognized his shape backlit by the central pillar behind his turntables and gear. He tapped his foot on the ground. When Joy looked, it wasn't a shoe, but a hoof. "This is the Hill," he said. "Under the Hill is one of the entrances to the Twixt, like a sliding door between worlds, get it? It's basically what makes the Glen 'the Glen' and not Middle-of-Nowhere, North Carolina." He waved a careless hand at the Carousel. "It doesn't take a genius to figure out why they built this thing here." His jolly eyes flashed. "Not everyone travels like your boyfriend, natch?" he said, hitching up his baggy jeans. "Or should I say 'ex-boyfriend'?"

Joy swallowed. "Word travels fast."

"Yeah, well..." He shrugged, headphones bouncing. "Not much else to do."

"Can you—" Joy stopped, twisting her fingers in her sweat-stained zip-up. "Can you tell me where he is? Can you tell him something for me?"

He shook his head. "I'm not one to get in the middle of a lover's quarrel...though I don't mind starting one." He leered mischievously. "But the smart bet is to let things take their course. Settle down. Get Zen. Listen to me on this one—go home, calm down, have a pint of ice cream, sleep for a day. Just turn around, little lady, and go home."

Joy threaded both her hands through the chain link.

"He *is* my home."

He threaded his fingers back at her. His fingernails were broken and cracked, speckled with dirt and glitter.

"Yeah, well," he said. "I suggest you move on." He pushed

back from the fence, which shivered as he let go. "See you when I spin you," he said and shot dual finger guns at her. "Don't let the night hit you in the ass on your way out and I'll do you a bonny favor and pretend you were never here, a'right?" He bobbed his chin as he strode back into the shadows of the old Carousel. He ran a finger along the length of his nose and shot her a wink. "You were never here."

Joy frowned and let it go. She heard the warning bright and clear.

"I was never here," she agreed.

"Good girl," he said. "Now go home."

Biting back her disappointment, Joy stepped away from the fence, feeling the young man recede from her at the same pace, continuing to share their mirror-moment as they both faded into the dark. She turned down the incline once she was at the foot of the green, only looking back as she left, wondering if she'd turn into a pillar of salt or if the Carousel itself might disappear like the Goblin Market or Atlantis.

"Later, little lady." The merry-mischief voice bubbled up from somewhere unseen. Joy didn't bother to look for its source. "Say hi to Stef for me."

Stef knocked on her door. "Ten minutes."

It was the closest he'd gotten to admonishing her. He knew that there was nothing to pull her out of bed except love and guilt—either one was good, but both were enough.

If it weren't for visiting hours, Joy would have stayed in bed. She burrowed beneath the covers, thick and heavy with smothering comfort. Her sleep had been a dreamless quicksand trap, sluggish and swallowing, and she'd had to claw her way to wakefulness more than once. Most of the time, it wasn't worth the effort.

She'd slept all day yesterday, only getting up to pee and eat cereal. Her hair was matted. Her tongue tasted awful. Her brain felt blurry. She smelled.

Ten minutes. She squinted at the clock. *Okay, nine.*

She stepped into the shower, got dressed and grabbed a cereal bar as she slowly forced herself out of the house. She tried not to think about anything between soaping, shampooing and toweling off to snapping her hair into a ponytail and stepping into clothes. She always wore mismatched socks so being semiconscious wasn't a problem. Joy hummed loudly when errant thoughts got too close to the surface.

It was something like gymnastics training and something like mourning and too much like everything was going to hell.

Joy drove to the hospital on autopilot with the music off.

For the third time, Joy gave her name at the visitor's desk. For the second time, she'd brought a book to try to read. For the first time, she was stopped at the nurses' station when she asked for room 218. The woman's face caught her attention. It looked pinched.

"I'm sorry," the woman said, looking up from her clipboard. "Someone should have called. Were you family?"

Joy froze hearing the past tense.

"Monica Reid?" Joy repeated it like a question. She felt hot then cold then sick.

"Hold on," the nurse said. "Let me check."

But Joy had already begun walking down the horribly familiar hall, past the green exit sign and the open doors and the odd knot of red-faced strangers holding balloons, crowding the door, faces blotchy with tears. Joy pushed past a woman holding a vase of Gerbera daisies, bouncing off a man in a rumpled suit and tie. The sunshine-yellow curtain was highlighted by the window's sun. The room felt cold. The first bed was empty.

The first bed. Empty. With clean white sheets.

Joy stumbled past the partition to the second bed, where Monica lay sleeping. Her facial bandages had been removed, the ugly half scar mocking, but she was here. Alive. Monica was alive.

Joy sat down hard, leaving the other girl's family and friends to their grief. She was grateful and sorry and guilty all at once, stealing all her polite nothings-to-say. The strangers quietly gathered the last of their things and left in a miserable hush.

She was too shocked for prayers or relief or tears. Joy stared at her friend's face, puffy with shadows under her eyes, grateful. Her heart slammed as if petulant at having to stop beating back there. *Too close. What if...?* Joy hugged her purse between her elbow and ribs, knowing that, for the third day in a row, the scalpel lay inside, unused. It felt like she had been too late. Too late to make things better, to make things right, to undo the damage made by her mistakes. Even though Joy knew that she could remove the rest of the scar at any time, sever her ties to the Twixt and the possibility of Ink's forgiveness, she hadn't prepared herself for the possibility of Monica not being here. Alive. Safe.

Joy started hyperventilating, a thin squeeze of breath.

Every day since the accident, Joy had forced herself to come, to suffer the same awful temptation, to make the same choice, again and again. Every day she left wondering if she'd made the right choice—the brave choice or the coward's choice. Joy berated herself: what else did she have to lose? Ink hadn't contacted her in three days. *Three days!* His hurt was made clear. His hurt was now hers. But each time, Joy left the hospital with her scalpel still in her bag and Monica's head still full of stitches, and the doctors powered up expensive lasers and wrote data on charts, trying to re-create that initial bout of flawless healing.

The Reids called it a miracle. The doctors told them that

Monica was responding well to the laser treatments with unprecedented results. The shallowest part of the scar had completely disappeared, as well as the area over most of the nasal cavity, and they hoped to repair the deeper tissue damage. Joy knew it was only because she'd started erasing the scar and hadn't finished.

She could finish it. She could erase it completely and they would never know.

But I would know.

Each night she was almost sure she would change her mind the next day. And the next day she would go through it all over again: Should she? Shouldn't she?

Ink had stopped her, but Ink was gone. He was gone and it was over and he wasn't coming back. She had clung to the idea that he would forgive her—that he *could* forgive her—and that there was a chance that he'd come back and see things her way and Joy could have everything be perfect once again. But beneath that, she knew—if she was being honest with herself—that he was right. She had started to do something without thinking, something that had risked Ink and Inq and two worlds attached to one another by tenuous strings.

That was it, really, beneath everything: she was wrong. Joy knew that by using the scalpel to erase Ink's mark, she'd stepped over the line; willfully placing everything and everyone he cared about in danger was not something he could forgive, not after all they'd been through to keep one another safe. Everything they'd done had been in order to maintain the illusion that the Scribes were flawless and that Joy was not a threat and that their worlds were still safe, and she had almost screwed that up. By beginning to erase one legitimate mark that bound their worlds together, Joy had proven—irrevocably—how irresponsible she could be. It didn't even matter that she'd stopped; she couldn't undo what she had done, couldn't take it back. As a human, she could not be trusted.

As a human with the Sight, she was also dangerous. And as a human with the Sight and the ability to erase *signaturae*, she was something that couldn't be tolerated to exist without chains. That was what the Tide had been saying all along.

Ink had tried to tell her that back in the cache, Graus Claude had tried to tell her that back in the brownstone, but she hadn't listened—she hadn't understood. Now she knew: Ink loved his sibling and Joy loved Monica and that was stronger than loving one another enough to forgive and that was that.

She wished she could feel more sorry, somehow. He was right; she'd made her choice and he'd made his. It was over between them. She had to face facts. It was time for her to cut the last cords that bound her to that otherworld, the Twixt, the Council and Ink. She still hadn't managed to get rid of the knight's tagger mark on her back, but she could do this for Monica. Joy could do this for her. There was no reason to let Monica suffer. If she was going to pay the price, why not do the deed? There was no one who could stop her now.

Now was her chance.

The puckered line that had once gouged Monica's pretty face, dividing her sloping cheekbone and her wide nose, had skipped over her right eye to cleave through the eyebrow and into her hairline, where a patch had been shaved away during surgery. Joy had made herself look at it every day, staring until she'd memorized every stitch and wink of pink that stood out on Monica's ebony skin. And there, still burning with fairy light, was the slicing, spearlike arrow that she'd left half-undone. Joy wondered what happened when a *signatura* was left unfinished—was the person still claimed? Was the owner somehow affected? Alerted? She was pretty sure that neither Ink nor Inq had ever left a job half-done, and she would likely never have the chance to ask them.

Joy hadn't much time before someone else came in.

The beeping monitor counted out a constant rhythm, like the ticking of a clock counting down. She couldn't pretend she didn't know what she'd be doing this time; she was aware of the consequences. Ink had repudiated her. Even the DJ knew it. She was free to do as she liked. She was free to be human and make human mistakes for her human friends. If the Twixt was not part of her life anymore, then this was: Monica, the Reids, Gordon, her family. Enrique was right—these were the people that mattered most. But it would mean purposefully undoing Ink's work, unmaking his client's mark, choosing to place him and Inq in danger by reneging on an assignment. Risking possible obsolescence. Possible death.

Joy sat back.

She couldn't do it. Even if they weren't part of her life anymore, she didn't want to hurt them. And yet, she didn't want Monica to suffer, either. Every time she saw the look in Gordon's eyes or the hitch in Mrs. Reid's smile, she wanted to die. It was worse when they hugged her or thanked her for coming, for saving their daughter, for being such a good friend.

It was the worst when they trusted her enough to cry.

Joy clenched her teeth and opened her purse. She felt the cool steel of the surgical instrument, the texture of its handle against her fingertips. She knew the blade with her eyes closed; it was almost like a part of her now. She squeezed it, feeling the tiny crosshatches dig in her skin. Joy knew that she could do this, and that she shouldn't and that she wanted it more than she'd wanted to draw the *signatura* that had stopped Aniseed from infecting the world. She hadn't known, then, what she could do. She hadn't known, then, what it felt like to be invincible, to change the rules, to unmake mistakes. But she knew, now, what it felt like to lose.

The room had gone quiet, or perhaps she had stopped listening. The world shrank down to Monica's sleeping face on the pillow and the sunlight on her bed. The mattress crinkled under Joy's hip, metal things pinging and clinking as she shifted her weight. Joy rubbed the scalpel against her thumb, examining where she'd left off at the side of Monica's nose, now taped over, and where it bisected her eyebrow. Joy exhaled a deep breath. Her hand shook.

I'm sorry, she thought to her friend. *I can't do it.*

"Joy!"

Joy wrenched around, saw Mrs. Reid's face—the whites of her eyes great Os of shock. Her whole body stood rigid. She wasn't looking at Joy—she was looking at the scalpel in Joy's hand. Joy lowered it, feeling sick, her heart thundering.

"I—"

"Get away!" Mrs. Reid shrieked and lifted her e-reader over her head like a mallet. *"Get away from her right now!"*

Mrs. Reid lunged forward. Joy fell back, off the bed, into the corner, slamming into something against the wall. Pieces of plastic rained down. She raised her hands, her left elbow caught in her purse strap, her right hand still holding the surgical blade as she cowered on the floor. Mrs. Reid hadn't hit her yet, but it trembled in her arms. A mother's heart warred with her eyes as she loomed over Joy. She screamed again.

"Don't you *touch* her, Joy! DON'T YOU TOUCH HER!"

"I wouldn't!" Joy said, a pain in her back blossoming. She inched across the wall. They both spoke through tears. The way Mrs. Reid looked at her... Joy shrank, sobbing. *"Please!"*

Mrs. Reid's teeth were white against her brown lipstick, her eyes still wild and livid with tears. She shrieked something wordless and smacked Joy as she jumped to her feet and ducked past, making broken sounds as if she'd hurt herself more than Joy. Mrs. Reid threw herself across Monica's body, shielding her with her arms, choking on her pleas.

"Go away! Lord, Jesus, protect us. Get away from my girl!"

Joy tripped over the wooden chair and caught her shoe

on the curtain, pushing off the wall, under the TV mounts
and past the vacant bed, all white sheets and emptiness as
she ran into the hall, chased by the echo of Mrs. Reid's sobs.
Joy pushed the scalpel into her purse and bolted outside,
face flaming, ears burning, head ringing, unable to think
of anything as she made for her car in the parking lot nearest the river walk in her usual section B. She ran to the car
and dived inside.

Slamming the door, Joy sat back hard. She pressed her
hands over her face and screamed. The scream echoed off
her palms, wet, hot and sticky, smelling of hand sanitizer
and metal and guilt. She pushed her knuckles into her eyes
as if she could blot out the look on Mrs. Reid's face the moment she'd seen Joy with the scalpel in her hand. Joy knew
what she must have thought—knew what had to come next—
and didn't know whether she should call Gordon or Stef or
Mr. Reid or the hospital and somehow explain, or if it was all
pointless and the cops would come soon. She should go. *No!
Stay or you'll look guilty.* But she *was* guilty. Yet she wasn't. She
ought to stay here. She had an obligation, a responsibility.

Joy crawled her fingers through her hair. She deserved
this for waiting. For trying. For thinking that she could get
away with any of it. She sobbed into her hands and grabbed
a series of tissues from the box in the back, wiping her face
and pressing them against her eyes.

The police would find the scalpel. And the stuff on her
phone. The Twixt would find out. The Tide would win.

No. She had to go. Had to get out of here. She pulled the
parking stub tucked under the sun visor, balling up tissues
and looking for somewhere to put them. Febreze stung her
eyes, its smell not quite able to cover the stale odor of old
food ground into the carpet. Joy threw her purse into the
passenger's seat, buckled her belt and wiped her face with

shaking fingers. She turned to look over her shoulder before backing out.

The roof smashed inward with a sudden crash.

Joy screamed and hunched down, enveloped in a sudden haze of yellow-gold sparks. Another crash, and the roof caved in at a sharp angle. The windshield fragmented, a sudden wall of spiderwebs. A third blow, and it shattered in a hailstorm of jagged glass.

Joy threw her arms over her face and saw the Red Knight, carrying an enormous hammer, stride past the broken frame. He strutted around the car slowly, the clank of armor gritty against the asphalt. Lifting the enormous weapon, he brought it down again on the hood. Joy jolted in her seat, bouncing off the collapsed ceiling. Her glyph-armor glowed, the light reflecting off chips of glass. They rattled against the floor as the Kia bounced on its shocks.

Tucking her knees, Joy yanked her feet away from the pedals just as another hammer blow smashed in the engine. Joy groaned as the steering wheel slammed into her side. She tried to open the door behind her, but it was wedged, buckled inward. She tried the lock. It wouldn't move. Joy scrambled on her elbows, pushing her hands and feet against both doors, trying to free the latches. Desperate wheezing sounds whistled through her teeth. The Red Knight drew closer with an eerie satisfaction; the helmet's eye slit fixed on Joy's struggles as he swung the hammer around, then down.

The impact forced Joy flat over the gearshift. The armor protected her from the roof, now crushed into the headrest, but couldn't help her escape out the crumpled doors. The Red Knight struck again. The car shuddered. Metal squealed. He was taking his time, carefully aiming his blows. Joy was being slowly crushed inside the car, the thin metal warping around her like foil. She kicked at the window, whimpering in her throat. The remaining glass was thick, toothy shards, and terror made her miss. She was lying prone. She was at the wrong angle. She could barely move. She was trapped.

The Red Knight circled the wreckage. She could almost feel him sizing up the angle, calculating the kill. She pounded her hands against the splintered plastic, against the twisted metal and the foam near her head. He raised the square war hammer high over his shoulders. Joy shot her left palm forward and *pushed!*

The passenger window exploded, shoving the knight back. He stumbled against the incline, thrown off balance, the hammer's weight pulling him back, his armored feet slipping on soft earth. Joy struggled to drag her purse across the car, up onto her belly, but the strap caught on a belt buckle and the zipper pull was out of reach. She needed the scalpel. She needed to *get him! Get the knight! Get out! He was so close!* She yanked the leather in desperation and tried not to cry.

Her head whipped sideways as the car slammed backward. The impact of the hammer caved in the front of the car, spinning it slightly on its wheels, adding to her panic and vertigo. A wave of nausea rolled through her, and she smelled hot rubber. Joy gritted her teeth and turned on her side, reaching to open the purse with her left hand. The car slammed forward, struck from the back. Joy's body flew sideways, protected from impact but not momentum. The backseat had crumpled; the seats snapped in half. Joy gasped, coughing dry filaments that powdered the air, feeling the closeness of the metal and the molding and glass. She was being violently crushed by degrees.

Another slam flattened the roof, pressing the ceiling flush against Joy's chest, stopped only by the armor: a hairsbreadth of golden light. The glyphs on her skin pulsed, swirling over limbs caught in awkward angles, still fumbling for the scalpel hidden somewhere in her purse. Her fingers struggled to obey the ragged tendrils of her last cohesive thought: that she needed to *get the knight* and *hurt him* and *get out!*

The steering wheel pinned her head against the seat cushion. She could feel her fingers move, feel the zipper catch and pull, feel the air blowing in from the open windshield. She held her breath and tried to stretch a little more—she could almost feel the handle—*not enough!* She wanted to scream, but her jaw was pressed flat and there was no one to call. She couldn't even imagine grabbing Filly's pouch of vellum notes and then lighting a tiny fire.

Joy's fingers closed inside the purse. Grabbed her phone instead. She nearly cried.

"Ink," she whimpered, trying to concentrate on locating the scalpel and not on the Red Knight, who was somewhere just outside.

There was a groaning shift and Joy felt gravity yank her forward. She would have tumbled off the seat cushions if she hadn't been pinned. Her feet scrabbled for purchase, heels catching on the armrest. The car tilted up at a dangerous angle, the fender shrieking and grinding against the cement. The Red Knight power-lifted the back of the ruined car and was pushing it forward with a scream of metal and asphalt.

Toward the edge of the lot. Over the incline. Into the river.

The Red Knight wasn't going to bother breaking her armor; she was going to drown.

Joy flattened her palm against the roof and mentally *pushed* and *pushed*—wind whipped at her hair and face, flapping her cheeks, but the metal was too strong and she was too scared. The world jerked upward and Joy screamed as keys and loose change and CDs slid over her face. One foot dangled out the broken window.

There was a moment of sickening weightlessness and then the car slammed down on four wheels.

Her head lit up like fireworks, limbs jostling around her

torso pinned in the metal pinch. Joy realized that she was still on land, although she felt the front wheels teeter. She could see it in her mind's eye: the slippery grass fell quickly over the sharp incline to the rocky riverbed below. Water lapped at the reeds where it dipped deeper offshore, full of buzzing dragonflies and burping frogs. There was more than enough room for the car to sink, and she was hanging on the precipice.

The wounded car gave a low, creaking moan.

There was a scuffling sound in the distance punctuated by a *shing* and *clang* on the wind.

"Help!" Joy shouted with what little breath she had. "Help me!"

She shuddered as the car listed. The front wheels began to dip.

There was a heavy thud against the back of the car and a tug that yanked the car slowly back onto the pavement. It evaporated suddenly when a crashing slam came down on the trunk, shaking the car as well as Joy's teeth. She squeezed her eyes shut.

She let go of her purse strap and fumbled for the lever, trying to push the seat back and give her elbow some room to move. Reaching behind, her fingers brushed the curved edge of the knob. She shifted her shoulders, twisting her spine expertly to gain another precious inch and tried again, using the side of her wrist to press down.

The seat moved. Joy gasped and reached toward the back to pull her legs free, digging her hands into the exposed stuffing. She kicked hard against the door.

Beyond the empty rear window, Joy saw the Red Knight fighting Ink.

It wasn't elegant or calculating—it was eager and brutal—but then Joy realized that this probably wasn't any of the previous knights. This Red Knight charged his way forward, sweeping his great hammer through the air and shifting its trajectory to drive Ink back across the yellow-lined parking lot through lines of imported cars. Ink parried with slashes of his straight razor, its power throwing musical sparks when it struck. Hunched forward, the Red Knight lunged, driving Ink like a lion, but the Scribe was a squirrel, a monkey, a fish, nimbly skipping over obstacles and easily dodging the hammer as if skimming through the water.

He's here! Joy kept thinking as she struggled. *He came!*

The Red Knight flung the hammer sideways, unearthing one of the security gate pylons that tumbled end over end, spilling great chunks of cement and soil. The shattered call box blew a geyser of fat sparks. Ink sprang over a Ford truck. The Red Knight pursued.

Joy swallowed thickly. Ink was playing bait.

She hauled herself forward, pulling her body through the cramped space between the front seats, using the lower edge of the rear window as a handhold to draw herself up and every bit of her body's skill to contort around the wreckage. She gripped the soft cushions, tearing stuffing and stitches, leveraging herself on one elbow, clawing for the crumpled trunk. Her upper body strength was more than enough to pull her up and out. Joy lifted her shoulders and felt her foot tangle on her purse strap caught on the belt somewhere. She kicked desperately, scraping her ankle against the emergency brake. The car buckled under her efforts and let out a squeal.

That was when the Red Knight saw her—half-in and half-out of the wreck—and that was the precise moment when Ink saw her, too.

The knight swung in a tight circle, lifting the hammer in both hands, grunted and let go. The hammer flew toward her. Joy cringed and braced herself against the car.

The hammer slammed into a ward and fell with an ominous clang on the ground.

Joy stretched to look. But the ward hadn't come from Ink.

"Get out of the car!" screamed Stef, who stood sweaty and rumpled on the other side of the parking lot, hands outstretched and flattened before him as if pressed against a wall. There were symbols drawn along the length of his arms and below both eyes. His arms shook.

Ink appeared beside the car, half crouched, having thrown himself through a breach somewhere near the ground. He exhaled as he slid to a halt, his eyes sharp as obsidian glass.

The Red Knight howled and charged. Ink spun to his feet, but not in time to stop the bull-rush impact of the armored shoulder hitting the car's left taillight, slamming the wreckage forward and over the edge.

Joy felt the sickening tilt as her ankle caught in her purse strap. Ink dived beneath the car and stabbed his weapon upward, piercing the floor. The Kia pivoted on the axis, circling, dragging its wheels through the dirt, smashing its front wheel into the divider, wrapping the fender around a pylon and lodging its headlight on the cap. The car stopped, torqued clockwise, Ink buried beneath the muffler.

Joy kicked off her shoe and pulled her leg free, slithering out of the car as fast as she could, but red mail gauntlets appeared, gouging into the trunk, gripping with fierce effort as the Red Knight clawed after her. Joy scrambled back over the corrugated roof. Beneath the blood-colored faceplate came a hollow, feral snuffling—a grunting, animalistic *need* that made Joy's primal instincts squeal. She stumbled, sliding backward, glyphs flaring on her skin.

There was a flash. Then another. And another.

Stef's voice called, *"Joy!"*

The car lurched. Joy grabbed the edge of a window. The Red Knight tightened his grip. She kicked him in the face. Her armor flared. The knight snorted.

Ink appeared over his shoulder, yanked back the helmet and stabbed wickedly under the chin.

A great gush of blood spewed across the trunk of the car, catching the edge of Joy's bare foot and spraying over the side. She flailed. The Red Knight pitched forward, head loose, then pitched back, falling with a heavy thump on the ground. Ink leaped away, eyes following the knight as its body tumbled down the incline past the teetering car, grinding to a clunky stop by the lip of the stream. Cattails bent lazily under his outstretched arm.

The car tipped. Joy stiffened. Ink offered her a hand and she took it. He quickly helped her down, and they retreated a few feet from the ruined, blood-spattered car.

Joy stared at his fingers instead of staring at him. He was here—she could feel him—but it didn't seem real. A tickling, trickling energy flowed up her leg, soothing and cool. She looked down and wiped her bloody bare foot in the grass.

"I didn't think you'd come," she whispered. Ink said nothing and dropped her hand. She swallowed and twisted her fingers in the edge of her shirt. She couldn't ask him the question she really wanted answered, so instead she asked, "How did you know?"

Ink didn't look at her, and she wondered if he was even willing to speak to her anymore. If he could stand to look at her after what she'd almost done.

"I placed a mark on your phone," he said. "I did not tell you, and when you exchanged it for a new one, I did not realize what had happened until..." Joy remembered his panic when she and Inq had returned from Mr. Vinh's. Ink unfolded the wallet and blew on the blade; tiny droplets of blood dissolved in the wind. He placed the clean arrowhead inside the leather and folded it back into thirds.

He'd killed again. For her. She tried to catch his eye.

"It took some time to place the next one," he said coolly.

His face hardened; his voice flattened to match. "I heard your call and I answered."

She flushed, still running on adrenaline, fear and shame. The feeling wore Mrs. Reid's face, and now Ink's. "Why did you come?"

Ink dug his heel in the dark, rich earth soaked in blood. "Because I promised that I would keep you safe from the Red Knight. I am bound by that promise, no matter what else has changed," he said, turning aside. "I cannot lie. And I keep my promises."

Joy folded her arms, hurt.

Stef was gaining ground, circling the parking lot, looking scared and sweaty and livid.

"I will ask Inq to update your armor with the *signatura* for the next Red Knight," he said. "And I will pay for it, since it was my actions here today that necessitated the change." Ink wiped a hand against his hip. "I would not want you further indebted to your former employer."

Joy swallowed against the tightness in her throat. She wanted to scream at him. She wanted to ask if he'd bothered to find out what she'd done for the Bailiwick, for people like Ysabel. Would that have helped? What did he think of her now? Did it matter? He was there and she was here, and it felt like there were miles between them instead of only a few feet. Joy felt awful and ashamed and guilty and scared. She wanted to beg him to *look* at her, to say something, to ask her why, to listen, to let her explain...

Ink watched Stef dive past the pylon. "I will go now."

"Wait." She had to say something. Find something to make him stay. He paused and she grabbed for the moment. "Why did the Red Knight go after you?"

"Because I would not let him hurt you."

Joy tried to ignore the past tense in order to make her point. "Graus Claude said that the Red Knight has no interest in anyone other than its contracted target. He said that my friends and family would be safe," Joy said. "Even so, he should have tried to kill me, not go chasing after you." She twisted her fingers together. "But this one went after you with a vengeance. I saw it. He wanted to *kill* you. I could see it in the way he moved."

"Yes. He was not very good," Ink admitted. "More brute force than experience." He turned to face her but glanced away into the ruin of the parking lot rather than look into her eyes. "As soon as I appeared, he dropped the car and came after me. That does not align with his contractual obligations or his reputation." Ink finally looked at her, but his eyes were not kind and his dimples were nowhere to be seen. "It was not until he saw you emerging from the vehicle that he refocused his attack."

A horrid chill crept up her sides. "So I should have stayed in the car?"

"No," Ink said. "I would guess that they are operating under old intelligence that I am bound to you for other reasons and not merely an impediment to success."

His voice was flat and matter-of-fact. Joy resisted biting back. Ink should know that she hadn't meant to hurt him or Inq and she hadn't done anything more to Monica's scar—shouldn't that count for something? Shouldn't that help? Shouldn't that prove something good about her? Even at that last moment just now, she hadn't—she couldn't—but now the Reids thought she'd attacked their daughter, and Ink thought that she'd purposefully risked his life and their worlds and everyone hated her.

The thought struck her full in the face, hot and horrid: *he hates me.*

She felt Stef's hands grab her shoulders, but she didn't turn around.

"That's it?" she said, her voice trembly and quiet. "That's all?"

Ink turned away, his fingers clenching into fists, the wallet chain swinging a silent metronome at his hip.

He kicked the car. There was a sound of tearing metal, a lurch of its innards, and the car broke free, dragged by its own weight down the hillside, rolling over the body of the knight by the stream. Its tires hit the water with a splash and listed. Ink tossed Joy's open purse at her feet.

"I will keep you safe from the Red Knight," he said as it hit the ground. "But that is all." He glanced up for a moment. He looked hopeful, intense. "Joy..."

Her heart lurched. "Ink?"

He shook his head, his slicing voice barely a whisper on the wind. "Do not let me lose you."

Joy stepped forward, but Stef's hands held her back. Ink flicked his wrist, slicing a clumsy tear in the world through which he made his silent escape. Stef hugged her shoulders tightly as Joy watched him go.

FOURTEEN

STEF'S FORK CHASED PEAS AROUND HIS PLATE, MAKING awkward scraping sounds that Joy felt in her teeth. They'd left the wreck, Stef had cancelled his plans and they'd stayed home and made lasagna with way too much cheese and not nearly enough sauce. Stef had boiled a bag of frozen peas to add some semblance of green. Mom had called, but Joy hadn't said much. She didn't know what to say besides "I love you." The image of Mrs. Reid shielding her daughter with her body kept burning in the back of her mind.

Stef's overshirt hung unbuttoned over his inside-out tee, and Joy tapped the floor with the toes of her shoes. It was a lot like having dinner with Dad during the Year of Silence before the divorce went through, but it was Joy who was now feeling weepy and quiet and grim.

"Eat," Stef urged, pushing the bowl of peas toward her. Joy accepted it through a fog, scooping sad pebbly orbs onto her plate. She rubbed the bruises on her arm. Stef still had runes on his. He chewed and swallowed. "Want to talk about it?"

"No."

A tinkly silence resumed: *plink, clink, scritch.*

"That's why you needed the armor?"

Joy swallowed peas. "Yes."

Scrape, clank, ping.

"I can see why you and Dad are so close," Stef said. "You're a brilliant conversationalist."

Joy slammed down her fork. "Who's the guy from the Carousel, Stef? The DJ from the Twixt? Because he said to say hi."

Unfazed, Stef shrugged and kept sawing at a stringy forkful of cooling cheese. "I don't know," he said. "Could be anyone. Probably an old client."

"Client?" Joy said. The word brought a rush of images: Graus Claude, the brownstone office, the files at Dover Mill. "You have *clients*?"

"Had. Yeah," he said and waved the fork at the long lines of glyphs drawn in marker from elbow to wrist. "Most wizards need ingredients of power." He poked his skin with the butter knife. "Mine's built-in, remember? Blood, tears, hair, skin. I learned enough on my own so I could freelance now and again, but when I signed on for my apprenticeship, my Master didn't like it."

Joy sputtered, "Your 'Master'?"

"Don't act all Voldemort." Stef spoke around another mouthful of lasagna. "I'm an apprentice. He's the master, hence the title."

Joy twisted her fingers in her napkin, ignoring her plate. "And your clients?"

Stef sawed more forcefully. "A few charms and potions here and there," he said. "Nothing major. It paid the bills, which is not something to sneeze at." He sighed and put down his fork, scrubbing his mouth with his napkin. "Speaking of which, I can't believe you wrecked the car."

"I didn't wreck the car," Joy said. "It was wrecked while I was in it. By someone other than me—literally *Other Than* me!" She'd been avoiding thinking about how she'd been trapped inside and nearly crushed to death and drowned; there were certain things like near-death experiences, Ink's dismissal and the look on Mrs. Reid's face that her brain didn't need to dwell on right now. "Besides," she said. "Better a used hunk of scrap metal than me."

"Is that the argument you plan to use with Dad?" Stef asked. "Or will that come after the story about how you lost your summer job?"

Joy winced. Everything in her life felt somehow too big and too small at the same time: real-life problems felt bloated in comparison and a totaled car ranked low on the totem pole of her life right now. The Reids thought she'd done something terrible, Monica was still in the hospital, Ink felt betrayed by her but was bound by his promise and she was out both friends and jobs while the Red Knight was out there trying to find new ways to kill her before Graus Claude could rescind the order.

"I was kinda hoping to avoid telling him as long as humanly possible," Joy said.

"Ah, avoidance. Very wise," Stef said, piling utensils on his plate. "Remember—one conniption fit at a time."

Joy picked at her plate, watching Stef clear his place. "Are you going to tell me how you made a ward back there?"

Stef scraped his plate into the trash. "No."

"Why?"

"It's not my design—it's my Master's. That's how wizardry works," he said. "Consider it patented material."

She ate more peas.

Stef turned on the water, washing the last smear of marinara off the plate. "Well, lucky for you, it's over now. No more knights in bloody armor, no more Twixt and a last gasp of debt-filled summer stretching out before you."

There was a sharp knock at the door and they both looked up. Stef shut off the water and Joy stood, feeling tingly right down to her toes. He glanced a question at her. She shrugged as she walked over to the door and peered through the peephole.

The heart-shaped face on the other side of the lens didn't look happy.

"I'm not in the mood," Joy said.

"Open the door."

Joy sighed and opened the door.

Inq strode in.

Stef nearly tripped over his shoes backing into the counter. Inq ignored him.

"Sit," she ordered. Resigned, Joy sat. Inq pushed back her chin, inspecting her neck. Glyphs flared gold in response to her touch. Stef choked out a word.

"You—"

"Quiet," Inq said. Stef froze. "You'll need to break the mark—" she pressed her forefinger hard into Joy's flesh "—here. I have the new one ready when you are." She pulled a slip of paper out of the pocket of her sleek black leather jacket. "Ink gave this to me and said to get here ASAP."

Joy swallowed. "I'll need a mirror."

"Just draw the blade across the skin," Inq said with a humorless smile. "It's like slitting your own throat. I'd be happy to help."

"Okay," Stef said, "this is officially no longer dinner conversation." There was no salt on the table, but Stef pointed with his butter knife. "You. Out."

Inq sized up Stef in one long, drawling glance. "Does he come with a leash?" she asked.

Joy lowered her chin. "Stop."

"Pity," Inq said. "It'd suit him."

Stef glared. "Not my kink."

"Enough," Joy said, getting up. "She's here to help." Joy looked between the two of them. "Sort of."

Stefan crossed his arms tightly across his chest and retreated warily to the counter's edge. The tag of his backward/

inside-out shirt wagged below his Adam's apple as he swallowed. He watched Inq carefully as Joy unzipped her purse.

"I thought we were done here," he said too loudly.

"Relax," Inq said. "This is just a house call. I'm here to
protect her."

"It seems to be that your kind's form of 'protection' keeps
almost getting her killed." Stef's angry retort came out more
like a plea. Joy paused and stared at her brother. He was
afraid. *Really* afraid.

Inq smiled at his evident discomfort. "It's not easy to love
a sibling, is it?" she said, turning a sideways glance to Joy.
"Their pain so quickly becomes your own."

Joy returned to her chair with the scalpel in hand, hair
hanging down to cover her face. She touched the tip of the
blade to her throat, cool and sharp. Stef made a strangled
noise. Inq held up a hand to stay him.

"Don't worry," Joy whispered. "I'm just..." She found that
she couldn't even begin to explain. Stef didn't know. She'd
never told him. She traded looks with Inq. "It's fine," she said
and brushed back her hair. Joy felt the light tug at the handle
as she slipped the blade beneath the Red Knight's mark and
cut. She felt the pressure evaporate with a wash of cool air,
an odd, unsullied kiss on her unprotected skin. She tilted
her chin to the side, like Ysabel on the couch, surrendering
to Inq. Again. "Did I get it?"

"Yes," said Inq. "Now sit still."

Stef hovered behind Inq as she drew her thumbs over Joy's
throat, sending the alien heat into her body, curling in warm
wisps of honeyed brandy beneath her tonsils.

"This is why I always have more than one of you," Inq said
as she worked. "Human hearts—fickle as the wind."

"I'm not," Joy said.

Inq squeezed her throat a little harder than necessary.
"You are."

Joy stayed quiet as Inq's fingers wound their magic. It was nothing like it had been before, and Joy knew that all the care and love and gentleness had gone out of Inq, reminding her of the veiled, dark threats the Scribe had issued back when they'd first met. Joy had broken something between them by upsetting Ink. Anger she could deal with, but hurting her brother was death.

"He made me promise—he made me *swear*—to make it perfect. To protect you," Inq murmured softly. "You who would so easily cast us aside, undo everything that we have worked for, what we have given you—you selfish, ungrateful *brat*." She curled the loop around the top of the sigil, muttering hotly under her breath. "Power, wealth, status, our integrity, my protection," she whispered a hiss. "His heart. None of it is good enough for you."

Joy felt the lines of power surge, a splash of light and heat as the newest *signatura* melded into her armor. The latest incarnation of the Red Knight was up and running, another assassin on the hunt for her blood. Who had ordered the contract? Would Graus Claude bother to stop it now that she was no longer welcome in the Twixt? Would the newest Red Knight still go after Ink? Would this moment with Inq be their last?

Before Joy could thank her, the Scribe wrapped her fingers around Joy's throat and gave her a quick shake. Stef grabbed Inq's arm and she threw him off, releasing Joy with disgust plain on her face.

"Don't make me do this again," she said. "You have a problem? Fix it yourself!"

"How?" Joy said carefully, coughing and rubbing her neck. "How can I stop it?" Stef's hands were on her shoulders, holding her steady, but she trembled with more than anger or fear. "They'll just keep coming—you know they will. How do I stop it?"

Inq smiled mockingly, her eyes devilish and sad. "Do what you always do—hide behind a ward," she said.

"The house is already warded," Joy said. "And so is my armor, but that won't stop the Red Knight."

"There are different kinds of armor, Joy—those that keep danger out and those that keep danger in," she said. "If you lock the Red Knight's Name in place so there cannot be any others, you can take care of him yourself. Force it upon him. Bind him to his mark. It's just armor, Joy—think about it. Consider it another gift from me to you." Inq slammed her palm flat against the kitchen table; the slip of paper with the scribbled *signatura* of the latest Red Knight was trapped under her fingers. "If you're brave enough, and can get close enough, you can carve his mark—bind him to his Name— make him wear it. Make it stick. Your armor will repulse him and he cannot touch you. I daresay you'll be the only one who has ever had the chance to try." She pushed herself upward, away from the Malones. "My brother will not always be there to save you."

Joy swayed in her own brother's grasp, wary and warm.

"How did you get in here?" she said. "His wards...?"

"Oh, they're still here," Inq said. "Despite everything, Ink has not abandoned you yet. And there is nowhere he can go that I cannot follow. Besides, my blood still lives on your threshold." She gestured to the open hall. "I can make it this far. And, just a heads-up, you let me in." Her eyes flicked to Stef, whose hands tightened on Joy's shoulders. "Blood calls to blood. Thicker than water, so they say. But even back in the Old Days, I never developed a taste for it." She snapped her tiny teeth together. "Too salty."

Joy felt Stef's hands tighten again, a tremor buzzing along her bones.

"Get. Out."

Inq winked and slid her palm up the edge of the door.

"Don't get your boxers in a twist," she told him. "I'm already gone."

The door slammed closed. Stef spun her around.

"Are you *insane?*" he snapped. "What was that?"

"That was Inq."

"No." He drew a slicing line across his throat. "That. What was that?"

"That was this." Joy held up the scalpel. "This was Ink's. He gave it to me for my birthday after we figured out what it could do—what I could do with it."

"What—?" Stef's hands were on his hips, like he was anchoring himself for something. He shifted his weight. He licked his lips. "What can you do, exactly?"

"I can erase marks," she said. "Remove them."

"Marks? Marks like those?" He gestured to her whole body, which still glowed faintly, fading as the Red Knight's link settled into place. "Then do it. Remove them."

"I can't..."

"You just said you could," he said. "You just did."

Joy tucked her bangs behind her ear. "I had to replace one of the links. That's why Inq was here." She pushed past him, gathering her plate and napkin for something to do. "The Red Knight's *signatura* keeps changing, so in order to stay protected, I have to update the glyph." Joy started scraping bits into the trash. "And I'm not supposed to be able to do that— no one is. That's what got me into trouble with the Council in the first place. It's what got me into trouble with Ink. And Inq. And the Reids." Joy started crying and put the scalpel and the plate down on the counter.

Stef sank into his chair and pushed away from the table. He cleared a small space to rest his elbows as he ruffled his hands through his hair and took a deep breath.

"Okay," he said. "I am officially beyond capacity." He adjusted his glasses, sliding his thumb over the glyphs scratched into the sides. "I want you to start at the beginning and keep talking until you get to right here, right now. Go."

What did she have to lose? Joy started talking, beginning at the Carousel with Ink and Inq and a razor in the dark up to Aniseed's plot to kill the bulk of humanity and bring about a legendary Golden Age, to Graus Claude and Kurt and those loyal to the Council finally taking them down. She talked about how the Scribes marked humans and the accidental discovery that she could erase marks and why it had to be kept secret from those who already didn't like her being a human with the Sight. She talked about the Tide and the Red Knight and her armor, skipping over certain sundry details like Hasp, Briarhook, Ilhami's drug bust and how far she'd gone shaping Ink's naked body. Joy explained how she'd saved herself from the magic disease by removing the *signaturae* on her skin and finished with why Ink was so angry because she'd put everything and everyone he loved at risk, how Mrs. Reid had found her with the scalpel over Monica's face and why Inq had had to come over since Ink had killed another Red Knight in order to redraw its reincarnated *signatura* on her invisible, illicit armor.

"I don't know whether I'll still have to go before the Council," Joy said after a long drink of water, "considering that I may no longer be part of the Twixt, but Ink's sworn to protect me as long as the Red Knight is still after me, and yet that still doesn't explain the weird mark on my back." She took another cool drink of water. She'd been talking for a while. "Maybe it'll disappear when the contract's lifted?" She looked over at her brother. His face had gone blank. "Stef?"

He pushed back his chair, calmly stood up and picked his keys out of the dish by the door. He didn't look at her, but he paused in the entrance.

"Stay here, Joy," he said.

"Stef?"

His eyes were hard. Not cold but hard. His voice was, too. "Joy Malone. Stay. Here." Stef blinked once. "Trust me."

She did. Of course she trusted him.

He walked out and closed the door.

Joy jumped out of her seat and yanked the door wide-open, aware suddenly of the edge of the wards and the fresh protections and the fact that Inq's blood must have seeped into the hall carpet or into the cracks between jambs. *Ew.* She stopped, unwilling to cross the threshold. She heard Stef's footfalls quickly disappearing down the stairs.

"Stef!" she called after him. He didn't answer. Joy stayed in the doorway out of respect or fear. *"Stef!"* She stomped her foot. "It doesn't matter! It's over!"

She leaned forward to call down the hall. Pain erupted in the back of her brain, crawling up her shoulders and wrapping like a hoodie over her head. Joy reeled back and slammed the door closed with her elbows, pushing the meat of her thumbs against her temples and grinding her teeth. Her neck and shoulders bunched with the runny feeling that she might have a nosebleed; she could almost taste the scorched-flesh flavor of Briarhook's branding by memory alone.

What's happening?

She clawed off her T-shirt and pressed it into her eyes. She breathed in the scent of her deodorant and gave a muffled groan. Blinking, she expected to see burned holes or blood, but her shirt was pristine, if rumpled. She dropped it to the floor and stumbled to the bathroom.

Leaning over the sink, she stared into her own face, flushed and feverish. She felt like she'd been gut-punched. She felt like throwing up. Images of cold melted cheese and marinara made her insides churn. She wiped damp bangs away from her eyes and sat one cheek on the sink, twisting sideways to take a look at the thing on her back.

The ghostly sigil burned with a peppery sheen. It glistened

along semicircular, sloping lines—a thin, squiggly shape blurred at its center, splitting and curving into a hazy circlet. It was morphing, becoming clearer if not clear. She ran her fingers over it. Grabbing a washcloth, she scrubbed at it, which only turned her skin pink. Joy twisted in both directions to try to get a good look, to see it in her mind's eye. Perhaps the Red Knight was nearby? If this was a magic tag to sniff her out, was the pain a proximity alert? A warning? Or something worse? Was something *happening* to her? She tried to remember when else she'd gotten sudden headaches, but it was becoming too hard to think.

Joy ran into the kitchen in her shorts and bra. Snatching the scalpel from the counter and her purse from the table, she ran to the door-length mirror in her closet to once again try to slip the blade underneath the shape and break the mark. She struggled on her tiptoes, straining her elbows and neck. It wouldn't catch. It was like trying to cut clouds with a knife.

She dropped her hand and rolled her shoulders. Her eyes in the mirror looked cagey and wild. Joy had the sinking feeling that time was running out. The Red Knight was after her and she was all alone, safe behind wards—for now—lost but not forgotten.

A thin smell of smoke penetrated her rising fear. Joy turned, trying to locate the scent, worried that she'd left something burning on the stove, and saw a tiny trickle of gray curling up from her purse. She spilled its contents onto the floor. Sifting through the mess, Joy found the small pouch from Filly—it was warm. Loosening the drawstrings, Joy fished out a tiny roll of paper from the small puff of smoke. Unrolling it, she read the words:

The Red Knight now hunts Ink. Orders from the Tide. Burn this after reading.

Joy blinked. Her mind fogged. The words didn't make sense, or, if they did, they wouldn't fit inside her brain. She couldn't make them fit. The Red Knight? The Red Knight was after Ink? That made no sense! The floor fell out beneath her and she stumbled against the counter as her knees buckled. Her mind swam. *Ink! No!* Joy focused on the last words: *Burn this after reading.* Okay. She could do that. She would start there.

Joy went back to the kitchen and, flipping over the note, wrote back, *Please come. I need help!-JM* and turned on the stove. She placed the piece of paper on the metal burner and waited, watching as the bit of paper curled brown then black then ash. She turned off the gas, put on her shirt and picked up her phone out of habit. She should tell someone, shouldn't she? She should call someone.

Who?

Monica? No. Stef? No. Dad? No. Mom? God no. She flipped over her phone, searching for Ink's mark, but she didn't see it. It had gone, disappeared. She held her cell phone in her hands, like a prayer, and said, "Ink." Then she searched through her call history and dialed Enrique. The phone connected and told her that the number was no longer in service. Worried, she tried Ilhami. Then Luiz. Then Nikolai— all the same. Even Tuan and Antony, whom she only knew by the smiling faces on her camera, had had their numbers blocked or changed. She'd been rejected, shunned. First Ink, and then Inq, Graus Claude and now the Cabana boys. Even Stef? Everyone was systematically shutting her out. Leaving her. Abandoning her.

Joy began to cry.

Wiping her face, she started searching through her contacts. Maybe Graus Claude would still take his messages?

Maybe Kurt could help? Maybe Stef took his phone? Maybe Filly...

There was a rumble that shook the kitchen window and a small sonic boom. A voice shouted from outdoors.

"Joy Malone!"

Her head snapped up in recognition and relief. She ran to the window and saw Filly outside the gate, hands curled into fists, vambraces flashing in the sun. The blue tattooed spots on her face showed livid against her skin. Her lips split in a wide grin as her cape of bones rattled in the wind.

"Joy Malone! Come outside!"

"I don't think I can!" Joy said. She drew her fingers along the sill and felt the tickle of the ward keeping her safe inside. The Red Knight might be out there, but she was surely stuck in here.

Filly grumbled and kicked a patch of dirt. She squinted up at the window.

"Then tell me quick," she said.

"The Red Knight is after Ink?"

Filly bobbed her head. "Yes, yes, I know. I was the one to tell you," she said. "But do you know why?"

Joy shrugged. "I'm not sure."

Filly stamped her foot like an impatient animal. "Think!" she said. "Do you know why?"

"Maybe," Joy said. "The Red Knight wants to flush me out. He can't get through my armor, but he can get around it as long as there's no one there to help. Now Ink's dumped me, Inq's furious with me, Graus Claude fired me and all my go-to numbers are gone. I've basically been kicked out of the Twixt." As she said it, Joy realized she wasn't sad about it. She was mad. *How dare they!* Her voice gained some heat. "It's like everything the Tide wanted has happened already!"

Filly crossed her arms. "Well, what are you going to do about it?"

"I'm not sure yet. Something."

Filly grinned. "That's why I told you," she said. "Because you will *do* something. Not like those nattering heads in the Halls—all talk! You and I, we make things happen."

"Yes!" Joy said, gripping the edge of the sink. She realized that she, Joy Malone, could do a lot, but not alone. "Will you help me?"

"Of course," Filly said in her boisterous, boastful crow. "I will agree to help you if you agree to help me."

Joy hesitated. "With what?"

"With payment only you can provide," Filly said. Joy's internal alarms started clanging, and Filly laughed at whatever look crossed her face. "You've already given me your most valuable possession, Joy Malone, but I need your help solving a riddle." She patted her nest of braids and grinned. "If you are willing to aid me in that, I will most certainly aid you now."

Joy twisted her fingers. She wasn't great at riddles, but the young horsewoman had only asked for her help, not on the condition that they succeed. If nothing else, Joy had learned to think through some of the loopholes of language when dealing with the Twixt. Joy took a deep breath, then nodded. "Done."

"Excellent!" Filly crowed and clapped both her hands. "You have a plan?"

"Not yet," Joy said.

"Aha. Well, first thing's first," Filly said, kicking the gate. A blue spark shot up. "You are well protected or well caged."

Joy considered the window ledge and the door and the glyphs she knew must be there, repelling the dangers, keeping her safe. *Wards. Glyphs. Sigils. Marks. She knew what she could do with those.*

She picked up her scalpel.

"Not for long," she muttered and slipped the blade through Ink's ward.

FIFTEEN

JOY FIDGETED IN THE PASSENGER'S SEAT, AWARE THAT every moment was another that the Red Knight might have already killed Ink. If this was all a ploy to flush her out of hiding, it was working very well. She could be playing into a trap. She could be running toward death. She was dropping her protections, her defenses, one by one. But she couldn't help it; even if he didn't want her anymore, even if the Twixt refused her, she had to try—she had to help Ink.

It was stronger than a promise. It was her choice. She chose him over feeling guilty, being scared or worried about making more mistakes. Letting pride get in the way would be the biggest mistake she could make. It was her own advice that echoed in her brain. *You love him, you don't want to break up, so don't. It's that simple.*

She loved him, he loved her, end of story. Really, it was as simple as that.

And she was going to save them both.

She'd told Stef she had to leave as soon as he'd come home—thankfully after Filly had gone off with her instructions. Stef had been none too pleased about their latest visit from an Other Than, and she'd needed him to listen. Once he'd gotten it into his head that the house was no longer safe and that he couldn't *make* her stay, he'd relented—albeit angrily—and insisted on coming along. Unfortunately, Joy couldn't *make* him stay, either.

Stef drove, sleeves pushed up to the elbows, arms riddled with drawn-on glyphs. Joy couldn't help staring at them any more than he could help staring at hers. Her brother hadn't liked the fact that she'd cut the house wards—and liked her urgent, desperate plan to leave the house even less—but he'd agreed to drive her wherever she wanted and to keep his mouth shut as long as he got to come along.

It was the perfect sibling outing: under duress.

Joy stared out the window, trying to follow every detail flying by. As long as the Red Knight didn't attack them en route, they'd be okay. Joy knew Stef would kill her if she wrecked his new car.

"For the record, I *really* don't like this," Stef said.

Joy sniffed and twisted her fingers in her shirt. "Duly noted. Keep driving."

He checked the GPS again. "I'm serious, Joy. Striking deals with Other Thans is a bad idea," he said. "Historically speaking, it's an *incredibly* bad idea."

"So says the apprentice wizard," she said. "'Sometimes we must choose immediately unpleasant things in order to prevent greater unpleasantness.'"

"Who said that?"

Joy sighed. "Ink." She stared grimly out the window and thought about Ink and Inq and the ugly, fearful churning in her stomach for what she was about to do. *Unpleasant* hardly covered it.

"It's up here," she said and pointed up the gravel lane past the nature preserve's brown wooden sign. Stef obligingly pulled up the road, small rocks pinging harmlessly off the underside of his car. His eyes craned around the lush forest.

"Are we going anywhere special?"

Joy nodded, keeping her eyes forward. "It's just up ahead. I'll tell you where."

They rumbled over a stretch of road, almost indistinguishable from any other stretch except for the thick wooden pole half-buried by weeds. Joy turned in her seat, the wrenching fear and doubt drawing tighter. She pressed a fist to her gut.

"This is it," Joy said.

"Here?" Stef asked as he touched the brakes. "You sure?" Stef couldn't see why yet, but Joy did.

"Yep," Joy said, her breath fluttering. "Positive. Look."

The Nissan slid to a stop with a crunch of gravel and dirt. A cloud of dust kicked up from the tires, parting like a curtain to reveal a lone thin figure in a camouflaged cloak, tied by a length of rope to the post. Joy shouldered her backpack as Stef tapped his thumbs nervously against the wheel.

He turned to look at her as she opened the door—there was the fear again, but also anger and resolve. Her armor glinted off his rectangular frames.

"Now remember," she said. "Don't freak out, don't say anything and keep your thoughts and opinions to yourself while I'm talking. Got that?"

His lips were a thin line. His hands squeezed the wheel. "Got it."

Joy frowned. "You promise?"

"I promise."

She stepped a foot out the door, paused and looked back at him as he opened his door. "And *please* don't be stupid," she said.

Stef sighed. "I remember. No Stupid."

She smiled with wished-for confidence. "I know what I'm doing, Stef," she said. "Trust me."

Joy got out of the car and circled the hood. The wind blew in her face, pushing her hair back as Stef slammed the driver's side door, squinting into the sun. It was eerie how bright and alone the woods could be. Joy was overconscious of how many conifers were around.

Kestrel rustled beneath her mottled cloak; the leather hood twisting querulously with little *pic-pic* noises as Joy stepped into the tall grass. She didn't want to get too close, knowing that Kestrel was both strong and skittish and she couldn't speak the tracker's language. She gave the hunter a wide berth as she approached the post. Joy dropped her backpack and checked her supplies as she waited for the others to arrive. The wind rustled the leaves. Birdsong tittered in the trees. The grass folded and parted off to one side of the road.

For some reason, Joy had pictured him dressed in his usual suit, which made her feel foolish. Kurt emerged from the brambles wearing desert khakis and a sleeveless muscle shirt. Chest straps crisscrossed over his heart, steadying the massive sword on his back. His black shoulder holster was threaded beneath it, a Maverick pressed into his side. He held a dull metal box in both corded hands, reflected sunlight hitting the ugly scar at his throat. He wore black tabi shoes. His face was grim. Stef stared at the bodyguard and said nothing.

"I've been expecting your call," he said.

Joy sighed and zipped up her bag. "I wouldn't have called unless I had a good reason," she said. "You told me not to."

"I did," Kurt agreed and glanced at Stef. "I thought that it might be you asking to gain my support with the Bailiwick or to pass a message on to Inq."

She shook her head. "I didn't think you would do that."

"You were right." Kurt scanned the perimeter with a wary eye. "This is a strategically poor location."

"Couldn't be helped," Joy said, jutting her thumb at the tracker. "This is the only drop-off point I know." She'd trusted Mr. Vinh to make the arrangements and to broker payment. Joy wasn't too familiar with dollars-to-dead-rabbit conversion rates. The fact that Kestrel was here gave her hope that she could do this. Even without Inq and Ink, she had her own ties to the Twixt, her own resources, her own allies, and she was going to use them all.

Kurt studied the tracker's hood with its topknot of braided leather and long cracked stitches. "I presume you have a plan." The Bailiwick's butler said the words as a statement rather than a question. Joy nodded as she scanned the overgrowth, avoiding his eyes.

"Yep."

Joy tasted the change on the wind, the metallic whiff of an ion charge at the moment she felt the hairs on her arms rise. Stef felt it, too, and eased to one side. Kurt shifted his shoulder, tilting the hilt, moving gracefully as he turned the box in his hands.

"I don't deny you have every right to ask for this," he said, scanning the treetops. "But I sincerely hope you know what you're doing."

Joy squinted, preparing for the flash. "Yeah. Me, too."

Stef glared at her.

There was a crackle and a clap of thunder and Filly strode confidently into view, escorting a hunched, grubby figure bristling with long quills and mealy rags. Joy's legs loosened and her stomach curdled—just the shape of him touched something nightmarish in her mind. The scent of his fetid-meat breath hit her like a fist. Her brother gasped, stepping back, and coughed for clean air.

Briarhook's smile creased his wobbly cheeks and his piggy eyes sparkled. He glanced eagerly between Joy and Kurt. His clawed toes raked the earth. Kestrel's hooded head perked up and she whickered with an all-body shudder. Stef regained his composure and flexed his fingers.

"As requested." Filly tossed Joy a plastic contact container with a screw-on cap. "Three tears per month, four months," she said. "Delivery included." Joy was grateful to the horsewoman; she'd forgotten to ask for that. She should be more careful when dealing with wizards. "And the Wizard Vinh said that your offer was only good for the one order, not the other, and not to confuse the two."

Joy nodded, thinking of what she was getting into. Mr. Vinh now had her on tap for a while. She stuck the container in her back pocket, trying her best to ignore Stef's look of shock and Briarhook's hungry stare. "And the other thing?" she asked quickly.

"Hmph." Filly snorted her displeasure. "Ladybird said he'd already named his price."

Joy frowned and then remembered. "That was for Ilhami's debt! And I said no."

"He said you'd say that," Filly said. "And that his price still stands."

Joy's insides squirmed. *Three drops of blood, willingly given.* That's what Ladybird had said. What would he do with them? She shuddered to think. She glanced at Stef, who said nothing, and she couldn't afford to ask. What else could she do? Her plan was shaky to begin with and she needed every advantage she could get. It sickened her to ask the drug dealer for anything, but she needed this plan to work.

"Fine," Joy said.

Filly smirked and reached into her side pouch. "He said you'd say that, too." She passed Joy a small glass vial with an address label and a tiny pillow made of peach silk, folded in plastic wrap. It sagged in her hand like a sigh. She tucked both into her other back pocket and wiped her hand on her shorts.

"Now you," Joy said to Briarhook. "I know what you want. Do you know what I want?"

"Want many things, you," he rasped. "But this want. Me." He held up a drawstring pouch and opened it with a careful claw; the satchel yawned in the thick of his palm, the briar seeds spilling over one another inside. Joy nodded.

"Yes," she said. "They're the same?"

He retied the slipknot. "Touch soil, seeds grow." His mouth curled in a hungry line, exposing wet yellow teeth. "Price, mine—half."

"No," Joy said, shaking her head. "No way. You gave me some for free."

Briarhook laughed. "Know Ladybird, you." He gestured at her pocket, quills rattling. His long hairless tail swished in the grass. "Know you—first time, free. Second time, pay." He leered. "Make message. You." He raised three hooked fingers. "Price, mine—third."

She looked at Kurt and Filly for some assistance. Both looked at her impassively with no hint at all. Stef stared intently at the thick metal plate in the hedgehog's chest. *Great.* She was trying to bargain with a nightmare monster and was no good at haggling. It was times like this that she really wanted Monica for backup.

"A thumb's width," Joy countered, her voice quivering. "That much."

"Ha!" Briarhook spat. "Joke, you. No. Third."

"An eighth," Joy said. "You burned your mark into my arm!"

"Scribe cut out heart, mine!" he seethed and bashed the metal plate fused to his chest. "Owe, you. *Lehman* to Ink!"

Joy felt her shoes grind deeper in the dirt. She wanted nothing more than to get away, forget all of this, run away—*run!* Briarhook's anger rattled something brittle inside her. Her instincts screamed, and she squeezed the pack straps to keep her hands from shaking. Joy forced herself to focus on his words: *Ink.* Yes. This was for Ink, and she hadn't time for this.

"A sixth," she said.

"Fourth," he said through a mouthful of spittle. "Quarter or no."

"A fifth," she said. "Or I stay empty-handed and you go away empty-hearted."

Briarhook growled. His feet scoured the earth. He grumbled. "Fifth. Yes."

Joy nodded to Filly, then Kurt. "Done."

Wordlessly, Kurt flipped the latches on the iron box. Both Joy and Briarhook edged closer to look. The beefy butler pulled a knife from its sheath tucked somewhere near the flat of his back; it had three wide holes like Swiss cheese and its blade was the width of Joy's wrist. He flipped open the lid and held it up for all to see: tucked inside a gray foam cutout was a living, beating heart, veined with blue-and-white fatty patches. Its aorta gaped, gasping, pumping nothing but air.

Briarhook salivated. Joy blanched. The heart kicked in its cage.

Glancing a cool confirmation at Joy, Kurt placed the knife at the point where perhaps it could be divided into fifths and cut a smooth line through the rubbery flesh. The muscle parted easily in a way that made Joy's own heart falter. After stabbing the gobbet on the tip of the wicked knife, Kurt held it up and closed the lid with a snap.

"First the briar seeds," Kurt said. "Then the bargain is witnessed and sealed."

Briarhook seemed to have forgotten himself and dropped the pouch in Joy's hand without a word of broken English or a backward glance. His eyes drank in the bloody scrap skewered on Kurt's knife. A thick spool of drool fell from his lip.

Joy pushed the pouch into her side pocket and took a wide step back, closer to Stef.

Kurt slid the bit of heart meat into Briarhook's waiting hand and withdrew the knife, wiping its edge against his pant leg, leaving a dark smear. Briarhook touched his thumb pads to the rippled red surface and giggled through his nose. Tipping back his snout, he dropped the piece of heart on his tongue and rapidly gobbled without chewing, his throat stabbing upward wildly at the mouthful as it choked its way down.

His quills clattered as he closed his eyes, the saggy flesh of his body shuddering grotesquely. A scrap of loose rag fell to the ground. Briarhook sighed and his eyes snapped open, cunning and clever and cruel. Joy flinched.

"Go," she whispered.

"Ah," he said, happily. "Next time, eh, *lehman?*" He shuffled into the thick grass, weaving his hand along the tasseled tops swaying gently in the wind. His tail swung contentedly. "This mine," he said. "Feel it, I. Lost kingdom, the Twixt. This bit— the forest, the wild woods—*mine.*" He pointed to Kurt and to Filly and to her. "Hear, you," he said. "I *will* have my heart." He struck a pose, claws curling into two shaking fists. "Never you free, Briarhook, 'til my heart, *mine!*"

His back bristled with a shiver as he lumbered into the woods, each breath sounding horribly like laughter, rusty and raw.

Kurt made a big show of securing the latches of the iron box and tucking it tightly against his abs. Filly flicked her thumbnail against the bone handle of her knife, and Joy watched him go with the cold, clammy splash of being too close to violence. Too close to danger. Too close to death. Kestrel's hood moved in short, quick jerks, searching for the rank scent that had now thankfully disappeared.

Stef was breathing hard, his arms behind his back, nostrils flaring.

"You know he'll kill you once he gets it all," Filly said. Joy didn't answer. She'd known it, of course, but this was the first time she'd actually seen it in the hedgehog's eyes.

"I'm beginning to doubt the wisdom of this plan," she said.

Stef raised a hand. "Am I allowed to say anything?"

Joy glared at him. "No."

"Well, I think it's brilliant," Filly said. "Bloody clever and bloody violent!"

This did not comfort Joy in the least.

"Very well," Kurt said. "I have delivered your property and witnessed your trade. My part in this is done. I must get back to my duties. Sir. Ladies." He bowed to Stef, Joy and Filly, his crisp suit and starched mandarin collar seeming to materialize over his rumpled camo and sweat-tinged shirt. "May you have every success."

"Thank you," Joy said, feeling increasingly nervous and uncertain. Kurt knew how to use that sword and the gun and the knife and who knew what else he carried on him, but she felt she couldn't ask him to stay. She knew what he'd say and didn't want to hear it, and part of her thought that, perhaps, he wouldn't want to say it. He was still part of Graus Claude's world and Inq's lover for more than a lifetime. While asking him for the heart was legitimate business, asking Kurt to fight the Red Knight for her was not. Still...

"Kurt?"

He turned. The look he gave her froze her tongue. She cleared her throat.

"Please tell Graus Claude that I am very grateful. And if you could tell Inq to protect her brother, please say that I'm trying to do the same." She swallowed a mouthful of fear and spit. "And that I'm sorry for what happened," she said. "I really am."

The bulky bodyguard said nothing for a long moment but lifted his chin in acknowledgment, flashing the long scar at his throat. "I'll do that, for you, Joy Malone," he said. "Good luck." Kurt gave a quick nod like a salute to each of them before stalking into the thicker wood. Joy lost sight of him in a shadowy copse of birch trees. Filly stepped forward; Joy hitched her pack on her back.

"Luck?" Filly snorted, testing her knife. "Skill is a warrior's luck."

Stef massaged his arms, smoothing down gooseflesh. "I wouldn't mind having a little extra luck." He pulled out a marker and drew a quick symbol on his wrist.

Joy patted her backpack. "Well, I've got a John Melton's boon, for whatever that's worth."

"Ah." The horsewoman nodded as if that explained everything. "And now?"

"And now," Joy said. "We see to our tracker."

Everyone turned to the lone figure still cloaked and hooded in patchworked bits of leather of shady browns and greens. The hood cocked to one side at their approach and an anticipatory foot pawed the ground. Joy saw that Kestrel's feet were bare and coated with mud.

"Are you sure she can track the Red Knight?" Joy asked.

"Certainly," Filly said. "Although you know he can travel through nettles—it's a trademark of the first Red Knight and why his *signatura* includes three pine trees, reversed." Filly exchanged a glance with Joy. "I like to know my enemies," she said. "But easier to find than to keep, and I'm uncertain whether she can drive him here."

Joy shook her head. "I'm not worried about getting him here," she said. "I just want to keep up with him once he does. Can she do that?"

Kestrel burbled a thick clicking noise through her hood. Filly shrugged.

"She says that she can," Filly said. "But in order to follow, we'll have to hold on to her lead. Lose your grip, and you could be left anywhere in the world." Kestrel burbled and burped. Filly added, "Or stuck halfway through a tree."

Stef hung his head and sighed.

Joy took out her fingerless weightlifting gloves, padded and worn smooth from use. She adjusted the straps and threaded her fingers with practiced ease. Nearly eleven years of gymnastics, half of it on bar, and here she was suiting up with invisible Folk in the woods.

"Don't let go," she said. "Got it." She picked up the leather leash and wound it over her padded palm. Filly took her position at the heavy rope around the post. Stef looked expectantly at Joy, who nodded.

"You won't show me how to build a ward, but will you make one for me?"

"Of course I'll keep you safe—"

"No," she said. "You don't need to keep me safe—I'm armored against him." Joy popped her hands together to warm up the pads. "I need you to keep *you* safe—you and Kestrel and Ink, if he shows." Joys pressed her need into her words as she tested the leash around her palm. "I don't want the Red Knight attacking anyone else, hurting anyone else, even by accident." Filly snorted and Stef moved to say something, but she raised a quiet hand. "*Please.* I can't let what happened to Monica happen again, okay? Got it?"

Stef closed his mouth and nodded. "Got it."

Yanking a thin finger through the knot at her throat, Kestrel threw off the cloak with a shake like ruffled feathers. The fabric fell like a curtain from her bone-thin frame. The tracker had a long wasted body only a bulimic ballerina would envy. Pale filaments trailed from her bare arms and legs, catching the breeze like underwater jellyfish tendrils. A thin, translucent shift barely covered her torso and breasts. The squat leather hood was a horrific contrast to her pale, questing, alien limbs.

Joy squeezed the leather leash; its end was secured to the ring in the collar at Kestrel's throat. Filly positioned herself behind the tracker, ready to remove the ancient leather hood, shaped like a falcon's head and topped in braids. Stef looked uncomfortable but steady, his feet planted wide. Joy lifted the rope twined around the post as Filly passed.

"Think this will work?" Joy murmured over her shoulder.

"Mayhaps not," the warrior agreed. "But, if you succeed, everybody lives, and if you fail, at least you no longer live in a cage!" Filly took inventory of her weapons, testing the slide of her knife. "The wizard said twelve drops. The drug lord, three. Think you can do that?"

Joy almost laughed until she saw the expression on Stef's face, which was grim. "That's a good chick flick with Monica on a Saturday night and a jab with a pin," she said, blinking to clear her eyes. "No problem." She tapped her pockets and her pouches to make sure she had everything within reach and threaded both her arms through her backpack, buckling the chest clasp hard against her breastbone. She rotated her shoulders and adjusted the Velcro on the backs of both gloves. She slipped the scalpel from the side mesh sleeve into the palm of her right hand.

Filly loosened the straps on the back of the molded hood and grabbed the topknot in one fist.

"Don't remove it until the Red Knight appears," Joy said. "I expect it will either charge or run. In either case, I'll need you right here by me."

"Indeed!" Filly said with vigor.

Joy hesitated at her obvious enthusiasm. Her insides felt coated with butterflies.

"You remember the plan?" she asked.

"I do."

"Don't kill him."

"I won't kill him," Filly said. "Until by your leave."

She turned to Stef. "You, too."

He nodded. "I understand."

Joy squeezed the scalpel between her forefinger and thumb. "No one kills him until after I seal him to his True

Name," she said steadily. "I have to draw it on his armor. Then there will be only one Red Knight locked to his name. Once that happens, I can ward everyone against him. I can even repel him if Ink or Inq shows me how." *Then Ink won't need to protect me anymore,* her thoughts added. *He'll be free, and I might never see him again.* Joy bit the inside of her cheek. *But I won't let him go without a fight.* She tested her grip. "If the Red Knight dies or gets away, then this will all be for nothing."

Filly licked the blue dot tattooed beneath her lip. "To kill the Red Knight would be a glorious thing."

"*Don't* kill him!"

"I won't kill him!" Filly shook her head like a horse, tossing her blond knot of braids; the tufted ends stuck out at crazy angles. "Yet." She curled her fingers over the hood's topknot handle. "But if, as I have heard, the contract's been changed, then how do you expect the Red Knight will cease pursuing Ink and conveniently stroll into our trap?"

"Simple," Joy said, trying to keep the tremble from her voice. She lifted the scalpel to her ear. Her Ink-like ear. "We use bait."

And she slid the blade across her neck, like slitting her own throat.

There was a flare of light as the Red Knight's sigil broke.

Joy inhaled sharply. She'd nicked her earlobe. The Red Knight's *signatura* disappeared from the armor. A cool breeze kissed the tiny drop of blood. Everything stilled. She could almost hear him sniffing, sensing her scent on the wind...

The forest exploded.

SIXTEEN

"AXE! AXE!" FILLY SANG. "HE'S GOT AN AXE!"

The Red Knight emerged from a fir tree and charged, a great wave of heat pushing pebbles and leaves before him as he swung a great, double-headed crimson axe. Joy backed up quickly. Kestrel cawed in her hood. Filly flipped her knife, handle-down. Stef slid his hands over the glyphs on his arms. Joy tried to stand bravely, but she cringed, exposing her back, her ears roaring with fear and noise.

The armor failed to light. There was a split-second wash of panic before a ward materialized, bathing the copse in gold. The fiery blast parted to either side, throwing bits of forest and earth and tickling the ends of her hair.

Stef snarled at her, glasses alight, arms outthrust, invoking the ward.

"You are an idiot," he said through clenched teeth. "A complete and total *idiot!*"

Joy coughed and meekly muttered, "Thanks."

He nodded, hands shaking, holding the beast at bay. "You're welcome!"

The Red Knight slammed his axe against the wall of magic and light.

Filly laughed. Kestrel shrieked. Joy tugged on the leash. Kestrel tugged back. She had trouble keeping her eyes off the

knight or, more specifically, his double-headed axe. The Red
Knight pounded at the magical shield like a thing possessed.
Stef held the ward, sweating with effort.

"He's going to bolt," Filly cried eagerly.

Joy nodded and squeezed the leash in her hand. "Okay.
Drop the ward!"

Stef paused, ignoring the sweat pooling on the front of his
backward shirt. Joy glared at him. "Stef!"

He shook his head. "No! No way!" he said. "I told you to
stay at home, Joy. You were supposed to stay safe!"

"I did! But I cut the wards to get out," she shouted. "It was
no longer safe. And I can't keep living in a cage of fear!" The
Red Knight began to circle, drawing his axe along the ward,
looking for a break, an edge to the spell. Joy watched with a
growing panic. Her brother's eyes turned in his head, nervously tracking the knight as he edged closer.

"You erased his *signatura* from your armor," he said.
"You're unprotected."

Joy nodded. "I had to draw him here."

"This is your plan?" Stef asked, arms shaking.

"This is my plan."

Stef grunted, elbows buckling. "I *hate* this plan!"

"I know," Joy said. "But I can do this."

Her brother groaned. Stamped one foot in mute frustration.

"I know you can," said Stef, exhausted, determined. "All
right. Hang on."

His permission scared her more than anything else. Her
skin tingled. Her lungs shrank. She tested the leash and the
scalpel in her hands. Filly rocked on her heels, a growl of anticipation crawling up her throat. Stef's fingers spread wider
as the Red Knight swept to the left.

"Dork," she muttered.

"Dweeb," he gasped.

Filly held on to Kestrel's hood as the head twisted, the tracker's filaments following the Red Knight like compass needles.

"Now?" the warrior shouted.

Stef nodded. Joy called out, *"Now!"*

Filly threw off the leather hood, exposing Kestrel's bald, noseless skull. She whooped and jumped back as the tracker's feathery antennae unfurled, exposing short, foxlike ears that rotated in spurts. Kestrel blinked at her prey, oval pupils contracting in the sudden light—her impossibly long, glassy eyelashes scraped against each other with an unnatural *shing* of sharpened knives. Her nostril slits flared. Her full lips parted. She gave an angry raptor's scream.

The Red Knight swept his axe and bellowed a challenge. The shield dropped. Stef collapsed, tossing salt in the grass.

Filly leaped with a yell, hungry for a fight. The Red Knight switched hands, raised the axe and charged. Filly lifted a downed birch branch the length of Stef's car and chucked it like a javelin. The Red Knight stopped and changed the angle of the axe midswing, chopping at the wood and batting it neatly aside with a *crack*. Bits of papery bark fluttered in the wind like battle flags. It bought Filly time enough to cross the gravel road and slam her buckler into his side.

Tucked neatly inside his weapon range, she jammed her pointed vambrace into the exposed armpit, throwing the momentum of the axe back and wrenching the knight at the shoulder. Filly grabbed the helmet by the eye slit and, yanking it down, delivered a hard knee to the inside of the groin, slipping neatly between plates. The Red Knight buckled, swinging an armored punch that spun Filly sideways, flapping her cape of bones around with a snap. She spat blood over his shoulder but did not let go.

The Red Knight turned, wrenching Filly around, finishing his turn with a violent swing of the axe. The shiny red blade cleaved the air with a hot, heavy hum. Filly twisted her midriff out of the way. Joy saw the edge of the blade trail fire.

"Look out!" Joy cried and pulled back hard on the leash. The tracker strained against her jesses. The axe chopped down, snapping the buckler strapped to Filly's left arm with a sound like cracking bone. Filly screamed. Her clothes sprouted flame.

"Down!" Joy said and Filly hit the dirt, rolling. Joy stuck the scalpel through the side of the backpack, lifted her left palm and *pushed!*

Nothing happened.

Joy swore.

She'd forgotten she was wearing gloves.

The Red Knight rushed her and the axe came down. Filly whipped a kick at his ankles, knocking him slightly off balance, and the axe head smacked Joy to one side. Her arm snapped back, jerking Kestrel to the ground. Joy slammed into a stump. The split second of pain wasn't her rib cage collapsing or her spine breaking; she coughed clean air, stunned. Glyphs glowed on her skin. Fire skittered along the surface of the wood and paved dirt, dying in wisps. How much could her armor protect her? Joy smelled burned hair and plastic.

The tracker screamed and clawed at her collar, making wild, high-pitched sounds.

The knight loomed, moving as if in slow motion, and Joy knew that this was what she wanted—what she had planned for, what Inq had dared her to do—but the moment was too real, *too much, too fast!* Her brain stalled, mind blank, forgetting what to do.

"Joy!"

Stef shouted and broke through the circle, throwing something toward her feet. Joy pushed back through the weeds on all fours as the Red Knight cleaved the axe almost level with her knees. The tops of grasses sprouted candlewicks of flame. Joy clawed for the scalpel. Stef slid in front of her, yelling something. The knight's helmet suddenly whipped back with a snap.

Another ward came up around Stef, Kestrel and her.

Filly had the knight by the helm again, this time with a thin cord caught under his jaw. The Red Knight clawed at the garrote. Filly, eyes wild and laughing, pulled, squatting deep. Tightened. *Pulled.* She popped a fast kick to his kidneys. And another. And a third.

"You waiting for an invitation?" she yelled at Joy.

But Joy didn't have the scalpel, and Kestrel had wound herself around Joy and Stef, tripping them up in a tangle of leash. Joy flipped onto her side; the backpack caught under her hip. Stef tried to move aside while keeping his hands raised, arms forward and out of Kestrel's way. Joy's fingers grabbed the handle, but it was as if the Red Knight smelled what was coming and tucked his hips under, reversing direction and tumbling backward, crashing into Filly as they both hit the ground. Man and metal fell hard. Filly choked as several things cracked.

Joy shouted, *"No!"*

The Red Knight had held on to the axe and was now using it to leverage himself up. Joy strained against Kestrel's wild lunges. Filly didn't move in the dirt.

"Stef?"

She needed to keep the Red Knight off guard and off balance; she needed more time. She needed to keep him here. Stef couldn't produce another ward—he was barely holding this one together, the strain bulging blue in his veins. Joy fumbled inside her pocket, grabbing seeds and scattering them everywhere. Briars exploded, blooming in jagged, thorny patches, ripping up turf and well-packed road; black branches extended like claws. Kestrel yelped and leaped aside, whipping her lead and catching Joy in the face as she struggled to hold on. Stef swore.

Filly snarled a weak curse. The grass was burning. The Red Knight stood up.

Joy looked at the briar patch—she had missed the knight entirely. Her heart faltered. The Red Knight gave his axe an experimental swing—black thorns caught flame and lost their shine, shriveling and curling in acrid smoke. Joy tried to switch pockets. Kestrel puffed up and cawed. Joy felt the heat on her back, on her face, in the air itself. Her fingers clawed in the dirt. A zing of shock ran through her arms. Her head snapped up. The Red Knight lunged. Joy threw dirt in its face as Filly curled forward, driving her knife into the back of his knee.

The Red Knight's howl echoed inside its helmet. Joy stumbled to her feet, still wrapped in Kestrel's leash. She tried unwinding her hand, her foot, her calf, stumbling over haphazard knots as the Red Knight writhed. Kestrel barked. Stef fell to his knees. She had to do this. She had to do this *now*.

Filly let go of the knife handle, aimed carefully and kicked, driving the blade deeper into the joint. The Red Knight's scream broke off sharply. He reached down, grasped the half-buried handle and yanked the knife out in a gout of bright blood. Filly laughed through a split lip.

"*Victory!*" Filly seethed.

The Red Knight whipped the dagger at her head. She flinched and caught it in the shoulder. Her legs spasmed.

Joy screamed something wordless. The Red Knight turned on its knee, rotating slowly in a puddle of his own blood, and lifted his axe through the haze of heat rising off the grass.

Something pink split their vision. Kestrel's tongue shot out, a long gooey tube, siphoning a quick lap of blood on the ground. It snapped back into her mouth, smearing her lips. Her yellow eyes dilated. She gave a cry that sounded like *"More!"* and lunged toward the knight, teeth stained pink.

The Red Knight dropped the axe and retreated, dragging the blade behind him like a plow, tearing a deep furrow that threw fiery sparks through the earth. The long groove filled with oozing fire, like liquid lava, cutting off their escape. The Red Knight slipped smoothly into a pine tree and vanished.

"No!" Joy yelled. Kestrel dived in pursuit. The smoke was thick and black as the brushfire went wild. Filly lay in the grass. Joy clawed at the leash.

"Hold on to her!" Filly snapped. She tried to sit up, choking on blood and smoke. *"Go!"*

Joy stared back at her brother. He was moving, hands extended, shouting at her.

"I'm trusting you," he called out. "I'll stop the fire. Go!"

Joy pulled on her backpack and grabbed the scalpel, tearing it free of the mesh. She took a standing leap, clearing the fire and then some. She landed smoothly, absorbing the weight in her knees.

"Come on," she said, grabbing Filly's outstretched hand. The horsewoman clamped on to her wrist and yanked herself forward, coughing up blood.

"I am beginning to doubt the wisdom of this plan," she said, spitting.

"Then you'll love this," Joy said and bent, hauling her under her armpit. After eleven years of Olympic-dreams training, Joy was *strong*. She squeezed Filly to her as Kestrel dragged them forward. Joy ran, leaving the flames behind, hoping that Inq was right and that this tracker was the best, because otherwise this was going to really hurt...

Kestrel dived like a hawk, tilted with speed, disappearing suddenly between the pine tree and its bark, her leash drawn tight, the tether spooling quickly into nothing. Joy held on.

Filly puked blood over her shoulder. The tree was coming up fast. Joy shut her eyes while running.

Cold!

The shock of it hit her as she skidded in the snow. The sunshine baked her skin, reflected blindingly off unspoiled snowdrifts. Kestrel snorted and tugged through the thigh-deep wasteland, undaunted by the mountainside, impatient in pursuit. Joy shivered. The hot, wet patch on her arm turned icy. Filly tipped her head back and laughed.

"Hoy," she said, catching flakes on her tongue. "Tastes like home!"

The Red Knight stood in the overturned path, steam pouring off the crimson axe against a pale sky. He was hunched over a patch of red snow. He had escaped through the pines to nurse his wounds and clearly hadn't expected pursuit.

Joy flashed the scalpel in the blinding sun. The sharp wind whipped her hair against her cheeks. She was hunting *him* now.

The Red Knight lifted his axe and spun it in a whirling disk of flame, all too bright against the colorless snow.

"Bad fighting terrain," the warrior observed. "We need to relocate. Watch this!" Filly said and heaved a deep breath, tipped back her head and *screamed*. Her face turned reddish-purple as her voice shattered and cracked; the world thundered with the reverberations, leaving everything shocked white and still. Joy gaped at Filly, her left ear ringing. The Red Knight buckled in the soft snow.

A section of the soft ice-cream puff near the very top of the mountain ridge broke with a slow-motion snap, giant sheets of whiteness separating, sliding, powder-edged shards of snow tumbling down.

Toward them.

"Now run," Filly urged hoarsely, although they were already running, the Red Knight leading the charge away from the avalanche that filled the sky with noise.

"I hate this plan!" Joy shouted as she pushed numb legs to run.

The Red Knight headed for the snow-laden evergreens. Sensing escape, Kestrel plunged forward, a greyhound in pursuit. Joy stumbled after them. Filly slid off her back and found her feet.

The sound of the avalanche was a living thing that tunneled through Joy's brain, pouring into her head with an awful cottony thickness that smothered her thoughts, filled her lungs, made her gasp for breath while she still could...

"*Move!*" Filly pushed her and they dived past sharp branches and torrents of snow, falling forward...

...into another forest.

It was muggy and dank. There was a flash of red and Joy was being pulled again, splashing. Through another tree. The smell of pine. Another. And another. And a third/fourth/fifth. Filly wrapped her good hand in the leash and wrenched back. Kestrel yelped. Filly loosed something over their heads. It hit the Red Knight in the helmet, shoving him off balance, short of the next copse of trees beyond a hedge.

Joy stabbed her scalpel through her belt loop and pocket, grabbing the few seeds left in her hand.

"Hold him!" she cried.

She heard the axe slice through the tree beside the knight before her eyes registered it. The trunk split like butter cut with a knife. Smoke curled from the break as the giant tree fell. Joy had the worst feeling of déjà vu.

She closed her fist and ran. The sudden slack on the leash surprised Kestrel and she tugged it, slick with blood, out of Filly's hand. Joy didn't notice until the wet strip slapped her leg. She glanced back.

"Filly!"

The tree was falling, about to cut them off. The horse-woman looked up.

She shook her head and shouted, "Go!"

The Red Knight moved. Kestrel moved. Joy moved. Filly stayed.

Coolness. Light.

Joy never heard the tree fall.

She was in another wood, with wider trees and higher branches that filtered the sunlight into a dappled fawn's hide of spots. The Red Knight was waiting and swung the axe through the tree they'd just come through, missing Joy's head by inches. She dropped the seeds out of fright. They landed at his armored feet, pinging sharply off the metal and spring-ing up like angry vipers from the fertile ground.

Joy leaped out of the way, twisting in the loam, smear-ing her body in mud and moss. She tumbled and came up in a crouch. The Red Knight stood skewered in a bramble of thorns wicked and sharp. He fought against briars, try-ing to bend his elbow and bring the axe down. The blade lit with its crimson flame, but the knight was trapped, one arm half-raised, the other snarled in the thicket. Kestrel wound around the back of the wounded tree trunk, her yellow eyes wild.

She hissed.

Joy couldn't feel her hand, tugged numb in the leather leash. She staggered back from the Red Knight's briar cage, disbelieving her own eyes.

I did it.

Joy fumbled for her pocket, scratching the back of her glove on the scalpel's edge. She grabbed Ladybird's plas-tic-wrapped packet of silk and powder, held her breath and shook it loose over the knight's head.

The pillow smacked into the helmet over the eye slit and pluffed sadly off the edge, snagging the tip of a thorn. Joy backed away from the wisp of sunset orange that hung far too still in the air. The Red Knight struggled, forcing his axe arm free. As he grasped the handle, the axe blade flared. The fire threatened its roar. The Red Knight gave a howl of triumph.

Which took a mighty inhale.

The pink packet caught fire and the tiny silk pillow went *poof!*

A giant cloud of grapefruit-colored smoke blossomed around the knight's head. Lightning flashes simmered where the axe blade pierced its underbelly, its bloody flames sucked right into the bright coral haze. The Red Knight stopped struggling. Its helmet lolled back. The arms fell slack as the body loosened, leaning back against the thornbush like a beanbag couch. The axe slowly tipped sideways and hung forgotten in the bramble. Joy waited until the snap and crack of briars slowed under the settling weight.

She pulled Kestrel back, worried about what would happen if the tracker got wind of the drug. Ladybird's warning sang in her brain, *One touch is all it takes.* The knight was tranquilized, insensate—as listless and addled as the horned toker on the couch.

The wind brushed the Sunset Dust aside in a gentle smear. The Red Knight didn't move. Kestrel cooed and scratched the dirt.

Steeling herself, Joy painfully unwound her hand from the long leather leash, fingers slipping on the end slick with blood. She tied the strap to a sapling as thick as Kestrel's post, keeping her eyes on the knight and listening to his even breaths, which sounded like "ah ah ah."

Having brought down her prey, Kestrel busied herself in the underbrush, rooting for something that slithered away with a rattle of twigs and leaves.

Holding her breath against any stray dust, Joy mounted the bramble, grabbing sharp branches with her gloved hands and clamping the scalpel in her teeth. It tasted like metal and blood and batteries and rain. She ignored the gently twitching hands and the axe that hung beyond its reach and perched herself above the Red Knight's breastplate. His head moved, but only just. Taking the scalpel from her lips, she scraped its blade against the armor with the sound of nails on chalkboard. Joy swiftly drew the Red Knight's *signatura*, its loops, its three inverted arrow-trees and the singular curl that defined this incarnation as the current Red Knight, the one that she had captured.

Panting in panic, her arms scraped with thorns, Joy tried to finish quickly as her fingers shook with strain and fear, a whimper curdling like a bad taste in her throat. The Red Knight shuddered. Joy drew faster. She half-expected to feel the axe blade or an armored hand at her throat. He tried to sit up, but she pushed him back with her forearm, giving her room to work. The final lines began to glow. The helmet turned. He stared at her mutely. Joy ignored him. She could do this. She could ward the knight off. She could lock him to his Name. She could keep everybody safe.

She cut through the last flake of rust.

The *signatura* flared.

The Red Knight vanished.

Joy pitched forward, suddenly alone in the briar. She sank into the bramble, arms scored to the elbow, spearing herself in many places as she fell. Joy felt the rake of thorns on her face, through her shorts, into her shirt. She gasped.

What happened?

Joy slowly extricated herself from the tangle of thorns, wincing at all the little pains as she tried to pick her way out. The hollow inside the briar formed a sort of crushed nest and she was struggling inside it, trembling, weak as a baby bird.

Stretching a leg backward at an improbable angle, she

carefully touched a shoe to land. Her foot sank in the soft earth. There was a touch on her shoulder.

"You okay?"

Joy spun on her feet. Inq steadied her with a hand.

"What—?" Joy said. She turned around, blinking. "What happened?" She wasn't quite sure.

"It's over now," Inq said gently. And when she let go, there was a new mark on Joy's arm.

She swiped at it angrily. Worse, she recognized it.

"I didn't—" Joy stammered. "I didn't *murder* him!"

"Didn't you?" Inq said. "Well, technically, no, but there's no category for erasing one of the Folk completely out of existence." She shrugged. "It's the closest thing I've got."

"I didn't..." Joy said and stared at the scalpel and the trembling hand that held it as if it belonged to someone else. "You said..." Joy shook her head. Inq cocked her button chin, looking genuinely concerned.

"Now, now," Inq said. "You can always take it off." Her eyes glinted a dangerous dare, a sidelong glance. "No one will know."

That wasn't true, and they both knew it.

"*I* would know," Joy said and frowned. "*You* would know."

"Yes," Inq purred. "That's right. And I think it's best if only the two of us knew what *really* happened here. Don't you agree?" The Scribe brightened noticeably. "It'll be our little secret," she whispered. "Just between us girls."

Joy retreated from the briar bush, pushing more distance between herself and the empty nest of thorns. The hollow was shaped roughly like a man. Joy turned away. Inq followed. Joy wished she wouldn't.

"That was a very brave thing you did, luring the Red Knight away from Ink."

Joy twisted her fingers together, not looking back. "How did you know?"

"I spoke to Filly," Inq said. "She's obstinate but very impressed."

Joy swallowed, covering her Grimson's mark with her right hand. "How's Ink?"

"He's fine," Inq said. "You pulled it off without him."

"But..." Joy said. "Why didn't he come for me?" The question hurt her more than she wanted to admit. He'd always come for her. He'd *promised*. And he could not lie. Even though she wanted to draw the knight away to keep him safe, she honestly expected him to show up before it was over. "And how did you find me?"

Inq licked her thumb and smeared it against Joy's jawline. She lifted her finger, which came away red.

"Blood calls to blood," she said. "You've touched our blood and we've touched yours—really, any good kiss ought to do it, and we've shared at least one." She winked and licked her thumb clean. "Thicker than water, so they say."

Joy wiped her ear. "Then why isn't he here?"

Inq sobered and walked alongside her. "He was...disillusioned with the idea that you aren't perfect, that humans are fallible in ways he cannot understand. He was afraid that you were courting death as a way to draw him out—a risk and a reasoning which he could not approve, although, obviously, that was not your intent." Inq shrugged elaborately. "In any case, he sought solace with the Cabana Boys and I'm afraid their solution involved a great deal of alcohol, which Ink hasn't learned to process any better than his emotions just yet. Regrettably, it was a poor combination." She leaned conspiratorially sideways in her high-heeled boots. "He tried, though, bless him, but didn't make it past the door. Pledged to protect you, tortured by your betrayal, yet unable to fulfill his pledge due to drink—he's positively emo over it."

Joy inspected Inq's face. "And you're not?"

Inq spread her hands, black-painted fingernails with diamond tips. "I got over it," she said. "Remember, I understand humans a lot better than my brother does."

"But the Cabana Boys all shut me out."

"That was my doing," Inq said. "For everyone's safety, given the Bailiwick's rant. But now, all is forgiven. Congratulations! You're back in the fold."

Joy stumbled over a tree root. Kestrel gave a little squawk in the grass. "And the Red Knight...?"

"Is undone," Inq said. "Erased completely and forever. By you."

"But I was trying to...to ward him away," Joy said. "Lock him to his Name so no more could come after me, keep him away so we...so I could be...safe."

Inq patted her arm gently, like soothing a child. "And now he will never harm anyone ever again." She smiled a self-satisfied grin. "Isn't that nice?"

"No," Joy said, which wasn't true, but she couldn't quite pinpoint why. Something buzzed like a cloud of gnats inside her head. She turned to Inq, frowning. "Did you know that this would happen?"

"Me? No," Inq said. "But I guessed."

A hot knot in Joy's chest broke and she burst into tears. She shook her head and rubbed her scratches and turned in tight circles, knowing that she had no idea where she was in the world and she was lost—so lost—and it had nothing to do with direction. She rubbed her gloves into her eyes, soaking the padding with tears. A little voice in her head whispered, *I probably should be bottling these for Mr. Vinh.*

Joy cried harder.

"They'll kill me," she muttered through her fingers. "The Council. The Tide. They were right—they were right about me! I could..." The scalpel sank point-first into the ground. "I shouldn't be able to do that, to *unmake* someone, it's... Ink told me..." She closed her eyes; her tears stung. "His job, your job, is to protect the Folk from harm—from *human* harm! Harm like this. Like me." Joy shook her head. "Ink will never, ever forgive me. *Never!* He'll…I don't know what he'll do," she confessed. "I've screwed up everything. I've destroyed *everything!* I made it all true!" The horror of the moment sank its teeth in and tore. It filled her blood with ice and smoky dread. "This guy, Sol Leander, the leader of the Tide? He warned the Council that I was the most dangerous human in the world."

Inq picked up the scalpel and gently blew on it like Ink. She pursed her lips and winked at Joy.

"That's right," she said. "You are. You, Joy Malone, are the most dangerous human in the world." Inq seemed to taste the words on her tongue. "But that's not the whole story, is it?" She offered the scalpel back to Joy, handle-first. Joy hesitated, took it, stuck the blade quickly into her backpack and zipped it closed. She sat on the forest floor, oddly comforted by the solid feel of earth and loam and pine. Kestrel snuffled somewhere on the edge of her vision. Inq patted Joy on the back.

"Don't worry about it. You're one of us now," she said. "And there's nothing anyone can do to take that away from you."

Joy glanced up, eyes swimming. Murder made her one of them? It was a horrible thought. She wiped the blood off her ear. "I don't understand."

"You will, in time," Inq said, smiling, and lifted Joy up by the shoulders. Kestrel, swallowing something long and slithery, cawed. "But right now, let's go get your Nordic friend. I think I left her bleeding under a tree."

SEVENTEEN

JOY PICKED UP THE LAST FILE AND DROPPED IT IN THE box. Everything else in Dover Mill had been packed up and cleared out. Soon the place would look like it had never been. Joy ran a finger over the sleek shelves and the tiny track lights, but she avoided touching the empty slate wall. Some things, like some memories, were best left alone.

Had she done anything good here? It felt like she had, but she still squirmed inside thinking about how part of her had always known it was wrong. Anything she kept from people who loved her, any secret that could harm one of them, was wrong by definition and there wasn't much that could justify it. She knew she couldn't tell her parents about things like Ink or the Twixt because those weren't just *her* secrets—they belonged to other people who had rights and feelings and would share the consequences. Stef had tried to warn her, Graus Claude, too, but now she got it—she couldn't have everything. She had to choose. And every choice had a good and bad; every freedom had its price.

A knock on the cache wall made her look up. Summer sun poured down from the entrance, backlighting the figure at the top of the stairs. The light filtered through the short beaded cape and gleamed off shiny vambraces. Joy smiled.

"We're closed," Joy said as Filly marched down the stairs.

"So I heard," Filly said. "But I came to see for myself." She set her hands on her hips and surveyed the empty cache. Minus the furnishings and paperwork, it looked bare as Stef's room back at U Penn. "The Halls are full of rumor thick as porridge and twice as tough to swallow." Filly poked through the folder tabs in the box. "Old hags are all as curious as cats, but don't like to stray far from their hearths." Joy picked up the box and fit its lid. Filly flashed a smile that stretched her tattoo. "Ach, well, they're not like me."

"No one's quite like you," Joy said, placing the box behind her to block it from further prying. "But as the former sole practitioner of this establishment, I can verify that we are well and truly out of business, starting now."

"Hmm," Filly said, crossing her arms and inspecting the walls. "So what are you going to do now that 'now' is over?"

Joy sighed and picked at her nails. "My father's due home in a few days and Monica is coming out of the hospital around then, too. Stef's still unbelievably angry at me and, as far as I know, so is Ink." She scraped her foot against the edge of the stair and twisted her fingers in her shirt. "Inq said he's safe, and that's all I really wanted to know." Filly stretched the tattooed lines on her eyelids to their utmost in surprise. "Okay," Joy said. "That's not *all* I wanted to know." She felt the tingle as she cut off the blood flow to the tip of her pinkie finger and let the fabric unwind. "I'm going to have to find some way to apologize before I'm dragged before the Council."

"Well, it should make it somewhat easier given that neither of you are currently being hunted by the Red Knight." Filly barked with laughter. "Even the Council will have to sit up and take notice of that! I wish I could be there to see it!"

Joy idly traced a split in the rock wall. "Yeah, well, at least there's that." Joy said the words carefully. She and Inq agreed to let it be known that Joy had killed the Red Knight after locking it to its *signatura*. Joy couldn't hope to hide Grimson's mark from Ink or Inq or anyone with the ability to fabricate Sight, but because it was in self-defense, due to an illicit decree, Inq had said that the Council couldn't fault her—even if she was a human—because otherwise it looked like they couldn't control their own people or enforce their own laws. "And a little status never hurts, either," she'd added.

There had been a loophole in the Edict and Joy had closed it. She wasn't sure if this would be a point in her favor or held against her when she was finally called in front of the Council—which Graus Claude warned could happen any day now—but she was certain she didn't want anyone to know the details. Inq was right about that, too. Unmaking one of the Folk was worse than just a crime, worse than murder; it was a power too awful and too easy to abuse. That was why the Folk were afraid of humans. That was why the Tide hated Joy. Humans had abused power and humans had abused the Folk—adding fuel to that historical fire would likely end up with Joy on a spit, so their deception wasn't so much lying as selectively neglecting to mention certain details.

Joy still had nightmares about blood-colored armor and black thorns and flames.

Despite the glow of fresh bruises and bandages, Filly looked healthy and full of good humor. Battle suited her like a cape of bones. "The Council won't take you to task. You won a fair fight with wit and valor as well as good people at your side." Filly raised a fist and slammed it against her chest. "Ink knows more than a little about honor and bravery. He'll come around. You'll see."

"And what if he doesn't?" Joy asked, voicing her fears.

Filly brushed a thumb over the horsehead pendant at her neck. "Well, then I'll be forced to knock some sense into his head." She grinned and Joy couldn't help grinning back. Filly clapped her on the shoulder. It stung. "But enough mooning—he'll get over it in time—today I've come for my payment!"

"Payment?" Joy said, feeling a stab of foreboding, but then she remembered. "Oh. The riddle?"

"Yes," Filly said. "You agreed to help me solve a riddle. Are you ready?"

Joy shrugged and stacked the last box. "I guess so. Sure."

"Fine, come with me." Filly leaped up the steps in gazelle-like bounds. Joy vaulted the stairs after her, feeling every ache and jolt in her body from their journey through the pines. The young warrior waited at the lip of the entrance, gazing through the thick brambles covering the overhang like a tablecloth.

Joy glanced around, seeing nothing but clouds hanging over the polluted river. "Your riddle's up here?"

"Not precisely," Filly said and took Joy's hand, grinning. "Come along!"

Joy felt the tiny hairs on her arms rise and the metallic taste of ions dance on her tongue.

"Wait..." she started to say and then the whole world *flashed!*

The boom of thunder came a split second later and spat them out into a fierce, whipping wind. Joy stumbled onto the loose sand, salt scouring her face, instantly drying her lips to a pucker. Salt was in the wind, in the sand, in the air and in the ocean crashing blackly far down below. Stubborn sprigs of crabgrass fluttered against the gale and nibbled at the rickety beach wood fence along the edge of a cliff. The wooden slats were jagged and powder-white against the water's inky darkness.

The wind yawned and swallowed, beating Joy's eardrums and whipping her hair every which way, pummeling her body with tiny fists. It hurt to listen. It hurt to hear. The wind sounded lonely and hurried and strange.

"Where are we?" she asked.

"The Crags."

Joy squinted around. "Should I know where that is?"

Filly ignored her as she scanned the horizon. "You agreed to help me solve a riddle," she said. "Are you ready?"

Joy shrugged. She'd promised to help the warrior woman, and Filly had more than delivered her end of the bargain. "Sure. What is it?" Joy shouted against the air. Filly stood by the fence post, poised and statuesque. Her face cut a sharp profile and her hair was drawn tight in its knot of braids, but even when a few stray hairs danced over her eyes, she did not so much as blink.

Joy was about to repeat herself when Filly pointed to a rock outcropping where several gray shapes moved.

"Do you see them?"

"Is this part of the riddle?"

Filly shook her head. "No."

Joy shielded her eyes with her hands. They could have been seals or sea lions or something altogether different, but it was pretty clear that she was far from any Carolina shore. The wind was cold and getting colder. That or the shock was wearing off. Joy shivered and tucked her hands under her armpits.

"Sea lions?" Joy guessed.

Filly shook her head again, this time laughing. "No." She turned more fully to Joy. "Can you hear them?"

"Are you kidding?" Joy said, cupping her hands over her ears. "I can barely hear you!" Joy had never realized how unprotected her ears were. She was unable to close them against assault—there was no escaping the punch and howl of sound.

Filly licked her finger as if testing the direction of the currents and drew it along the fuzzy purple edge of the horizon. "Doubtful air, then," she said and glanced at Joy's feet. "Take off your shoes."

"My what?"

"Your shoes, Joy Malone." Filly pointed. "Take them off."

Obligingly, Joy toed her shoe loose. She knew her toenails were chipped, making her twisted and malformed toes look particularly ugly today. She didn't want to be barefoot.

"Is this the riddle?" Joy asked.

"No, it's an order!" Filly said impatiently. "Do it!"

Joy shucked off her shoes. Cold sand quickly covered her toes.

"Grind your feet." Filly pulled off her own boots, smashing her foot against the earth, twisting her heel back and forth. "Like this." Joy complied and felt the earth grow colder, zinging icy sparks up her calves. Filly watched her, then snorted annoyance. Joy stopped. She wasn't sure what she was supposed to be doing or hearing or seeing or feeling, but mostly she was confused and cold. Her ears hurt. Joy yawned to pop them. The waves below banked and crashed, tucked almost silently under the blanket of wind.

Filly stepped through a break in the crusty fence posts, standing at the very edge of the cliff and looking all the way down. Joy felt queasy when Filly gestured for her to come closer to the precipice. Squeezing her arms tighter, she kept her eyes on the skyline, only pretending to look down as she shuffled forward, unwilling to pick her feet up off the ground. A jellylike quiver pooled in her knees and puddled in her stomach. Her mouth was dry. She blinked against the salt in the wind.

"It is a riddle," Filly said. "And a tough one, no doubt." She looked over at Joy and wiped at the tattoos on her eyes. "But I'm not one to give up so easily." She smiled slyly. "Curious as cats—it's our curse."

She clapped a hand on Joy's shoulder and pushed.

Joy screamed and twisted, tumbling off the cliff backward, her hands flailing around her, hopelessly grabbing empty air. The wind buffeted her body, whipping her hair and cries skyward as Joy saw Filly perform a graceful dive after her, the end of her bandage flapping behind her like a tail. Joy scrambled to grab hold of something, her arms and legs fighting gravity and the force of the wind, but she was too far from the cliff face and there was nothing but open air and the cold spray of the waves below her, crashing white and coming up fast. She was going to hit the water and she was going to hit it hard if she didn't get control of herself. Joy crunched her ab muscles around a screaming ball of fear and forced her arms straight and her legs to a point, slipstreaming into a passable dive. She prayed as she forced her head downward, straightening her spine, gritting her teeth. She saw a flicker of Filly falling past.

She was grinning like a madhouse on fire.

Joy hit the cold water with a splash. Breath collapsed, her head rang and she sluiced underneath the waves, spearing down through the darkness and the shock of sudden silence. The air had been slapped from her lungs, and her body loosened in a spray of bubbles, her mind blank of anything beyond the immediate need to breathe. The press of water on her skin pushed her urgently to reach the wobbly sunlight overhead. Following the bubbles, she kicked and clawed toward the surface, pulling herself up through the green-black depths and kicking against the waves that tugged her impatiently toward the cliff. She broke through the ocean with a gasp.

She coughed and spat, the salt water in her mouth and nose making her retch, the roll of the churning water doing nothing to help. She choked on her own phlegm in the back of her throat and shook her hair out of her face. Filly was treading water lazily beside her.

"*Are you crazy?*" Joy screamed through a mouthful of spray. She sputtered and gagged. "*You could've killed me!*"

Filly bobbed on the waves, her hands winding effortless circles. "Not air or water, then," she said conversationally.

"Maybe fire? With that temper, I wouldn't be surprised. What do you think?"

Joy's anger flared past her chattering teeth. "What do I *think*? I think you are *completely insane!*" She splashed feebly in Filly's direction, already growing winded. She wasn't much of a swimmer and hadn't the rhythm of endurance in the water. Her limbs were tingling with cold.

Filly sniffed, unimpressed. "I wasn't talking to you."

Something moved beneath the water. Joy saw its shadow slipping under the waves. It was *big*. Joy pulled her knees close to her chest as it slid beneath her, imagining the feel of it gliding past her feet. It coiled, growing closer, growing larger, threatening to surface. Joy wanted to climb out of the water. She wanted to throw up. She wanted to scream and cry, but didn't. Couldn't.

A head broke the water, pale green and dripping; black shark eyes gazed out of a massive horse's head. The snout was long and ridged, its dark mane tangled with kelp and foam, nictitating membranes flicking over its eyes as its forelegs churned the water. An impossibly long and sinuous tail corkscrewed down into the darkest depths. Joy stared into its glassy gaze.

"She is not one of the Water Folk," a voice oozed in her ear. "Perhaps Earth?"

Buffeted by a sudden swell, Joy fought to keep herself upright. "What? Of course I'm not!" She spat out a foul mouthful of salt water. "I'm not...I'm not *anything!*" she said. "I'm not one of the Folk! I'm human!"

Filly rode the waves like she was standing still. "You heard what he said?"

Joy's anger and fear coiled into suspicion. Suddenly, she understood. *She* was the riddle, and Joy didn't like the idea of being solved.

"I heard...something," she admitted, trying to ignore the

penetrating glare of the monstrous sea horse looming over the waves. Her head ached, having been deafened by the wind, drenched in ocean water and exposed to sudden cold. Salt crisped her hair and stung her cheeks. She helplessly looked up at the beach, but it was a long, cold cliff face with only scraggly bits of grass along its height.

"She has an *eelet*," the voice said. Joy could hear the thrumming clearer on her right, as if it spoke just over her shoulder past the gulping waves. Joy spun herself around, fighting the current, but all she could see was the horse, staring down. Its mouth hadn't moved. She noticed a fluttering by its neck where small fins rippled. The giant serpentine tail slithered beneath them. The voice came again. "You placed a shell to your ear, perhaps to listen to the ocean?"

Joy was about to deny it, but she realized that it sounded familiar. She *had* held a shell up to her ear...but not to listen to the ocean. She remembered a kind, elderly face under a rumpled umbrella that tinged her memory with curiosity and betrayal. Something about the sea and a siren's song...

She splashed at Filly. "What's going on?"

Filly treaded water with the same calm grace. "You tell me," she said as she patted the slick, muscular body of the horse beside her. His side rippled with water and thin, papery fins. "Better yet, tell the hippocamp. His name is—" And she made a sound like waves crashing together, driving flotsam into the undertow.

Joy clamped her mouth shut. It *had* been the horse. She was talking to an enormous water horse while trying not to drown on the ridge of an unfamiliar ocean. Joy fought the waves and the nausea and lifted her head, trying to ignore everything but the intelligence behind the flat, black eyes.

"A man gave me a shell," she said, spitting out salt water. "Back when I first delivered messages for Ink. Something about roses for his wife, or maybe his daughter— I forget."

Honestly, what she'd forgotten was whether she'd delivered the message at all, not that it had mattered in the end. He was dead. That was back before she'd known about becoming a *lehman* for Ink. Back before the elderly man had betrayed her and Graus Claude. Back before she'd begun working for the Bailiwick. Back before she'd betrayed Ink.

Joy wrenched her thoughts to the present where she was wet and cold and growing colder. She pumped her legs and tried to keep away from the giant leaf-shaped fins.

The hippocamp reared out of the water, hooves stippled with barnacles crashing through the spray. Joy splashed to one side, evading his upset. "The siren's get!"

Filly jerked a thumb at Joy. "Who? Her?"

"No." The hippocamp's voice sang a buzz in her head. "An *eelet* is a rare gift. It burrows inside your ear, attaches close to the bone, adjusting our sonar into sounds humans can hear." Joy quickly stuck a finger inside her ear as if she could feel the alien thing squirming. The horse tossed its head, spraying Joy's face with water. "Leave it! As I say, it is a rare gift, a deepwater breed—one of the royal pedigrees, I suspect."

Joy switched positions, spitting salt. Her arms were getting tired. "He said that his wife was a siren."

The nictitating membranes blinked. "That man was Dennis Thomas," he said into her brain. "And that would make you Joy Malone."

Joy was too cold to be chilled by fear. "How do you know that?"

The hippocamp whickered hard-edged bubbles. "I know many things."

"I don't understand," Joy said. Her teeth clattered as her jaw quivered. "I don't understand any of this."

"You understand enough to have come this far," he said in a voice that slid into her ear. "And with the *eelet*, you can understand me." A massive undulating of its flanks and giant frond-like fins and its scales slid into view, rolling lavender, green, purple, turning indigo-black near the tip of its tail. The hippocamp was covered in leaflike flippers from its mid-section all along its dragonesque tail. It circled Filly easily. Its eyes bore down on Joy.

"I cannot lay claim to her as she is not Water," the hippocamp said. "But I will send word to our representative of her esteem. Perhaps you should try Earth? They would most likely know."

"As you say," Filly said and patted the hippocamp's mane. "We'd best be off before she turns blue."

"The color doesn't suit her," the hippocamp observed. Joy was shivering too badly to reply. It was as if the churning water was liquefying her bones. She couldn't feel her fingers or feet. The oozing voice warbled in her head as cold water plugged both ears. "I'd best take you to shore."

Joy felt the tug of something grabbing the back of her shirt along with a hank of hair that should have hurt but felt more like a distant ache. Her limbs floated behind her as she hung loose as a kitten, uncaring and unfeeling as the waves flowed beneath her, spraying her face and lapping over her chest. Too soon she felt as if she were being dragged over sandpaper. The wind bit like mosquitoes, sandy pinpricks all over her body. She curled against the cold and water dribbled out of her mouth, swallowed instantly by the hard, wet sand.

"Definitely not Water Folk," the hippocamp muttered. Filly rolled her roughly over and Joy flopped onto her back.

"Still alive, Joy Malone?"

Joy cracked her eyes open. Her lips were chapped. "Enough to want to kill you."

"Well enough, then," Filly said, laughing, and dripped ocean water into Joy's face. Joy flinched and protested meekly as the horsewoman pulled her arm over one shoulder and hoisted Joy to her feet. They left long smears in the darker sand behind them that were swept clean by the surf. Filly squeezed Joy's ribs in a way that felt like a warning, or maybe payback. It hadn't been that long since their positions had been reversed. "There's still the riddle, and it's not solved yet."

"What do you...?" Joy coughed, stumbling after Filly as she walked up the beach. "What are you trying to prove?"

"What I know is that I know, and others don't know yet," she said cryptically. Filly pointed a finger at Joy, her vambrace flashing in the sun. "When I told you to remove my mark, you did it, despite not wanting to, and despite the possibility of earning the Bailiwick's ire. When I bid you follow, you obeyed, although not completely and not unthinkingly—you heeded my words, even including removing your shoes. And I've told you before that no coin you could give me would outweigh what you've already given me, your most valuable possession." She snapped the water from her cape of bones with a self-satisfied grin. "Have you guessed?"

Joy shook her head. "No."

"Your True Name, Joy," Filly said. "I know your True Name. And you gave it to me willingly."

Joy froze without feeling the cold.

Filly nodded. "Yes. You see? I wanted to know who you are. Or at least whom you belonged to before the ravens circle to claim you as their own."

"But I'm not..." Joy struggled to make the words combine. "I'm not one of you. I'm not one of the Folk. I'm human." That is what they'd fought for: her human freedoms. Because she was *human*. Filly had to know that. Her theory about Joy having a True Name made no sense. "I'm a human with the Sight."

"And who is to say that a human with the Sight is not somehow somewhat related to the Twixt?" Filly said while drawing great semicircles in the sand with her toe. "It would explain a great many things, would it not? Perhaps the rumors are true and those with the Sight have a drop of faery blood in their veins? Or perhaps you are something entirely new? I imagine the change began when Ink marked you, or when you began traveling through the Twixt, or when Aniseed splashed you with her potions that set fire to her web of glyphs. I don't know, but I made up a test and you passed every time. You have a True Name and it is Joy Malone."

"That's...that's impossible," Joy said, mind whirling. "That makes no sense! By your logic, everyone I've ever met could control me like a puppet and I've done *lots* of things that people told me specifically not to do!"

"People knowing your True Name isn't the same thing as *giving* them your True Name," Filly said. "You have to do it willingly—offer your full name to that person, yourself—in order for it to work. That is why polite circles demand things like formal introductions and calling cards. You cannot be controlled through secondhand information." She tossed her head in the wind. "But I met you early on and when I asked for your name, you gave it to me." The blonde warrior stood back and considered Joy frankly. "Who have you given it to? Do you remember?" Joy stared into space, thinking carefully: *Ink, Filly, maybe Inq? Graus Claude?* Her insides rolled over as the implications swam through her head. *How many times was I told to trust someone or not to worry, to hand something over, to let it go...* And Joy had done it, willingly, obeying without thinking, every time. Had they known? Had they always known? Filly nodded as if she understood perfectly.

"I am your friend, and you can trust me, but offering others your True Name has made you vulnerable. Controllable. Not entirely, but then again, you're not entirely one of the Twixt, and yet not entirely human, either," she said. "You pose a danger to yourself and others who would seek to use you as one of Ink's tools." Her blue tattoos accented the sly glint in her eyes. "This is unacceptable to warriors like ourselves, so I wished to make you aware of it and offer you a choice."

"A choice?" Joy asked. "What choice?"

"The choice to claim yourself for yourself," she said. "The Folk have found a way to protect ourselves—it's written into the Edict of all those who dwell in the Twixt." Filly nodded again solemnly. "Even you."

Joy could feel it like a hot brand between her shoulder blades: the alchemical smudge that was slowly morphing, becoming something irreversible, irrefutable, set into her skin. *My signatura.*

Filly watched understanding dawn. "It won't manifest if you don't complete it," Filly added, letting the unsaid go unsaid. "But you are stronger, lighter, fiercer than when I met you. I see it in you—you have begun to change. The Twixt has started to claim you, to protect you, but a half-built wall is no wall at all." Filly raised her chin. "As I said, I am your friend. And I will tell you how to claim it, if you want to do so."

Joy curled her arms, hugging herself, walking faster and faster as she tried to outpace her thoughts. Revelations and epiphanies bubbled and popped in her brain. *What if it's true? What if I'm not human? Then what am I? What about Great-Grandma Caroline? What about Stef?*

They weren't fully human. They had the Sight.

They had True Names.

They were vulnerable, controllable.

And the Tide would kill them all if they ever found out.

"What happens if I don't? Would it stay unfinished? Would it fade away? And what happens if I do? Would some part of me still be human? Or will I become invisible, too?" The questions shot out rapid-fire, matching her growing panic.

"*Hel* if I know," Filly said. "I just wanted to be the first to solve the riddle. I'm surprised the others haven't figured it out yet." She picked up a piece of driftwood, curved and worn smooth. "Maybe they have and haven't told you. But it's your choice and yours alone. I don't know the answers to your questions, but I can tell you what happens to those who choose not to shield their True Names. You think you'd survive long enough to defy the Council thrice over? There's no one still here who hasn't locked the power of their True Name into a sigil. Once that happens, the words *Joy Malone* will be only sounds that you can choose to answer or not. They will hold no power over you." She swung the stick back and forth. "Of course, you can also choose to be human and leave all of this behind, but you should at least know your options before making that choice."

Joy pushed back her salted hair. It crackled. She was reminded suddenly of a sign hanging in church: *God grant me the serenity to accept the things I cannot change; courage to change the things I can; and wisdom to know the difference.*

It was her choice.

"Tell me."

And Filly did, looking eager as a storyteller with a gruesome campfire tale. Afterward, Joy stared at her while rubbing her arms in an effort to keep warm.

"That's it?" she said. "That's all?"

"There's a song, but it's unimportant, and a ritual bath, which is even less important, but the one thing that you *must* do is give up something of yourself—something uniquely yours—in order to bind you to your Name." She straightened the horsehead pendant at her throat. "All true magic demands a sacrifice. And it must be done, as they say, willingly, sealed in blood." Filly broke the knot of wood between her thumbs. "Declare the words, have them witnessed and prick your thumb. One drop of blood is all it takes." Grimacing, Filly scratched her scalp under the wet braids. "I don't know if that last part's important or if the Council just likes to see us bleed." She eyed a smear of storm clouds heading in over the cliff. "The choice is yours, but best do it soon," she said matter-of-factly. "I'm not the cleverest of the lot and others will guess." Her eyes blazed in the hazy sunlight. "You have many powerful enemies as well as many powerful friends—neither will likely enjoy the decision you will have to make."

Joy couldn't help asking, "Then why do you care? Why tell me this?"

Filly stepped into Joy's personal space, larger than life. "Because I am a warrior, not a politician or lover. Because the others don't understand, except maybe the Bailiwick—I cannot change what the Nornar decree, and I know a fighter when I see one. I know that and I trust it." She clapped a hand to Joy's arm, unaware that Grimson's mark lay beneath her wet sleeve. "You will fight. And you will do so with honor. You will *do* something, Joy Malone, and it will change the world."

And, knowing that Filly spoke her True Name, Joy could do nothing but accept that this was true.

EIGHTEEN

SHE'D BEEN SUMMONED WITHIN THE HOUR. SHE WAS lucky that she'd had a chance to take a shower and change out of her ocean-soaked clothes. Joy didn't know whether the timing was due to bureaucracy or her four-leaf clover, but she was grateful nonetheless.

The grand amphitheater curved overhead like a giant flower, cavernous and awesome with sloping, petal-shaped walls. A central, star-shaped skylight glowed with the dregs of summer sun despite it being late and, as far as Joy could tell, several miles underground. Green sparkles moved lazily along the ceiling like drunken fireflies. Golden strands, thin as tinsel, hung at varying lengths from tiered heights. Mosaics of semiprecious stone covered the walls, glittering black, red, ochre, green and a deep blue turquoise down to the rows and rows and rows of gallery benches surrounding a central dais. The Council seats sprouted from the ground in a semicircle of smooth, white shoots facing a desiccated stump whose rings were worn smooth with age. Whether by guilty feet or countless years, Joy couldn't guess as she craned her head behind the heavy green curtain to try to take it all in.

She stood waiting in an arched alcove off to one side of the ground floor, level with the central stump, stage left. If the Council chamber had been built to impress, it had done a splendid job.

She let the curtain settle and twisted her fingers in the edge of her wrap. She'd worn a halter dress, the one she'd worn to Stef's graduation, along with a matching pashmina, strappy heels and hose. A breeze touched her back. She pulled the shawl tighter. Squeezing her clutch purse, Joy wobbled in her shoes and squirmed.

With her toes squashed into fashionable triangles, her ankles were feeling the pressure after a summer of flip-flops and flats. She fiddled with the strange fabric of the curtain, her planned speeches and practiced defenses muddled thick in her head. She wished Inq hadn't left after escorting her to the chamber. She glanced back at the grand staircase by which they had appeared. She wondered where Inq had gone. She wondered if Ink had come. She wished that she could catch a glimpse of them before everything she had to say was said and there would be no turning back. But she was alone.

This was it: Joy Malone versus the Twixt.

Stef couldn't come with her. They both knew it, but for very different reasons. He'd walked her to the Carousel on the Green; its massive carnival features loomed dark and quiet behind the fence. He'd held her hand as long as he was able before Inq appeared.

"You don't have to do this," he'd said.

He was wrong, but she hadn't told him so.

"I can do this," she'd said.

Stef had sighed and nodded. "I know you can. And I know you will." Then he'd glared at Inq, the Other Than waiting to take Joy before the Council of the Twixt. "Bring her home soon."

"I will," Inq had said. "Trust me."

But Stef didn't.

Joy had tried to look brave as Inq took her hand and walked them both Under the Hill.

The last thing she wondered was whether the DJ was there, lurking somewhere in the shadows. And then the world folded in on itself as the Carousel blossomed open, drawing her into the heart of the Twixt.

"Are you well?"

Joy turned. A young man with a shock of white hair and a pale, open face glanced at her with concern. His eyes were an odd color, green-gray like the sea, and his clothes were from another century, a pale double-breasted suit with swallowtails peeking out from beneath a high-necked feathered cloak.

"Thanks, I'm just..." Joy surprised herself by being honest. "Nervous."

"Don't be," he said gently. "Whatever you have to say, it is important that the Council hear it. That is why they invited you here, after all." He twitched aside the curtain with his right hand as the seats began to fill. Joy watched a bronze-skinned man with incredibly large antlers speaking to a creature that looked like a cross between a peacock and a flamenco dancer, all jewel-tone colors and crested crown. Several fat, jolly men in bulbous hats chittered among themselves as a green, sticklike figure waved at them to shush. What could only be a gryphon cawed loudly from an aerie seat. A knot of black-skinned elves argued, punctuating their angry voices by waving silver staves. Joy's stomach fluttered as her brain balked. It was hard to separate the panoply from the noise.

"I remember the first time I saw these Halls," he said, gazing up at the ceiling. "I thought my head might twist right off my neck—there was so much to see! I tried to take it in all at once." He gave a self-humoring smile. "I think the Council Hall is meant to be overwhelming, so don't be surprised if you're feeling overwhelmed—it's built into the design." He shrugged. "Of course, I believe it should also be welcoming and encompassing, to allow you to feel part of something larger than yourself—to let you know that you are not alone." His voice was kind and coaxing. "You belong here as much as anyone." The curtain closed and Joy let out a little sigh of relief. "There, now," he said. "Feeling better?"

"A bit," she admitted. "Thank you."

"Then my good deed for the day is done." He did not offer his name or ask for hers, which she now knew to expect—and why—but the strange etiquette made its absence less noticeable. She was still agitated, sensing a latent hostile threat beyond the curtain, as if something slithered in the shadows, waiting to pounce. Right now, Joy would take any small kindness that she could get.

"Thanks again," she said, wondering if he'd be so gracious if he spied Grimson's mark upon her arm. She hadn't removed it. Like Monica's remaining scar, she knew better—some experiences left a mark. For better or for worse, they'd been earned.

The feather-cloaked gentleman gestured toward the curtain a final time. "I must go now, but know that after this first sorry business is concluded, the Council is open to anything the Folk here have to say. It's important that all our voices be heard in order that they may govern wisely." He smiled graciously. "You are important to us." Joy gave a shaky smile. He obviously had no idea who she was, and, for a moment, she was grateful for that much. That last small protection of anonymity would be gone all too soon, and she would stand before them, vulnerable and alone. He seemed nice, but what she really wanted was Ink by her side.

He gave a quick bow and mounted the gilded stairs, his cloak sliding elegantly behind him. Joy fidgeted on the carpet, thick and rich as soft earth.

The murmurs beyond the curtain grew louder so that she could make out individual voices talking, some speaking in languages she didn't recognize and others speaking in sounds she didn't recognize as language. She peeked again, scanning the hundreds of inhuman faces, looking for a pair of all-black eyes, telling herself that she was part of this—that this was by design.

There are no accidents.

A sharp rapping split the air, startling her. The voices smothered to stillness.

"Order to our Order." A reedy voice cut through the vastness, buoyed by the ringing, unnatural acoustics. The entire Hall rose in their seats as hundreds of Folk spoke as one, "We present ourselves as representatives of our most noble Houses, whose collective oaths constitute this, the Council of the Twixt." The sound of their declaration was a force, like the ripping cliff winds or the crashing ocean waves. Joy rocked on her heels and grabbed the archway for support. "Which, in accordance to our laws, ascribes and mandates an onus to grant counsel, judge fairly, decree wisely and transmit faithfully the will of the Court so to best govern those who uphold the last vestiges of our stronghold and honor upon this earth." The recitation included one collective breath. "To this end, we thus remain your humble servants and stewards until the Imminent Return."

Everyone sat with a sound like thunder.

Again, the reedy voice sliced through the sudden silence. "The Council calls forward Joy Malone."

Joy knew this was her cue and forced her feet to move. Her hands parted the thick curtains as she walked toward the stand, her consciousness floating above her body in a surreal cloud tethered by an awed, impossible fear. Even competing for Olympic qualifiers, Joy had never had an out-of-body experience—she felt literally scared out of her skin.

The sudden vastness of the chamber woke her senses to uncomfortable sharpness; she could hear the creak and rustle as Folk strained to catch a look, the low murmur of gossip skittered along the benches, and she felt the press of hundreds of eyes dissecting her every move. Mutters whispered in the darkness, reminding her of Aniseed's trap, of shadows and blood and coffee cake. She kept her gaze on the rings of the stump, thinking of mahogany eyes ringed in foxtails and an evil, malicious grin. Aniseed had been a member of this Council.

Joy took a deep breath and looked up.

Graus Claude was resplendent in a formal robe of aquamarine silk, embroidered in cuffs of gold fitted with pearls. He sat behind the small partition and stared at her with an unreadable expression. She thought, perhaps, he still hadn't forgiven her for her latest trespass. A thin, elderly man sat center stage with snakelike scales along his throat and a long, wispy moustache that wafted in a breeze that wasn't there. A dark redheaded pixie with scalloped ears and swollen lips bright as cherries sat next to a squat woman reclining in a bowl-like seat—her soft, doughy face was the color of mushrooms and her brown hair hung loose to the floor. A sexless figure of faceted crystal stared down at her with eyes of molten flames, its every movement giving off a sharp *ping* and *crack*. An elderly dryad sat nearby and stared at her, his face a knot of woody vines and his hair braided with twists of berries like beads. Something indistinct floated in a teardrop-shaped tank, suspended gently over its seat, and near the end of the row stood a severe-looking man with sunken eyes and a dramatic widow's peak—he glared down at Joy like a physical push. At his left stood the young man with the feathery white hair. He wore an expression of shock and disgust. When she saw him, it was immediately clear that he wished she hadn't.

She shifted her attention away from the Council's stares and stopped twisting the edge of her shawl. Clutching her purse and pashmina, Joy steadied herself for whatever came next. She reconsidered her plan as her thoughts scattered like leaves. She was standing before the Council of the Twixt. The stares of the assembled Folk were real and unfriendly. They could take out her eyes. They could tear out her heart. Or they could do none of these things if Filly's riddle was correct and she was somehow one of them, if only just. But Joy stood on the stump as if it were the edge of the Crags, because no matter what happened in the next few minutes, she knew that her life would never be the same.

"The Council formally acknowledges Joy Malone," the old man said, and Joy tried not to wince as he said her name. His voice warbled out of a throat that stretched and lengthened as he spoke, and she noticed that his eyes had slits for pupils. She felt more human than ever. "You present a difficult case, Miss Malone. Having been born a creature bestowed with the Sight is a remarkable quality, one that we have old laws to address and control. Having been chosen by the Scribe, you were granted leniency as well as your gift—a rare honor—yet once you shirked the bonds of *lehmanship*, we found it difficult to excuse your continued actions within our demesnes without the onus of proper guidance and enforced restraint." The speaker failed to keep the contempt from his voice. "However, your deeds upholding the balance between our worlds as Accorded by the Twixt were recognized by this Council and we awarded you and your family proper protections under the Edict via our Decree. Despite our word and recent recriminations—" the slitted eyes flicked to the severe Councilman and his pale-haired page "—we cannot continue to ignore the flouting of our authority, both by your person and those persons who wish to do you harm. These are transgressions which the Twixt cannot abide." His head moved in a way that reminded her of snakes, slithering hypnotically on his well-muscled neck. "Therefore, we, the Council, felt it best to invite you forth to settle our disquiet in a time-honored manner upheld by both laws of our peoples in ancient times." The elderly man stroked the heavy stone gavel with long fingernails filed to points. "I confess that your situation is without precedent. You have been cited with improprieties unequaled since the days of the Rhymer, and that is no small accomplishment. But we acknowledge that the crimes committed against you by the employ of the Dreaded Red Knight were in defiance of our Edict and herewith forgive any action of yours that necessitated defending your person or persons of your blood or acquaintance against him." Joy exhaled slowly and was surprised to see Graus Claude do the same. *Is this his doing? Or Inq's? Or both?* She didn't know if she should be grateful, but she was glad that she didn't have to defend her actions or her Grimson's mark. A great swell of talking forced the Council leader to rap the stone in sharp rebuke.

"The Tide's representative moves for a redress."

The elderly man's head turned, his moustache tips fluttering to either side of his ears. The man with the widow's peak had bent forward slightly, his elaborate, stardusted cloak catching winks of firefly light.

"Indeed," the Council head said. "I would not expect any less from you, Sol Leander, but as you are newly admitted to the Council, I would also not expect you to be familiar with the common considerations accorded to persons who have been wronged by actions against the Accords or, in this case, our own Decrees." The reedy voice thrummed with an iron undercurrent. Joy saw great ram's horns curved along the sides of the old man's skull. Or were they part of his skull? Joy shivered. "Understand that at this time, there is no need for redress or reconsideration." The scaled chin turned back

to Joy and she saw the barest nod from Sol Leander acknowl-
edging the dismissal. The young man in the feathered cloak
looked even more affronted and his anger found a target
in Joy.

So this is the Tide.

These were the people who wanted her dead.

"Now then, Miss Malone," the Council leader resumed.
"We are given to understand that you have been presented
with several options for your consideration, those which
have been suggested and approved by the Council in private session, and we wish to acknowledge your human laws
by offering you a choice." His face twisted around the word
and Joy saw tiny wisps of smoke curl up from his nostrils.
"By voicing your preference in our presence, you will exercise that right. I urge you to consider the full ramifications
of this allowance before you answer. To that end, we, the
Council, offer the following options..."

There was a ripple among the Council members and the
Folk assembled in the massive stands, and Joy wondered if
everyone already knew the answer and it was only she who
didn't quite know what to expect. Did they know? Did they
suspect? Filly thought she was the first to guess the truth
about Joy, but she was wrong. Ink had known the real truth
about Joy, before anyone—before Joy knew herself—and it had
nothing to do with her being human or not. He knew that he
loved her and that she loved him. *No matter what.* It buoyed
her in a way she hadn't experienced before, her body and
mind suddenly feeling light and carefree as a pink balloon.
Joy realized that there had never been any other choice she
would make.

This is my choice. I choose this.

It really was as simple as that.

"To willingly return that which was bequeathed by Master Indelible Ink, which has been proven to affect *signaturae,*

a singular crime within the confines of the Twixt, to accept the yoke of *signatura* from one of the Folk and thereby be bound to our laws under their Name and auspice, answerable for your actions within the confines of the Twixt, or to willingly abandon all contact and future interaction with the Folk and the Twixt, up to and including the use of your gifts, both innate and acquired, for as long as you shall live."

There was a general hubbub, but Joy had lost track of what had been said as opposed to what she had been preparing herself to say. She glanced around hastily, trying to catch a hint, a glimpse from those she knew, but only when the voices had quieted down did she hear the words "...means taking the blade *and* her eyes..."

Joy shuddered, squeezing the clutch purse harder, feeling her body contract. Carefully memorized words dissolved into a white mist of panic. Fear hammered in her chest and spots of terror winked behind her eyes. All she could think was that whatever the Folk were, they weren't human. They would blind her, cut her, kill her without a moment's hesitation—her life meant nothing more to them than a dust mote in a breeze—but they also envied and feared her, and that made her powerful. She still had freedoms—human freedoms and human choices.

"And now, Miss Malone, we invite you to voice your preference for our consideration."

Joy swallowed her misgivings and a sudden lack of spit. The words she'd been planning to say fractured like bits of refrigerator poetry. She caught Graus Claude's icy glare and the Council leader's crocodile gaze.

"For your...consideration?" she said, surprised at the volume of her own voice amplified back at her from the high, glittering walls. It sounded high and weak.

"You have the right to voice your preference." The crystalline figure with the molten eyes spoke like steam escaping, shifting in its seat with delicate *pings* of broken music. "But this does not obligate the Council to grant it."

There was another murmur, this time of approval, and Joy bit back the retort that came to mind, *That's not fair!* Joy knew more than a little about "fair"—in Olympic training, it was a banned word. There was nothing in the rules about anything or anyone being "fair," and she was sure this was the closest to "fairness" that she could expect in the Twixt. She tried to ignore the flush of heat and sweat that blotched her face and the pinch in her toes as she shifted her feet.

Joy cleared her throat and tried to stand tall under the collective gaze of the Twixt.

"Thank you," she said, her whisper amplified to fill the Hall, "I am honored to be invited here by the Council of the Twixt, who have graciously protected my family and I under your Decree," she said, ignoring the ridiculous boom of her words. She knew more than a little about showing deference before a panel of judges. "I know that it has been difficult and that many unforeseen things have happened to bring about this decision, and I wanted you to know that I appreciate being included in the process." She licked her lips. "However..." She swallowed again. "For reasons that I hope will become clear, I am unable to accept any of your stated offers."

There erupted a sound unlike any she'd heard since the battle on the fiery warehouse floor: screeches and shouts, roars of outrage, snaps and barks and howls of hundreds of berating voices and hissing curses. She buckled on the stand, slipping in her shoes. The rapping of the stone split the chamber, chopping at the noise like an axe.

"Please," Joy said. "Please let me explain!"

"ENOUGH." Graus Claude's bellow wasn't a shout so much as a clap of thunder. He'd half risen out of his chair, four hands gripping the edge of the partition wall. He settled back, two arms crossing over his chest and his browridge lowered, the ice-blue eyes searing into Joy with unspoken warnings and worse. "Let her speak."

"I..." In the quiet, Joy's voice shook. She scraped her fingernails against the inside of her arm and brushed back her hair from her eyes. She placed the Olympic mask over her face: this was the beginning of her performance, as routine as a routine. She straightened her shoulders, centered her spine, raised her rib cage and started again. She could do this.

"I am sorry, but I can't give back the scalpel as it was a gift willingly given, bequeathed to me by use of my name," she said. "And while I would be tempted to swear to you that I would never use it again, recent experiences have proven that I *would* use it in self-defense, to protect myself or those I care about most." She faltered at the momentary flashes of Stef and Monica and Ink. "And I would not want to insult you by offering up any false or hasty promises."

There was a general murmur; an acknowledgment that a human promise wasn't worth much and that she was wise to admit it up front.

Humility.

"Furthermore," Joy continued, "while I had the honor of being chosen as *lehman* by the Scribe, Indelible Ink, I was ignorant of the responsibilities and obligations of that position. Knowing what I do now, I could not accept that role again from any other in the Twixt," she said. "Nor did I realize that my actions would strip me of that title and the respect I had not yet earned. To that end, I offer my sincerest apologies to the Council and to him." Joy didn't turn around but was sorely tempted. Was Ink in the stands? Had he heard her most public apology? Would he care? Did it matter? It was from the heart.

Sincerity.

Again the clamor of debate, lower this time, and again came the knock for silence. Joy matched the reptilian glance of the Council speaker, whose scaled face was now wreathed in smoke. It made her heart flutter, but her words did not falter. She had committed herself to this course—she would see it through. *This is my choice.*

"But even then, I could not accept his *signatura,* or the mark of any one of the Folk as my bond to the Twixt, because..." Joy faltered as the Council head grew more serpentine and awful as the moments ticked by. She found it hard to breathe in the smell of smoke, slightly damp and organic, and stand before the collective anger in the Hall. The tension had a taste to it. If she succeeded, it was over. If she failed, she was dead. She drew her palms across the fringe of the pashmina, wiping them dry, remembering the words that Filly had made her recite over and over until she knew them by heart.

"Because, I, Joy Malone, do seal my soul upon my Name and thus upon my sigil." She'd had to raise her voice over the rising outcry. "I offer my armor and accept this decree by blood and by word and by deed."

Taking the scalpel from her purse, she stabbed her thumb.

A wash rippled over her body, lighting her entirely in glyph-drawn light that spun and swirled, unzipping and collapsing, a chorus of undoing, ending with a final punch between the shoulder blades. Joy pitched forward, gasping. Her pashmina fluttered to the ground. The Council and all assembled could see the mark blazing in the center of her spine—fully formed, fresh and new: a circular pictogram of a bird's outflung wings, its pointed beak raised to the sky. Even as it faded from view, save from those who had the Sight, they had witnessed its birth. They could not remove it and they could not deny it.

It was hers. Her. *My True Name,* she thought. *Mine.*

Joy Malone.

NINETEEN

PANDEMONIUM.

Joy kept her head down as the Hall erupted. She was glad she'd listened to Graus Claude's advice and stayed bowed, conciliatory, allowing everyone the time to react without looking directly at her face. *The Council is more impressed with a show of vulnerability than strength.* She shut her eyes and tried to ignore the chaos boiling all around her, quietly holding on to her scalpel as well as her bleeding thumb. She sneaked her hand to her face and sucked at the cut. It tasted deep. It might even leave a scar.

"Joy."

She lifted her face and looked up at Ink. Tiny flickers of firefly light swam in his eyes. Was it wonder? Hope? Fear? Awe? He stood nearby, shielding her, like he had with the *bain sidhe*, like the Red Knight—always by her side.

"I am here," he said.

"I'm sorry," she said into the quiet cave of his ear. "I'm sorry—I didn't know. I didn't understand." Her voice bounced quietly between them under the uproar. "And now I do. Erasing your mark erases a part of you—your integrity, your purpose, and tears at both our worlds, harming everyone, everything, and that's wrong. It was wrong for me to do and wrong to try and excuse it and I'm sorry." She pushed her heart into her words, trying to close the distance between them. "And now you know that I know," she said. "I'm part-Folk. I cannot lie."

It took a moment for her words to register, and his eyes grew incredibly deeper.

"I..." He touched her hand, the barest brush of his fingers. "Joy? How?" he said. "How did this happen? When?" His voice sliced through the noise like the sweep of his razor, crisp and clean and sharp. "When did you know?"

"I didn't," she confessed as the stone gavel banged. "But Filly did. I'd given only a few people my True Name willingly—including her and you." Joy shook her head, caught between laughter and tears. "Inq, too, probably, since you seem to come as a set." She was feeling something very big, but she couldn't quite decide how to define it. Her body quivered as she whispered, "I don't know how, I don't know when, but I chose you then and I choose this now." She pushed the scalpel into his hand and squeezed their fingers around it. "There are no accidents."

Joy picked up her shawl and rose to stand as the Order was brought to order. Ink stepped behind her to her left, much as the feather-cloaked boy stood next to Sol Leander, who sat smoldering in his seat.

"The Council must consider your claim." the elderly man's voice was no longer reedy, but slithered ominously like smoke issuing from a deep pit. His eyes burned a startling golden-green that hadn't been there before. Joy swallowed. "But we cannot ignore that you come into our chambers bearing armor and weapons in defiance of our laws."

The redheaded pixie chirped, "Which laws?"

Sol Leander spoke easily. "No human can appear here bearing weapons against the Twixt."

"She isn't human," Ink said, the words costing him more to say than even he realized until they rang out in the Hall, his crisp voice tight. Joy could hear the loss of something she might have never known. "She is not entirely human. She bears a *signatura*. She completed the ritual. She is one of the Folk," he said. "One of the Twixt."

"It's been long rumored that those born with the Sight have a drop of faery blood flowing through their veins," mused the crystalline figure aloud, its eyes burning with fire. Joy was startled to hear the words phrased exactly as Filly had said them, as if it was an adage or a nursery rhyme... or a well-paid bribe.

"Unh," grunted the little mushroom woman, pointing at Joy with a grin. "An' there's yer proof."

"I move that all rulings pertaining to those with the Sight be suspended immediately pending a thorough investigation." Graus Claude's rumbling bass soothed like water over stones. He glanced at Joy, and she caught a glimmer of a smile. "If this theory proves correct, we would not want to unintentionally harm those who are our own."

Joy knew that the Folk were few, and their safety was the Council's top priority, which was why *signaturae* and the Scribes had been created. If she were one of them, they would have to protect her and her family and all those like her. Everyone with the Sight would be spared!

The Council had no choice in the matter. No choice at all.

"Falsehood! Trickery!" Sol Leander seethed with his fist on the wall. *"Lies!"* The word was like a slap in the Twixt, and his young associate shot Joy a scathing glare. "This human is an affront to the very nature of the Twixt!" he said and Joy could all but feel the glyphs no longer humming against her skin. "She stands before us as a warning—a sign of what's to come—a harbinger of war! *This...*" His voice rang out. "This is the infestation humanity represents. This embodies the very circumstance that the Council endeavors to shield us from!" He stood, an imposing figure in an imposing Hall, and leveled a finger at her brow. "This before you is our death, incarnate!"

She flinched and buried her bleeding thumb in the meat of her fist. The Tide could not know what she had done. They could not possibly know that their Red Knight was more than dead, but completely *unmade*. They could never know how close Sol Leander's words were to the truth.

But then she saw something: the glow of *signatura* on his skin, Sol Leander's True Name etched on the side of his throat: a familiar-looking spear-shaped arrow striking down like a slash. It pulsed with a hot, itchy light, looking swollen and painful, and all at once she knew that she had insulted Sol Leander more personally than anyone else in the Twixt. *His auspice is survivors of unprovoked attack.* She dropped her eyes and sighed miserably with the realization. *Monica.*

"I sincerely apologize," she said. "For any upset I may have caused." Her words were carefully phrased. Joy could no longer tell a direct lie, but she knew how she could bend the truth—and even this little falsehood hurt her with a tiny niggling ache. The pains she'd experienced these past few weeks were just the beginning, and she knew, instinctively, that a lie could kill her now. Joy glanced around the Council seats, noting what they'd said and left unsaid, feeling like she already had friends and allies forming around her, tied with invisible strings. "I did not know who I was or what I was, only that I had to live to see this day," she said, grateful for Ink's closeness and his soothing scent of rain. "But I no longer need protections from my own people."

The silence was as thick as night. Green firefly twinkles hung in the air.

"We once had practices in place for acclimating change-lings," Graus Claude said with lazy grace. "For inducting those born outside back into our world, even before the advent of the Twixt. Could these not be applied in such a case as this?"

"An acclimation?" the vine-faced man said, his berries swinging.

"Preposterous," Sol Leander scoffed. "It's archaic."

The mushroom woman raised her head, black hair brushing the chair back. "Who're you callin' 'archaic,' boyo?" she said with mock surprise. "Yer new to that chair an' those of us who've been warmin' them longer than you know 'tis the Old Ways we've been holdin' dear till the glory days of the Imminent Return." She sniffed. "So if'n this be 'archaic,' then I says 'twere most assuredly the right thing to do!" She banged the edge of her chair with a knobbly stick and grinned at Joy like a wise baby.

The old man's moustaches drifted, smoke still seeping from his flaring nostrils. His eyes were mellower gold. He stroked his beard with overlong nails.

"And do any claim her?" he said.

"I claim her," said Ink.

"Denied," Sol Leander said with a wave of his hand. "She has already repudiated the Scribe. Was once not enough?"

The head of the Council said nothing, but it was clear he thought the same thing.

"I volunteer to be her sponsor," Graus Claude said, surprising the squat woman beside him. "As I am most familiar with the Scribes and their positions in the Twixt, it seems only fitting that I oversee the training of the third Scribe."

"The third Scribe?" The treelike man wove himself around his seat, tendrils hugging the post with a sound similar to creaking wood—it was a sound that still gave Joy chills. "I see no Scribe!" he said, gesturing at her with a cluster of vines. "I see a small girl with a *signatura* and a scalpel and a Grimson's mark."

Panic slithered up Joy's spine and plugged her ears.

"Nevertheless, she completes the set," Graus Claude said with a conciliatory smile. "One whose marks can be seen, one whose marks cannot be seen and one who can remove obsolete marks." He smiled wider, exposing pointed teeth. "She is undoubtedly one of the Scribes."

"Hold," the elderly man said, his voice receding into the thin, reedy trill that he had demonstrated when they'd first assembled; his neck contracted, his smoke all but gone. "We shall consider the motion to formally acknowledge the one known as Joy Malone as one of the Folk, deserving equal rights and protections as any in the Twixt." He noticed the gazes and glowers all around him. "But first I propose a short, but necessary, recess."

The motion was quickly seconded, and the gavel snapped down. Chaos descended, funneling down stairs and rows of benches on stampeding feet.

Officiates fled their seats, spinning into waiting chambers or swiftly addressing their delegates in the stands. Sol Leander swept into a back chamber, his feather-cloaked assistant casting a black look over his shoulder as he shut the door behind them. Crowds swarmed, awkwardly and eagerly, but Joy was quickly escorted through the alcove where the curtains had been drawn, nearly tripping over her heels in the hurry to escape. Stumbling, Ink pulled Joy against him and kissed her forehead.

"I'm sorry," he said. "I'm so sorry. I should have been there."

She hugged him closer. "You're here now."

"Quite a spectacular show, Miss Malone," Graus Claude said as he ambled into the alcove, shiny silk shoes poking out from beneath his embroidered hem. Two hands rolled up a scroll as the third gestured toward the dais. "I do not believe I have ever seen such a display of equal magnitude and gravity. I pray you know what you're doing."

"I have no idea," Joy said, arms about Ink. "But I'm learning."

There might have been a quirk in the Bailiwick's cheek. "Well, that is all anyone could hope for."

"Do you think they will acknowledge her?" Ink asked. "Formally accept her as one of the Twixt?"

Graus Claude spared a glance over his hump at the glittering chamber doors. "I imagine that they will have to—there is clear precedent for halflings coming forward to claim their birthright, but none quite so dramatic as this." He eyed Joy critically, his four arms tucked behind him. "And yet you remain remarkably tidy, despite your recent mishaps, even going so far as to be properly dressed for the occasion. Perhaps there is some justification of you remaining under my influence and tutelage, since the results are proving favorable and you are unusually apt at heeding my advice." He smiled then, displaying his wide range of pointed teeth. "If you would deign to have me as your sponsor, that is?"

Joy beamed. "Gladly!" She could ask for no better benefactor than the Bailiwick of the Twixt. *Lucky me!* The great toad shook his head a little as he assessed the kicked-anthill antics of his fellows.

"You have given them much to debate, for this night and for ages to come; a welcome distraction from outmoded matters such as the Tide's Golden Age, wouldn't you agree?" He sighed contentedly. "And I find that things are rarely boring where you are concerned, Miss Malone." His ice-blue eyes took on a delighted gleam. "I look forward to watching this situation develop."

Joy rested her head against Ink in her arms and smiled. "Me, too."

"Very well, Miss Malone, Master Ink." Graus Claude stepped back and gestured with two hands to the waiting chambers. "I believe I am needed for a lengthy discussion behind closed doors. Perhaps it is best if you are returned home, Miss Malone. Few of my colleagues take notice of mortal time passing, and I suspect that this will take quite a while. I will contact you when a verdict is reached." He nodded to Joy with deep sincerity. "Please accept my apologies for my earlier conduct and know that all channels are open to you once again."

Joy bowed a little. "Thank you, Bailiwick."

He inclined his great head, his twenty fingers pausing along the curtain's edge. "A last bit of advice concerning members of the esteemed Council and your fellow associates in the Twixt," he said. "You might want to ruminate on how you shall conduct yourself among the Folk in the future as you are now permanently without protections, by your own word and deed." His eyes flashed. "Remember that and heed it well, for the Folk are known to have long memories and are very, very patient."

The massive shape turned, a mountain swathed in silk and pearls, lumbering past packs of gibbering Folk shouting for his attention. Joy watched his tread with a mixture of admiration, pride and awe. Above the chamber doors, high in the stands, Joy saw a pale figure in a black motorcycle jacket and a length of pearls wave her hand and mime applause. Joy couldn't quite make out Inq's eyes twinkling in mischief, but she could easily imagine it.

Ink placed his hand gently on her back where her *signatura* lay burning bright.

Joy traced her thumb over his heart line; her breathing came easier, but her voice was still too loud in her ears.

"Ink?"

"Yes?"

"I love you."

He smiled. "And I love you."

"No matter what?" she whispered.

"No matter what. Nonnegotiable."

"Good," Joy said and squeezed his hand. "Take me home."

EPILOGUE

"CAN YOU PASS THE MUSTARD DOWN HERE?" DAD called from the adult's picnic table. He waved a hand over Shelley's head as she talked about local politics with Mrs. Weitzenhoffer and Mrs. Reid. Stef picked up the yellow squeeze bottle and handed it to Joy.

"You're the waitress," he said around a mouthful of hot dog. "You've had practice."

She pushed it back at him. "I'm retired," she said. "Now I'm a happy wage slave at Nordstrom Rack." Stef poked the mustard across the table in her direction, millimeter by millimeter. She pretended not to notice. Stef sang the *Jaws* theme under his breath. Monica laughed. Joy rolled her eyes.

"Fine." She snatched up the mustard and walked through the grill smoke thick with onions and kielbasa and sweet potato fries. The sun shone warm and wonderful across Abbott's Field and the sky was picture-perfect robin's-egg blue. They couldn't have asked for better weather for a Welcome Home picnic to celebrate Dad and Shelley returning the same weekend Monica got to go home.

Joy traded the mustard bottle for a basket of butter rolls. Mr. Reid handed it forward while Mrs. Reid looked for something in her purse. Joy smiled stiffly and hurried back to the kids' table; she was still uncomfortable around Mrs. Reid despite Monica's reassurance that everything was fine.

"I told her that I made you promise to take a lock of my hair and wrap it in a poppet if ever I was hospitalized," Monica had said with a shrug. "Aunt Meredith was old-school Creole—she basically put the 'super' in superstitious—Mom bought it because she *wanted* to. She loves you, Joy. She knows you'd never hurt me. She just needed an excuse." Her friend's voice was as firm as ever, despite the last vestiges of bruises and tape. "But one day, I expect to hear the story of what *really* went down or I swear I'll raise my aunt's ghost to haunt your marriage bed. Remember that."

Joy nodded and poured more Sweet Baby Ray's sauce on her fries. She knew that she'd always remember this summer. Even now, it was hard to look at Monica and not be reminded of it every day. Although Joy's first attempt had removed a lot of the scarring and the plastic surgeons had done a great job on her nose, there was still a permanent chip in Monica's right eyebrow, a thin line of skin bisecting the black that stood out like an accusation every time Joy saw it. This was what she had done. This was what was at stake: a reminder never to forget that Joy had to protect others as well as herself and her world from the unseen dangers of the Twixt.

And while she *could* undo the scar, even now, she knew she never would. There was far more to consider than just her, just love, just Ink—there were the laws of her people, both people in both worlds. Somehow, she was one of the Folk, and yet she was still human, too. She had to be very careful, more careful than ever before, because Graus Claude was right: the Folk had long memories and time meant nothing to them.

Stef speared another sausage and Joy let him have it with only nominal fighting with the tongs. He laughed and took a bite. Despite everything that had happened, she hadn't told her brother yet. She didn't know how he would take knowing that he, too, was part Other Than. She decided to keep that a secret...for now.

Monica smiled up from the cradle of Gordon's arms. Three of Gordon's sisters hooted a chorus in the grass as they played with a red kickball and a giant Wiffle bat. Mr. Weitzenhoffer moved over to make room for Joy. She placed the rolls in front of him and he smiled—the man was an identical older version of his youngest son. Joy wondered if he'd been the one to introduce Gordon to Nordic bubblegum punk. Scary thought.

"Thank you, Joy," he said and offered the basket to Gordon, who took two and offered one to Monica. "So are you still planning to go back for another round of laser treatments?" he asked her politely.

"I don't know," Monica said, breaking one of the rolls in half. "It seemed to be really working when they started, but now the results have gone way down. The doctors say it broke up a lot of the scar tissue, but this last bit's being stubborn." She slathered some of Mrs. Weitzenhoffer's homemade sour cherry jam on the crust. "Mom says I shouldn't be surprised since the rest of me is stubborn, too."

Gordon ran his finger along the thin line of stitches disappearing into her weave. "I kind of like it," he said. "I think it gives you character."

Monica elbowed his gut. "You're a character!"

And they were at it again—poking and giggling in front of their parents, cute as ever, which made it twice as nice.

Joy tried not to be too jealous.

She picked up her lemon water, still beading cold against the glass, listening to the birds, the adult chatter and the distant kids at play. The sunshine was warm where her *signatura* burned. Stef had seen it but didn't yet know what it meant. How long could she keep that safe? She had Grimson's mark, too, her own little reminder that sometimes keeping "safe" had a high price.

An invisible tickle, an imagined tug, made her turn around. She swiveled on her elbows and leaned against the table, watching Ink come toward them from across the field. He smiled at her, the sun fading the shoulders of his black, formfitting T-shirt and sparkling off the ever-present wallet chain swinging at his hip. He brushed his fingers through his hair nervously as both dimples appeared.

Joy grinned. Even if he was a secret, even if no one else knew, it meant a lot to her that he'd come—that in some small way, everyone who mattered to her most was here, together... with a little room left over for Mom. And Doug? Joy heard laughter from the grown-up table. *Maybe someday.*

Ink came closer. Joy paused. There was something different about him. Joy couldn't put her finger on it until she saw the mark on his bicep, like a *signatura*—like *her signatura*—but drawn in dull matte black, like an ordinary tattoo. Stef stopped chewing. Of course, Stefan could see him, but he should know enough not to let it show. She smirked a little to herself, wondering how her brother would handle any invisible PDA shenanigans.

"Um...Joy?" Monica sat up straight and Gordon wiped the crumbs off his lap. Even Mr. Weitzenhoffer turned around, looking mildly interested. Joy followed their stares and felt her pulse thud inside her chest. She glanced at her father, who was getting up from the table, a hand tapping on Shelley's shoulder to get her attention.

And still Ink came closer, black eyes dancing, stopping to stand next to the bunch of Welcome Home balloons.

"Sorry I'm late," he said. Joy gaped up at him, absolutely unable to speak. Ink turned to Monica and offered his hand across the table. "Hi. You must be Monica. I'm glad to hear you're feeling better," he said in his smooth, slicing voice.

Monica shook his hand with the widest grin ever and actually giggled at Joy. Gordon offered the next handshake: two sets of hands met with knuckles, fingernails, fingers, all of it. Joy felt herself smiling and tried not to cry.

"I'm Gordon," the giant blond said. "Gordon Weitzenhoffer."

Joy put a hand around her boyfriend's glamoured waist. He curled an arm around her, natural as anything, and shook Gordon's hand again.

"I'm Mark Carver," he said with a dimpled smile. "But most Folk call me Ink."

* * * * *

ACKNOWLEDGMENTS

THIS IS BOOK TWO OF THE TWIXT, A BOOK THAT I promised would be made after *Indelible* sold in 2011. It was my first sale of a book that didn't yet exist, so in a very real sense, it was *Invisible*. I want to sincerely thank my editor, Natashya Wilson, my agent, Michael Bourret, and my critique partners, Angie Frazier, Maurissa Guibord and Susan Van Hecke, for helping me keep my promise. Thanks to Mark and Kris Apgar, Angie Moore and Matt and Jenny Bannock for friendship and patience above and beyond the call of sanity, with shout-outs to Tessa Gratton, Kim Harrington, Georgia McBride, Diana Peterfreund and Carrie Ryan for sharing professional savvy on this side of the keys. Heartfelt thanks to Jim Wheeler for gruesome details and medical expertise, and special thanks to Coe Booth, who made me take a stand for Monica, and Holly Black for her advice about sequels—this was *exactly* what I needed to hear!

The story itself would not be visible if not for many people behind the scenes and between these pages, namely, the Harlequin TEEN Dream Team—Melissa Anthony, Jenny Bullough, Fiona Cunningham, Jean Delaney, T. S. Ferguson, Natasa Hatsios, Amy Jones, Gigi Lau, Fion Ngan, Kathleen Oudit, Michelle Renaud, Mary Sheldon, Annie Stone, Larissa Walker, Lisa Wray, and also Anna Baggaley of the U.K. Mira Ink team.

And this would be absolutely nothing without the support of my family, whose love is the theme for every book I ever wrote. Thanks to my parents, Holly and Barry, my other parents, Marilyn and Harold, my siblings and sibling-spouses Corrie, Richard, Adam, Michelle, David and Shari and my beloved husband, Jonathan, whom I love more and more every day (where will I ever keep it all?!) and to my children, S.L. and A.J.—I love you more than all the words.

And if I forgot anyone, I deeply apologize. Blame it on yetis.